distance

THE BENEATH THE MASK SERIES

BOOK 1

LUNA MASON

D1521694

Copyright © 2023 by Luna Mason.

All rights reserved.

No part of this book may be reproduced in any form or by any electronic or mechanical means, including information storage and retrieval systems, without written permission from the author, except for the use of brief quotations in a book review.

This is a work of fiction. Names, characters, events, and incidents are the products of the author's imagination. Any resemblance to actual persons, living or dead, or actual events is purely coincidental.

Cover Design: Coffin Print Designs

Editing: Indie Proofreading

Formatting: Unalive Promotions

Formatting background art: DAZED Designs

author's note

Distance is a dark, standalone mafia romance. It does contain content and situations that could be triggering for some readers.

This book is explicit and has explicit sexual content.

It is intended to be for readers 18+.

For a full list of triggers, please visit the author's website: luna-mason-author-tr6ads.mailerpage.io

Or visit the author's Instagram: https://www.instagram.com/authorlunamason

You can join the author's reader group to get exclusive teasers, be the first to know about current projects and release dates. And also a chance to win giveaways.
Luna Mason's Mafia Queens

This book is dedicated to all my readers out there who need to escape reality. To be told you're a 'good girl' by a morally gray, tattooed mafia hitman.

Keep flicking those pages.

I've got you.

Keller is waiting for you...

CHAPTER ONE

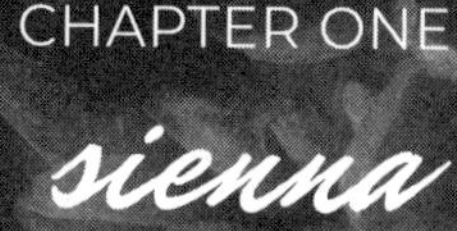

That's it. Ten days is long enough for this pity party.

My tiny bedroom is shrouded in darkness thanks to the wonderful invention of blackout blinds. I'm cocooned, snuggly in my duvet, surrounded by snotty tissues. The Salvatore Brothers being the closest I've come to human interaction. My life is just one disaster after another.

Ten days ago, I walked in on my fiancé–now ex-fiancé–balls deep in some leggy blonde as he bent her over the kitchen counter. My world was crumbling as my heart shattered. He was too busy entertaining his guest to notice me hurl my engagement ring at his head and storm out. I shudder at the memory.

The persistent prick is obviously now racked with guilt, as despite being blocked in every way possible, he continues to reach out.

During my ten days of avoiding sunlight and wallowing, the realization dawned on me. My sadness wasn't for

Jamie cheating, specifically. I think I was in love with the idea of him, rather than truly him.

Maybe I am just unlovable. I sigh, tucking the duvet up even tighter around my neck. Being abandoned by your own father and neglected by your alcoholic mother doesn't muster much for self-esteem. Something my therapist and I are trying to hash out. Somehow, I'd let the illusion of love and needing a man cloud my judgment. All I wanted was for someone to show me I was enough.

I'd spent my whole life caring for myself before leaving my toxic family home in London. At eighteen, I uprooted my life for a sociology scholarship at Columbia University. That teenager I was then, with a spring in my step, would be pissed to see me in this state now.

I snatch my phone off the bare nightstand, the light from it almost blinding me. I have to blink through my teary eyes to focus. Twenty-four missed calls and three texts. I rub my temples, trying to ease the pulsating headache as I open up the latest onslaught of Jekyll and Hyde messages.

UNKNOWN

Babe, please call me back. I am so sorry. It is not what you think.

Wow, I didn't realize you could confuse watching his cock slide in and out of another woman. This one almost makes me chuckle.

UNKNOWN

I need you, I miss you, please call me

You know you NEED me, just get over it

ME

Fuck OFF.

Rage jolts through me as I hurl my phone to the floor with a thud. Tossing my head back with a huff against my pink fluffy pillows, the tears are now free-flowing down my cheeks. I was so almost happy, with a good steady paralegal job at a top ten law firm in Manhattan. It just wasn't my dream job of working in social care. I had a fiancé. It wasn't an all-consuming passion and love, but I felt safe. I knew something was missing. I didn't want to face it because at least I had managed to run away from my old life in London. At least this was *better.*

It is always my problem. I crave more–more out of life, more out of relationships–and it has gotten me this far. I have a fire within me that tells me I can do better, so I work my ass off to not become my mother.

Just chuck me a bottle of vodka right now, though, and the resemblance is there. An absolute shit show.

"I will always choose you." Damon's deep voice booms through my room from the small flatscreen plonked on my dresser. Don't we all secretly love a bad boy?

Jamie was sweet, reliable, and secure. Three things I thought I needed, not wanted. He pushed me to find my job for financial security to build a base to pursue my dreams. He took me on dates. He asked how my day was when I would get home from work. But there was always something missing. There was never that spark. That's one thing I'm relieved about. I'll never have to fake an orgasm with him again. He wasn't a bad partner in that department, he just wasn't enough. After asking him to grab my throat, he stopped and looked at me like I had two heads. It's safe to say I never bothered asking him for anything else again, sexually speaking. Boy, did I fantasize about finding a man who would.

He'd open doors for me with a cute smile, but never slap

my ass on the way through. I don't crave sweet affection; I never really got so much as a hug from my mom on my birthday. I crave the feeling of being claimed, owned, and used. It might be wrong, being so fiercely independent in every other aspect from such a young age, but this one part of me, I needed to be brought to life.

Maybe one day.

Now don't get me wrong, I have read my fair share of romance novels. But not the sweet swoony type, with a perfect happily ever after. I read the darkest of the dark. You know, the kind where her alpha hole lover sends her the enemy's hand in a parcel with half the book smothered in dirty kinky smut. Maybe I'm getting this whole romance thing wrong.

The apartment door crashes open, followed by the clang of keys being hurled into a glass bowl. The clicking of stilettos on the oak flooring echoes throughout the apartment, becoming louder and louder. Shit, I promised Maddie that today is the day I get my shit together. My current position looks the exact opposite of that.

"SIENNA ANDERSON, I swear to God, I better not be hearing Damon Salvatore on that TV coming from your room or so help me!" Maddie bellows from down the hallway, and I cringe. I must be the worst roommate in history.

I pounce to the bottom of the plush double bed, rifling through the insane amounts of decorative pillows piled there, frantically searching for the TV remote. Suddenly, my eyes burn from the stream of natural light as the door flings open. *Christ, maybe I am turning into a vampire.*

I bring my gaze up to my best friend and give her my best *please forgive me* pout.

"Nope. You are done, Si. I can't watch you do this to

yourself any longer." She stomps over and snatches the remote from under a pink frilly pillow.

"Don't you dare turn that off, Maddison," I growl, yes growl, trying to make a ninja move to snatch the remote back, but it is no use. The silence is almost deafening.

Maddie glares at me, her brows furrowing.

"Sienna, I know you have had a shitty time, but please, I need you back. I need my best friend, and most of all, you need to stop punishing yourself for Jamie's mistakes." Her face softens as she perches at the foot of the bed.

"Ha! Shitty is one way to explain it, Mads. I mean, look at the state of me!" I exhale, throwing my hands up. "What is wrong with me? Why don't I deserve to be loved?" I'm sniffling now because just hearing Jamie's name feels like I am being speared in the heart.

"Look, Jamie is and always was a douche-bag. Now, walking in on him fucking some blonde, snorting cocaine off her tits, was not ideal, but you need to realize that you deserve so much more."

I wince at her words. Not only had I been cheated on, but I was also clearly thick to not realize he was an addict. Sweet and predictable Jamie wasn't who I thought he was at all.

Maddie's silky hair spills over my shoulder as she rests her head there, offering me comfort.

"Please tell me you are done with this wallowing now. You absolutely fucking stink. The room is covered in snotty tissues, and you have not seen sunlight in over a week."

Peering down at her, I grin and sniffle my nose. "It has been ten days, actually," I sarcastically respond with a smirk. She's right though. I am a fighter, and I wouldn't let this knock me down. I can't.

I nuzzle my head into Maddie's shoulder, taking in her

warmth and the smell of her signature sweet floral perfume. As if noticing my body relaxing, she flies back up off the bed, knocking me backward. Her grin is so wide, it creased her eyes.

"Exactly!! Get the hell out of bed, get in that shower, and glam yourself up. You have exactly one hour before the birthday eve events begin!" She's saying this while tossing her curly platinum blonde hair over her shoulder and quickly turning on her heel to leave, not waiting for my response. "Love you, Si," she excitedly giggles, already down the hallway.

Maybe a girl's night out is just what I needed.

An hour later, I have a clean room, my collection of snotty tissues in the trash, the bed perfectly made, and I no longer smell like crap.

Maddie was right. I smelled like a cheap burger, and when I caught my reflection in the mirror, I hardly recognized myself beneath the red puffy eyes and greasy, limp hair.

In my little pity party, I'd completely forgotten today was our birthday eve celebration. These were always mine and my dad's tradition. Since he decided to pack up and desert me over fifteen years ago, I continued the tradition with Maddie.

Giving myself a final once over in the mirror, I finish the look off by dragging my favorite red lipstick across my plump lips. Being all dressed up, I can't stop Jamie's words from taunting me.

"Is that really what you are wearing, Sienna? It's a bit

fucking tight." My grip on the lipstick gets tighter and tighter, remembering it.

Making my way into the living room, Maddie clocks me a genuine smile that lights up her features.

"Fuck me. Sienna was still in there somewhere. I knew it," Maddie taunts, wiggling her eyebrows. She's clearly overjoyed by her sass.

I roll my eyes and waltz straight past her, bee-lining to the fridge, where I bend down to grab the crisp bottle of rose that's calling my name.

"Is that dress short enough, Si?" Maddie laughs from behind me. "I can see your asshole near enough from here."

I quickly straighten my spine as I tug on the hem of my dress, shooting her a glare. Until recently, I had never been self-conscious about my appearance. I work hard to keep my figure in check whilst eating and drinking whatever the hell I want. I am, by no means, model material. My love for food and wine wouldn't let me. I definitely don't have the height or the long legs for days, unlike Maddie. What I do have is a mighty fine ass and a good pair of tits to flaunt. Looking down to check the length of my dress, I quickly snap myself out of that. Weeks of Jamie subtly gnawing at my confidence clearly have taken its toll on me. But damn, I look smoking hot tonight.

"Well, what do you think? Good enough to get some free shots tonight?" I ask, giving her a 360 spin of my final look.

"Oh, hell yes. You look totally fuckable. Maybe just ask me if you need to tie your stilettos up in the club."

"Piss off." I can't help but laugh. This dress is short, but it's staying on.

Catching a glance of myself on our floor-length mirror in the living room, my make-up gives me the smokey-eyed temptress look, highlighting my icy blue eyes. My lightly tanned skin is glowing thanks to a dab of bronzer, and I've painted my lips in a deep maroon to pop against my *short* black dress. My hair sits just above my bra line. I recently added some caramel highlights to contrast against my natural chocolate brown locks, which are more visible with these bouncy curls. My hair was so greasy earlier that I couldn't even see them. Maddie was right. I look like a totally new person.

I lean over the white marble counter, grab two large wine glasses, and aimlessly stare at the liquid pouring in. It made that glugging sound that always reminds me of my mother and thereby makes me wince. Taking Maddie's glass over to her, we lift our drinks to toast.

"Cheers to being single and sexy!" she giggles, giving me a wink, and tosses her head back, downing the whole glass of wine.

"The Uber will be here in five. Get your shit together and down that wine," Maddie announces, frantically pacing around the apartment, collecting her coat and bag.

"Mads, where are we actually going tonight? Am I going to need my entire week's wages?" Knowing Maddie, it's going to be somewhere high-end, full of corporate assholes for her to bat her eyelashes at.

Basically, a room full of Jamies. Just what I need.

"The new nightclub on 10th Avenue. Have you not been on social media in the last week, Si?" She lifts an accusing eyebrow. "It's called The End Zone. Apparently, it's owned by some sexy, mysterious, unattainable boxer, according to a New York magazine's most eligible bachelor article. The opening night is tonight, and I managed to nab us tickets from a client at work."

"That actually sounds really cool."

I grab my phone out of my clutch and look up The End Zone. As I predicted, it's high-end yet sexy, so I best master my best flirty smile for those barmen and free shots tonight. With a newfound spring in my step, grabbing my leather jacket, we make our way out of the flat and off to my first night being single in the City.

CHAPTER TWO

sienna

My legs bounce erratically up and down in the Uber all the way over to 10th Avenue. I try to quiet the noise going on inside my brain. This is the start of my new life, again. I'm free.

I failed to mention the darker details to Maddie–the recent nights when Jamie would have complete breakdowns, shouting and smashing the apartment up. After days upon days of reflecting on our relationship, the realization dawned on me I had completely lost myself.

Maddie was concerned enough about me already, which is why I needed to concentrate on breathing to calm the rising panic coursing through my body. I promised her, her bubbly best friend would be back, and that is what she will be getting.

I tap my fingers on my wrist, trying to ground myself to the present. Despite the freezing temperatures outside, I notch down my window a couple of inches and take a deep breath. The cold air makes my nose run. The fumes of the traffic almost choke me.

Facing the window, I close my eyes and continue to

breathe, calming my thoughts. My body instantly starts to relax into the leather seat. I can control my anxiety if I catch it quickly enough, like right now. It's always there in the background, waiting to creep up on me.

"Si, are you ok?" Maddie whispers.

I place my hand on top of hers and let out the deep breath I had been holding in.

"I will be, promise. Just need to get my head in the zone and get ready to party with my bestie." I flash her the best fake smile I can muster. She seems to sense this as she slowly nods, not wanting to press me any further.

Maddie was the first person I met when I moved here seven years ago. I remember tiptoeing into my new dorm with just a small pink suitcase of all my belongings. Not wanting to disturb anyone in the middle of the night. Maddie leaped straight out of bed screaming with excitement, wrapping me up in the tightest bear hug I think I had ever had in my life. I knew in that moment we were twin flames. They do say every Scorpio needs an Aquarius in their life.

The Uber coming to an abrupt stop shakes me from my thoughts. "Thank you. Have a good night," I say, as I open the car door, the cold air almost taking my breath away.

"Mads, hurry up! It's fucking freezing. I need a better alcohol blanket," I shout over the Uber as I wrap my arms around myself to keep from shivering. Also partly to hide the fact my nipples are way too obvious in this dress. Ugh, my brain is starting to sound like Jamie. *Shut up, shut up, shut up*.

"Well, it's a good thing I got us VIP passes, so we don't have to stand in that."

Her perfectly manicured finger points to the queue of people winding along the sidewalk. Maddie steps in front of me, her high heels clicking against the tarmac, and links her arm through mine. “Let’s go get our party on,” she shouts for the whole street to hear. A laugh escapes me. She is always the party starter.

“Too right.”

We head towards the red carpet leading to an oversized gold door. Excitement is jolting through me. God, I need a shot of tequila, pronto.

We breeze past the queue of people freezing their butts off, waiting to gain entry into the club. The place is buzzing, and the music is filling the streets. We pass the big burly bouncers our ID cards. The bald older man snatches it from my hand, stealing a quick glance at it, then my face. With a grunt, he thrusts my ID back out.

I flash him a big smile and walk through the entrance, following the red carpet. The warm misty air of the club wraps around my body and stops the shivering. With Maddie’s arm still linked through mine, we hand our coats to the barely legal woman chewing on a pen in the booth, and she passes over our tickets without even so much as a glance in our direction. I shoot Maddie a side eye as we turn on our heels and make our way through the next set of glass double doors.

The beat of the music hits me first, almost taking my breath away as the bass slams through my body. We stand on the sidelines of the club and I take it all in. Yep, this place is *faaancy*. But not in a pretentious, boring way, no. This place is exciting and sexy. This place is wow.

The walls are painted a deep red, with massive crystal chandeliers reflecting the strobe lighting. The dance area is in the center of the room. Black flooring, speckled with glitter, surrounded by black leather booths with gold tables–solid gold, I would bet. This place is dripping with wealth.

It is filled with unimpressive, mostly dark-suited men with hooded eyes that are standing by the dance floor, watching, like lions hunting their prey.

My glance quickly darts around the room, zoning in on the most important part of the club: the bar. I snatch Maddie's hand as her gaze travels the room, the excitement bubbling on her face.

"Wow, Sienna, this place is incredible, and have you seen how hot all these men are? I have not seen one who isn't a complete sex God yet."

Looking at, or even thinking about, men is the last thing on the planet I want to do tonight, but I'm not below plastering a smile for a shot or two.

"Let's get this party started, shall we?" the DJ announces from the tall, mirrored booth in the corner, as Eminem's Real Slim Shady now blasts through the speakers.

I turn and give Maddie a cheeky grin, and her eyes light up in amusement. "Shall we?" I say, as I hold out my hand to her.

"Oh, we shall."

The nights we spent reciting his every lyric whilst downing wine were about to pay off.

We beeline to the center of the dance floor, shaking our hips, our hair flowing around us as we recite every lyric word for word. Clearly, most of these women are of a higher class than us because they all fade away to the sides of the floor, giving us 'the look' as they do, obviously not knowing a word of this filthy rap song.

We might be completely out of place here, but we don't care. Thrusting our hands up in the air, we let out the last verse, both erupting into a fit of giggles as the DJ moves on to the next song. I slam my hands to my knees and bend over, trying to regain my breath. My lungs are burning from shouting over the music.

"Mads, we need to get some booze down us. That wine has worn off now." She giggles in response, her cheeks flush.

"Si, I forget how British you are, and then you go and say shit like that."

I roll my eyes and spin on my ridiculously high stilettos toward the bar behind me.

My legs start to wobble. These damn heels. The world goes in slow motion as the bar comes closer to view. My ankle folds from underneath me and I start to tumble sideways. Squeezing my eyes shut, I shoot out my hands and brace myself for the inevitable impact of the floor. Pain radiates from my ankle.

My fingers jab into something rock-hard in front of me.

An electric jolt passes through my body as a strong hand cups my left ass cheek, creating a burning sensation beneath. The air crackles around me, and a strong musky aftershave assaults my nose. I squeeze my eyes tighter, not wanting to face the utter embarrassment. I can feel his chest rise and fall steadily beneath my hands. Bar the squeezing hand on my ass, he is still.

I trail my left hand slowly down, blindly searching for something to grab onto to hoist myself back up. My hand settles and grips onto the hard bulge I'm assuming is the table. I take in a deep breath, ready to make my exit, and feel him hiss. No wait, that feels familiar. Realization dawns on me and I am 99.9% certain I am grabbing a rock hard penis, a fucking massive one at that.

I'm as still as a statue, not wanting to make this scenario any worse for either of us.

Okay, Sienna, we needed to get this over with. Rip that

band-aid off and run away, far, far away, and never return. With all the courage I can muster, I squint out of one eye, trying to assess who I'm dealing with. My hand is still tightly wrapped around a now throbbing cock.

I scan my way up his dark tux, his body a mountain of muscle. My gaze is met with the face of a man who could literally have jumped out of one of my smutty books. His liquid dark eyes search mine. I've never seen eyes so dark; it's like they are piercing into my soul. I can't stop staring, mesmerized by the hottest man I have ever laid eyes on. His jet-black hair is just long enough to grab a fistful of on top, and shaved short on the sides. A chiseled jaw is emphasized more by the dark angel wing tattoo that spans up his entire neck. I hold in a breath and open my eyes completely. I need to get a proper look. As I do, he clears his throat. This quickly slams me back into reality, the one where I still have my hand on his cock, which is aggressively pulsating in my hand.

I snatch my hand back as if I had been scolded and push myself back. The grip on my ass only tightens as he tips me forward, bringing his lips down to my ear. His breath tickles against my sensitive skin, leaving goosebumps. My whole body shudders in response, heat creeping up my cheeks.

A fire ignites within me as his lips smile against my cheek. My eyes flutter closed, and a small moan falls from my lips.

Fuck.

CHAPTER THREE

keller

Fuck me, how much longer of this charade do I have left? I glance at my Rolex. Three hours and counting–great. I tap my fingers on the solid gold table in annoyance. If I have to make small talk with one more of these pompous twats tonight, I'm going to end up punching someone in the jaw.

Tonight is the opening night of my new nightclub–well, that's what this façade is to the media. To me, it's another step in paying my debt to Luca. I smirk just thinking about this arrangement. My foster brother turned leader of the largest mafia organization in New York, had the bright idea of faking to the mob that I am taking legitimate steps to repay my debt to them. The small debt for saving my fucking life.

No longer am I Keller, the street rat boxer, scraping a life prison sentence for *almost* killing someone underground. Enter, instead, Keller 'The Killer' Russo, lined up to fight to become the undisputed heavyweight champion of the world. I live and breathe fighting. Nothing beats the euphoria of releasing my inner beast and pummeling the shit out of my opponent. It's all I've ever known. Only now, I get to do it for multimillion-dollar deals.

I run my hand along the plush leather headrest of the booth next to the dance floor, tip my head back and close my eyes. *Just three more fucking hours*, I think, as I take a deep inhale. The bass of the music thuds throughout my body. I take a drawn-out sip of scotch, letting the burn draw deep inside my throat, and then I survey the room. The place is filled with desperate women and these corporate assholes pining over them.

A cackle of women stops and crowds next to my booth, giggling to try to get my attention. I roll my eyes and keep my focus forward, ignoring their advances. I'm not in the mood tonight.

They obviously didn't read the latest bullshit article about me. *New York's most eligible bachelor is off the market.* Or even better, they did, and they just don't give a fuck. I am off the market, but not for the reasons they think.

The bad boy rags to riches story really gets them going; trying their luck to be the woman I finally let my guard down for and fall in love with. Just the thought makes me shudder. Most women use my wealth to fund their lavish lifestyle, pretending to be happy whilst I disappear into the night, hunting in the shadows for the mafia and sticking my cock in the first available hole after. The only women I am interested in are the ones who scream my name while riding my cock and then make a swift exit, never to be seen again. Simple transaction, no drama, and absolutely zero feelings.

Although, I suppose that's one way to speed time up. My office is upstairs and yet to be christened. Maybe that's something I can change tonight. That polished oak desk would look good with a woman bent over it. The thought has me shifting uncomfortably. Fuck, I just need to get out of this booth. I might have designed the place, but standing at 6 foot 5, there is nowhere near enough leg room under the table to sit here all night waiting for Grayson.

The club is pulsating, bodies grinding on the dance floor. I can smell the tequila oozing from their pores. The lights fade, giving the room an erotic vibe. I knock the rest of my scotch back in one and slam the tumbler on the table. If Grayson's gonna be late, then I am going to have to find other ways to pass the time.

This fucking tux–it's making my skin crawl. Even when tailor made by the best in New York, it's hard to squeeze my bulked out frame into. I undo the button under the bow tie, instantly becoming less claustrophobic.

Icy air brushes against the back of my neck, causing my jaw to clench as I whip my head round. Fucking useless bouncers. Last entry for gold VIP was half an hour ago. I clench my fists and shuffle to the edge of the booth to go lay into them. I come to an abrupt halt and all the air barrels out of my lungs.

Holy fuck.

The room stands still as I watch her flit through the door, arm-in-arm with a leggy blonde. The kind I can imagine gives you a fucking headache after being around for an hour.

I can't drag my eyes off this goddess.

I watch bouncer dickhead number two smirk and stare at her ass as she walks by, winking at dickhead bouncer number one. Just that alone makes my blood boil, and I want to rage over there to smash their ugly mugs together.

My gaze instantly lands back on her. She is stunning, like no woman I've ever seen. Women rarely spark immediate interest from me; I make them work for the privilege. But this one–just one look and my dick is twitching.

Rubbing my cock under the table, I try to tame him. Nearing thirty and I'm sitting here with a hard on over a stranger. Perfect.

Her dark hair bouncing around her face is a perfect length to wrap around my hand. Which would give me perfect access to pull her head back to expose her slender collarbones.

Even from this distance, her bright blue eyes are captivating, piercing straight into my chest. Her frame is toned in all the right places, with an ass I'm itching to grab. That tight black dress is teasing me. Just the thought of ripping it off and seeing what is underneath sends electric shocks straight to my dick. *Fuck, I need to get a grip.* I groan into my hands as I rub them down my face.

I need to stay the fuck away from this woman. I don't know what she has done to me, but it fills me with unease. I squeeze back into the booth and re-adjust myself under the table, abruptly whipping two fingers up, signaling my bartender to get me another drink. *I need to drown this out now.*

Two more scotches later and my head is back in the game. Grayson the late prick is on his way, thank fucking Christ. I need the distraction. I can't stop my gaze from finding her in the sea of people; I'm mesmerized by her passionately rapping to Eminem with absolutely no shame, right in the middle of the dance floor. From this angle, I am getting a front-row seat to one of the best shows I've seen. Her perfectly round ass has been taunting me for the last half an hour. Fuck Broadway, this is the best seat in the fucking house. I could watch her all night.

I am clearly not the only horny fucker to notice her.

Every man watches her, admiring something they can never have. While the tight-lipped women scowl at her from a distance. She's different from the other women here. She doesn't belong, and she clearly doesn't give a single fuck about that. It's refreshing.

I huff and swallow the remains of my glass, instantly pissed off at the possibility of being in the same boat as them. But if I can't have her, sure as hell no one fucking else can.

I need to leave and have a cold—fuck that–freezing shower and go to bed. I reach into my pocket to pull out my phone to text Grayson:

KILLER KELLER

Wait till I see you in training tomorrow. Get some ice packs ready. Where.the.fuck-.have.you.been?

Instantly, he responds:

GRAYSON

Look forward to it 😉

I let out a laugh. The cocky asshole.

I shove the phone back in my suit jacket, going still as I do. Pure electricity shoots through me. *What in the fuck*?

A shriek next to me instinctively sets me into fighter mode. I whip my body around and thrust out my hand, grabbing the flailing woman who's crashing toward the floor.

As soon as my hand connects with her body, a fire ignites within me, shooting straight from my hand into my cock. *Fuck, I know exactly who this is.*

The one woman I mentally decided I can't and won't have, lands straight on my lap, using my dick as a joystick.

I peer down and scan her scrunched-up face, witnessing the horror flashing across it. She is now completely squinting as if she is trying to muster the strength to look me in the eye. Her hand still death grips my cock as if she is going to fall to the ground if she lets go. Little does she realize what these hands can do.

Her body pressing tightly against mine sends a warmth through me. I bring my head down slowly so as not to startle her and take a long breath in; she smells delicious, like peaches. No doubt sweet, just like her. *Again, Keller–not the girl for you,* I remind myself.

Smirking, I catch her left eye slightly opening. She is stiff as a board, her eyes roaming my appearance. She must like what she sees as I feel her breath hitch and her heart fluttering, visible in her slender neck.

Not thinking clearly, I lower my mouth to her ear and move her soft curls to the side. Honestly, I don't know what possesses me: the heat flowing through my veins, her hand holding on so tight to my hard cock, or just the sheer beauty of her. A breathy moan escapes her as I breathe in the sweet smell of her. It makes me imagine all kinds of ways to make her moan even more.

"Hey gorgeous, aren't you supposed to buy a man a drink before grabbing his dick?" I back away, smirking and anticipating her reaction.

Like a deer in headlights and her breathing heavy, the goddess attempts to leap off my lap, but like fuck I am letting that happen. I tighten my grip on her ass to keep her firmly in place where she belongs.

Something about this woman draws me straight to her. I don’t want her to leave my lap.

“Is this how you treat the man who saved you from

smashing your face into the floor? I can think of a few ways you could repay me."

I push her further to see how she will react to me.

I expect a look of disgust to appear. She seems too pure to put up with my shit. Instead, shock overtakes me as her features soften with a mischievous twinkle in her eye. I open my mouth to speak and she grabs the neck of my suit to hoist herself over me, bringing her smooth leg around to straddle my lap. Now her face is just inches from mine. My breath gets more shallow as we stare into each other's eyes. While groaning, I bring my hand across my face to try to regain some of my sanity and kick my brain back into action.

She chews her bottom lip between her perfect white teeth as she surveys me, glancing up and down my body, eating me with her eyes. Ever so slightly, she leans back, rubbing her ass right on my cock. Jesus Christ, where did this woman come from?

I cock my eyebrow up at her, enticing her to speak while trying to distract my brain from thinking about those plump red lips wrapped around my cock.

She pulls herself in closer, so we're flushed together when she brings her lips to my ear. *Concentrate, Keller, ignore the feel of her breasts squashed into you.* Her breath tickles my neck.

"Well *Sir,* thank you for saving my ass," she rasps.

Instinctively, I groan and lick my lips with the tip of my tongue, gripping her ass and keeping her in place on top of me. Just as I am about to reply, she slides herself off my lap, straightens out her dress, and gives me a wide smile, showcasing her perfectly straight white teeth. She then throws me a quick wink and spins on her heel, heading for the bar with an extra sway in her step as her ass moves from side to side.

I cannot take my eyes off this woman. Her innocent smile and that unawareness of how truly sexy she is masking an inner hunger. I bet she'd respond perfectly to me tightly wrapping my hand around her throat as she sinks down on my dick. Just the thought has me shifting in my seat again.

I crave more.

I want her.

"This isn't the last you'll see of me," I whisper to no one. Drowning in the remains of my scotch, my stare trains on her like a hunter on his prey.

I've set my sights on this mystery, and I always fight for what I want.

CHAPTER FOUR

What the hell was I thinking? Not only did I grope the man, but I also winked and called him Sir. My mind is reeling, embarrassment heating my cheeks, but my body doesn't care. It's still on fire from his touch.

I finally make it to the bar on unsteady feet. I drop my head into my arms, resting against the cool metal surface of it in an attempt to lower my temperature.

His stare penetrates my ass the whole walk over there. I made sure to put an extra sway in my step for him. I've *never* behaved like that; a confident, sexy Sienna has risen from the ashes.

I think I like her.

His touch lit a match in me. His deep, raspy voice made my pussy clench. His hooded eyes hold darkness behind them, way beyond the color. This man is trouble, but that gives me a whole new buzz.

"Four tequilas, a double vodka, and coke please," I fire out to the barman, almost breathless, as he gives me a wink and starts pouring.

One shot after another, I throw my head back, welcoming the burning sensation seeping down my throat. That's nothing compared to the fire burning in my body from *his* touch. I need the buzz from the alcohol to gain the confidence to walk back past him.

Ugh, why hasn't Maddie made her way over here already? That would make my life a hell of a lot easier.

I guess she's still on the hunt for her Prince Charming. Now, *she* reads far too many soppy romance books, always dreaming of her fairytale wedding with two kids and a white picket fence. She'd spent the last year dedicated to kissing lots of frogs to find her prince. Just a couple of weeks ago, after a long day of work, while kicking my feet up on the sofa, my ears were deafened by the screaming throes of passion. Parker, I think his name was–wait, was it, Peter? Whichever it was, he clearly wasn't the one. Just seeing her dedicate her free time to finding love exhausts me, but when her eyes light up as she describes what she is looking for, it stops me from actively rolling my eyes at her.

Scanning the room, her platinum blonde hair floats around the dance floor with her latest tall, skinny man pining after her. The next potential Mr. Prince Charming leans down and whispers in her ear. I can tell by the lack of enthusiasm etched on her face she needs an out. I grab our drinks, take a deep breath in while counting to four, and then release it slowly.

I set my sights on Maddie, and take it step by step, keeping my eyes focused on her. *Do not look at him, do not look at him*. It's no fucking use. My eyes are magnets to his body, hell–I am magnetized to his body. I can't help it.

He is the most gorgeous man I have ever laid eyes on. His presence seeps power and danger, but that just entices me more. A god in his own way, even as he sits with his ankle resting on his knee, sprawled out in the booth with his tattooed hand bringing the scotch up to his lips, the man oozes sex, and not the vanilla type. The kinkiest, dirtiest you can imagine. His deep, gravelly voice is so fucking hot, and the thought of him commanding me in the bedroom makes my pussy pulse. Now that's a man who knows what he's doing. I would bet everything on that.

I hadn't even noticed I had stopped dead in my tracks, ogling this beautiful man, until his gaze daggers into mine, the internal conflict evident on his face, flickering behind his eyes. I affect him just as much as he does me. That in itself makes my cheeks heat. He brings a glass up to the air and nods his head towards me in acknowledgment, with a smirk, as if to tease me. I give him a quick smile and continue past him to the dance floor.

I don't have time for this. I am done with men. I try to force myself to remember.

Maddie whips around, giving me a knowing look, dismissing the man behind her who backs away onto the next woman.

"Fuck, Sienna, that was *hot.* Just watching him stare at you right now is turning me on," she yells over the music while dramatically fanning herself with her hand.

"Don't, Mads. I don't know what came over me," I reply, trying to poke light of the situation, not to egg her on.

"You mean you want him to *come* all over you?" she giggles. God, this girl. I can't help but laugh.

"I mean, look at him. Who wouldn't?" I answer while raising my brows. "But remember, I am on a ban from men for the foreseeable," I add, trying to change the subject.

"No, Si, a ban from relationships, not from a hookup. Remember, you have to get under someone to get over someone."

I roll my eyes. Imagining him slamming me up against a wall and devouring me is getting me all hot and bothered.

"Si, you're blushing."

Wanting to kill this conversation, I toss the straw out of my drink and down the contents. *I'm far too sober for this shit.* Then I snatch her hand and twirl her around, dragging us deeper into the dance floor, because she can't grill me if she's too busy dancing. She just belly laughs in response, wiggling her brows. She knows what I'm doing.

Time passes in a blur. We dance, laugh, and drink. It's up to full capacity, too. Almost like a can of sardines, there is no room to move. I've spent the last half an hour with different men gyrating up against me. Not one caused a stir in my body, not one touch set my soul on fire enough for me to even want to turn around. The whole time, I've been too focused on not making eye contact with him. Like prey being stalked, I can feel his hungry gaze on me. Something inside tells me if I go over there, I will not return.

Lost in my thoughts, I close my eyes and let my hips sway to the music, forgetting the heartache, the embarrassment, and the pain of the last few weeks. I just allow myself to be free, with the music flowing through me, inhaling the mix of booze and musky aftershave and feeling the sweat beads roll down my forehead. I feel free.

I'm crashing back into reality as I hear "Baby girl!" shouted at me from behind. My back immediately stiffens and my hands ball into fists. *This cannot be happening.*

"Sienna!" His irritating voice is getting closer, but before he can open his mouth again, I spin around and cut him off.

"What do you want, Jamie?" I snap, coming face to face with my prick of an ex-fiance, keeping my chin held high.

His eyes open wide at my tone and then soften as he leans in towards me, making my skin crawl.

"You haven't been answering my calls or texts, so I used the tracking app we had to find you. You finally left the house."

An icy chill runs through my body. *He has been tracking me? He knows I've been home crying my fucking eyes out? But today is the day he decides to approach me?*

"Please, Si, come and talk to me outside. We need to sort this out," he desperately pleads, inching closer and closer to my ear.

I'd almost believe it's genuine, but my brain quickly catches up. Immediately, I remember him nailing that bitch on the counter. I scoff. "How about fuck off and leave me alone, Jamie. We. Are. Done," I snap at him, jabbing my acrylic nail into his chest. Fuck, that feels good. Looking at him now, I don't know why I stayed with him for so long.

Now, don't get me wrong, he's not bad looking. Your typical lawyer look, just over 6 feet tall with a lean but muscular build and slicked back blonde hair–suited and booted always. He doesn't look as fresh as usual, his stubble is a few days old, his eyes are red, and his hair is a mess on top of his head. His emerald green eyes dart to mine in horror.

"Come on, Si, this isn't you. You don't go out drinking, and you certainly don't speak so crassly." He looks me up and down. "Wearing slutty clothes like that," he scoffs, zoning in on my legs.

I don't need this shit tonight. I turn to walk away from him, but a hand forcefully grabs my wrists, squeezing tight, yanking me back to him. I'm suddenly flush against his chest.

I let out a shaky breath and wince as the pain in my

wrist radiates up my arm. My heart pounds in my chest. His breath blows against my neck while he's still squeezing my wrist in his hand. "I only have so much patience with you, Sienna." His tone drips with anger.

My rage erupts. How fucking dare he talk to me like that, like he owns me, after months of him putting me down, cheating on me, and lying to me.

I forcefully yank my hand out of his grip and elbow his stomach. He groans in response, letting me go. I quickly move away from him and turn to see him doubled over. His eyes are now dark, glaring at me as his jaw ticks.

Oh shit, I know what that look means.

Blood pounds in my ears as I swallow down the bile that rises in my throat.

"You fucking bitch!" he yells, as he lunges forward into the small distance I created between us, grabbing both my upper arms so tightly his knuckles turn white. His nails are now digging into my skin, almost cutting it. The pressure reaches all the way into my bones. I squirm at the pain.

"You're hurting me! Get off me!" I shout, my body trembling. *Why is no one helping me? Where the hell is Maddie?*

Jamie's grip on me slightly loosens, his eyes darting past me, filling with fear.

"You heard the lady. Get your hands the fuck off her. Now!"

Without turning to look, I know who it is. I sense him closing in on me from behind. Jamie lets me go. *Finally*, relief washes over me as he lifts his hold. Thank God he came. I feel so much safer now. *That's going to bruise*, I think, as I look at my arm where his hands held me.

"Calm down, I was just having a friendly conversation with my fiancé."

My protector stiffens behind me, just for a second,

before he wraps a protective arm around my middle, pulling me flush against him. His musky aftershave, laced with scotch, fills my nose. My body tingles in response to his strong hand splayed across my stomach.

"If I so much as see you lay a hand on her again, I will fucking end you. Do you understand?"

Jamie starts to back away, his eyes pinned on my protector's hand. I glance at his hand, covered in dark tattoos. His white shirtsleeves are now rolled up, the tattoos snaking up his forearms. As his hand slips further around my stomach, the veins in his forearms protrude. Shit, even his forearms are sexy.

I turn my neck up towards him; he towers over me and Jamie. He must be over six foot five inches, his massive muscular frame owning the room.

Jamie shoots me a glare, followed by a devilish smirk, which makes me stop breathing for a second or two.

"Yeah, whatever," he spits, as he turns and walks away into the sea of people, and I let my body relax.

"Are you okay?" he asks, concern laced in his tone.

Am I?

I'm flushed, my breath is shaky, and my legs are slightly trembling. *Can he feel me trembling?* Not from what happened with Jamie. No. My body is reacting to his touch.

I give a small nod, the back of my hair sweeping against his solid chest. I shuffle around in his tight grip to face him. His strong hand is now firmly on my ass. That alone makes my panties wet. Tipping my head back, my eyes meet his hooded dark eyes.

"Thank you. For saving my ass twice tonight." I smirk, using the heels that have given me the height advantage I need to be able to wrap both of my sore arms around his neck.

I plant a soft kiss on his cheek, leaving a dark lipstick stain just above his jaw. A low groan leaves his lips in response. I can feel his bulge rubbing up against me, which only lights my fire even further.

I want this man.

"Come with me," he says, his face remaining straight as he laces his fingers through mine and pulls me off the dance floor. My legs take double steps, trying to keep up with his large strides. Past the bar, we take a side door at the back of the club.

"Do you work here or something?" I quiz.

"Or something," he responds bluntly, not stopping in his mission.

"Oookay," I reply, trying to lighten the mood. "So I'm guessing you wouldn't actually kill Jamie if he touched me again?"

I ramble when I'm nervous. Obviously, he's not going to murder my ex, but maybe it's a good idea to gauge if I'm walking off with another fucking lunatic tonight.

That question stops him dead in his tracks, and I nearly crash into the back of him as he spins around. His hard gaze meets mine, and with fire in his eyes, he invades my space, his warm breath now tickling against my neck.

"I never make empty threats, princess." His deep voice causes ripples through my body. His words *should* scare me. I think that's what he wants, but it's having the opposite effect. I don't know whether that's the alcohol or his whole dominating alpha male act, but my panties are *soaked.*

Not waiting for my answer, he grabs my hand again, and we continue marching along the dark corridor. We must be in the employee's staff rooms or something as the black doors are all shut. He reaches into his pocket and pulls out a card, swiping it along the side of the black door.

When a green light blinks, he throws open the door and drags me inside. When the heavy door slams shut behind me, it makes me jump.

My body immediately sags as he lets go of my hand, the loss of contact leaving me cold. Maybe that's a good thing; I need space from this man. He is obliterating all my senses and fogging my mind.

Opening up a fridge next to a solid oak desk, he gestures. "Drink?"

"Anything with alcohol in it will do."

Pulling down on the hem of my dress, I survey the room around me.

Like the rest of the club, this room is also swanky, with black velvet walls, a soft leather sofa–black of course–and a massive desk fitted with gold features. Continuing my nosing, at the back of the room, I notice a bathroom, pristine and shining. This room alone is probably worth more than my entire savings. I plop myself down on the sofa and sink in, the leather cooling me down. The room smells freshly painted and masculine, like him. Footsteps snap my attention as he stalks towards me with two drinks in his hand.

"Is tequila okay?"

"Hmm, yes, my favorite. Thank you." I take the glass and swirl the ice against the crystal. I offer him a genuine smile.

"My name's Sienna, by the way. Sienna Anderson," I say, reaching my free hand out to him, cringing at my corporate awkwardness.

Clearly, I'm a bit out of the game, so to speak.

He glances down and back to my face. Then his dark tattooed hand clasps over mine, so large it completely covers it, bringing my eyes back to his.

"Well, Sienna Anderson," he says in the best British accent he can muster, "pleasure to meet you." Then he gives me a slight curtsy.

Why Americans think all British people are posh, I'll never understand. Coming from a council estate on the outskirts of East London, with an alcoholic mom and runaway dad, I am as far from posh as you get in England, I think. I try to hold in a laugh and give a slight nod, rolling my lips through my teeth.

"And your name, *Sir?*" I remember his reaction the last time I called him that.

"Keller Russo," he retorts with a smirk to match mine.

It's becoming so hard to concentrate. My whole body is buzzing with anticipation. I've never been so bloody turned on in my whole life. My fight-or-flight mode is kicking in and adrenaline is pulsing through me. This man, Keller, does things to me that I can't comprehend. He's searching my face. I wonder if he can see my mind going a thousand to the second. I wish it would just stop.

As if noticing my inner turmoil, he takes hold of my arm to inspect the marks. I wince as he does. A look of pure anger flashes across his eyes. I'm starting to think his threat wasn't a joke.

"Is this the first time he's laid a hand on you, princess?" he murmurs, now caressing the marks with his thumb.

"Hmm hmm," is all I can muster. I can't stop looking at those damn lips.

"It will be his fucking last, trust me," he replies, and I'm sure he means it.

He leans his head into the crook of my neck, so close I can feel his warm breath brushing my skin. "I can hear your heart beating through your chest, Sienna. Is that from the shock or because you're imagining me fucking you over that desk?"

I can feel him smirk against my neck. "Maybe a bit of both," I answer truthfully, hoping that wasn't a mistake. He brings his hand to the side of my face, gently turning it to face him, our noses just inches away.

"You, Sienna, are breathtaking, but you are far too good for me."

"Ohh?" I draw out, edging my face away from his. That's a rejection if ever I've heard one. He quickly grabs the other side of my face, pulling me back in towards him, his breath heavy. He is so close I can smell the expensive scotch when he growls.

"Well, it's a good fucking thing I don't play by the rules."

He crashes his lips down on mine. An all-consuming kiss, no gentleness; he's kissing me like he wants to ravage me. I've never been kissed like this in my life and fuuck, it's hot. His tongue swoops into mine, upping the pace of the kiss. I can barely fucking breathe and I don't want to. I don't want this to ever end. To hell if I suffocate; what a way to go. His hands are clawing at my hair. Breaking the kiss for a second, he gives me a devilish grin before continuing his assault on my neck. Kissing, biting, and sucking. Pain and pleasure in one, causing me to moan as I tilt my head back.

"Fuck, Keller," I moan, imagining what those lips could do elsewhere. Jesus.

"Get out of your head, baby. Back with me." I meet his eyes and can see the pure lust raging there. Giving me his best panty-dropping smile, he says, "Good girl."

Those words, coming from his lips; I almost combust right there and then on the spot. His eyebrow raises for a second as he watches me.

He knows.

Smashing his lips back onto mine possessively, his hands wrap around my neck, giving me no movement to escape. Then one hand slowly lowers, skimming the top of my dress and cleavage. The cool feel of the metal from his Rolex leaves shivers in its wake. He never breaks the kiss as his hand dips inside my dress. He caresses my breast, rolling my nipple between his thumb and index finger. He squeezes my nipple, making my breath hitch. Feathering kisses along my jaw, he continues playing with my breast, inhaling my scent.

"Fuck, Sienna, tell me to stop. Tell me this is a bad idea."

I snap my eyes to his. They are almost pleading with me, like, if I say 'no', he won't be able to control himself. "I'm not a good man. In fact, you don't get much worse than me, but I can't seem to control myself with you."

The words on the tip of my tongue shock me. I certainly don't want another relationship, but I am a woman, and I have needs. For the first time in my life, I'm going to take what I want. "Keller, I don't give a shit. I want you to make me feel good and then you never need to see me again. I'm not looking for another Jamie in my life anytime soon." That makes his jaw tick as he contemplates my response.

"Don't *ever* compare me to that prick again. I would never cause you pain." Then raising an eyebrow, he adds with a lopsided grin, "That you didn't ask for."

He brings both hands to my cheeks, his eyes blazing into mine. "I can hear your thoughts screaming from here. Just get out of your head for one evening. You'll be amazed where that can take you, princess."

"Show me."

That is enough to tip him over the edge; that last straw of self-restraint, gone. His strong arms lift me to straddle him. His cock rubs against my pussy; pleasure tingles in response.

He grips hold of my ass, and I lean down to press my lips to his. Our lips smack together as we deepen the kiss, our tongues dancing as I start to grind on his lap, pleasure coiling at my center already.

"Baby, if you keep going like that, I'm going to come in my pants," he groans out, tipping his head back against the sofa, his chest heaving up and down.

I have never been so turned on in my life. I could literally come with my panties still on. I'm breathing heavily. "Keller, I need more... now."

"Patience, baby. I have plans for you all night," he taunts, lowering his head to my neck and piercing my skin with his teeth. The pain only intensifies the pleasure building inside me.

"Fuck, Keller."

I tip my head to the side to give him better access to my neck. He switches between biting and kissing. Pain and pleasure. Taking me to the edge and bringing me back again.

My eyes squeeze shut as electricity flows through me. My hips speed as he sucks along my bra line. Rubbing his hands up and down my thighs, I grab his hand, moving it closer to where I *really* need it.

He flips my hand under his and tears his mouth away from my breasts.

"I get to decide when you come. Not a second before I tell you. Understood?"

I nod, lowering my head, but he immediately tips it back up to his.

"No hiding from me."

"Please, Keller. I need more."

My voice is throaty and needy.

"Fuck, begging sounds fucking perfect from those full lips. I can't wait to have them wrapped around my cock."

I lick my lips at the thought.

"Since you asked so nicely."

He smacks his lips over mine, stealing the breath out of my lungs. His hand slowly, too fucking slowly, teases up the inside of my leg, causing ripples through my body, almost shaking in anticipation.

His hand cups my throbbing pussy and uses his index finger to move the panties to the side, giving him access to my bundle of nerves.

"So wet for me, Sienna," he hums in my ear, satisfaction dripping from his voice. He nips at my neck as he slides one finger in, then another, the third almost tipping me over the edge as the blood hammers in my ears. I ride his hand. Oh my God, we've barely begun, and I can't control myself.

I feel the orgasm building up in my body as I ride his fingers. I am so close. He continues his assault while nipping at my breasts. My walls clamp around his fingers; my legs tremble around him.

"Keller, I'm so close. Let me finish. Please!" I emphasize the 'please', as he's nuzzling his nose into my neck.

"Come now, my filthy goddess." And that's it. It's all too much for my senses. That sends my head back, and I'm moaning his name, not giving a shit who can hear me, still riding his hand. My orgasm rips through my body, tearing me apart as his fingers slam in and out of me.

I slow down the pace as I crash back down to reality, my legs limp and my ears ringing. I shift on his lap, allowing him to retrieve his hand. He slips his fingers out slowly, an ache forming in their wake, then brings his hand up between our bodies, to his mouth.

His eyes twinkle with mischief. Shit, no, he is not about to... His shimmering fingers reach his mouth and he sucks them clean, one by one, making a pop as he removes them.

"Goddamn, you are fucking delicious, Sienna." He groans, bringing the same fingers to my lips, and pulling my bottom lip out.

His throbbing cock hits against my soaking pussy, arousing me all over again.

A loud knock startles me. Keller doesn't even flinch, just glares at the door like he wants to murder whoever dares be on the other side.

I immediately attempt to move my leg, to un-straddle him, but he quickly pushes my leg down, pulling the back of my head to nuzzle into his chest.

"Shh Sienna, you stay like this, okay?" That wasn't a question.

"Come in," he shouts with annoyance.

Peeking through my hair, I see a tall figure waltz through the door, definitely of Italian descent, with his olive skin and dark features, a cigarette resting behind his ear. He's eyeing us up with intrigue. "Keller, is this why you failed to answer your goddamn phone this evening?"

"It's the opening night of my fucking club, *brother*," Keller mocks with a heavy New York accent. "Leave, and we'll talk later."

There's an authority in his response. Wait, hang on. He *owns* this club? Oh shit! It's Mr. Unattainable, the boxer guy Maddie mentioned.

"Fine. You finish having your dick sucked and throw her my way when you're finished." I stiffen and feel Keller rub the outside of my thigh in reassurance. His touch is calming.

"Give me five minutes and I'll meet you out the back. Now. Fuck off," he orders. I guess that's me dismissed, too.

The door slams shut, rattling throughout the room as we sit in silence, the sound of our heavy breathing filling the room.

I slowly peel myself off his chest, avoiding eye contact. Standing up, I straighten my dress and bend to pick my purse up from the other end of the sofa.

Keller now stands up. Towering over me, he grasps my wrist, tugging me back to him, bending to whisper in my ear.

"Me and you. We're far from finished. I gotta go, but don't doubt me when I say I will find you and finish what we started. Remember, baby, I don't make empty threats."

Placing a soft kiss on my lips, he turns on his heel and strides out, not even looking back as he leaves. I suck in a deep breath and compose myself. My fingers rub my swollen lips.

He won't find me.

He will be back on to the next woman tomorrow, and that's fine. I have a life to rebuild. With that, I snatch up my bag and start my search for Maddie. I need my bed and to forget about this.

Somehow, I don't think it will ever happen. That scene will replay in my head for the foreseeable.

CHAPTER FIVE

keller

Fucking Luca. Now, of all the times he needs to throw his weight around talking to me like I'm some sort of lackey. Don't get me wrong, I love the man like a brother. Hell, he is the only brother I've ever had, fostered or not. But seriously, I could have punched him square in the jaw for interrupting. Let alone insinuating I'd pass Sienna over to him for his enjoyment. Think again, motherfucker.

He needs to remember he fucking needs me. He's established his title in the mafia by using his masked ruthless enforcer to elicit fear in anyone that crosses him. I am the monster he unleashes in the shadows; the reason his mob stays at the top of the chain.

No one outside the immediate circle knows the next undisputed heavyweight champion is also their masked enforcer.

My office door slams shut behind me. *Maybe stopping when we did is a good thing,* I tell myself. I can't fucking have her, but after having just a taste, I don't know if I'll be able to stop. My addictive personality gets the better of me, and

I usually need to inflict pain and let my deep-rooted anger out. But with her, she is a whole new addiction unto herself, one I need to stop before it cuts too deep.

I drag my hands over my face before I enter the room. I can't let him see how affected I am by her. The last thing I need is Luca prying. Striding through into the club VIP lounge, I spot him in the far corner, sprawled out like he owns the place. He's dragging on a cigarette and sipping his whiskey, his gaze pinned on the blonde, busty waitress. After spotting me, he gives me a smirk and summons me over with a flick of the wrist. *What the fuck is up with him tonight?*

"Yes, Luca?" I ask, keeping the tone neutral, my fists clenched by my sides.

He flicks the ash from his cigarette slowly and brings it back up to his lips, not bringing his gaze to me; he's pissed.

"I have a job for you. If you'd have answered that fucking phone of yours, I wouldn't have had to drag myself out of Melissa's to come here–very selfish of you, brother."

"I am fucking busy," I spit. "Look around. It's the opening night of my club. The same club I'm letting you funnel your fucking money through–remember that? I'm fucking busy. You'll have to get someone else." I don't have time for this shit tonight.

He flicks his head back at me, throwing his cigarette in the ashtray. Smoke covers his face as he leans forward, elbows on his knees.

"I don't fucking trust anyone else in the organization; you know that. They need to understand I am their fucking boss, but they go against me at every turn. I can't fucking deal with their shit anymore, and I'm sick of walking on eggshells. I need to make a statement: they listen to me or they die."

I don't like where this is going already. Whining Luca is the worst kind, and it seems to happen more and more often lately.

"Dante was caught meeting with the Falcones earlier today. I hear it's not the first time either. He thinks he can walk all over me. He needs to be taught a fucking lesson. I need you to send the message. These fuckers need to be put back into line pronto, and you need to do it. You need to bring the fear of God into them to prove we run this mob, not them. My father is gone and they need to fucking accept that. It's been six fucking years already."

And there it is. He wants the monster to come out and play. Fucking gladly. I need a distraction, and I can't think of a better way to end the evening than cutting some asshole's tongue out. Scrap that. I'd much rather be sinking my dick into Sienna's sweet pussy, but I'll take what I can get.

"Fine. Text me the address, and I'll leave now." I watch him slip his phone out of his pocket and tap at the screen.

"Thank you, brother. I owe you." There's sincerity in his tone.

"Of course. You know I owe you my life. But remember our deal. I want out once this dies down. I win my fight, and I go on my own. So you better use me while you can," I say with a grin.

I do. I owe this fucker my life. If it wasn't for him taking over the mob six years ago, dragging me off the streets, and funding my boxing career, I would either be in jail serving life or dead. So being his enforcer is hardly worthy of the debt I owe him, but we make it work. I have a lot of rage I need to rid, and he needs someone out on the streets; somewhere I'm at one with. Behind the charade of being the boss, Luca is a mirror of me, an angry foster kid fighting to make something of his life. He never planned–hell, he never fucking wanted to run a mob, but unknown family ties meant he had to. No wonder the rest of the mob is pissed after years of working and killing for his father. But Luca is a fighter, and he is fulfilling his duty, even if it means I have to go out and do the majority of his fucking dirty work.

It was the same when we were kids on the street. Luca would pick a fight, but he was never a good hands-on fighter. He has always been the brains. I was always there in the background to beat the shit out of anyone who upset my brother. And still, fourteen years later, we are the same. Just now, the stakes are much higher, and it's a lot darker than a street fight.

"Of course, brother, you know I will stand up my end of the deal." And I believe him, I have to. He is the only family I have, mob or not.

As I turn to leave, he finally asks, "Who was that hot piece of ass on your lap earlier? Is she still here? I'd love a fucking go on that." I clench my fists in response and take in a heavy breath. I couldn't let him know she's not one of my usuals, but over my dead body is he going to ever touch a hair on her head.

"No, she's gone. We won't be seeing her again." I try to keep my voice calm. His eyebrow raises as he looks at me, searching my face for more.

"That's a shame."

I take that as my cue to leave, heading back to my office to grab my shit together. Good thing I keep supplies and my signature black balaclava locked in the desk. Tracing my hand across the smooth oak, I shake my head. Damn, it's a shame I never got to bend Sienna over this tonight.

Grabbing my gear, I text my driver to meet me at the back entrance of the club. I don't have time to say my goodbyes; that's one thing I can thank Luca for tonight. He responds that his ETA is three minutes. Guess I'll get myself some fresh air while I wait. Nothing beats the cool air of New York in November. It's fresh, almost cleansing on the lungs, as I spark up a cigarette. I am not a smoker of habit. I'm a professional boxer at the peak of my fitness. But some habits die hard. I'm sure Grayson will give me a kicking for this tomorrow. After the events of tonight, I need this to clear my head and unleash my inner demons.

Dante's in for it tonight. I'm a pent-up ball of anger after Luca interrupted me getting my release earlier. Exhaling the smoke into the frosty air, I can still hear the music pounding from the club. I can't fucking wait to have a moment of silence.

"Get the fuck back here," a loud voice booms from down the street. Great, now the drunk fuckers are filing out. I step back into the shadows with my back against the wall, leaning my foot up along the brickwork. This should be interesting; I love a good street fight.

The sound of high heels clicking against the pavement piques my interest. It gets quicker and quicker. Almost as if they are running. Shit. I observe my surroundings, hoping I am wrong. I can't get involved in shit that I don't need to. I have everything riding on the title fight. I can't fuck this up, and street fighting certainly would. I'm already in shit with Grayson and Stacey for being pictured with 'too many women'. Why the fuck they care, I don't know. Public image isn't my problem. I pay good money for that shit to disappear.

By this time, the clicking has stopped.

"Get off me, Jamie! What the fuck is wrong with you?"

Fuck, I recognize that voice. No, it fucking can't be.

"I said, get your hands off me now!"

Nope, that's it. Fuck this. I push off the wall into a jog. It may be dark out, but it's New York, and everything's lit up all night long. Making my way on the sidewalk, I follow the voices that keep talking.

"I fucking told you I need you back, and you didn't fucking listen. So now I'm going to have to take you."

What in the fuck? I try to remain calm and focus on my surroundings. I'm certain I know who this is.

Bingo. I see two shadows in the alleyway just off the street. I can't make out faces, but I see right away–a woman being held up against the brickwork by her throat as a hooded man leans into her. Looks like I'm about to get some anger out before the torturing tonight.

As I pace up the alleyway, softening my footsteps not to startle this prick, my heart is thumping in my chest, and my nerves are on end. It's the same feeling I had when I saw her earlier. Shit, no. I hope I'm fucking wrong. I edge closer and her voice guts me straight in the heart.

"Jamie, please don't do this," she sobs.

He's a dead fucking man. Puffing my chest out and retrieving the blade from my pocket, I shout, "I fucking told you, *Jamie.* If you so much as touched her, I'd fucking end you."

I hold the knife up, giving him a wild smirk. That's it, fucker. I've got your attention now. He lets go of his grip around Sienna's throat where he was pinning her up against the wall, and she takes this opportunity to pull her knee back and slam it straight into his balls. That's my gorgeous firecracker.

Jamie throws her against the wall and doubles over in pain. I dart at her as quickly as I can and catch her before her head hits the pavement. Jamie, the limp prick, takes his opportunity to run. Oh, don't worry. I'll fucking find you later, you cocksucker.

Immediately turning my attention to Sienna, I gently brush the hair from her face. The alleyway only has dim lighting, so I can't access the full extent of any injuries, but she's shaking in my arms. She must be in shock. Her piercing blue eyes are boring into me, but no words are coming out. Fuck.

"Sienna, baby. I need you to talk to me. Are you okay? Where did he hurt you?" Every muscle in my body is tensing, trying to hold in the burning rage I'm feeling in my chest. How fucking dare he? She wraps her arms around her chest and lets out a cough. Fuck. She's freezing.

"Keller, can you take me home please?" she asks weakly.

"Of course. Can you wrap your arms around my neck?" She does. Scooping her up, she's as light as a feather snuggled into my chest. I feel her breathing start to steady. I'm fighting an internal battle to stay calm, so she relaxes when every instinct in my body wants to hunt him down and rip him apart. *Later, Keller.*

So many thoughts are wracking through my brain as I stride to the back entrance of the club. My gunmetal gray Aston Martin waits, shimmering under the streetlights. What did Jamie mean when he said he needs her back so he's taking her? That sounds like a lot more than just a breakup. The prick sounded desperate, panicking.

I store this information to dive into later. With my mob connections, I'll drag out everything there is to know about this fucker in no time and put a big red mark on his head. I bring my focus back to Sienna, still snuggled into my chest. Now that we've reached the club, the crimson on her arms draws my attention. He fucking made her bleed. For every cut she has, he will have two to match, ten times deeper.

We reach the Aston Martin in no time. Using my muscular frame to my advantage, I grab the keys from my driver standing by the passenger door and give him a nod to dismiss him. I'll drive her myself. Bending down, I crouch and softly place Sienna into the red leather passenger seat. Taking the seat belt, I move it across her body.

My gentle caressing of her skin makes her instantly shiver. Fuck, she feels this, too.

Taking off my jacket, I place it over her, stride around to the driver's seat, and slide in. The engine roars to life, making the car shake. God, I love the thrill of this beast. Rubbing my hands along the leather of the steering wheel, I pull the stick into reverse, snaking my hand behind Sienna's headrest as I turn to look out the back window. Catching her watching me intently, I see the desire burning in her eyes. Now really isn't the time.

Once we are away from the club, being the early hours of the morning, the roads are quiet.

"Are you not going to ask me where I live? You're going the totally wrong way."

I have no intention of letting her go back to her apartment on her own. Looks like my second rule is going to be broken; no women in the penthouse. This is dangerous.

CHAPTER SIX

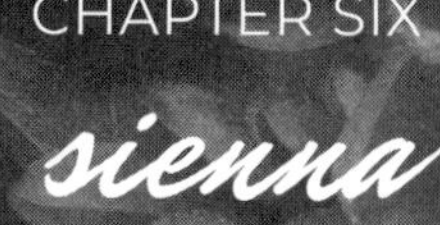

sienna

Keller keeps his eyes on the road, avoiding my question, but I'm too tired to push further. Despite only knowing him for a few hours, I feel safe with him.

I have a feeling the man he shows to the rest of the world is very different from the true man hiding beneath. I can tell from the gentleness of his touch tonight. I know there is more, deep down. He wouldn't ever hurt me physically.

I'm so tired I can barely keep my eyes open. The heating is on full blast, subsiding the shivering but making me drowsy.

I recline my seat slightly so I can get comfy and watch Keller. I should not be turned on right now. Just moments ago, my ex attacked me down an alleyway, and now I'm being raced back in an Aston Martin with my drop-dead gorgeous savior.

Watching him handle this beast of a car is so sexy. He drives with complete control and power, his hands gripping the wheel so tight his tattooed knuckles peak with white beneath the ink.

Every now and then, he shoots me a worried look, as if checking to make sure I am still okay, but beneath that, I can see the fury wreaking havoc. There is a darkness within him that wants to come out, and he is completely tense in his attempt to try to keep it all in.

I lightly rest my hand on his thigh. He seems to be as uncomfortable with being my protector as I am with needing to be cared for. Needing care is an alien feeling to me. He rests his hand on top of mine and gives it a light, reassuring squeeze. Who'd have thought a man with such darkness and power would have such a gentle side? Either that, or he just feels sorry for this stupid damsel in distress.

Saving someone three times in the same night is a bit much for anyone's standards.

A few minutes tick by in silence as we drive past Central Park, hand in hand. Of course, we're heading to the posh area. I'm in an Aston Martin for Christ's sake. He owns that bloody nightclub!

Removing his hand from the top of mine, I instantly feel empty from the lack of contact. Electricity sizzles in the car. It really shouldn't. I'm covered in cuts and bruises. The air suddenly doesn't seem to be reaching my lungs quickly enough. Panic runs through me as I try to catch my breath. *Fuck, Jamie attacked me.*

Until this point, he's never physically attacked me; he's scared me, but never touched me. *Why is he doing this now?*

Taking deep breaths, I try to calm the rising panic. *What would have happened if Keller didn't save me? How far would he have gone?*

The car begins to slow down, distracting me momentarily from my inner worries. We approach the Park Avenue skyscrapers. Surely he doesn't live in a fucking skyscraper–*wait, do people even live in them?*

He hits a button on the screen of the car and the garage door next to the building opens. He gives a nod to the two security guards sitting in the booth outside. We enter the brightly lit parking area, his hand snaking behind my head-rest as he reverses into a spot. I am unable to form a coherent sentence, so I just keep quiet. I do have one burning question.

"Keller, what level are we going to? I'm terrified of elevators. So, we need to take the stairs." I'm babbling now.

"If I tell you, it will only make it worse, Sienna. Just trust me, okay? You have nothing to be scared of with me," he replies, hitting the button in the center console, which shuts the car off. He slides out of the driver's seat, walking around the front of the car. Never taking his eyes off me. The passenger door flies open, the cold air taking my breath away as he holds out his hand. Instead of helping me up to my feet, he bends and scoops me back up into his arms, cradling me into his chest. His steady heartbeat pounds against my ear.

He walks us to the elevator. Shit, maybe if I just shut my eyes, it will be fine. Visions of my mom shutting me in the crappy elevator to our flat back in London invade my mind. Every time I pissed her off when she was drunk, she would shove me in there and leave me crying. That was until she remembered to let me back out. Sometimes I would spend the whole night in there and cry myself to sleep. I was only a little girl. Everyone in the block of flats assumed it was broken, so no one ever came to my rescue. I was petrified.

The elevator doors ping open and he strides us in, distracting me from my past.

Even despite the fear, I can't deny this lift is absolutely

stunning. Around twenty people could fit in here easily. The calming music, though, is having the opposite effect, reminding me of the waiting room for my therapist. Turning his back, Keller presses the button, attempting to use his large frame to hide it from me. I peek around him and see the 86th number lit up in green.

"Are you fucking kidding me, Keller? That's going to be like ten fucking minutes in elevator time. I can't do it. Let me out," I pant. Beads of sweat form on my forehead.

He places a soft kiss on the top of my head and wraps me tighter in his embrace. I close my eyes and focus on my breathing, listening to the steady beat of his heart.

"We're nearly there, gorgeous," he reassures me, now stroking my hair.

The tender side of him throws me off guard. *Maybe he just feels sorry for me*. There is no denying the anticipation in the air; the electricity is almost crackling in here. Being smothered against his chest, I smell his musky aftershave laced with scotch and cigarettes. Before I can respond, the elevator pings and the doors open.

Softly lowering me to my feet, he laces his fingers in mine and leads me out into the most stunning penthouse I could imagine. Floor-to-ceiling windows surround the living space, overlooking the Manhattan skyline twinkling in the night. My stilettos echo on the white marbled flooring that accents the black and dark oak furnishings. The smell of paint is still fresh. The penthouse is open-planned and my sights set straight on a state-of-the-art kitchen, the kind I can imagine you'd find in a palace back home.

A large U-shaped black leather sofa scattered with lighter cushions keeps with the black, white, and neutral tones of the house. God, what I would not give to cook in that kitchen; it even has one of those taps that give you boiling water!

"Keller, this place is absolutely stunning. The view, the kitchen–fuck, all of it. It is heaven." I groan in amazement.

Keller's gaze sweeps me up and down. "The only view that is heavenly here is the one standing in front of me."

"Don't be ridiculous." I blush. My cheeks are on fire. There is no point even trying to deny it.

His gaze holds, assessing the grazes all over my arms. Closing the space between us, he gently traces his fingers down my arms, leaving shivers in his wake. He lifts me like I weigh nothing and lays me down on the couch as he crouches beside me.

His fingers find the zipper on the side of my dress.

"Can I?"

I nod, my emotions wavering.

He gently pulls the dress down my body and over my stilettos, turning his attention straight back to me.

His finger trails down my arms, stopping at each cut and graze. He dips his head and places a delicate kiss on each mark.

"For every mark left on your beautiful body, I'll snap one of his bones. He will pay for this. I promise you," he rasps, violence dripping from his tone.

I should be scared, but I'm not. What's worse is I think he means this.

A phone ringing pulls our attention away. *Shit, I need to phone Maddie.* I told her I was going to the bathroom. That was until Jamie decided to drag me out of the club and assault me.

Keller frowns at the screen. "I need to take this in the other room. Make yourself at home. I won't be long."

He places a quick peck on my forehead and turns on his

heel, walking down the hallway. In nothing but my drenched panties, I sigh and grab my dress.

I make my way over to the kitchen and start opening cupboards–there must be over thirty here–now on a quest to find a glass. The sixth attempt brings success. I reach for one of the tall crystal glasses and fill it to the brim with water before going to rummage through my bag for painkillers. My arms are starting to sting and my head is pounding. I toss the pills back and down the remains of the water, welcoming the refreshing cold against my burning body. I grab my phone and see the screen filled with missed calls from Maddie. Without reading the messages, I quickly redial her.

"Sienna, where in the fuck are you?" she shouts, music blaring in the background. "I'm still at the club, in the bathroom. I couldn't find you anywhere. I've been worried sick."

God, I feel so bad. "Maddie, I am so sorry. Jamie turned up at the club and kept begging to talk to me. He was doing my head in, so I agreed. But once we got out through the side exit, he dragged me down an alleyway. I tried to run away from him, but he pinned me up against a wall. Luckily, Keller found me before he did anything else. Now I'm back to his. I'm about to get an Uber home," I explain, without making her worry too much.

"Jamie fucking did what? Where is he now? I'll fucking stab his eyes out with my heels. Shit, Si, are you okay?" Her voice is almost hysterical.

"He ran off Mads. It's okay. I'm okay. A bit cut and bruised, but I'll be fine. I did kick the twat in the balls, though. I'll meet you back at the apartment soon, okay? Text me when you're on your way. I need to say bye to Keller first." I'm hoping that will calm her down.

"Okay, okay. Shit, Keller. The guy you straddled in the club? I can't wait to hear more about that. Send me your ping when you get in the Uber, okay? Love you."

"Love you, too, Mads," I reply and cut the call.

Keller still isn't done with his call, so I bring up the Uber app and request a ride. After booking, I perch on the bar stool at the breakfast bar. I need a distraction. The adrenaline is clearly wearing off and I'm crashing, spiraling out of control. My trembling hands come into my blurry vision, the cuts covering them make me want to scream. My lungs are burning as I frantically try to catch my breath.

What the fuck is happening to me? What did he do to me? Why are there so many cuts?

I stumble off the barstool, needing to get to the bathroom. On wobbly legs, I head towards the first door I can just about make out. The closer I get, the more it feels like the air is sucked from my body.

Fuck, I'm going to die.

I slam open the door and tumble into the dark room. I can barely make out where I am. My whole body is aching; pain soars through me as I struggle to breathe. I give up my pursuit for a bathroom because my body physically can't take me any further. I drop to the floor in a heap and drag my legs into my chest. Pressing my forehead to my knees, I'm fighting for air as tears stream down my cheeks.

I'm a petrified mess.

I squeeze my eyes shut and let the darkness consume me as sobs rack from my trembling body.

I feel a thud next to me and warm hands pull my face out of my lap.

"Fuck, Sienna, what happened? Are you ok?"

"I-I–" My lungs fail me. I can't get the words out.

Strong arms wrap me up, and it's like I'm floating. His hammering heartbeat, oddly, brings me comfort.

"Shh, it's okay, baby. I've got you," he says as he gently lays me down on a soft mattress. My head rests on a silky pillow. My muscles start to relax as I sink into the mattress. The bed dips as Keller slips in next to me, grasping me by the waist and pulling me flush against his chest.

"Just breathe. No one can hurt you now. You're safe. I promise."

The softness in his voice and the way he strokes my hair slowly start to allow the air back into my lungs. I continue to take deep, steadying breaths and feel my heart rate return to a somewhat normal beat. We lie there together, his muscular frame caging me in, making me feel safe.

By now, my breathing has returned to normal. I find the courage to speak, embarrassment creeping up my cheeks.

"Shit, that was scary. I'm so sorry you had to see me like this. I bet it's the last thing you need after already saving me three times tonight. I'll get out of your hair soon."

"Don't apologize. You were attacked. I wondered if you were taking it all too well on the ride here. Sometimes you have to let it all out some way or another." He places a kiss on the back of my head, spreading more warmth throughout my body.

"Hmm," is all I can muster in response as my tired eyes flutter closed.

Shit. The Uber.

My eyes fling open, and I push myself out of his hold, then drop off the bed and dart towards the door.

"Sienna," he growls.

His low voice stops me in my tracks.

I slowly turn to face him.

"Where do you think you're going?"

"I forgot I booked an Uber," I respond, fidgeting with my hands, my eyes avoiding his.

His jaw ticks as he stalks towards me. For every step forward he takes, I take one away, until my back bumps up against the door.

"Sienna. Don't mistake my kindness for weakness," he rasps, making me shiver. "You are not going anywhere. For one, it's not safe out there this time of night. And two, because I fucking said so. Do you understand?" His firm words are a contradiction to his soft lips, peppering kisses along my jawline.

Fuck, this is hot, for all the wrong reasons. This man and his filthy, domineering voice do things to me I never imagined possible. But I sure as hell don't need protecting.

"No," I answer, tipping my head up in defiance. I've just about had it with men today.

"Sienna," he growls. "Don't fucking test me. I am already on the fucking edge."

The conflict is clear in his tone. He wants me, but he doesn't know what to do with me. That much is evident. He's used to demanding what he wants in every aspect of his life.

"Fine, you drive me home and then go and do whatever that was about," I gesture, pointing to his phone in his pocket.

Taking his hands away from the wall behind me, he creates some distance between us. "Okay," he huffs and storms off into the room, slamming the door behind him.

Great. I've managed to piss off the beast.

After a few minutes, the sound of drawers slamming echoes through the penthouse. Keller reappears, this time dressed in black joggers and a tight black hoodie, a sports bag slung over his shoulder.

Fuck-me, I honestly don't know which is sexier. Keller in a fitted tux or in casual sportswear. The way the hoodie clings tightly emphasizes the sheer size of his biceps and the joggers don't leave much to the imagination as to what's underneath them. If I wasn't so pissed off with him, I'd want to jump into his arms and smash my lips to his.

Keller, clearing his throat, snaps back my attention.

Perfect. He's caught me ogling him.

He tosses me a shirt and walks straight past me, nodding forward as if summoning me to follow him. I slip on the black shirt, which hangs off me like a dress. Looks like all the niceties are out the window. The whole time we ride the elevator, and then the car, there is no eye contact.

He pulls up and stops the engine. I reach to open the door, but his strong hand stops me. He leans across, squashing me into the seat.

A strangled sigh leaves his lips.

"Sienna, wait a sec. I'm sorry. I have a lot of shit going on, and I don't ever entertain women like this. I don't know what this is, but I can't explain this pull I have toward you. Give me your phone?" His tone is sincere as he turns his palm over.

"Please, I think you mean to add," I mock him with a grin.

He gives me a lopsided grin in return. "Fine. Please, Sienna."

I jab my passcode in to unlock the phone and place it in his palm. He quickly types on the phone and his pings.

He hands it back. "You have my number, princess. If you need anything, you call me. If Jamie so much as breathes the same air as you, you call me." A second passes. "Please."

Trying to hide my smile, I say, "Okay, Keller. Thank you."

I don't know what's gotten into Jamie, but he really scared me tonight. He was acting crazed and desperate. The complete opposite of his usual calm and collected demeanor.

With that, I remember how the man who sits in front of me apologizing saved my ass three times tonight. I grab both sides of his face and bring his lips down to mine, giving him a quick peck, just intending to say thank you and goodbye.

I know this can't go on any further.

I pull away and reach back for the door handle. Keller is stealthier than me. He whips me back around and crashes his lips to mine, fisting his hands in my hair. He deepens the kiss as I moan, letting his tongue enter, and our teeth clash. We are like two starved animals, clawing and ravaging each other.

Every emotion tonight has ignited is being put into this kiss.

When Keller breaks away, my lips are swollen, and I'm trying to catch my breath.

"Fuck, Sienna. We need to pause this for now. I have to go," he says through heavy breath, which I can still taste as his lips are mere inches from mine.

The windows in the Aston have fogged up, and the smell of pure desire fills the car. I give him the best fake frown I can, but it's no use as I end up laughing.

"Okay, well, I suppose I'll speak to you soon?" I murmur, wistfulness in my voice.

"Sooner than you think, baby." He winks at me, leaning over to open the door for me. God, even as he rubs his body against me, I just want to jump on his lap.

"Trust me, if I didn't truly have to go, I'd be carrying you into your apartment and making you scream my name, forgetting any other man existed before me," he whispers in my ear, sending shivers down my spine.

God, if only.

I slide out of the car and walk to my apartment, turning to give him a quick wave as I go.

Finally, I make it up the five flights of stairs to mine and Maddie's studio apartment, panting by the last floor. As I unlock and then throw my keys on the side table, I fling off my shoes next to the door. *Fuuuuck, that feels good.*

I pad along the hallway to the lounge, peeking through the wooden blind slightly, looking down to where Keller dropped me off a few moments ago. He's still there. I can sense his glare from here. My phone pings, drawing my attention to the lounge, and I jog over to retrieve it.

SEX GOD KELLER

Go to bed princess, sweet dreams of me x

I quickly type out a reply, chuckling at the name he's given himself in my contacts.

ME

Night Sex God, thank you again for tonight. I hope you have sweet dreams of me, too xx

He responds immediately.

SEX GOD KELLER

There is nothing sweet about the dreams I'll be having about you 😉. Now sleep x

I shoot a quick text to Maddie to let her know I'm home. I drop myself back onto the bed, grabbing the nearest cushion to cuddle as I fall asleep, thoughts of Keller dancing on my mind as I drift off.

CHAPTER SEVEN

keller

After leaving Sienna, I drove straight to Dante's restaurant, Rico's, over in Brooklyn. It's safe to say he won't be speaking out of turn for a long fucking time. Try the rest of his life.

Luca wanted me to deliver a message to the rest of the mob, and so I fucking did. Dante was just unlucky that I had rage burning inside me, needing to be released. Anger that should have been inflicted on Jamie.

Pushing open the wooden restaurant door, the chipped red paint scrapes off under my fingers. The chattering of Italian, and laughing, goes dead. Four older men and Dante are perched at a wooden round table in the middle of the restaurant. Playing cards and dollars are scattered over the table. Cigar smoke clouds the air and as I harshly inhale, the toxic chemicals burn the back of my throat. Without a word, I stride over to the table, dragging out the white metal foldable seat. It scrapes across the uneven wooden flooring before I flip it around and straddle it. All eyes in the room are on me. Not a sound leaves their mouths, and each is looking like they have seen a ghost. Slowly, I empty the magazine of my gun, bronze bullets clinking one by one onto the pine table we sit around. The only noise in the unit is water dripping second by second from the hole in the back corner. Slamming my now empty gun on the table so forcefully the bullets jump in the air, I notice no one so much as flinches because they're too scared to move.

They know why I'm here. They know who I am and who sent me.

Picking up a single bullet between my thumb and index finger, without saying a word, I hold it up for them all to see. Then thrust the bullet between my fingers into Dante's chest.

"Swallow," I command.

"What, no." His voice trembles.

"I won't repeat myself again. Swallow," I demand without hesitation.

He really doesn't want to piss me off tonight.

Slowly, he retrieves the bullet from between my fingers. I can feel a slight shake as he does. His eyes are wide, pleading for a way out.

Well, he isn't getting one.

Lifting the bullet, he holds it between his lips, his Adam's apple bobbing up and down. Snatching the shiny metal blade from my sock, I put it up against his carotid artery just on the left of his neck. With slight pressure, it digs in enough for the sharp blade to break the layers of skin and crimson starts to slowly drip.

That seemed to give him the motivation to get on with my command. The bullet enters his mouth as he swallows. A cough stutters as the bullet makes its journey down his throat.

I loosen the pressure of the knife against his neck. His body sags slightly at the relief.

Picking up another bullet, I thrust it into his face, his eyes wide.

"Again."

His so-called friends watch on in horror.

Quicker this time, he grabs the bullet and swallows it, holding in the gagging as it penetrates his insides.

"Good. Now open your mouth and stick out your tongue."

He does as I say, his jaw shaking as he obeys.

Grabbing the small but deadly blade, I carve the tip off his tongue. It feels like cutting through a rough bit of well-done steak, blood gushing out of his mouth and down his chin.

Holding out the tiny bit of flesh, I dangle it above his open mouth.

"Last time, I promise. Swallow"

Luca wanted a message delivered. I think this will do the job. The fear is palpable in the room.

Clamping his mouth down, he swallows the end of his tongue, spluttering blood all over my jacket as he does.

"You can fucking pay for the dry cleaning on this," I say in disgust as I throw my blood covered jacket on the damp floor.

"Now, that will be the last time you speak of Luca's business to the Falcones. Do I make myself clear? If we so much as hear a whisper you have even stepped foot in their territory, you'll have a bullet wedged right between your eyes."

He frantically nods in response, his hand covering his mouth that is pouring with blood.

By the time I get home, the sun is rising over Central Park. My bloodied clothes have been discarded in a bag to deal with later. I have an ice-cold shower, trying to get the image of Sienna riding my hand out of my head.

It doesn't fucking work.

The rest of the week, I train with Grayson. I have to keep my hands busy to stop myself from contacting Sienna. God, I want her.

I want to possess her, claim her, and make her mine.

I want to protect her and care for her.

That's what stops me from making contact.

She doesn't need to be wrapped up in my shit. Being involved with me would be dangerous. Having a woman in this lifestyle is a weakness. One I can't afford.

And that makes me fucking angry. Who is this woman and why does she have such a hold over me?

The memory of her pinned up against the wall by her ex stirred something deep inside me, something completely foreign. Then witnessing her smash him straight in the balls made me proud. There is definitely a fire that burns inside of her, pure perfection wrapped in a neat goddess-like form.

I'm going cold turkey. If that's what people do to get off drugs, surely it works for a woman you haven't even fucked.

Which is why I spend the entire week exhausting every muscle at Kings Gym. Every combination I nail provides a distraction from my thoughts.

Kings is mine and Grayson's training gym. We set it up when Luca first assigned him as my trainer. He was fresh out of the Marines, and I was just plucked off the streets after Luca managed to orchestrate a deal to keep my ass out of jail.

Grayson's been kicking my ass into shape ever since. He takes no shit and is the only opponent I've ever struggled to knock down on their ass in the ring.

We may have started off on unsure footing when I was a foster kid fighting on the streets. Discipline wasn't my thing. Let alone from a guy no bigger than I was and only five years older. Now, six years later, I couldn't be without the grumpy asshole. He and Luca are the closest thing to brothers I have.

There are only two months until my unification title fight. Already holding three belts, the WBC is the one I've got my sights on. Only a six foot four inch Russian machine stands in my way. He is an inch shorter and leaner than me, so he has quicker punches and is lighter on his footing for defense. I have pure power and skill. Boxing is 90% a mental fight. Once I get in the zone, there is no one that can stand in my way. I'm undefeated for a reason.

This fight holds more than the unification. It is the key to my freedom. A life away from the mafia. A chance to solely focus on boxing and live out the rest of my life without always looking over my shoulder. Grayson knows what's at stake, and fuck is he killing me for it.

Tossing my gym bag on the bench press, I head over to the office. As much as I should knock, I won't; it's our office, not just his. I'm going to bet on the fact there wouldn't be someone in there on a Monday morning, but Grayson, the ultimate playboy, doesn't listen to society's restraints on sex.

Barging through the door, I call out, "Knock knock, motherfucker."

Fuck, I love winding the big guy up.

Grayson shoots me a glare, taking his attention from his phone. We have those leather swivel office chairs, but neither of us can actually fit in the fucking things. Grayson is just an inch smaller than me, set with the same heavy, muscled frame. Still keeps an ashy blonde buzz cut. I guess old habits die hard from the Marines. Not that I'd know. He never fucking talks about it. I've tried to dig over the years, but he just shuts down and avoids the questions. I take that as he doesn't want to talk about it. I know something happened, but it's just passed by with us and Luca. The same as Grayson knows my ties to the mafia. Hell, he is also friends with Luca, so it's hardly a secret.

Maybe that's why we're like brothers. We understand each other's pain, but don't dredge it up. We don't need to be fucking therapists, just punching bags.

"I heard you had fun with Dante over the weekend," Grayson smirks.

"You won't be hearing much from his mouth now," I laugh.

"You're a sick fuck, Kel. I heard he exploded the toilet, shitting out those bullets." Tell me something I don't know. "Are you training today?" he asks.

"Why the fuck else would I be here? We have a big fight coming up in two months. Remember?" My tone mocking.

"Oh, fuck off. Of course, I do. You just don't ever grace this place with your presence on a Monday. I'm sure the ladies' boxercise class won't mind getting an eyeful of you, though." He winks, snickering.

Now, Grayson is a complete ladies' man. The lopsided grin and cheesy chat up lines make me fucking cringe when we go out. I've not yet actually seen him with the same woman more than once.

He will be lapping up the ladies' attention.

I don't flirt, I don't chase, and I certainly don't engage in small talk while I'm fucking. I imagine Grayson whispers sweet nothings into their ears as he fucks them. I don't do any of that. That is, until *her*, and I've barely tasted her yet.

Her being the reason I'm training on a Monday.

Monday I usually use to deal with all my other shit, like promos, club openings, and Luca's shit. But my brain can't concentrate on anything other than her. So instead, I go do what I do best.

Beat the shit out of people to stop myself from feeling.

Do I need a therapist? Fucking probably. But these methods have worked for me so far.

In just two months' time, I can focus on boxing and The End Zone. No more enforcing for Luca, no more watching my back constantly.

Wrapping my hands up and getting the gloves on, I step into the ring. Over on the mats are a bunch of middle-aged moms pretending to punch the air. I forgot my gym became a fucking mom's club in the day.

Grayson steps into the ring with pads on and a protective helmet. "You scared I'm gonna knock you out, you pussy? Take that fucking helmet off!" I shout across the ring.

"Na, I'll keep it on. You're in a weird ass mood today, and I don't want any shiners on this pretty face," he goads.

Jogging up to the center of the ring, I start my first combination of jabs on the pads. Left right left, ducking as Grayson swings the pad at me. We keep going and going until my lungs burn, sweat is dripping over my eyes, and my tank top is drenched.

Once I get in the zone, the whole world is silent. It's perfect.

My mind goes blank, and the only thing I see is my opponent; a dangerous headspace to be in.

The power in my punch can kill. If my mind switches off, there is nothing to stop the devil that dances in my veins.

Catching my breath, the room is deadly silent. I look over to the moms' class and all of them are staring at me open-mouthed, avoiding my gaze. They are petrified. I can smell their fear from here.

Grayson's voice echoes in the background.

"Keller! Keller, snap the fuck out of it! Now!" he bellows next to me.

Fuck.

Ripping off my shirt that's clinging to the sweat, I use it to dab my forehead, trying to steady my breath. Without acknowledging Grayson, I duck under the ropes and storm to the showers.

If he's shouting at me, I clearly didn't kill him. Shit. I could have.

After a cold shower and getting dressed, I hunt down Grayson, who's now throwing his own punches on a bag. I must have pissed him right off.

"Grays!" I shout, getting his attention.

Pushing the bag away, he stalks over to me.

"What in the fuck was that up there, Keller?" he demands, pointing to the ring. "You completely clocked out. It's fucking dangerous. You have to get your head in the game. Otherwise, you'll fucking kill someone," he spits, rubbing his hands over his face in frustration. "Go home; sort your head out. Christ, go get fucking laid. Now is not the time to lose it, Keller. A boxer is nothing without a strong mind. Remember that." Turning his back to me, he starts hurling punches into the bag. One guess he's imagining I'm that fucking bag.

The rest of the week, I immerse myself in training, avoiding Grayson for a couple of days for us to cool off.

Whenever my mind isn't focused on training, it wanders to Sienna. I wonder if she's thought about me. Has she thought about texting me? Is she dreaming of fucking me like I do every night of her?

It's not healthy; it's almost becoming obsessive.

I found her Instagram. I couldn't help myself. I thought if I just saw her, that would sedate the need, but it didn't. I just ended up beating one out with images of her posing on her feed flashing through my head.

I need to get this woman out of my system before it's too late.

CHAPTER EIGHT

Monday rolls around quicker than expected. Before I know it, I'm making my way through bustling New York traffic in rush hour. London may be busy, but it has nothing on the crowded streets of New York. I'll never get used to the chaos.

After I jog up the steps from the subway and head toward the cafe opposite my office, I'm met with the sun beating down through the clear skies. But the air is crisp, perfect weather to wear a tight black turtleneck jumper tucked into a pencil skirt. The top is ideal for hiding the bruising and grazes spotted over my arm. Instinctively, I start rubbing the sore patches. At least the bruising has faded from the red angry marks I woke up to on Saturday morning. What a perfect birthday gift that was. The high neck of the jumper masks the bite marks dotted along my neck–Keller's primal mark.

As I wait for my flat white to be poured, I open up my last messages from Keller and hover over the keypad to type out a morning text. I haven't heard a peep from him since he drove off in the early hours of Saturday morning. I don't want to come across as desperate, yet I can't rid the man from my every thought.

Maybe I'm just horny.

I spent the weekend lounging on the sofa with Maddie, watching Netflix and eating popcorn. I felt good, normal even. My birthday was on Saturday. I didn't even get my annual drunken text from my mom, telling me how I ruined her life by being born. I can't say I missed that.

Maddie knows how I feel about celebrating my actual birthday, so we kept it small with a little cake and a glass of wine. As a joke, she got me a fucking rape alarm and pepper spray, just in case Jamie re-appears and I don't have the chance to kick him in the balls. I can always count on Maddie to poke fun at anything serious. Although, it did make me laugh.

She kept trying to dig into the events with Keller, the nosy cow. I gave her some details, but kept most to myself. Otherwise, she won't stop.

"Flat white for Sienna," the blonde barista shouts, distracting me from my phone. I give her a smile, take my wake-up juice, and head to the Chrysler Building, downing the contents of my takeaway cup. The amber leaves scattering the pavement crunch under my heels. The cool breeze whips my hair into my face as I walk into the office foyer.

The reception area is dead. *Shit, am I late?* I check my watch–7:50 am. I'm ten minutes early, *phew*. Giving a quick smile to Harriet, our bubbly red-headed receptionist who's busy rambling down the phone, I head towards the stairs. The family law department is only on the fifth floor, so I don't mind the trek up to avoid the elevator.

By the time I reach the floor, my breathing is heavy.

Swiping my keycard, I make my way over to my desk, plonking down in my swivel chair.

"Morning, gorgeous girl," David declares with a grin that creases the corner of his eyes.

"Morning, David. New hair I see," I say, returning the grin.

David quickly became my best friend at work and now outside of work. Taking me under his wing from my first day over four years ago. At one stage, our boss, Alan, banned us from desking next to each other as we were too loud and distracting together.

We can't help it. We get on like a house on fire.

Don't get me wrong, David is a very attractive man to any woman with eyes. Tall and muscular build, with mesmerizing emerald eyes complete with a panty-dropping smile. He's no Keller, though.

We've been there and tried that.

One night a couple of years ago, we decided to get super drunk–prosecco drunk, no less–and Maddie dared us to kiss. Now, I don't have a brother, but that kiss was what I can imagine kissing your brother would be like.

It felt so wrong.

So, we made a pact to never discuss that again. At least we tried it.

On paper, we would be the perfect couple.

David coughs, grabbing my attention, and now sitting at his side of our connecting desks, he slides over a steaming hot coffee. *God, do I need the caffeine today.*

"Ooooh, what flavor did you pick for me today?" I ask. I never get the same coffee flavor twice from David. He knows I like, in his words, 'sickly sweet coffee', and is always pulling his nose up at my choice.

"Well, seeing as it's nearly Christmas, I had no choice but to let you try the Gingerbread latte today."

"Oh my God, thank you," I say before blowing him a kiss. Grabbing the cup between both hands, the steaming drink warms my insides, the cinnamon lingering in the air.

Shifting in his seat, he presses his gaze to me. "Maddie texted me over the weekend," he starts, his voice quiet. "Are you okay? I heard about what happened with Jamie. You should have texted me, Si. You know I'd love to punch him square in the jaw." Concern drips from his tone.

I know David hates Jamie.

David and Jamie's history goes back way beyond me. They used to work together at Jamie's dad's law firm until Jamie stole David's promotion from under him.

"I fucking wish I never introduced you two. I'm so fucking sorry he did this. I could kill the prick for laying his hands on you, Si," he says, placing his hand over mine.

"Honestly, it's fine. I'm okay, just a little shaken up. I'm more bloody embarrassed than anything. I don't even recognize the man he's become. The hatred in his eyes and his anger at the club Friday was fucking weird," I explain, rambling. "Have you heard anything? Why is he so obsessed with trying to get me back? He cheated on me;clearly, he didn't love me that much."

"I'll ask around, Si. I have a hunch this little drug problem of his goes back longer than we think. He's a snaky asshole. Just be careful."

"Yes *Dad,*" I mock, raising a brow.

He tips his head back, laughing. "Jesus, Si, are you really calling me Daddy now?"

"You two! It's barely the start of the day. Shut the fuck up and log on to work. Don't make me move you to separate ends of the office. Again." Alan points at us, disapproving, as he stands in his office doorway.

He shoots David a look, and we smirk and turn to face our computer screens.

"Sorry Alan." I try not to giggle.

The door slams shut. David leans over onto my side of the desk.

"You still up for drinks with me and Maddie Friday? Please come," he pleads, giving me those puppy eyes.

I can't resist those sparkling emeralds. I fake roll my eyes dramatically. "Oh, if I must."

THE REST OF THE WEEK FLIES BY. I KEEP MYSELF BUSY WITH WORK during the day and the new series *Good Girls* in the evenings on the sofa with Maddie. Still, every day I'm receiving apology texts from Jamie from unknown numbers. On Wednesday, a box of one hundred blood-red everlasting roses is delivered with a note.

"Everlasting roses just like my love for you. I'm sorry."

Maddie and I spent the evening chopping the roses up into a bin bag.

He always bought me red roses, thinking they were my favorite. Because every woman likes red roses, how original. Well, I don't.

If he'd have taken the time to even ask, he'd know I hate them. My dad used to buy a bouquet for my mom every week on his way home from work. After he left us, if anyone happened to buy her roses, she'd be off on a week's bender.

Now it's Friday. I'm standing, wrapped in a towel, dripping wet, swiping through the dresses in my wardrobe, deciding what to wear tonight.

I'm feeling something black, tight, and sexy. My fingers run down the black sequined cocktail dress, the tags still hanging from the label. I bought this dress for a charity dinner for Jamie's firm a few months ago. But he'd told me I looked like a stripper, so I changed into a longer red dress, not wanting to ruin the evening and piss him off.

Ripping off the tags and throwing them in the small trash can, I place the dress on the bed and focus on my hair and make-up. The events of last weekend invade my mind, as I dip the eyeliner in the black ink. I guess Keller really wasn't interested in seeing me again. *Sigh.*

The whole week, the memories of his touch, his power–hell, even his deep raspy dirty voice, made me hot as fuck. Every night, I had to use my purple friend to find some sort of relief.

But every night, I was left feeling disappointed. I need to get over it. I can't keep imagining being with a man I haven't even had. He isn't and can't be mine. Tonight I need to find someone to scratch this itch. I doubt they'll even come close to Keller, but I have to try.

Maddie comes strolling into the room, dressed to the nines. Her platinum blonde hair is straight, resting just over her boobs, like a mermaid. Her make-up is natural, emphasizing her contoured cheekbones, and clear gloss draws attention to her plump lips. She's wearing a metallic silver dress, with spaghetti straps, that just about covers her butt. I suppose being taller, with legs for days, most dresses come up short. I don't have that problem.

Plonking the prosecco next to me at the dressing table, the bubbles spill over the rim of the glass.

"Si, we only have half an hour before we need to leave.

Let me do your hair," she says, as she's already grabbing the hair dryer and brush.

Thirty minutes later, we're ready to go.

The sequin dress fits like a glove. I've paired it with some blood-red heels and matching lipstick.

Maddie braided the front of my hair in two French plaits and gave the rest big bouncy curls to emphasize the lighter ends of my hair from the dark roots. It's different for me, but it looks sexy.

Posing for a quick selfie, I upload it to my Instagram and lock my phone, tossing it back in my black leather clutch. I run and grab a black fur coat. Last week it was fucking freezing and tonight feels even cooler.

"David just sent a text. He's on his way to The End Zone with a couple of his friends from the gym now. I said we'll be there in about twenty."

My body instantly freezes when she mentions The End Zone.

What if he's there?

No. Last week was the opening night. The owner doesn't need to go to the club every weekend, right?

Maddie links my arm through hers. "You might get to see your sexy boxer friend tonight with any luck."

That's exactly what I'm afraid of.

CHAPTER NINE
keller

It's Friday night. I promised Grayson a VIP night at the club to make up for being 'an absolute cunt' this week–his exact words.

I get to the club early, pour myself a scotch in the office, and pull up the security feeds. Memories flood back to me of last Friday in my office with a certain firecracker coming apart on my fingers. I can almost smell her sweet scent now. It's addicting. Dangerous.

Here I am sitting and watching people enter the club on a Friday night, wondering, no, hoping she might make an appearance. What the hell has happened to me? This woman is turning me into an absolute pussy.

I know I shouldn't want her. I can't have her, but I can't resist this urge.

I saw on her Instagram that she was off on a girls' night tonight. I can only hope her fine ass ends up in my club.

Now on my third measure of scotch, Grayson texts to tell me he's on his way. I continue to study the monitor until something catches my attention. Zooming in on the main doors, I squint. *Is that you, princess?*

I know from the hammering in my chest it's her.

She's in the queue with her blonde friend from last week. I can see through the screen her eyes light up when she talks. *Why am I bothered to know that she has friends to take care of her?*

A pair of masculine arms wrap around Sienna's neck and she snuggles into them, turning to flash the prick her bright, infectious smile.

Fuck. This.

Slamming my drink on the desk, I charge out of the office, fists clenched by my sides. Grayson's walking down the hall towards my office. I don't have time for him right now. Cutting him off before he can start, I say, "I've gotta sort something real quick. Your booth is set up in the VIP area. Give them your name. I'll meet you there in a minute."

Without waiting for a response, I continue on my mission: get that bloke the fuck off Sienna.

All week I've almost killed myself physically trying to get her off my mind. Just one look at her and it's all flooding back. Every cell in my body is warning me against this, screaming at me to leave it.

My heart may be working in the sense it pumps blood around my body to keep me alive, but it's dead in the sense it doesn't feel.

It doesn't feel anything other than darkness.

There is no light.

I don't deserve light.

To be the beast in the boxing ring, the enforcer on the streets, I can't allow light into my life. I crave the darkness.

But I'm fucking taking it anyway, even if it is just for one night.

The rage courses through my veins, blood hammering in my ears, as I push past the crowd in the club.

It's the second weekend we've been open, and the place is overflowing. I should be proud; it is my vision come to life. In the long run, it's a means to an end, part of my deal with Luca. He funnels his dirty cash through the club, keeps the mob happy, and sets me free. After the small job of becoming World Champion.

The fight is booked. Just seven weeks left until my debt is paid. But I can't concentrate on that until I fuck this goddess out of my system.

The number one rule of boxing: *Fight with your head.* Right now, it's all over the place. I can't afford to lose my head in the ring.

Fuck, I need to calm down.

The chances are, Sienna is going to be pissed because I haven't contacted her all week. But I'm hoping I can sweet talk her into agreeing with my proposal.

One night of pure sinful sex and then we carry on with our lives. Easy, right?

Barging past those useless bouncers, the ones I still need to fire, I scan my way through the crowd. Like a wolf on a hunt, I zone in on my prey.

I can pick her out of a crowd of thousands. My body reacts before I even see her. If I didn't know any better, it's almost as if she's cast some kind of spell on me. Never has a woman had this effect on me.

I spot her easily. She stands out from anyone else around her. Absolutely no man in this universe could ignore her beauty. Quite simply, she is stunning. Her piercing icy blues lock onto mine, realization etches across her face as she gives me a wide smile, her face lighting up.

Fuck, I swear when she smiles at me I forget how to breathe. All the air is knocked clean from my lungs.

I return her smile with a teasing smirk.

Her hair is braided at the roots with curls bouncing around her, flowing right down her back. Under the luminous red signs of The End Zone entrance, I can see her sinful sequined dress shimmering against the lights, emphasizing her killer figure. I bet she looks even more delicious out of the clothes.

The prick still has his arms locked around her neck, his head resting on her shoulder. He's a reasonable-sized man, but no match for me. She cocks her head to the side and whispers in his ear.

Watching this makes my skin crawl; seeing another man's hands on her creamy soft skin makes me murderous. He looks at her with concern, setting his sights on me with a worried glare. Yes, asshole, hands off. I'm still standing by the entrance to the club. I should know better. The last thing I need before a fight is more bad press. Grayson's already pissy with me after my outburst this week.

The prick finally takes his arms off her, her eyes searching for mine. Oh, she's caught on quickly. I don't fuck around.

It's now or never.

I stride over to her and plaster on my best fake smile for the crowd. To them, I'm a celebrity, a billionaire boxing playboy, and that's the story we're sticking to.

I reach her just as she turns to face me. Her blonde friend smiles at me in recognition; I guess she knows about last weekend. "Hey, Keller." Sienna speaking breaks me from my thoughts.

"Hey, baby," I whisper against her ear, just loud enough for her to hear. A crimson blush creeps up her cheeks. I set my sights on the rest of her group. "I have some space in our VIP area tonight. You'll have to put up with my asshole trainer. Drinks are on the house all night to make up for that."

Her friends all cheer in response, and Sienna eyes me suspiciously. And she should. I have plans for us. I'm just being polite, offering her friends an alternative to her company. Fuck knows why. I don't ever care about other people, but with her it's different. I don't want her to fear me. I don't want her to know my darkest side.

The blonde one is the first to pipe up. "Urrrr yes! Of course, we'd love to. Wouldn't we, guys?" She emphasizes her words while shooting them all daggers.

Prick with the cuddle complex is unreadable, and my patience is wearing thin. He's already had his hands on something that doesn't belong to him. The fact I'm offering an evening on the house is a miracle, when all I want to do is smash his head against the pavement.

"Yeah, sounds good, pal." The prick finally responds, and Sienna gives him a soft smile, which pisses me off.

I move the red rope barrier and signal for them to come through, catching Sienna's wrist as she waltzes past, stopping her in her tracks.

"Not so fast, gorgeous. We have other plans." And I feel her shiver under my touch.

The only solace from this predicament I find myself in is it's clear she's under the same fucking spell as me. Her body can't help but react to me, no matter how much she may will it not to.

Releasing her wrist, I shut the barrier, which gets me some moaning from the queue of people. I cock my eyebrow in annoyance at their whining and turn my attention back to Sienna. Placing my hand at her lower back, I lead her into the club, nodding to the bouncers as we pass.

Once in the club, we make our way by the dance floor,

bar, and then the VIP area. I clock her friends walking in, good they will leave us alone for a bit now. I'm sure Grayson will keep her blonde friend company. I lead her down the hallway, heading towards my office. Déjà vu of last Friday flashes in my brain, automatically sending all the blood rushing straight to my dick. As we make our way into the office, a waft of her sweet peach scent smothers my senses. Fucking delicious.

Her perfect ass is teasing me as she edges into the room just inches away from my dick touching her. *Fuck, I need to get it together*. She makes herself at home and plops onto the leather couch, legs crossed and arms folded. But I can see her perky nipples giving away her true feelings. She wants me as much as I want–no–crave her.

I walk past her and around my desk; I need a second to compose myself.

"So, to what do I owe this pleasure, Keller?" she asks. Even her British accent turns me on, despite the angry undertone.

"I have a proposal for you." I get straight to the point, reminding myself this isn't an offer of marriage. Although, have I ever had to ask a woman to have sex with me to get them out of my brain so I can focus on anything else? No.

"Ok, and that proposal is?" she presses, shifting in her seat.

I lean over my desk, my palms flat on the smooth oak. "I won't beat around the bush, Sienna. I want to fuck you. Hell, I haven't stopped thinking about you all week. I have a big fight coming up, and I can't afford any distractions. Therefore, my proposal is one night. I will give you the best night of your life. Any number of orgasms you want, you've got."

Tapping my fingers on the desk, I watch as she soaks in

my proposition. Chewing the inside of her mouth, her brows furrow. I can hear the cogs turning inside her head from here.

"What do you say?" I ask, holding my breath. I really fucking need her to say yes. For my own sanity.

"Say 'please'." She smirks, eyes twinkling.

Fuck, this woman is going to kill me. Raking my hand over my face in fake annoyance, I let out a huff. "Please, princess. I'll get on my knees and beg if you need me to." I groan. Of course, she's making me work for it. The woman's a firecracker. I should've expected no less.

Looking me dead in the face, desire burning behind her eyes and giving me a devious smile, she simply replies, "Yes, Keller."

And that's all I need.

Pushing myself off the desk, I stalk over to her. I can't kiss her here. If I do, I won't be able to stop, and I don't want any interruptions. She promised me a whole night and that's what I'm taking.

I grab her by the waist and hoist her over my shoulder. She screams while whacking me on the back. "Keller, put me down. I can walk!"

"I know, but it's a lot quicker if I carry you when you've got heels on," I reply, slapping her ass. I hear a small moan escape her lips as I do.

Oh, tonight's going to be electric.

There's not a chance in hell one night is going to kill this obsession.

CHAPTER TEN

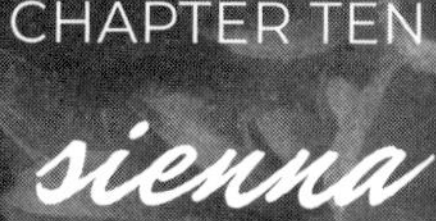

I'm twiddling my thumbs in the passenger seat. *Does this man not own any modest cars? I get he's rich, but who needs a different car for each night of the week?*

"So, Russo. Italian-American right?" I ask in an attempt to make small talk. I have always rambled when I'm nervous.

He eyes me suspiciously from the driver's seat.

"You'd be correct," he drawls. "I'm not Italian-American, though." His features are straight as he grips the wheel with both hands.

"Oh, okay." I'm cautious, sensing it's a sore subject so not wanting to press.

"My birth mother was a drug addict. She gave me up when I was a baby. No, I don't know who she is, and I don't want to."

The hurt is laced in his tone.

"I spent my childhood being tossed from foster home to foster home. No one wanted to keep a kid with my kind of 'darkness', as they described it. It's bad for their real kids."

My heart hurts for little Keller.

"By the time I was in my early teens, I'd made a name for myself on the streets in underground boxing. I met Luca around twelve years old. The kid couldn't stop pissing people off, so I'd have to fight all his battles."

He chuckles, which instantly brings a smile to my face.

"By the time we were fourteen, we were inseparable, so we were placed with Mrs. Russo, a recent widow. A little Italian lady with an infectious smile and one hell of a backhand."

His eyes light up when he speaks of her.

"We stayed with her formally until we turned eighteen, but on that day, we both changed our last names to Russo. She didn't have a family of her own. Her husband died young. She loved us boys so fiercely, like her own. We didn't want to leave her at eighteen, so we stayed. Plus, she made mean Italian food, so who could possibly ever want to leave?" He smiles.

I rest my hand over his. "That's so lovely. I'm glad you found her. She sounds like an incredible lady." I nod, giving him a small but genuine smile.

There is so much more to this man underneath his hard exterior.

"Yeah, yeah she is," he mumbles. Keeping his eyes on the road, stroking his thumb over my hand.

A few moments pass in silence. "So, Londoner?" he asks, now sporting a cockney accent and a smirk.

"I do not sound like that!" Hitting his bicep with the back of my hand, a giggle escapes.

"How long have you been an honorary New Yorker?"

I guess this journey's turning into a get-to-know-your - history chat. I'm not entirely convinced this is one night stand pre-chat, but fuck it.

I take in a deep breath, readying myself to answer. For some reason, I feel comfortable opening up to him.

"I moved here the second I turned eighteen. I was awarded a scholarship to study sociology at Columbia University. I lived in the rough ends of East London. My dad walked out on us when I was ten. Not heard from him since."

"Fucker," Keller mumbles under his breath.

That makes me chuckle.

"Then my mom turned to vodka as her companion. Hence why I got on the first plane out of there. I'd grown up taking care of myself pretty much my whole life. Figured moving countries wouldn't be that hard." I shrug. Deep down, it hurts.

I might be rambling, but shit, did it feel good to let it out to someone who genuinely asked about me rather than someone being paid to care.

"So, now, I work as a paralegal at Chambers & Sons, specializing in family law. But the real dream deep down is to go into social care. I want to help kids from disadvantaged backgrounds achieve, you know? I was lucky to get my scholarship and start a new life, but not every kid has that. Those are the kids I want to help."

Shit, of course, he fucking knows.

Pursing his lips together, he slowly nods.

Crap.

Keller takes a sharp left and my body crashes into the passenger door.

"Shit, Keller! What the fuck are you doing?" I exclaim.

My body hurtles forward and smashes back into the seat as the car comes to an abrupt stop.

I slowly turn towards Keller. Shit! Were we in a crash?

The fucker presses the off button of the car, not even looking at me.

Is he fucking psychotic?

Before I even get a chance to ask him if he's a psychopath, he turns his head to look at me, lust burning from his gaze. Heat rushes through my body, channeling straight between my legs. I squeeze them tightly together, so tight it's creating more friction. He's staring at me like I'm worthy, like I'm the sexiest woman on the planet. At the same time, like he wants to fucking devour me.

I drag my eyes from him so I can scan my surroundings. From what I can make out from the dimly lit street, we're definitely in a residential neighborhood, near 5th Avenue. A quiet one at that.

Not one light is on in the apartments surrounding us on either side of the sidewalk. Not one car passes us by. I mean, it's kind of an ideal place to murder someone and not be seen. But by the heat radiating off Keller, I think the last thing he wants to do is murder me, not unless you count death by orgasms.

I stare out the passenger window. I swear his gaze is burning holes into the back of my head. I'm scared to turn back around. The sound of each deep inhale he does draws me back to him.

This pull we have between us, with him so close to me, I can't focus on anything. *Am I even breathing?* I turn back to him and watch the cords in his neck and the veins popping as the tension rises in the small space. I'm desperately fighting the urge to bite him. The thought alone makes my pussy burn. *Jesus, how am I so wet just thinking about him?*

A moan escapes me, and he looks dead at me.

Oh fuck.

We might have agreed to fuck to get it out of our

systems, but somewhere deep down, the feelings stirring in my chest might not leave after just one night. I'm going to crave more; more and more until it fucking breaks me into a thousand pieces.

Oh, but it will all be worth it.

I slowly turn my body around to face him, rolling my lips between my teeth. Keller's dragging his thumb along his jaw, his sight not leaving my mouth. It seems as if he's having the same inner debate.

"Fuck it," is the last thing he says before his hands grip around my neck and his lips crash down onto mine.

A throaty moan escapes me in response to the ferocity of the kiss. I don't even recognize my own voice. I'm putting everything I have into my response, a subtle way of showing him I feel the same way.

I may not fucking want to, but I do.

We've set the wildfire now.

It is either going to burn down our whole world or we are going to dance in the flames.

"I couldn't fucking take it anymore, Sienna," he rasps between kisses. "I've tried to stay away, but I can't seem to get you, my fiery goddess, out of my every waking thought. I have to have you now."

There's urgency in his tone as his almost black eyes burn into my soul.

"But I don't think I'll ever be able to give you up."

My eyebrows raise and my lip forms an 'O'. *He does feel it, too. I knew it!*

Not waiting for a response, as if he didn't mean to add that last part, he slams his lips back onto mine, pouring every ounce of desire into his kiss. He is demanding. I have no control over it. He is taking what he wants and I'm laying it out on a platter for him.

"Spread your legs for me, baby," he growls, sending shockwaves straight to my throbbing pussy.

God, his deep voice is enough to just soak me.

I straighten my back as awareness shoots through me like a lightning bolt

"Keller, we're parked in a street. What if someone sees us?" I'm cautious, but truthfully, I'm so turned on right now, I don't know if I could actually stop this.

"Do you think I'd let anyone else have a glimpse of what's mine, Sienna?" Annoyance laces in his tone.

His fingers trace up my thighs until his hand creeps up the hem of my dress. I lift my bum off the chair to give him better access. He grabs my panties and rips them clean off, leaving me bare. I can feel the cold air against my heat. Bringing his lips down to my neck, he bites, the pain intensifying the desire.

"I'll fuck you when and wherever I want, but I don't share, not even with a passerby on the street." He teases me whilst nipping at my neck. My whole body is on high alert. With every touch, every nip, pleasure shoots straight through me.

I have never felt more alive.

I bite my lip to hold in a moan as he traces his tattooed finger down my arm, watching with intent as goosebumps appear under his touch.

"Do you understand?" he breathes softly into my neck.

"Yes, *sir,"* I whisper, my heart fluttering in my chest.

"That's a good fucking girl."

The zip of his pants echoes in the car.

I can't help it. Those words uttered from his lips, with his deep voice, undoes me. It is so fucking hot. I have never been so turned on in my life. Unable to move my gaze from his cock, pulsing against his pants, I chew my lip in anticipation. From the outline in his pants, I can see his cock is fucking massive. *Jesus, will it fit?*

"It will." His chuckle breaks me from staring. *Fuck, did I say that out loud?*

Oh well, I'm intrigued now.

"What is it? Like thirty centimeters or something?" I ask, quickly trying to calculate how that would fit inside me if I am right.

"I don't have a clue what that is, but mine's eleven inches, baby."

Holy Shit.

With that new information, and the fire burning through me since he uttered the words '*good girl*', I'm getting impatient. I need a release. I need him.

"Keller, please." Fuck, I sound needy, but I don't care.

"So greedy," he teases, giving me a devilish grin and tapping his fingers on my thigh.

Yes! Just a bit higher.

I lift my butt just a few inches off the seat to encourage his fingers to go where I need them.

He wraps his hands around my thigh and presses me back down flat to the chair. Tossing my head back, I let out a frustrated groan. I can't fucking take much more of this.

My breathing heavy, I place my hand on top of his. I can't help it. I need to touch him.

"Put your back up against the door and spread your legs across the console," he demands.

I do as he says, as quickly as I can, scooting my butt until my back connects with the cold metal frame.

Not even that can put out the fire within me.

I slowly lower myself, opening my legs and placing one next to the gear stick and the other on the armrest. It's the best I can do.

Good job he took the G-Wagon tonight. Maybe his flash array of cars will be useful after all.

Rubbing his hand over his face, he lets out a breath as he stares at my naked pussy. "Fuck, Sienna. I can't wait to get a taste."

Slowly, too fucking slowly, he slides his seat back and rests his body over the center console. His eyes, still on one place, look ready to devour me.

The anticipation nearly gives me a heart attack.

He lowers his face towards my pussy, placing soft kisses on my inner thighs, his slight stubble brushing against my skin, almost burning. The warmth of his breath hitting my sensitive skin makes my breath hitch.

He crashes his lips onto my pussy, shooting an electrical current up my body. The instant his mouth connects, my back arches and I cry out.

Jesus. Fucking. Christ.

He laps his tongue like a man starved, swiping up and down, biting on my clit, which sends my eyes rolling to the back of my head.

"Fuck, Keller," I rasp through heavy breaths.

He doesn't let up his assault with his tongue.

Shifting slightly, he traces his hands up my leg, sending shocks through me as he slides a finger down my slit and enters me slowly with one, quickly adding another. Both are now thrusting in and out of me as I buck my hips to match his pace. Fuck, I need more.

I twist my fingers through his hair and push his head back down. His eyes meet mine, almost sparkling.

"My greedy, greedy goddess," he chuckles.

I don't even need to respond; his tongue finds that sweet spot over my clit and laps it up, finding the perfect rhythm with his fingers slamming in and out.

I can't take any more.

My legs are shaking violently, my heartbeat is hammering in my ears. I'm trembling around him but still manage to keep moving my hips up and down. I throw my head back against the window as the most intense orgasm rips through my body.

"Oh my god, Keller!" I cry out.

Gently pulling my dress back down, Keller slides his fingers out of my throbbing pussy. I immediately feel empty.

My whole body is tingling and trembling. I lift my leg, brushing the top of his head. I'm too exposed; I need to close my legs. Keller cups my cheek, nuzzling his mouth to my hair, as my breath only mildly starts to return to normal.

Fuck, him breathing in my ear is enough to send me off again. I have never orgasmed more than once with any of my other partners. Yet Keller just breathing on me is almost sending me into orgasm number two. *Fuck, he's good.*

"Princess, don't you ever hide from me. That was the goddamn sexiest thing I've ever seen. You losing control on my tongue made me almost come in my pants. There is no embarrassment here, only pleasure." He whispers this, and I slowly nod in reply.

Keller moves back over to his seat, and I spy his erection and can't help but stare. Even through his trousers, it's a fucking monster. As if sensing what I'm thinking, Keller turns to me, chuckling, trying to readjust himself awkwardly.

"When I come tonight, it's going to be inside your tight pussy, with you screaming my name as you take every last drop from me. Okay?"

His lips turn into that sexy lopsided smirk he does.

God, his mouth.

The thought makes my heart jump; my whole body is aroused again. Fuck, this man is something else. I don't just want more; my whole body craves it.

"My place or yours?" He smirks, turning his attention to his wing mirror as the ignition roars the car to life.

"Yours," I respond instantly.

I've had dreams of being fucked on his kitchen island all week. I'm not sure what he'd think of my poxy double bed smothered in pink fluffy cushions. I'm not even sure he'd fit in my bed.

It's a stark reminder we live in two different worlds, his being one I don't belong in.

I chastise my inner thoughts. *It's only for one night, Sienna. It's not as if you're going to marry him. He wants you for sex. He's hardly going to care about your bank balance.*

Always the over-thinker. Sometimes I wish I could just shut my brain off for five minutes.

I'm starting to doubt that just one night will ever be enough of him.

CHAPTER ELEVEN

keller

I couldn't help myself.

Listening to her talk about her passion to help disadvantaged kids struck a cord close to my heart. She's absolutely perfect in every way. Far, far too perfect for a monster like me. But I'm in too deep now. And nothing is going to stop me from claiming her as mine tonight. Even if it's just this once.

On the drive back to the penthouse, anticipation sizzles in the air. After devouring her pussy in the passenger seat, my cock has not gone back down. It fucking hurts. Being near her is a constant hard on.

Now, I'm not just getting turned on by her looks or sassiness, but by her dreams, desires, and intelligence. It's fucking dangerous. Keeping my eyes on the road, I can't risk catching a glimpse. I'm not sure my cock can take it.

Just a few minutes' drive feels like a lifetime. I open the passenger door for her as she slips out of the car, grabbing her by the waist to lift her down. The car emphasizes how petite she is. My fingers are almost touching around her ribcage.

Placing my hand back to its favorite place–her lower back–I guide her into the elevator. It's fucking freezing; plumes of vapor come from my mouth as I breathe. I left my jacket at the club in my haste to get her back here. She must be freezing in that short figure-hugging number she has on.

I move my hand from her back and wrap an arm around her shoulder, pulling her into my side, hoping that will warm her up. I can feel her shivering against me. Either from the cold or from my touch.

I hit the button for the 86th floor, and the realization hits me of her fear of elevators. From the corner of my eye, I catch her twiddling her thumbs, her clear tell of anxiety. There's no one else in here, and I have the perfect distraction tactic.

My hands find her waist, and I hoist her up to rest her ass on the gold metal railing that runs along the walls. Spreading her legs with my body, I step in towards her and she wraps them around my back. Her bare pussy rubs against the zip of my trousers.

Jesus Christ, this woman.

I start peppering kisses along her slender collarbones and up her neck. She hums in approval, and I watch as her eyes close and her head tilts back slightly. She is breathtaking.

"You are so fucking beautiful, Sienna," I rasp between kisses, inching closer and closer to her lips. Cupping her jaw with my hand, I bring my lips down to hers. This kiss is unlike the desperation and desire from earlier. This is intimate, our lips caressing each other. I have never experienced a moment like this in my life.

She moans with satisfaction into my mouth as I part her lips with my tongue and enter. The sweet taste of her is still on my tongue from in the car. She tightens the grip of her legs around my body as best she can. Her legs barely reach around my frame.

I take that as an invitation to deepen the kiss. I press my chest up against hers, my free hand moving up to cup her ass, and continue to explore her mouth.

A ding of the door opening breaks us apart. I lift her off the railings with both hands under her ass, keeping her legs tightly snaked around me, and walk us into the apartment.

"See, elevators don't have to be scary," I tease.

Hmmm, where do I want to fuck her first? I plan on nearly every surface.

The first available space I see is the kitchen island. Something Sienna doesn't know is that I have never had the company of a woman in this penthouse. This is my personal space, my solace. I've never wanted to bring a woman here.

Until now.

I place Sienna's feet on the ground and spin her around to face the kitchen island.

Dark, intricate fine line work spirals down her spine. The tattoo clearly goes lower than the dress. Fuck, I need to see the rest.

Slowly unzipping the dress, I inch it down, exposing more of the artwork that laces along her pale skin, all the way down to the dimples at the base of her spine. The dress pools around her feet on the floor, leaving her completely naked in front of me; her perfect, round ass taunting me. Dipping my head to the back of her neck, I lick all the way down the tattoo, her chest falling up and down as I do. She is so responsive to me, almost as if she's made for me.

A moan escapes her lips as I reach the base of her tattoo, then drop to my knees on the hard marble flooring. I take both cheeks in my hand and I bite down hard, causing her to jerk forward. Red primal teeth marks tainting her skin stare back at me, and pride rushes through my chest.

"Fuck," she grits out as she bends herself further over the counter, clear liquid dripping down the inside of her thigh. Fuck, she's dripping for me.

Not wasting any time, I rip off my shirt and unzip my trousers, finally freeing my cock. *Fuck, that feels better*. I grab the base of my cock and give it a couple of tugs–habit, I guess. My cock has never been more ready to go than right this second.

Her pussy is glistening. I quickly dart my tongue out to lap up some of the juices. I can't help myself; she is delicious. I stand up and grab her ass to line up my cock with her entrance, slowly rubbing against her slit, covering myself in her wetness.

"Baby, are you ready?"

Turning her head slightly to face me, she takes a quick breath. "Fuck me, Keller," she rasps as she wiggles her hips. That's all the invitation I need. I sink into her tight pussy slowly, inch by inch, letting her adjust to my size.

"Fuccccck. Oh my god, Keller."

I'm barely able to form words. "Your pussy takes me so well," I grit out, looking down at our bodies joining. "It looks fucking perfect holding my cock."

My greedy girl inches her ass backward, taking the rest of me, shouting out as she does. Pleasure soars through my body. We've barely even started and I'm so close. Her walls are pulsating against my cock, wetting it in her slick juices.

Shit. Shit shit shit.

When I grab her ass to stop her from moving any further back, she flings her head around to look back at me over her shoulder, the annoyance in her eyes shooting daggers at me.

“Sienna, I didn’t use a condom.” Even I can hear the hint of panic in my voice. “I’m clean. Are you on the pill?” Like fuck do I want to tie her down with having a kid with me.

“Yes, it’s fine, Kel. I'm clean, too. Just don’t stop,” she grunts.

My body sags in relief. Thank fuck.

I finally thrust in the rest of my cock, and she screams out my name. Grabbing onto her ass, I slam in and out, my knuckles turning white. Shit, that might leave a mark. But the pure thought of leaving marks for her to see when I’m gone makes me possessive and want to fuck her raw.

I won’t fucking last long like this, with her pussy taking me for everything I have. Her legs start to shake, so I quickly flip her over onto her ass. Her eyes are full of desire as she grins at me, and that smile pierces me straight through my black heart.

I pull her back down onto my cock as she uses her arms to hold herself up on the counter, bouncing up and down, her tits matching the movement, just begging to be touched.

Unable to resist, I bend my head down, take one of the rosy buds in my mouth and suck, still thrusting in and out. Her legs start to tremble around me.

Lifting her head, she brings her hooded gaze to me. “Keller, I’m so close.”

“You don’t get to come until I tell you.”

Gritting my teeth, I up the tempo. Our bodies slam together, beads of sweat delicately slip down her forehead.

“Keller, I can't.”

“Yes. You. Can,” I grunt out between thrusts.

Furrowing her brows, concentration etched across her features, she arches and throws her head back. Bending in, I grip her throat. "Good girl," I whisper against her delicious neck, as her pulse hammers against my palm. I squeeze my hand slightly tighter, which only spurs her on more. I groan at the sight before me. I'm right on the edge of my own release, every muscle in my body tight. I yank her head towards me and crash my lips over hers.

"You can come now, gorgeous."

Tipping her head back, she revels in her orgasm, her whole body quaking, sending me straight over the edge. I join her, tipping my head back as pleasure rips through me. Her walls pulsate against my cock as I spill my seed into her.

"Fuucck!" I roar. Her screams are ringing in my ears over the blood thumping.

Our breathing is heavy, yet in sync, while I bring my sweaty forehead down to hers and we stay there, my cock still twitching inside her.

While tracing my thumb across her flushed cheek, she gives me a sweet smile. Her hair is wild, and her makeup is starting to smear, yet she still looks perfect.

"Jesus, Keller, that was something else. I can't even feel my legs."

I'm not wanting to delve into the emotions swirling around in my chest. But seeing her like this, exposed and freshly fucked, stirs up feelings inside me I don't recognize. I don't want her to go home. I don't want this to be the last time I sink my cock inside her perfect pussy.

Exactly what I'm afraid of is happening. I'm craving her, I'm fucking hooked. Line and sinker.

Shit. This wasn't part of my plan.

"Do you want to know a secret?" she asks, resting her head in the crease of my neck.

"Go on."

"You're officially the first man to ever make me come twice in the same day."

Pride fills my chest. I shouldn't give a shit, but knowing that makes me want to delve in and see what number we can get up to. At the same time, part of me is angry that any other man got to experience her before me.

"How many do you think you've got left in you tonight, baby?" I tease, hoping and praying it's a high number. I'm not a religious man, but watch me drop to my knees and pray for this.

Have I ever been interested in fucking a woman more than once in a night? Not particularly. Sienna is different. I have an all-consuming need to take care of her. I want to protect her when it's me she needs protecting from.

I watch her sigh; I think I actually feel it.

"Keller, I really don't think it's possible. I think my body is just broken. I've never been able to."

Well, that's a challenge if ever I've heard one.

"That's because you've never been with a real man."

With that, I lift her off the counter and stride down the hall toward my bedroom.

Never has a woman been in this bed. This place is my sanctuary. I don't let people in. Yet here she is, her hair sprawled out over my bed, laid bare, just waiting for me. I give her a quick kiss and turn around to the en-suite.

"Hey, where are you going?" she shouts behind me.

"You'll see. Don't you dare move."

I have a freestanding gold bath. It's the centerpiece of the room, surrounded with floor to ceiling windows. My favorite part of the entire penthouse. There's nothing like watching the world go by as you relax your muscles, immersed in the bathtub, the room lit up purely by the stunning New York skyline.

I've never thought of it as a sexy setting before. The thought of getting Sienna in here has my cock standing to attention.

Turning on the warm water, I rummage through the cabinets. Surely I have something sweet smelling like her to put in there. Coconut and vanilla sounds sickly. Somehow, though, I imagine it laced on her soft skin will be a heavenly combination.

The shimmering moonlight falls through the windows directly on Sienna, sprawled out across my bed. Her body glistens, and her curves are highlighted perfectly. Running a hand through my hair, I let out a breath. Fuck, I'm in trouble.

Every time I look at her, my heart does this weird jumpy thing. My heart isn't supposed to do these things. Shit, maybe I'm ill. It's almost the same feeling I get before I step into the ring–pure adrenaline and excitement laced together.

I stalk over to the bed. Her eyes never leave mine. I can see the amusement and desire written all over her face as she gives me a sexy smile, catching her lips between her teeth. Without saying a word, I bend to her and pick her up–she's light as a feather–and walk us back into the bathroom. Her breath hitches at the sight. I get it; I never get sick of this view.

"Keller, this is so beautiful," she says through a smile, her eyes zoning straight in on the bath, which is now almost overflowing with bubbles.

I gently submerge her into the bath, and she lets out a little moan as the water surrounds her. The bubbles dance across her silky skin. A view I'll have burned into my brain for the rest of my life. Her head leaning back on the side, her hair draping over the edge of the tub, she purrs to me while swishing water through her fingertips.

"Are you coming in?"

Crouching down, I bring my head to the same level as hers. She opens her eyes, those piercing blues dagger into me, stealing my breath, as she searches my face. Too stunned to speak, emotions swirling in the air, I do what I know best and lean in, bringing my lips to hers, raking my hands through her soft hair. Her manicured finger traces down my chest, down to my abs, and back up. If that isn't the most erotic feeling I've ever felt, I don't know what is.

My cock is pulsing, and not being able to wait any longer, I jump into the bath. Water spills over the sides as I do. I barely fit in the bath on my own, let alone with another. Lacing my fingers through hers, I pull her towards me so she can come and straddle my lap.

As soon as her pussy connects to my lap, she lifts slightly, positioning the head at her entrance, fire burning in her eyes.

"Fuck, baby," I groan, dragging her head to mine, searching for her lips as my cock slides into her. I need as much contact as I can have with this woman; just even fucking her isn't enough.

I want more. I want it all.

She sinks onto my cock and that's it, the tiny thread of self-restraint I have flies out the window.

"Ride me, princess. Take what you want from me," I grit out.

Her hips rock forward and back, and fire dances through me. I grip her ass as tight as I can, needing to center myself. Her nipples taunt me, her tits bounce up and down as she grinds on me, her eyes burn into mine.

Water sprays out of the bath, slapping against our skin.

Only the moonlight and glistening specks from the skyline light up the room.

I take over the pace as I chase my release, using my grip on her ass to pound into her. Her hands cup my cheeks as she gives me a sexy smile before claiming mine for a ferocious kiss. Her tongue explores my mouth as I struggle to hold in a moan. I'm losing it. Together, we are unstoppable.

Like a match being lit, a fire burns between us.

An orgasm aggressively rips through me. "Now," I pant.

That sets her over the edge. My perfect goddess, coming along with me, writhing above me, riding out her third orgasm of the evening.

Fucking perfect.

A perfect that's not mine to keep. No matter how much I want to.

THREE ROUNDS LATER, WE ARE WELL AND TRULY SPENT. I HAD NO intention of letting Sienna go back to her apartment tonight. So, now, she's curled up in the fetal position, tucked neatly into my side, lying on my arm. Her even breathing indicates she's fast asleep.

Another first: a fucking sleepover.

Her lying next to me, her sweet peachy scent wafting up my nose, brings sudden calm. Usually, I sleep a couple of hours max. My brain is usually a whirlwind of chaos, the chattering so loud I can't switch it off. Tonight, my brain is silent.

In fact, it's so silent I can hear a phone constantly buzzing in the other room. Mine is always on loud. I can't miss one of Luca's demanding calls. It must be Sienna's. No doubt one of her friends checking in on her. Sienna doesn't strike me as someone who wouldn't let her blonde friend–Maddie, I think–know she was leaving.

The buzzing piquing my interest, I gently slide my arm from underneath the sleeping goddess's head and slip out of bed, padding into the lounge. More than anything, I need to silence this fucking phone; it's giving me a headache.

Her phone illuminates on the counter, an unknown caller flashing on the screen. I check the time on the stove–2 am. *Who the fuck would be calling her off an unknown at this time?*

The buzzing stops, thank God. Her home screen displays an onslaught of messages.

I scroll through, skimming the texts.

UNKNOWN

Answer your fucking phone, you whore.

I fucking told you I was sorry. ANSWER or you'll regret it.

You won't be so tough when you haven't got the new man you're whoring yourself out to to pick you up like the pathetic bitch you are.

I bet he's enjoying the boring sex.

SLUT

The more I scroll, the more my blood boils. I'm clutching the phone, willing myself not to shatter it into a thousand pieces.

The phone vibrates in my hand. I smirk.

I answer on the first ring.

"I know you couldn't fucking resist me, Sienna. Stop fucking around and get over yourself."

I clear my throat. "Jamie, I take it."

Silence.

His heavy breathing is the only response.

"Jamie, you are going to listen to me very fucking carefully. If you contact Sienna again, I will hunt you down and cut off each of your fingers so you won't be able to use a fucking phone again. Three warnings are quite enough. You have no idea who you're dealing with."

A few seconds pass.

"Look, buddy."

"I'm not your fucking buddy," I growl, cutting him off.

"Whatever, look. You don't know Sienna. We are meant to be getting married. I need her back, and I won't stop until she's back where she belongs. I'm not scared of you. If she won't come willingly, I'll just fucking take her. "

"Do not fuck with what is mine, Jamie. I will burn down the earth to protect her. You have no fucking idea. You threaten her again, I'll hunt you down myself," I spit out, blood hammering in my ears.

He really has no idea.

Fucking ending Jamie would just be another one on the long list.

"Yeah, we will see," he muses, as he cuts off the phone.

Slamming the phone on the counter, I'm surprised nothing smashes.

I feel her presence without even turning around. She's leaning against the entrance to the kitchen, sporting one of my Kings Gym training shirts that hangs off her like a dress, with freshly fucked hair and glowing skin.

Her eager eyes assess me.

"What was that about?" she says, stifling a yawn.

She pads her way over to me slowly. I imagine I look as

murderous as I feel. Yet she comes to me anyway, wrapping her dainty arms around my humongous frame.

"Baby, look. I don't want to scare you, but something needs to be done about your ex. That was him threatening to force you back to him. Something's off. I'm starting to sense there is more to his desperation. Even my threats don't seem to faze him," I explain, trying to keep my tone calm, when deep down inside, I want to unleash the monster and go rip his head off his shoulders.

Sienna tenses against my chest and tries to hide her face away from me. That just ignites the fire inside of me even more.

"Tell me what's going on, baby." I mask the rage burning inside as I gently stroke her hair, willing her to open up to me.

She sighs into my chest.

"It's ok, just talk to me."

"Don't worry about me, Keller. You already have a lot on your plate, by the looks of it. You don't need to be fighting battles for a one-night stand."

My jaw ticks at her response, at the reminder we agreed to one night. *What a shit idea that was.*

She starts placing soft kisses on my tense jaw, clearly attempting to avoid the conversation.

"No, we both know that's a bullshit answer. Please, just talk to me. I need to know."

Her eyes go wide as I move my head away to stop her attempts to kiss her way out of this. Hurt flashes across her face, followed by a single tear, and her eyes dart to the floor.

"He's scaring me now, Keller. I caught him cheating on me a few weeks ago. I ran out and never looked back, but since then, he's pretty much started stalking me. Texting, phoning, sending hundreds of flowers to the apartment. He has a drug problem I just found out about, which could explain the split personality. I never thought he'd physically hurt me, but look how wrong I was."

She's sobbing as she speaks the words, just managing to force them out, her hands grabbing the faded marks still visible on her arms.

That reminder just makes me want to kill him, slowly and painfully.

I reach out and cup either side of her head, making her look at me. I mean, really look at me.

"Sienna, I swear I won't let anything happen to you. Let me do some digging. I have some, let's just say, connections that might be able to help."

She sighs into my hand.

"I don't know, Keller. I'm not used to this. I don't want to be a damsel in distress. I've managed to look after myself just fine my whole life."

"I get that, Princess, but I'm here now. I can take care of you. I *want* to take care of you. *No* one is ever going to hurt you again, I swear." Leaning in, I lick the tear away, the salty liquid burning on my tongue.

"Baby, I fight for a living." That's all she needs to know; she doesn't need to be witness to the true darkness that hides behind the mask. "Sorting Jamie won't cause me an issue. I promise."

In fact, I'll get great pleasure in watching the fear dance in his eyes as I torture him. *I can't fucking wait.*

Something tells me I need to assess before I act, drug problem or not. It's unusual for a corporate lawyer to start behaving so deranged over a woman. One he clearly didn't care about, as he stuck his dick into someone else. Fucking idiot.

Grabbing Sienna's hand, I pull her back down the hall

into bed, lifting her side of the duvet as she tucks herself in. She pats my side, inviting me. I chuckle at her. Fuck, this woman is something else. She belongs here. Scooting up next to her in bed, she turns her back to me and pushes back against me, her ass rubbing against my dick, which immediately stands to attention.

Great, now I'm going to bed with a hard on.

Feeling her breathing start to even, I press a light kiss to the exposed skin on her neck. "Night, baby," I whisper. And for the first time that I can remember, I drift off into an easy sleep, no demons to fight tonight.

CHAPTER TWELVE

sienna

The natural light burns against my skin, which quickly reminds me I'm not in my blacked-out bedroom. Nope, I'm eighty-six floors up, with a giant, sexy boxer wrapped around my body, breathing softly against my neck.

Holy fuck, I'm pretty sure I had sex with the hottest man on the planet. Not only that, he comes with the dirtiest mouth and an earth-shattering desire to bring me pleasure.

I didn't know it was possible to climax so many times in a row, each one more intense than the last. But boy, does Keller know what he's doing. Boxers know how to go the full twelve rounds, that's for sure. It's like he was created and formed on the basis of my dirty book boyfriends, made to fit perfectly with me.

The sunlight penetrates my closed eyelids. Ugh. Like a vampire, I can't stand it. I carefully peek to confirm that the shutters have automatically opened. Is this his routine? Then I realize I've never seen this man in daylight before, so in wanting to get a good look, I slowly roll over to face him.

I use this time to my advantage, taking in his sleeping

form. I'm mesmerized by him. His razor-sharp jawline, that dark wing tattoo that spans his neck right up to that sexy jaw. I'm not usually into neck tattoos, but holy shit, does his look hot. With his eyes shut, he's less daunting, the blackness of his eyes is too penetrating sometimes. In his slumber, he looks peaceful and sweet. Lowering my gaze, I am mesmerized by his body. Every muscle is defined. I can't begin to imagine the hours of blood, sweat, and tears that have gone into becoming so perfectly sculpted. Even resting, those sexy veins of his arms protrude, and his shoulders sport so much definition. He truly is a masterpiece.

Just thinking of him owning and dominating the space inside the boxing ring makes me clench my legs. I bet he is an incredible force. Any opponent must shit themselves coming face-to-face with him. Just one devious glare from him would be enough to make a grown man run away.

Unable to resist, I start tracing my fingers along the masses of ink covering his chest. There is barely any space left for more, other than the small square of olive skin peeking through above his heart.

The tattoos, like him, are dark and powerful. They make a statement. Continuing my quest, I take my hand lower, tracing each of the abs on his–Jesus–8-pack, finally settling in that famous V just above his boxers.

I can feel his heart rate spike as I find my way to the edge of his shorts. I know if I look up from the crook of his neck, I will find his stare penetrating me. I know he's now awake.

"Morning, gorgeous," he murmurs in a sleepy haze.

"Morning," I quip back.

Not giving him the chance to take control, I search lower and wrap my hand around his massive cock. My hand is tiny in comparison.

I stroke up and down his shaft, still avoiding his gaze. That earns me a low groan, which only gives me the confidence to keep going. Pushing myself up, I trace kisses along his chest, slowly descending with each one until I'm face to face with his dick.

Now I look up, my gaze meeting his. Desire burns through his eyes, making them almost black. He's looking at me like I am the most beautiful woman on the planet. His features soften as he gives me a nod to continue. Lowering my head, I take the tip of his cock in my mouth. I can taste the remnants of last night's passion.

"Take me deeper, baby."

I do as he says and take as much as I can of him to the back of my throat. My mouth is full, and tears start to pool in my eyes as he fucks me. And my god, if it's not the hottest thing, I don't know what is.

I can barely breathe and he doesn't let up. Fisting his hands through my hair, he pushes me further down, completely ravishing my mouth, taking everything that he can get.

And I give it willingly to this man.

Slowing the pace, I take this opportunity to lick up and down the shaft. I feel him shiver in response as his breathing gets heavier and heavier, his balls tight as I cup them.

"Fuck, Sienna, you're such a good girl, taking so much of my cock in your mouth. You greedy, greedy girl."

Oh, there it is. *Good girl.* I'm drenched. Squeezing my legs together, I try to hold in the building pressure. Yanking me by my hair, pain sears through my skull as he pulls me up to straddle him. His hungry eyes burn into mine.

"If I'm coming anywhere, it's tight inside that sweet pussy of yours."

He fists his cock and swipes it up and down the length of my slit, lapping up my arousal. With one hard thrust, he enters me, letting out a low groan as he does. Arching my back, I slowly ride him, rising as far as I can and slamming back down, the pressure building on each pulse. He wraps his firm hands around my throat and I lean into his grasp.

Whether it's the fear of not being able to breathe or the orgasm simmering, I lose it.

Ever so slightly, he tightens his grip around my neck. It's sure to leave marks but enough for me to inhale, and so firm he is basically holding me upright as I quicken the pace. Sliding his other arm between us, he reaches down and pinches my clit, sending shock waves through my whole body. I start to feel my walls tightening.

"Do not come until I tell you to, goddess."

I squeeze my eyes shut in response, willing a way to concentrate enough to hold off. I don't think it's possible–but I try.

He meets me thrust for thrust. I'm so close, my whole body shakes. I hear curses come from Keller's deep voice, his breath quickening. Releasing my neck, I drop forward, falling onto him. He grabs my face and slams his mouth onto mine, nipping my bottom lip.

"Come now," he rasps.

His own orgasm rips through him, too. In that moment, my whole world explodes, my body is on fire, and the most shattering orgasm fractures through me.

"Fuck!" he roars, spilling into me, still peppering kisses along my jaw.

We lay there for a few minutes, both breathing heavy, our sweaty bodies intertwined. He hasn't removed himself from inside me. I can feel it pulsing. Lazily wiping a stray hair off my forehead, he places a soft kiss there, giving me a sexy grin.

"You are incredible, Sienna."

Not sure how to respond to that comment, my cheeks flushing, I nuzzle my face into his neck.

"Sienna, look at me," he whispers.

His gentleness, after such ferocity, throws me off. I've never been treated like this after sex. Especially with Jamie. Without a word, he would leave the room to clean up, eventually returning to say goodnight and rolling the other way. I slowly turn my face to him. His eyes are still burning with desire but also now, with awe, as he gently cups my jaw.

"That was the sexiest fucking experience of my life. Don't you dare be embarrassed with me. Hell, every taste I've had of you so far has blown me away. I mean what I say, Sienna. You are a force to be reckoned with. Incredible."

His tone is laced with sincerity. I give him a small nod. It's all I can formulate at this point. His kindness and reassurance take me by surprise. The thought of leaving this morning and never looking back, never feeling this again, forms an emptiness through my body. How can any other man ever compare to this? In my twenty-five years on this planet, not once have I felt this kind of all consuming connection with another man. I let out a sigh as I cuddle into his side, his strong arms pulling me in close. I can feel his brain ticking as he stares up at the ceiling. We're both silent. Our breathing is the only noise filling the room.

Once Keller gets in the shower, I decide it's time to rip the band-aid off. I can't deal with goodbyes or empty promises. I know if he asks me to stay, I can't say no. I don't think I could ever deny this man. I quietly pick up my clothes from the floor, tiptoeing out of the room towards the front door. The private elevator mocks me. *I know I can't get in there without him.* I could do with the cardio. What're eighty-six floors, anyway? I need a distraction from my sadness.

My calves are burning from the mission down. The icy breeze beating against my exposed skin makes me gasp as I finally make it out of the skyscraper. I should have taken one of his jackets.

Time to return to reality, I suppose.

"Oh, look who finally made it home," Maddie shouts from her room as I walk into the apartment.

Crap. I was too wrapped up in Keller to even tell the guys goodbye. Bracing myself for the lecture, I slowly open her bedroom door, expecting a scowl. I'm surprised when she's beaming at me while still tucked in bed. Her usual blonde curls are wrapped in a messy bun on the top of her head.

"Did you have a good night?" I ask, eyeing her suspiciously.

"I may or may not have. The VIP area of that place is incredible!"

She has a grin beaming from ear to ear. *Phew, at least she isn't angry at me.*

"Unlimited champagne all night, Sienna. The works. Plus, Keller's friend was there providing the eye candy material for the night."

A blush spreads across her face.

"Ooooooh, you like him?" I tease, sinking into her memory foam mattress.

"Oh my god, Sienna. He is gorgeous, tall, ripped, with a blonde buzz cut. And the most mesmerizing blue eyes."

There's definitely lust in her voice.

"So, why are you here in bed on your own then, Maddie?" If he was so dreamy, did he not make her fairytale fantasy criteria?

"He is a complete playboy and nowhere near ready to settle down. The most I got from talking to him was a gruff 'hello'. He seemed constantly pissed off, unless one of the servers was showing attention. That's the only time he smiled. Hence the eye candy, not husband material," she explains with a pout. "Oh well, the quest continues. Anyway, tell me everything about your night with Mr. Boxing Extraordinaire. Leave nothing out–you owe me for ditching us last night," she says, poking me in the arm.

"Put it this way, he made me come multiple times in multiple different positions," I say with a smirk.

"Shut. Up. I thought old lady Sienna could only do it once."

She smacks her hand against my forearm, her bubbly laughter filling my ears.

"I know! Turns out nothing was wrong with me down there. Must have been Jamie," I say with a chuckle.

"So, when are you seeing him again? Multiple orgasms look good on you, girl. You can't let him escape your grasp, giving this kind of five-star service to anyone else."

Her comment makes me feel physically sick. The thought of Keller with another woman gives me a stabbing pain at my core. He's not mine. I have absolutely no claim to him. Yet he will always own a piece of me.

Attempting to fake a smile, I tell her how we agreed last night to get it out of our systems so we can get on with our lives.

"That sounds like an incredibly stupid idea by two completely clueless people. You clearly have an insane connection and epic compatibility. Why not delve into it? You can't let a chance of true happiness get away."

Christ, I feel like I'm back at school being told off.

Immediately, that gets my back up. "I'm not looking for a fairytale, Maddie. Last night was perfect. Why ruin it? I'm not letting another man trample on my heart and ruin my self-esteem. So, one night is all we can be. Christ, just search his name. You'll see a different woman draping off his arm like a lost puppy in every article. The man isn't a one woman kinda guy. So it looks like Nana, one orgasm Sienna, will have to stay." I try to get my breath back from my explosion of words.

I'm right. I know I am. I have to be.

Even as I say the words out loud, I truly don't believe that was the last I'll see of Keller. He's a ruthless fighter. If he wants me, he's going to have to work for it.

"Okay, whatever you say," she laughs, giving me an eye roll.

"Right. I gotta go shower and have a nap. I'm exhausted." With that, I slip off Maddie's bed with a thud on the floor.

"I bet you are," she calls out after me.

Flipping on the hot water, I slip out of yesterday's clothes and step in. The harsh droplets beat down against me, the temperature so hot, I'm almost instantly red. Reaching for the shower gel, I lather my hands and make my way up my body. The remains of the marks Keller left dot my skin like artwork, and I trace over them. His fingerprints are now burnt into my skin, claiming me.

He knew what he was doing, reminding me of the power he has over my body, my soul, and my thoughts.

Looking down at my breasts, my eyes go wide in horror at the angry-looking bite marks scattered across them. The memory of the pain, and the pleasure, dancing in my brain.

I wonder if he's as caught up in last night as I am.

I step out of the shower and grab a towel, wrapping it snugly around my body. I spy myself in the mirror. Maddie was right; I look freshly fucked. More than that, looking at my reflection, with those fresh marks glaring red. I don't feel ashamed or self-conscious. No. I look hot. For the first time in a long, long time, I feel desirable.

After drying off my hair and lathering my face in my whole skin care collection, my skin is practically shining. There's nothing a bit of vitamin C serum can't solve.

Finally sprawling out in bed, my head hits the pillow and I grab my phone off the nightstand. I haven't checked it since I got home a few hours ago.

No more messages from Jamie. Perhaps he has finally got the hint. Thank you, Keller.

A text pops up from Grayson, and a smile passes over my lips.

GRAYSON

Hi pretty lady, just checking in to make sure we're all good for tomorrow. I've even managed to rope in a celebrity appearance for them. He's agreed to help out with the session if that's ok? Speak soon.
Grayson xx

Grayson Ward, co-owner of King's Gym over in Midtown and boxing trainer to the stars. We've only ever spoken a few times over the phone. He certainly has a way with the ladies. Flirting seems to be necessary in every conversation he has with the opposite sex. Not that I mind, I imagine by the sound of his thick voice laced with flirtation that he won't be bad looking, that's for sure.

Quickly tapping back my response, I keep it as professional as I can.

ME

Hey, Grayson. Yep, all still on for tomorrow. Thank you so much for all your help with this. We really appreciate it. The kids are going to love meeting a famous boxer! See you tomorrow. x

He responds immediately:

GRAYSON

Great, see you tomorrow. ;) x

I chuckle. The man can't help himself. I bet his whole text chain is full of those winky faces, ha–and the rest.

I started speaking to Grayson a couple of weeks ago. I volunteer a couple of weekends a month at a local start-up charity–Young Minds. A charity dedicated to giving kids in low-income families educational tools they wouldn't necessarily come across any other way. Some of the kids come from loving homes which just struggle to scrape by, not affording luxuries like kids' clubs, or being able to pay for hobbies for their kids. For other kids, this charity is a lifeline. Their parents choosing, much like my own mother, to hit the bottle rather than care for their kids. It breaks my heart. Seeing these kids' faces light up at the smallest acts of kindness indicates that isn't a normal thing for them. *I wonder if I would be less fucked up if I had something like this as a kid.*

I've helped organize, with the help of Grayson, a boxing training day for the kids at King's Gym. They are going to lose their minds when they get to meet this celebrity boxer

Grayson's talking about. Each weekend, we let them try either a different sport or hobby, and if they love it, we try to help them go regularly.

Working with these kids has just solidified what I already knew. I need to pursue my passion; I need to try to find a way to make it work, build a career. I sigh. For now, it's just not possible. I have to pay the bills. At least I get the weekends to feel like I'm making a difference.

My mind can't help but spiral back to Keller. All this talk of boxing, I can't help it. God, what I'd give to see him in action in the ring. Maybe, just maybe, I'll have to start watching his fights.

Just as I'm about to drift off to sleep, my phone lights up the room. Snapping it up to close it off, I see an unknown number. Fear pits in my stomach.

UNKNOWN

You think you can avoid me forever, Sienna? I've tried being nice to get you to you come back to me willingly. Looks like we gotta do this the hard way. You never make anything easy for me, do you?

I'll be seeing you very soon, sweetheart. J x

I blink, staring at the phone for God knows how long. A shiver runs down my spine. It alarmed Keller how deranged Jamie sounded on the phone yesterday. Now this?

This isn't the Jamie I knew. I was never scared of him. He was Mr. Cool and Composed. Mr. Corporate America. His designer suits are always perfectly tailored, with crisp white shirts. He was the perfect gentleman when we first met in the coffee shop opposite our offices.

It was only recently things started to change. He started commenting on what I wore and where I went. Storming out and giving me the silent treatment for days if he didn't like my responses. Then he'd bring me those God-awful red roses to apologize and take me to dinner. A vicious cycle.

The Jamie texting me now is behaving like a psychopath; he clearly didn't love me enough to keep his dick in his pants. I throw my phone back on the side and close my eyes, my mind taking me back to that explosive night with Keller as I drift off to sleep.

THE RAIN PELTING MY WINDOW WAKES ME. *SHIT. WHAT TIME is it?*

I have to meet Paula and the kids at King's Gym at 9 am. Reaching for my phone, I'm horrified that the time is 8:30 am already. I jump out of bed and run to the shower.

I pull on my black leggings and quickly pair them with a burgundy oversized sweater. I'm going to a boxing gym, not on a date, so I'm guessing workout gear is acceptable. Peeking out my bedroom window, the rain is hammering still. The sky is gray. Yep, this is a good outfit choice for sure.

I have to look somewhat presentable. I can't be looking like I've just rolled out of bed. That's hardly the role model these kids need right now. I slide a brush through my hair and slap on a thin layer of silky foundation to brighten my skin. I dig out a burgundy lip gloss and with a quick pout, I'm done. From homeless to glamourous gym fit in fifteen minutes.

I slide my trainers on, throw on a puffer jacket, and fly out the door, making a light jog down the stairwell into the pouring rain. Great, I'm going to look like a drowned rat by the time I get there.

Hailing down a yellow cab, I fling the door open and jump in. “King’s Gym, please,” I ask breathlessly, rain dripping off my nose. If I keep being late, I’m going to run out of money pretty quickly, jumping in taxis like this.

8:50 am. I should be there just in time, thank God.

CHAPTER THIRTEEN

sienna

By the time the cab pulls up outside the gym, adrenaline is pumping through my body. I can't quite put my finger on why. Maybe it's the excitement of spending the morning surrounded by male testosterone. Or maybe, just a tiny bit, this place reminds me of Keller.

I dart for the doors and barrel through them as quickly as I can to get out of this weather. The scent of musky sweat and leather assaults me first as I enter, then the echoing of punches being slammed into the punching bags. Thud, thud, thud. Makes me wince. The place is open plan. A boxing ring takes center stage with various mats and punching bags surrounding it. Over in the far corner, there is even a kitted out gym. Straightening my spine, I make my way over to the noisy group of very excited kids, plastering on a big smile. I spot Paula first and give her a little wave and a smile.

She is just the sweetest lady you could meet, rocking long white hair and bright red lipstick. You wouldn't believe she is over sixty. She is always perfectly put together and manicured. I just hope when I am her age I can look as flawless.

"Sienna, darling," she gushes, as she wraps me in a tight embrace, instantly relaxing my nerves as she does.

"Hey, Paula. Hey, kiddos," I excitedly reply, the kids now rushing over to tackle me.

Max, who's currently wrapped his little arms around my leg, is hanging on for dear life. I know I shouldn't have favorites, but I have a massive soft spot for this kid, and I ruffle his blond mop of hair. He has a heart of gold, yet absolutely no filter when he talks, always making me laugh. He's had a rough start, that's for sure, but he's getting there. His confidence has been building in masses each week.

Bending down, I reach his eye level. "Are you okay, bud?" I ask gently. He avoids my eyes, shuffling on his feet.

"I'm just nervous. Miss Paula said if we were good at it, they might let us train. What if I'm bad, miss? What if I can't do it?"

Oh, bless his sweet heart.

I wrap my hand around his tiny ones. He's only seven and has the weight of the world on his shoulders.

"Max, listen to me. You can put your mind to do anything. The guys here, their job is to help you, not judge you, okay? Just go and have fun," I answer in a gentle tone. He gives me a perfect, wide grin.

"Okay," he chirps, and with that, releases my leg and runs back to the group of boys crowding around the boxing ring.

My body instantly stills, blood hammering in my ears. No, it can't be. The way my body is reacting, I know exactly who that is.

He has his broad muscular back to me, his tattoos glistening with sweat. With each punch he throws, the room almost echoes. His grunting hits me straight in my core. He is a complete powerhouse. It oozes from him. Every punch is thrown with perfect composure, his muscles rippling with each strike. Despite his height and muscular frame, he moves delicately. He absolutely owns the ring. *Of course he does.*

The poor guy getting punched seems to, weirdly, be enjoying winding Keller up, laughing in response to each punch that connects. Like a crazed animal, he keeps coming back for more despite the fact he is getting his ass handed to him.

"Is that all you got, big guy?" he muses.

"Fuck off, Luca. You know I'm taking it easy on your weak ass."

"Fucking hit me already!" he shouts, his voice bellowing throughout the gym.

Luca–I recognize him. The guy who rudely interrupted us in his office a couple of weeks back. He might be getting beaten by Keller, but he is by no means weak. Not quite the powerhouse Keller is, but he's fit. Maybe just not a boxer's standard. Don't get me wrong. He is a very attractive man, but anyone next to Keller is subpar.

I clench my legs together. God, he is hot, but the way he commands the ring is making me even hotter. A blush creeps over my skin. Thank Christ, he's too occupied to spot me. I'm near drooling at him.

I can't rip my eyes away from him. He is mesmerizing.

I faintly hear my name being shouted. It doesn't matter. I am so engrossed in watching Keller's every move, I hardly recognize the voice getting louder until a large chest blocks my view. I scan my way up the wall in front of me. *Christ, is everyone in here a giant?* Bright blue eyes search mine with a lopsided grin.

"Something got your attention?" he chuckles.

"Oh, hey." I frown. This is an unwelcome distraction.

He puts out his hand, an invitation to shake. All I can see is the veins popping out of his forearms. That always gets me.

"Grayson–we spoke on the phone," he explains.

Shit, Grayson! Giving him a small smile, I grab his hand, and he takes that as an invitation to pull me into a friendly embrace. It's honestly like hugging a brick wall. I quickly release my hold and step back. For some reason, I don't want to upset Keller. That's assuming he cares, which I doubt.

"Thank you so much for helping organize this. The kids have been out of their minds." I gesture towards them, all still engrossed in Keller's fight. Screaming in excitement at every punch, they are truly amazed. Grayson follows my line of sight.

"Ah, yes. I brought the big guns out to impress you." He coughs. "You all," he corrects with a wink.

This man is a terrible flirt.

"Big guns?" I question.

"Don't tell me you haven't heard of Keller 'The Killer' Russo?"

Genuine shock radiates off him.

"Should I?"

I have, but not for the reason he's thinking.

"He's a World Champion Heavyweight Boxer. Come on, I'll introduce you. Be warned–he has absolutely no social skills. He's more used to punching people than actually making conversation. But he means well. Most of the time."

With that, he wraps his arm around my shoulders and guides me toward the ring with a big grin on his face.

Shit, this is going to be a disaster.

I plaster on the best friendly smile I can and try to avoid bringing my gaze to Keller's. I know with one look from him all shirtless and sweaty, I'll be in a puddle on the floor.

"Kell! Luca! Quit it. I have someone you need to meet," Grayson shouts, getting their attention.

Keller breathes heavily, his ribcage moving deeply in and out. Luca spots me first. A knowing grin sweeps across his face as he licks his bottom lip, lapping up the blood dripping down his face. Like Keller, Luca has a darkness behind his eyes. Power radiates from him. Unlike Keller, Luca insights fear in me, whereas Keller sparks every cell of my body.

Darting his head around, Keller's eyes meet mine, his eyes lighting up as I give him a small wave. His attention immediately drops to Grayson's hand, squeezing my shoulder. I can see the hurt flash behind his eyes, and then quickly his entire face turns emotionless, except for his jaw ticking.

I can't take my eyes off him. For some stupid reason, I think my eyes can tell him that I'm his. That I want his hands all over my body, not Grayson's. It's no use. Keller can barely look at me.

Luca rests against the ropes, suspiciously eyeing Keller's reaction, yet not saying a word. His glance flicks between me and Keller.

Grayson weaves his fingers through mine and leads me up the steps, then lets go of my hand to pry apart the red ropes, urging me to step forward as he places his other hand on the small of my back to help me through.

I can feel Keller's murderous stare on us from here as he

mutters curses under his breath. I straighten my spine. Sod him, thinking he has some sort of claim over me. Why can't Grayson touch me? I am not, nor will I ever, be his property. I inch my chin a notch higher. I'm not letting him get to me. Grayson's hand is firmly back in place on my lower back.

"Keller, meet Sienna. She organized this charity training session today. Sienna, this is our champ, Keller. Keller, play nice, please."

Keller grumbles a response. I can't even make out what he's saying. Luca stays on the sidelines, taking in this whole interaction. I really hope he doesn't actually recognize me, but the small grin he's sporting and the way his eyes light in amusement, no doubt at my awkwardness, tell me he knows.

Seconds tick by with our eyes clashing while we both refuse to make the first move. It is becoming more and more uncomfortable. The room has gone silent. All I can hear is the rain beating against the glass and the clock ticking on the wall. Now, of all times, the kids decide to be quiet.

"Miss, why are you so red?" Max announces, as the rest of the group giggles.

Now I must be the color of beetroot. I can feel the flush creeping up my chest and across my cheeks. Keller's clearly enjoying watching my suffering as a deep chuckle escapes him.

I reach out my hand to him. "Hi, nice to meet you, *Keller*. Thank you so much for taking time out of your busy schedule to train the kids." I give him a sarcastic grin.

Not missing a beat, he grabs my hand between his gloves. The leather sticks to my skin as he slowly inches the back of my hand up to his lips, his dark eyes never leaving mine as he softly places a kiss there. I shuffle slightly to clench my legs together. Jesus Christ, this man is insatiable.

Then he gives me a little curtsy. How can a man so tall and muscular pull off a curtsy? I don't know, but he does.

"So lovely to see you again, m'lady," he drawls out in a posh British accent.

I feel Grayson go stiff next to me. Could Keller be any more obvious? He might as well scream, "I've already fucked her; keep your hands off," for the entire room to hear.

Snatching my hand back down to my sides, I turn to Grayson. "Great, well, shall we let the kids get on with the training? I give them two more minutes before they all start fighting each other. As much as I love them, I really don't have the energy to be dealing with that right now."

"Right! Everyone pair up and get over to the mats. Sienna, you're pairing with me." Keller's domineering voice carries over the rest of the chattering. The room now descends to silence.

Well, fuck.

CHAPTER FOURTEEN

keller

Rage burns through my chest.

Why the fuck does Grayson have his hands on her? I can almost guarantee he's picturing her bent over the desk. That man gets every woman he flashes his playboy smile at.

Sienna appears to be oblivious, which calms me slightly. She made no genuine effort to shake him off, though.

I shouldn't be bothered. We agreed to one night.

The fact that she cut it short with her little 'Cinderella leaves the ball' episode didn't really allow us to truly get each other out of our systems.

One night wasn't enough. I'm starting to think there aren't enough nights left in this lifetime for me to get my fill of her.

Leaving the shower to discover an empty penthouse left a gaping hole in my ribs. Not just my ego hurt, but my heart felt empty. Life immediately reverted to a cloud of darkness. Sienna seems to bring light into my world with her infectious laugh and sexy attitude.

Seeing her with Grayson confirmed my fears. She is well and truly under my skin, and I don't want her to claw her way back out anytime soon. I want to keep her–to own and worship her in every way possible. She doesn't realize that once I want something, I don't stop until it's mine. And now, that something is her, and I'm not letting her out of my sight. She doesn't know what's coming.

She looks uncomfortable, tapping her wrists with her index finger as she watches the kids pair up and begin sparring.

Grayson gets the kids to start warming up, and now that he's fully distracted, I wrap my arm around Sienna's shoulders, ushering us into the office and slamming the door.

She barely says a word to me or even looks at me, and fuck, it hurts. She's pressed back against the office door, still tapping away at her wrist, chewing her bottom lip as she eyes up the room.

I close the distance between us, and my wrapped hands connect with the door on each side of her head, making it shake. She sucks in a breath as her piercing eyes meet mine. Desire flashes through them. Heat is radiating off her as I watch the crimson flush spread up her chest. It's taking every ounce of self-restraint I have not to devour her mouth.

No matter how hard I try, I can't let this woman go. It's a selfish dick move, bringing her into my world.

My lips press against her ear as I run my fingers across her collarbone. The instant my fingers connect to her ivory skin, electricity shoots through my fingertips, straight to my dick.

"You left without giving me a kiss goodbye. I'm very hurt," I say, raising my eyebrow at her.

She lets out a whoosh of air. "I thought we agreed to one night, Keller. You didn't sign up for a breakfast date, too. I thought it would be best to rip the band-aid off and leave. I couldn't stand the thought of a goodbye."

I'm actually surprised to hear this much sadness in her voice.

"Then don't say goodbye."

"This between us is all-consuming. I'm not ready for a relationship. Hell, I'm pretty sure at this point, my love life is cursed. But I can't deny how much my body craves you, Keller."

She whispers this, sending chills down my spine.

"One night was never going to be enough for us. I can't stay away; I don't want to stay away. I want you in every possible way. I can't even fucking explain it. I can't offer you the fairytale happily ever after. That's never been in the cards for me. I can offer you earth-shattering orgasms. Let me claim that pussy as mine, Sienna."

The words are out of my mouth before I contemplate what I'm saying.

Desire sparkles in her eyes. Her tongue licks her burgundy glossed lower lip.

"Yes," she breathes. "Make me yours."

I don't hesitate before slamming my lips onto hers like a man possessed. I give this kiss everything that I have. When I pick her up by the ass, she wraps her slender legs around my middle, her fingers clawing at my back. I can feel her nails piercing my skin and that just spurs me on with my assault of her mouth. Spinning her around, I swipe the contents of the desk to the floor, the clattering of all Grayson's shit vibrating through the room. Not that I can focus on that, as my blood is hammering in my ears. I drop her ass on the desk. She looks as desperate for me as I am for her.

I can't wait any longer. She's wearing too many clothes. She gives me a knowing smile as she raises her arms up straight, inviting me to peel her sweater off, revealing her toned, porcelain stomach. Her breasts are cupped in a black sports bra. Hurling the sweater on the floor, I dip my head straight between her perfect tits. They fit just right in my hands to squeeze, as if made just for me.

Sienna lets out a low breathy moan, aware just a few feet away are a bunch of kids no doubt punching each other by now. I muffle her mouth with my hand.

"Baby, not a sound. If you so much as make a peep, this stops. Do you understand?" I demand.

Her eyes wide, she gives me an excitable nod. Fuck, she is perfect.

"Good girl," I growl.

I know that gets to her. She sucks in a breath under my palm. The naughty goddess has a praise kink I just can't wait to exploit. Sliding my hand down her torso, I inch under her lace thong, sliding my middle finger along her drenched slit.

"You are absolutely soaking, gorgeous. Is this all for me to feast on?"

She gives me a slow nod, desire glistening in her eyes.

My hands slowly trail back up her stomach. Her pants snap back onto her skin as I bring my finger up to my mouth. I need a taste of her sweet nectar.

She watches intently as I do, her juices swirling on my tongue. It's not enough. I need to bury my face between her legs. Pushing her head back so she's spread out over the desk, her legs still wrapped around either side of mine, I yank off her pants in one motion.

She gasps as I do.

"Not a peep. Remember the rules," I command between peppering kisses over her stomach.

Gripping her lace thong between my teeth, I inhale her sweet scent. Fuck, I am obsessed. Sienna is watching, her top half propped up on her elbows, hunger etched all over her face.

I slide her thong down her slender legs between my teeth and slip them off her feet and straight into the pocket of my shorts. She cocks an eyebrow and opens her mouth to speak, quickly snapping it shut, remembering my rules. Then I lick all the way up the inside of her leg. I make my way to her center, swiping my tongue from her entrance all the way up to her clit, taking the small bud in my mouth and sucking. Her legs shake while resting on my shoulders.

She is delicious.

A forceful knock at the door tears my attention from her. Without thinking, I jump on top of her. Fuck if anyone else is seeing just an inch of her flesh.

"Fucking hell," I growl.

Anger boiling inside of me; my rock-hard cock now rests against her pussy, invading every thought. Sienna's body is as stiff as a board underneath me.

Grayson waltzes in. I guess this serves me right for always invading his privacy. His eyes immediately go wide as he realizes what–or better, who–I'm hiding under my body, and the contents of his desk are scattered all over the floor.

"Goddamnit, are you fucking kidding me, Keller?!" he yells. "Get the fuck out of my office and clean yourselves up. I need you out there. I'm sure you can wait a few hours to get your dick sucked."

His face flashes with anger as his fists clench by his

sides. Then he turns away and slams the door shut behind him.

I know better than to poke the bear right now.

Resting my nose on her forehead, I take in the coconut scent of her hair wafting up my nostrils.

"Fuck, I'm sorry. I shouldn't have done this here. I just can't fucking help myself when I'm around you," I whisper, hoping she understands.

Her small hands cover her face, hiding the horror no doubt etched beneath them. I lift off her, giving her some space. She launches off the desk and darts around the room, picking up her items of clothing tossed around the floor. Every time she bends over, her perfect ass is on display for me and my cock threatens to explode. I watch as she throws her sweater over her head, then bends from her hips to pull her leggings on, stepping into one of the legs. Stalking over, I settle behind her, grab both her hips, and rub her ass against my rock-hard dick.

"Keller, we can't. You need to get out there and train those kids. They are so excited to see you. I can't get in the way of their happiness today."

An annoyed groan leaves my lips as I ruffle my hands through my hair, trying anything to get some composure. Any time she's around, I seem to lose it.

She straightens, pulling up her leggings, covering her perfect, round ass. Then, turning to face me, she brings her hand to my cheek. Intimate moments like these usually turn me off instantly. When she does it, the opposite happens. It's like she knows how to tame me without even trying–hell, without even truly knowing the depth of the monster whose cheek she's caressing.

Her face softens as she raises up on her tiptoes and gives me a quick peck on the lips.

"I'll still be here after everyone's gone home. We can finish this then," she says with a wink. Then she turns on her heel and walks out with a spring in her step, leaving me open-mouthed, gaping at her.

Fuck, I may not know what love is or how to love, but if I did, I'm certain she could be the one to show me.

THREE HOURS. FOR THREE FUCKING HOURS, THIS TRAINING SESSION went on. Three hours of holding back the blood rush to my cock every time Sienna throws a punch at my face. My girl knows how to throw a punch, that's for sure, and she enjoys every second of laying into me. Then there's every time her face lights up when one of the kids smashes a combination. The way her whole body lights up around these kids shows she has a passion and a love for them. This truly is her calling.

One kid in particular clearly has self-confidence issues. He spent the session second guessing every combination he copied from us. Sienna just knows instinctively what he needs and how to help him cope. So I make sure I give him extra attention, showing him one to one how to nail each combination, even if I have to spend the whole time boxing from my knees so he can reach the pads.

I know from our encounters, underneath all of this compassion, she is a complete firecracker who takes no prisoners. Hell, I watched her knee her ex in the balls. Any other woman I know would have been a complete wreck. Not her. She is a fighter, wrapped in a petite, lovable frame. I guess it's similar to me, even down to the shitty childhoods. *Maybe that's why I'm so drawn to her.*

The kids are now sparing with each other, possibly a disastrous idea, but Sienna trusts them, so we trust them, too. I mean, I'm weeks away from being a world champion. Surely I can deal with a few boisterous kids, right?

I've been in many of their shoes; from what Grayson told me, these kids have shitty upbringings. Which gives me a brilliant idea. As all the kids are packing up to leave, I beeline over to Paula and Sienna, who are chatting away. Interrupting them with a cough.

"Hi, Keller," Paula says, resting her hand on my forearm.

Resisting the urge to flinch, I give a tight grin, raising my eyebrows to Sienna as she holds back a laugh behind her water bottle.

Oh, you won't be laughing in a minute, princess.

"So, I was thinking," I say, giving myself some distance from Paula. Sienna is still amused, watching on. "I run a two week evening session with my foundation, Street Champs. It's set up to get kids away from fighting on the streets and channeled into learning to box. I think we could tie in with your organization and take on any of your kids who might be interested in joining. Obviously, there is absolutely no cost and the kids can continue for however long. I'm happy for them to use this gym like a second home if they want. Anything we can do to help, just let us know. Grayson will sort out all the details if it's something you would be interested in."

Paula shrieks with excitement, enough to pierce my eardrums, and I wince at the noise. The next minute she's wrapped her arms around my torso. I stand there like a statue, looking down at her gray bun, then over to Sienna, my eyes willing her to remove this woman. I let out a low cough to get Paula's attention. I only want one woman glued to me, and she's standing there smirking, offering no help whatsoever.

Jumping away from me, Paula brushes her top. "Oh, sorry, I got a bit excited there. Yes! Of course! That all sounds fantastic. Sienna, are you okay to liaise with Grayson to organize the finer details for me, please?"

"No, it's okay, Paula. Sienna can deal with me directly. It's my charity, after all. I can make time for her, always," I cut her off abruptly.

"Oh, right. Okay. Thank you." She shoots Sienna a look, but she only continues to stare at us open-mouthed, like Paula and I have two heads. The older woman scuttles off, shouting at the kids to hurry up.

I stalk my way over to Sienna, who is frozen on the spot, staring at me.

"Keller, I-I can't thank you enough for offering to help. We've been really struggling recently with ironing out a regular schedule for them. This will be an absolute game changer for some of these kids," she gushes.

"It's fine," I quip, lowering my head to her neck. "Don't go anywhere. We need to talk," I whisper in her ear. I hear her breath hitch as I speak.

Twenty minutes later, the gym is finally empty. Grayson left without even speaking to me. He's pissed, so I'll leave him to it. Luca left during the time I was AWOL in the office with Sienna. So, finally, it's just us.

It's late, the only light coming from the warm hanging industrial lighting. There is nothing better than an empty gym to let loose in. No distractions, no noise, just me and the punching bag. Now that will have a whole new meaning.

Sienna lies on the mat, scrolling through her phone. She's been nudging the punching bag above her head in a slow rhythm, letting it sway back and forth above her like a pendulum. She always seems so on edge. It's nice to see her relaxed for once. I stay hidden in the shadows behind the ring, watching her. Beauty radiates off her, the sweat lightly coating her skin from the training today. Making my way to her, our eyes connect, but she makes no attempt to move. The bag still swings above her head.

"On your knees," I command, already rock hard from just the sight of her, the release on the edge all afternoon. If I last more than five minutes, it will be a miracle. She doesn't hesitate now as she bashes the punching bag out of her face and sits up on her knees. Rolling her tongue over her lip, the punching bag swings through the air behind her.

Fuck, make that three minutes.

Her glistening lips look ready to fuck, still painted with a burgundy gloss that I want smothered around my cock. I rip off my shorts and grab my throbbing dick, rubbing up and down.

"Take off the sweater, baby. I want the full view while I'm fucking your mouth."

She quickly tosses the sweater over her head and follows with the sports bra, leaving her perky tits bouncing, her rosy nipples already erect. I stay where I am, my hands now on my hips, and my erect cock dripping with pre-cum.

"On all fours, crawl to me."

"Really?" she rolls her eyes. She actually rolls her fucking eyes at me.

Pinning her with my stare, I give her the answer. I'm deadly serious. As if realizing what we're doing, still on her knees, she leans on her left hip and pulls her leggings down over her ass, spreading her legs as she does, giving me the full view of her perfect pussy, glistening from her arousal.

Swooping her legs back around, now completely naked, she makes a slow crawl toward me, while licking her lips. My dirty goddess. She sits back on her knees as she reaches me, her eyes not leaving my dick.

"Good girl," I rasp as I stroke her face, her tongue licking my thumb as it rolls her bottom lip. "Suck."

Her eyes twinkle with desire. We exchange no words as she opens her mouth and closes it over the tip, sucking and rolling her tongue over. *Jesus Christ, it feels like heaven.*

She continues to go deeper and deeper, all the way down to the base, her eyes watering, but she carries on, her dainty fingers cupping and stroking my balls as she picks up the pace. Every nerve in my body is on the edge, the veins in my neck almost popping from the pressure.

"Fuck, Sienna, you are magnificent," I huff, barely holding in a groan.

I don't want to come in her mouth. If I'm doing that, it's going to be in her perfectly tight little pussy. I wrap her ponytail around my hand and yank her off.

"Keller, I need you inside me," she desperately pleads.

I don't waste any time, spying the punching bag behind us, chained to the ceiling. It gives me an idea–my ultimate fantasy.

"Turn around and wrap your hands around the bag, and bring your ass back to me," I demand.

She immediately does as I say, her perfect ass now taunting me. Closing the distance, I rub my cock up and down her slit, coating it in her juices before I slide into her entrance. She lets out a gasp as I do. She's so tight, so perfect. I'm fucking coming undone. She screams as I thrust in and out of her with all my might, grabbing those perfect ass cheeks of hers.

"You hold it for me, princess."

This is what she gets for leaving early, for having Grayson's hands on her, for all the days of my fucking life that I didn't get to fuck her. I don't know how long I'm lost in the feel of her, my dick stretching her extremely tight pussy. It sucks my juices out drip by fucking drip.

"Keller, please." I hardly hear her over the loud slaps of our hips, our heavy breaths, and my groaning.

"Keller? Keller!"

I tighten my grip on both her ass cheeks. By the time I gain some sense and open my eyes, hers are overflowing with tears, and she's wincing. She is not even breathing.

"Come for me, baby," I roar.

The squeezing and releasing of my dick is almost violent. I don't stop. Her whole body trembles. I can't stop.

God, she looks gorgeous hanging like this. I have to hold her body upright.

"Keller. God, please, *Sir!*" she whispers, barely any energy left in her.

The minute she says 'sir', I spill into her. Pins and needles cover every part of my body. I can't do anything but feel her breathing start to settle against me. Our bodies slipping against each other, covered in sweat.

This woman is going to be the death of me, I swear.

"Jesus, Keller, if that's how a boxer likes to fuck, I want five of them," she teases, still panting.

"Don't even fucking think about it. I don't share. Not you, not ever. Understood?"

Pulling herself away from me, there's a twinkle in her eye, on her flushed face.

"Yes, *Sir.*"

Slowly slipping out of her, I yank her naked body into my embrace. "Unless you want me to fuck you again right now, don't call me Sir."

She giggles in response and leaves my embrace. I'm left with an icy feeling in my chest. She bends down and starts crawling across the floor to collect her clothes.

"Really, Sienna? Do you think you could give me a couple of minutes' break before you flaunt that perfect ass in my face, making me hard again?"

She flips me off and starts dressing. Mine is easy, a pair of shorts I can whip off in one swift movement.

She steps over to the front window, staring out into the night.

"Uh, Keller, would you mind, umm, giving me a ride home? It's a bit dark out now."

I furrow my brows and walk toward her. "Has he bothered you again?"

Her eyes stay pinned to the window as she fiddles with the sleeve of her sweater.

"No," she answers quickly.

"Promise me, Sienna."

"No, I just–"

I wrap my arms around her middle and pull her into me. She melts into my hold.

"I just feel like sometimes I'm being watched. I don't know. Maybe it's in my head."

Fuck.

"I'll sort it out. Let me go get changed and we can grab the car. I can't promise I won't spread you across the console again, though, but it's a risk you'll have to take." After giving her a kiss on the top of her head, I quickly make my way to the locker room to dress in my gray sweatpants and hoodie.

I still have an hour before Luca needs me; plenty of time to drop her home and get my shit together.

Not that I can concentrate on tonight's job. My

thoughts are clouded with the implications of what we've just done. We've opened a can of worms. Something in the back of my mind is bugging me, reminding me I can't keep her. I can't drag her into this life. But my heart isn't getting the memo.

I'm fucked.

CHAPTER FIFTEEN

keller

Pulling to a slow stop outside Sienna's apartment, I kill the engine, letting the darkness envelop us. 57th Street is dead this time of night.

That doesn't stop me from noticing a hooded figure leaning against the building next door. Since I turned onto her street, he hasn't moved. Wearing all black, thinking he fits into the shadows. I am the monster that hides in the shadows at night, so I can sure as hell spot him a mile off.

He could be waiting for someone. Unlikely–not just anyone hides in the shadows of New York this time of night. That is when the monsters come out to play.

His frame is tall and lean. I can't make out any other features. I draw my attention away from the figure, not wanting to freak out Sienna. She is already on edge after Jamie's performance. She's too busy twiddling her rings on her thumb to even notice, anyway. She's nervous, I can tell. Her leg is bouncing. Her main tell is the way her hands fidget without her even realizing it. Clasping my large hand over both of hers, she lets out a deep sigh as I do.

“Did you–did you want to come up?” she asks, not bringing her gaze to me.

I cup her chin and make her look at me. Her expression is passive. Does she really think I’m just going to reject her? *Have I not made it clear enough that I’m borderline obsessed with her?*

“Baby, I have work to do tonight. I have to meet Luca.” I sigh as she attempts to turn her face away from me. Tightening my grip on her chin, I bring her back to me.

“That doesn’t mean that I don’t want to. Fuck, I want that more than anything. Spending the night wrapped up in you sounds like fucking heaven. I meant what I said earlier. This,” I gesture between us, “is not over. I can’t even picture the day we can give this up. So get used to me, sweetheart.”

Relief flashes across her face as she gives me a smile from ear to ear.

“Now, let me watch you get into your apartment. And get some rest. Before I spread you across the car again.” I give her a wicked grin and bring my lips to hers to show her how much I mean what I say.

“Good night,” I whisper, my forehead resting on hers as I steal a quick peck.

“Night, Keller,” she says, as she opens the passenger door. The icy air fills the car, reflecting the coldness I feel when she leaves. Giving me a small wave as she enters her building, I spy the hooded man watching her walk past. He doesn’t move, but he’s positioned to look straight at my car.

Something inside is screaming at me. I’m now nearly certain it’s Jamie watching her. I didn’t think that phone call would be the last of this. If I don’t scare him, there must be something seriously wrong with him. He doesn’t strike me as powerful or as a fighter, which means it’s worse than I thought. Worse, because that means he's desperate.

Like with any fight, you need to know everything about your opponent. The fuck am I letting him anywhere near Sienna. I need to know all that I can to protect her and make this asshole go away.

I itch to grab my gun from the glove box and slam it into Jamie's head. But I can't risk it, not this close to my fight. Irritation burns through me. Instead, I touch the dial for Luca's contact. If anyone can find out Jamie's deal, it's him. The mafia boss himself.

He answers on the first ring.

"Oh, hello brother, are you on your way to the meet yet?"

His voice echoes through the car. I can hear him blowing out smoke as he speaks. I turn the volume down. The street doesn't need to hear any of this conversation.

"Yeah, I'm just leaving Sienna's apartment now. I'll be there in twenty minutes."

"The woman from the club; I knew it. She's special."

Letting out a sigh, because there's no point hiding it now, I nod. And seeing as I need his help, I agree with him. "Yes, Luca." I sigh again. "But I can't have her to keep. I can't bring her into this world. I don't deserve someone so pure."

"Keller, you need to extinguish this ball of anger inside you. You're not that kid on the streets fighting to prove himself anymore. You've made it. You deserve love. You deserve her."

Dismissing his comments, I get to the point. "Look, I need a favor from you. Her ex, Jamie, attacked her last week. I found them in an alleyway outside the club. Turns out he's been basically stalking her since their break-up.

I'm pretty sure he's hooded up outside her apartment now. From what I gather, this is out of character for him. He's acting desperate. I have a suspicion there's more to his behavior than wanting her back. He's a lawyer, for fuck's sake, hardly a mobster."

"Sounds like she's already being dragged into something. Why not be our world? At least in ours, we protect our own. No harm will ever come to her here. You know that. Text me what you know about him and I'll do some digging. Just because they are suited, doesn't mean they aren't hiding something darker. You should know that."

"I'm worse. I'm a monster, Luca. A monster who slips out in the night to hunt people down. I can shoot a man between the eyes, watching their life drain away, and feel nothing. How is that man worthy of happiness?"

"You're a fighter, Keller, inside and outside the ring. Everything you've done up to this point has been a necessity. It's not who you are. Don't let that define you. You may wear a mask, but beneath that, you're a fucking good man."

He pauses. I can almost hear his brain ticking; I didn't think he'd be so passionate about this. I honestly thought he was going to talk sense into me and tell me to stop being pussy whipped and get on with my life.

"What's the point of being a billionaire with no one to share it with? We've fought to build an empire. Build a family worthy of that, and never let them go."

Fuck it, he's got a point.

"What if she abandons me, Luca? What if I can't control the evil inside me anymore?" I ask while running a hand over my face, letting out a ragged breath. He laughs.

"Then the world better plead for mercy against you, brother. But what if she doesn't? What if she's the one to pull you out of the darkness and into the light? You know your true self. Ask him if he's worthy. Ask the man beneath the mask if he's worthy. That's your answer."

Who knew he was so philosophical?

I hear sadness in his voice.

"I'll look into this Jamie for you. I agree that threatening to kidnap your ex for leaving you is extreme. Well, for outside the mafia. We know we should never underestimate the underdog." A deep chuckle escapes. "I'll get back to you as soon as I can. Now go to the meet, shoot that fucker in the head, and go claim your girl once and for all. I can't have my star fighter distracted, pining over some pussy."

"Shut the fuck up, Luca."

A full bellied laugh fills the car. Prick.

"Knew that would get ya. I'm joking. I like seeing you all soppy. Makes a change to your usual glittering personality."

"Right, I gotta go, then." I pause. "Thank you again."

I cut off the call and slam my head into the steering wheel over and over, as if it might knock some fucking sense into me.

I PULL UP OUTSIDE THE ABANDONED WAREHOUSE ON 1ST AVENUE. Graffiti covers the surrounding gray stone walls, and the warehouse is covered in rust. The perfect late-night mafia meet spot. The area is barely lit–who's going to pay for lighting in such a fucking dump?

I spot Luca's Bentley and park next to it, killing the engine. Luca is still in the driver's seat, hands gripping the wheel. Slamming my door shut, I walk over to him. *Let's get this shit over with.*

He slips out of the Bentley and straightens his black Armani suit jacket. You'll never see Luca dressed in anything less. The man screams every inch a mafia boss.

"Boss," I nod in greeting.

"Ah, Keller, you ready to pull on the mask and go fuck shit up in there?" He has an evil glint in his eye.

We're meeting with Carlo and his gang–the organization we have an agreement with for our cocaine shipments. Carlo is a short Italian chef by day and a drug runner by night. The perfect disguise behind his Mario-inspired mustache. Recently, there's been word on the street that Carlo is also now supplying the Falcones, who in turn, managed to have a whole load of their shipment stolen, leaving Carlo and us pissed. Carlo knows he needs us. He can't afford to lose his relationship with, undoubtedly, the largest mafia organization in New York. The Falcones don't, and won't, ever have shit on us, no matter how hard they try.

Tonight, we show him you don't fuck with the Russos. I grab my semi-automatic from Luca's trunk. The air is still and darkness surrounds us. Just like when I walk into the ring, I'm freakishly calm, despite the adrenaline coursing through my veins. Tonight, I have a nagging voice in my head screaming at me, taunting me. '*What would Sienna think if she saw the monster you are right now?*'

I shake my head. I can't afford to let whatever this may be with her distract me right now. *Mine and Luca's lives depend on the monster coming out from behind the mask,* I think as I slip on my signature black balaclava.

Striding over towards the warehouse, I follow Luca's lead as he kicks open the iron door that's hanging on by its top hinge, and we enter. Immediately, I spot Carlo and two of his henchmen in the center of the room. Both of his men are fucking massive, around the same height as me. Probably in their late 30s, with shaved heads. No doubt there is only a single brain cell to share between them.

I slowly aim the gun straight at Carlo's head as we continue to stalk towards them. Carlo instantly flings both his hands up in surrender. Fear dances across his bloodshot eyes.

It's a known fact, if Luca brings his masked right-hand man, someone's about to die. Little do they realize, Luca is on the same deranged scale as me. They just haven't had the pleasure of meeting him yet.

"Luca. Luca, please. I can explain. This was a complete fuck up on our part, but it will never happen again. You have my word," Carlo pleads.

An evil chuckle leaves Luca's lips as he reaches Carlo, a deathly glare shooting daggers at him.

"A fuck up, Carlo? Really? You're telling me, giving my shipment to a rival mob, only to have it fucking stolen, is a fuck up?" He snarls. "You've cost me a lot of fucking money, Carlo, and given Marco and the Falcones a reason to believe they're taking over. You understand what this means?"

"No, no, Luca please. I'll make it up to you. The next shipment you keep for free? Please, just let me go. I have children, a family. I can't die tonight!" His voice is shaking as he trembles on the spot. His useless fucking henchmen staring blankly at us. They know if they so much as make a move, I'll shoot them point blank between the eyes with not an ounce of remorse.

Carlo's words hit me. He has children and a family. What the fuck is he doing getting involved in drug shipments for the mafia if he has that at home? How can he be that desperate to risk that? Fucking selfish bastard.

Luca grabs him by the throat as Carlo lets out a cry,

which snaps my attention back. He's lifting him up as if he weighs nothing. "The next two shipments are for free. If I hear any word of you even talking to the Falcones, that man there," he points at me, "He'll find you, your wife, and your children and make you watch as he slits their throats one by one. Do you understand me?" he shouts, spit landing on Carlo's face.

Would I shoot Carlo? Yes, without hesitation. Would I kill his family and make him watch? Probably not. That's a bit extreme, even for me. But as I watch the piss seep through Carlo's trousers while Luca dangles him in the air, I understand the threat had the desired effect.

Luca loosens his grip on Carlo's neck, letting him collapse onto the stone ground with a thud. Without bringing his head up to look at Luca, he simply responds, "Okay, okay."

Clearly satisfied with his answer, Luca nods at the two useless men with Carlo, then to me, as he strolls past. I walk backward towards the exit, my gun still pointing at Carlo, balled up on the floor.

Luca throws open his car door, about to slide in.

"Slitting his wife and kids' throats? Jesus, Luca," I chuckle. The man certainly has a deranged side.

"What, not to your taste?" he asks, cocking an eyebrow at me just before letting out a laugh. "Fucking pussies. Did you see how soaked his jeans were in piss? I mean, for fuck's sake. The man deals in multimillion dollar cocaine shipments."

"I'm out of here; that's enough fun for tonight." I give him a nod as I go to close his door.

"You off to go get your girl now?" Luca asks with genuine interest.

"Tomorrow," is all I give him.

I need a shower and sleep. But Carlo's words will not stop repeating in my head. Since when did I suddenly become conscious of dragging other people into this world? Sienna is making me see my life from a whole new standpoint. I know it's dangerous, but I can't bring myself to let her go. Not now, not ever.

What would I do if someone threatened to slit her throat in front of me? Well, I wouldn't piss my pants, that's for sure. I'd kill them before they even got the chance to finish their sentence.

My car screen wakes up with a text, sexy Sienna's name flashing across the top. I tap to open the message.

SEXY SIENNA

As requested, I'm in bed. Naked. xx

Visions of her perfect, silky smooth body naked, spread out in bed, cloud my brain. I swipe the message away and roar the car to life. Maybe if I wait until after my world championship fight, I can have her then. No mafia, no real danger. Rubbing my hand over my face, I shake my head. Shit. I don't think I can leave her alone for another six weeks. That sounds torturous.

CHAPTER SIXTEEN

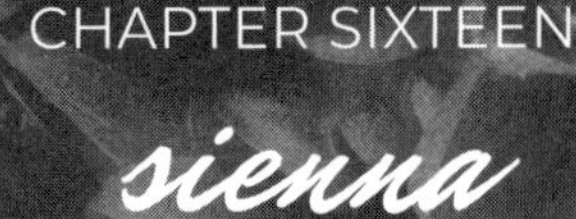

The last two days passed by in a blur–work and straight home. Repeat. I keep checking my phone, but nothing. Maybe him not coming back to my apartment was his way of cutting me off. The way his eyes ate me up, the desire that flashed across his face when around me, I really believed he felt this, too. *Then why hasn't he bothered since?*

I texted him the night after the training to say 'good-night'. Well, that, plus the fact I was naked in bed. I never got a peep back. Maddie tried to reason with me. I caved and gave her the entire story, and she gushed the whole time, pure excitement radiating from her. She truly is a sucker for love. I just wish she would hurry up and find someone worthy of her; someone to worship the ground she walks on. By God, does she deserve it.

David's picked up on my new foul mood in the office. Even his black cherry hot chocolate offering can't cheer me up. I am pining over a man. Not just any man–a man who worships me when he is with me, but then forgets about me as soon as I'm out of sight. I just don't understand.

Maybe my mom was right; I'm not good enough for people to stick around.

Recently, it has become clearer that financial security isn't a big part of my dream. I need to pursue my passion, which has only grown since the training day at Keller's gym. I need to speak to Paula and see if there is any way I could go full time. There is enough money to see me for a while.

I am tapping away on the computer, reading these boring ass mediation notes. Don't get me wrong, usually I find these juicy. We are currently representing the poor, betrayed, angry wife, trying to obtain funds she rightly deserves after being cheated on. Most of the time, the couples can't keep their cool. They storm out of the meeting room red faced, shouting expletives and complaining about each other, almost every time. I thought family law would be focused more on the family aspect, like looking out for the children and not ripping the family apart. In reality, it's all about money–who can get or keep the most, and how much damage could they put on the other person. Another tick in the box for why Sienna won't be partaking in this marriage crap. I've been that child in the middle of a family splitting up, and now I witness it daily. People are selfish.

Or maybe I am just bitter because I have never gone down the aisle and recently can't even keep a man interested in more than just having sex with me. Hardly the morale boost a girl needs.

"Could you tap any louder, Sienna? I'm sure they can hear you smashing the keys on the floor below," David chuckles, poking me in the arm.

"Oi, you know I'm just sooo engrossed in my job. I just need to get the words out," I tease. He knows full well this isn't my career of choice. But that doesn't mean I'm not bloody good at what I do.

"Har-har. No, something clearly pissed you off. You forget I know you. How about some fresh air? We haven't had a chance since you abandoned me at the club last week," he says. I know he means well.

Checking the time in the corner of my computer, it's 1 pm. Perfect time for lunch. I nab my coat from the back of my chair and motion for David to hurry up, not wanting to run into our boss, who would just eat into our lunch break, requesting updates on what I have already emailed him. He is utterly useless with technology and doesn't read his emails.

Once outside, David loops his arms through mine, giving me a big grin. It's so easy spending time with him. I just don't know if I'm ready to tell him the real reason I'm upset. He's going to think I'm mad for jumping out of the fire into the pan so quickly.

The crisp autumn breeze whips around my face, making my cheeks blush, but the sun is beaming. It's beautiful out. We walk along the sidewalk arm in arm for a few minutes, just taking in the fresh air. It is nice and peaceful. Just what I need to clear my head.

David runs into the Starbucks on the corner to grab us a couple of lattes, perfect to warm my hands up. The office is only a ten-minute walk to Sheep Meadow in Central Park, our favorite place to wander around on our lunch breaks. Although this is close to Christmas, it's packed with tourists, so grabbing a bench isn't always easy.

I don't celebrate Christmas anymore. Having a mom who got pissed the whole day, burned the turkey, and had a meltdown, throwing my presents in the garbage, kind of ruined the whole holiday for me. But I do have to say, New

York at Christmas is spectacular. The twinkling lights, the tree at Rockefeller Center, and the insane amount of parties. They sure know how to celebrate here. If I wasn't such a grinch, it would be incredible. Maybe one day.

"So, baby girl, want to tell me what's bothering you? Does it have something to do with a certain man who whisked you away after looking like he was going to murder me on the spot for touching you?" He wags his eyebrows.

Letting out a sigh, I resign. Here goes nothing.

"I know you probably think I'm ridiculous entertaining someone so soon after Jamie. I really thought there was something there. I'm not sure what exactly, but the sex was mind blowing. Like, I don't think I'll ever experience anything as good as that again." I cringe, realizing I'm going into details about my sex life with David.

"Oh, baby girl. There are plenty of men out there who know how to use their dicks, you know. Don't write yourself off too soon."

I playfully hit him on the arm.

"But honestly, that guy looked seriously into you. Jesus, he scared the shit out of me. Who gives a shit how soon it is after Jamie? You need to get him out of your brain ASAP, and what better way of doing it?" he teases.

"Why don't you shoot him a quick text? The guy doesn't always have to do all the chasing, you know? If you're in need of some sexy servicing, just tell him. What's the worst that's going to happen?"

Hmm, he has a point.

"Look, being totally honest, the connection with Keller–"

His arm whips from mine as he stops dead in his tracks, gawping at me.

"Shut. Up. You are not fucking Keller Russo. World Champion Keller "the Killer" Russo? No fucking way."

"Jesus, do you want his number or something? Yes, that's him," I huff.

"Well, get your phone out and text him now. Fuck, how didn't I recognize him Friday?" He pauses. "It must be because I was too distracted, trying to avoid him murdering me."

I laugh. "He's not that scary."

"Are you fucking kidding me? Although you could be right. I am not sure there are many men out there who could compare to him. Maybe you can stay angry for a while longer. I'll allow that," he teases as he bumps his elbow into my side.

We walk and chat a while longer, arms now linked back together as we laugh and organize the details for our night out Saturday. David's pretty insistent we go back to The End Game, if I can sort out VIP again. Crafty little shit.

A buzzing vibrates against my ribs as my phone sparks to life inside my black fitted blazer. Quickly unzipping my coat, I grab it out to shut it off.

My screen lights up with text after text.

1:26PM SEX GOD KELLER

You look fucking stunning today, baby.

1:27PM SEX GOD KELLER

I suggest he get his hands off you before I rip them off.

1:28PM SEX GOD KELLER

I mean it Sienna; I wasn't fucking around when I said you are mine.

1:29PM SEX GOD KELLER

Have it your way.

A shiver runs down my spine as I scan the area. Surely he's not following me. He can definitely see me, though. How else would he know I'm walking arm in arm with David? Completely platonic, but he doesn't know that.

Shit.

My heart pounds. I know he's near; I can feel him. I don't even know how it's possible, but my body reacts to him involuntarily. It's as if we are magnets that cannot stay away from each other. The attraction is too wild and strong. There is no point running from him. I have the feeling he will always find me. Maybe when he wants to, I suppose.

But if he thinks he can tell me who I can spend my lunch with, he has another thing coming. He might own me in the bedroom, but only I own me outside, especially after ghosting me, yet again, this whole week.

Heavy footsteps jog behind me, and David eyes me suspiciously. I frown and subtly shake my head. David may be tall and muscular, but he is by no means anywhere near Keller's league.

The footsteps come to a halt, and heavy breathing fills my ears, his musky aftershave assaulting my senses. Slowly, I unlink my arm from David's and do a one-hundred-eighty degree turn. My nose brushes past his chest. God, he smells divine.

Taking a small step back, I take him in.

His gray sweatpants, hanging perfectly off his hips, are paired with a muscle hugging black T-shirt that details perfectly every ridge of his abs. His entire frame is ripped and powerful, emphasized by the glistening of sweat.

I quickly snap my mouth shut when I realize I'm basically drooling over his body. His liquid dark eyes bore into mine. This is the first time I've really taken him in, in broad daylight.

There's a faint scar visible, only a centimeter or so, vertically down his left eyebrow. *How have I not noticed this before? Oh, probably because his head is normally buried between my legs.*

The memory sends ripples down my body, and I shiver. His jaw ticks as he takes me in, shifting his vision between David and me.

"Hey! I'm a big fan," David pipes up, interrupting us from our staring competition.

"Nice to meet you," he says through gritted teeth, as he sticks his hand out to David.

"David. I er–work with Sienna. I was with her last weekend at the club," David explains, grabbing his outstretched hand with a firm handshake.

Keller gives a nod and turns his sights back to me, ignoring David, who is only two steps away from us.

"Well, it was nice to–"

Before I can even finish my sentence, Keller smashes his lips onto mine, cupping both hands around my jaw. Then, just as quickly, he's pulling away from me, looking down at me through hooded eyes, giving me a lopsided grin. A grin that makes me forget why I'm pissed at him in the first place.

Now I'm hot and flustered. I feel like I need to rip my coat off to let the cold air wrap around my body.

"I'll pick you up outside your office at five."

Coming out of my haze from the kiss, I blink up at him. "Wait, how do you know–"

"I'm a resourceful man."

"Well, if you would have actually spoken to me this week, I would have told you." I bite back now. The haze from the kiss gone.

"Oh, princess, don't be like that. I had some things I

needed to sort out. I don't intend to go that long without you ever again."

Talk about putting my head in a complete spin. *Maybe he does want me?*

"So, I'll see you at five, yes? I believe I have some making up to do, baby."

He gives me a knowing wink, planting a quick peck on my forehead, and launches back into a jog without even so much as a goodbye.

I stand there blankly, watching him jog off toward the New York skyline. *What the fuck just happened?*

"You're blushing," David nudges me out of my haze.

Linking my arm back through his, I march us back to the office. Now, I'll be counting the hours until I can continue that kiss. Damn you, Keller, for making me horny at work. Oh well, an afternoon of divorcing couples arguing will soon douse the heat inside me.

THE AFTERNOON GOES BY AT A SNAIL'S PACE. I'M WATCHING THE seconds pass by. The off-white walls and cool-down lights almost giving me a headache. I'm still mad at Keller for ignoring me all week, but damn, all I can think about is being fucked into oblivion by him again. Just the thought has had me squeezing my legs together at my desk all day. He's quickly consuming my every thought. *I need to be careful not to get too attached. I can't let him break my heart.*

The second five o'clock hits, I fly out the door, offering David a quick goodbye as I swipe my coat and make for a jog down the stairs.

The ground floor heaves with businessmen making

their way out of the building. I beeline straight to the revolving doors. I can spot him a mile off. His black jumper with the hood up and those delicious gray sweatpants, as he leans up against his gunmetal Aston Martin.

I see the envy in the eyes of the businessmen admiring his car. I roll my eyes–*men and their toys.*

Keller's face lights up, relief flashing over his features as he realizes I'm coming to him. Quickening my pace, I'm now almost jogging toward him; everyone around me is a blur. All I can see, all I can focus on, is making my way to him.

When I finally do, I literally leap into his arms and wrap my legs around his waist, dropping my lips straight to his. I just can't help myself.

"Well, that's one hell of a greeting, baby," he rasps. "Now I'm fucking hard in the middle of the street in broad daylight."

Wiggling my hips down slightly, I feel his rock-hard cock against my pussy. He wasn't joking. Good job his pants are baggy. Nothing would hide the massive bulge he's sporting; nothing could hide that.

All that does is ignite the fire within me. Knowing this man wants me this much makes me feel more alive than ever.

I slide my legs down his sides. He takes my weight as my low-heeled stilettos touch the pavement.

"Thanks for giving me a lift home," I say as I open the passenger door. Keller's hand slams on the cool steel, his body towering over mine.

"I'm only taking you home so you can pack a bag of all your shit to bring to mine. I want you in my bed every night. Non-negotiable. Two days and I can't function without you, and I'm not doing a second more."

Damn.

My eyes look over his face. This is moving fast. I haven't even had time to be mad about him disappearing, but... *How do you argue with that?* It may feel dangerously close to a *normal* relationship. But the thought of being worshiped by my own sex god every night for a while is something I won't deny myself. I deserve this, even if it ultimately is going to shatter my heart into a thousand pieces.

"One week trial period." I point my finger at him. "But I stay at mine when or if Maddie needs me."

"Fine with me," he huffs, as he grabs the door handle and gestures for me to get in, then leans over to secure the buckle. I swear he purposely grazes my breasts as he does.

I CAN'T HELP BUT ADMIRE THE SHEER LUXURY OF HIS PENTHOUSE. With the size, elegance, and beauty of this place, I feel completely out of my league. Keller could have any woman he wants at the drop of a hat. *Why me?*

The place neatly reflects Keller, the dark furnishings contrasting with natural light and white marble. That's him, dark and brooding, but underneath all of that, there is light. I can see it, although he might not.

But I have yet to see any photographs or personal touches, not even any boxing memorabilia. It feels like an empty shell, just waiting to be filled and brought to life.

"This place is magnificent, Keller."

"Well, get used to it, baby. If I have my way, you won't ever be leaving this place," he says as he sneaks up behind me, wrapping his heavy arms around my waist.

I lean back into his embrace and just take it in. It feels

right. With him wrapped around me, I feel like I can take on the world.

"Well, now might be a good time to tell you I can't cook for shit. I was brought up on ready meals and takeaways. Maddie's practically all but banned me from making anything other than coffee in the kitchen. So, if you're expecting a doting housewife, then you may be severely disappointed."

"Wife? Mmmm, I like the sound of that," he mumbles into my neck.

I feel his lips slide against my skin into a smile. I can't help the smile that creeps up my face. *Maybe being a wife wouldn't be so bad after all.*

"Good thing Mrs. Russo taught this boy how to cook. Don't worry. I'll make sure we're both well fed. Your sweet, sweet pussy is going to provide me with dessert every damn night."

Now that sounds perfect.

"In fact, I think I'd like something sweet before dinner," he says as he hoists me up and then drops me down to sink into the cool leather sofa. Ripping my jeans and little black thong off in one yank, he leaves me exposed. Wasting no time, he dives in, lapping me up, sucking on my clit as his fingers start to thrust in and out, bringing me to orgasm in record speed. He certainly knows how to push all the right buttons. He whips his mouth from my pussy and gives me a hungry kiss. I can taste the sweetness of myself on his lips. It's fucking hot. His erection strains against those sexy gray sweatpants. I want more and attempt to bring my hand up to the waistband, but he quickly swats it away.

"Patience, baby. Food first, then fuck. Deal?"

"Fine," I huff. Despite just orgasming a few moments ago, I crave more. I crave him. But food does sound good.

Keller works the kitchen like a pro. I'm yet to find anything Keller can't exceed at.

Boxing–check. Can find my clit–check. Cooking–check. Surely a man can't be this perfect.

The aromas of a creamy garlic chicken make my stomach rumble. Steam fills the kitchen as Keller flits from one pan to another, spatula in hand, his face stern as he concentrates.

I just perch on the barstool, drooling over the sight in front of me. Damn, I could get used to this.

"Do you need any help? I'm sure I could manage dishing up, if you want?" I ask.

"Nope, you just sit there and look pretty. Let me show you how a real man cooks."

I roll my eyes. That's fine by me.

Dinner is, by far, one of the most incredible meals I've ever had in my mouth. Well, bar his cock, but that doesn't count.

Each mouthful is a burst of flavors dancing on my tongue. I can't hold back a moan for every bite. Keller grips his fork more and more tightly as we eat. Until he can't take any more and slams his fork on the countertop, making me jump out of my skin.

"Fuck, princess, if you moan one more time, I won't be able to help myself from bending you over this counter and fucking you until you scream."

"Sorry," I pout, heat burning my cheeks. "It's just so fucking delicious; I can't help myself. I'm clearly not used to anything beyond pizza and grilled sandwiches," I add, as I stuff another mouthful in, letting out another involuntary moan, though I try my hardest to stop.

His heated gaze burns into me as he slips off the barstool and beelines toward me.

I clench my legs shut and squirm on my seat, pushing my near empty plate away from me, and spinning my barstool around to face him.

A word doesn't even pass his lips as he crashes them down onto mine, causing another moan to slip out. Jesus, this man makes me so vocal.

"That fucking mouth," he mumbles low under his breath. I give him a knowing smirk, dipping my finger in the sauce and popping it between his lips. His eyes go wide in response. I try my best not to break out into a fit of laughter at the sheer shock on his face. It's priceless.

THE NEXT WEEK FLIES BY AS WE SETTLE INTO OUR NEW ROUTINE. I can't remember the last time I smiled so much. The last time I felt so safe and secure. Every day I feel more and more loved, like I have never felt before in my life. I don't want this bubble to burst.

Every morning, we sit and have coffee together before Keller drives me to work, giving me an earth-shattering kiss that makes me extremely horny all day at work. At 5 o'clock on the dot, Keller is stationed outside my office, his hungry eyes watching as I make my way out of the building.

Then we spend our evenings cuddled on the sofa watching crime documentaries, seeing which of us can solve it first. So far, I've not won that yet.

He lights up when we talk about his boxing career and his unification fight in a few weeks. He's absolutely exhausting himself training every day. The pure fire and grit that he has are clear as day.

Let's not forget the rounds and rounds of passionate

sex. Christ, I knew that man was fit. I can confirm he is more than able to see out the twelve rounds. I don't think there is a surface left in his ridiculously large penthouse that hasn't been christened.

Every night, I fall asleep snuggled into his frame, yet every morning, I wake up to an empty bed. His side barely crumpled, like he doesn't even sleep there.

Everything is starting to almost feel too perfect.

By Friday, my whole body is sore, and I'm exhausted, but I've never felt more alive. Keller wasn't in the penthouse this morning when I woke, nor did he appear for coffee or to give me a lift. I tried calling a couple times with no luck. Not wanting to sound like a nagging, needy girlfriend, I pull up my big girl pants and decide to walk myself to the subway. Not that I particularly want to. I can't shake this strange feeling I am being watched. David has been off sick this week, so I've been doing my lunch break walks on my own. Anxiety runs through me every time, making me quicken my steps and get back to the office as soon as I can. I lost my nerve after the second time and haven't bothered since. *Maybe it's all in my head.* I sigh.

It's worth reminding myself again not to slip into relying on a man. I've come this far only relying on myself, and I sure as hell am not going to change now. I'm falling deeper and deeper for Keller. I know I shouldn't, but my heart can't help it.

We were clear that we both don't want a relationship, but it's starting to resemble one more and more each day. If I'm not with him, he's all I think about. When I am with him, I just want to rip my clothes off and let him devour every inch of me. We light each other up through our own brand of darkness.

I stand in the kitchen, tapping my foot as the coffee

machine buzzes to life, the dark liquid filling my takeaway cup. Even just the smell of coffee is enough to wake me up.

I open up the washing machine to throw some more underwear in. I thought I had packed enough. Keller's caveman need to rip off every pair I own means I am down to the last two pairs of satin black thongs. Pulling out the mound of clothes stuffed in the washer, I hurl them on the floor. I turn my nose up as some kind of metallic stench assaults my senses.

Picking up each black item piece by piece and tossing them in, I notice crimson covering my fingertips. *What in the fuck*? I try to hold in the vomit creeping up my throat. Deep red liquid drips on the white marble. Through shaky, blood covered hands, I hurl the soaked black hoodie into the washer as panic takes hold of my body. Stumbling back to the sink and whacking on the hot water, I aggressively scrub the red from my fingers.

Shit, what if he's been hurt? What if he's in hospital? *Shit, shit, shit. Please be okay.* Taking a deep breath, I turn off the scolding water and grab my handbag off the counter. Shaking the contents all over the side, I quickly swipe my phone and dial him.

Keller answers on the first ring, his deep voice booming through the speaker.

"Morning, gorgeous. Are you okay?" he asks softly, clearly unaware of the sheer panic I am in.

"Morning?! Are you fucking serious, Keller? I thought you were fucking dead!" I shout through heavy breaths. My hands are still trembling.

"Awe, are you worried about me, baby? I had to get up and out for an early training session. I left you a note on the plate of fruit in the fridge." He chuckles, like this was some sort of laughing matter.

"Keller, I found your clothes in the washer, dripping with blood. I thought... something happened to you. Why didn't you just call me like a normal person? You know I can't stand food first thing in the morning," I whisper down the phone, as if someone could hear me sounding like such an overreacting cow.

The line goes silent. I can hear his breathing becoming heavy.

"It's okay, Sienna. Calm down. I'm fine, I promise. I was training late with Grayson last night and took a bit of a battering from him." He quickly switches the conversation. "I can head back now and drive you to work."

Everything is suddenly becoming all too much. The walls are closing in on me. *Why do I feel like he is lying to me?*

"No-no, honestly, it's fine. I'm running late, anyway, and you have training to get to. You don't unify World Titles without a little bit of hard work. Especially with all these late night sessions you've been getting in," I ramble, my brain working a thousand times a second. He doesn't respond, so I continue, "I-er said I'd meet Maddie and David tonight, so I'll probably just stay back at mine. She misses me. Maybe it will be good if we just have a little space for a couple of days." My voice is trembling.

"Nope. How about me and Grayson meet you at the club later, then we go *home* together?"

"I'll meet you there at 8 pm. Have a nice day." I try to sound chirpy and cut off the call before he can even respond.

A text immediately flashes on the screen.

SEX GOD KELLER

Cut me off like that again and you won't like the punishment. I'll see you tonight, my goddess x x x

With shaking fingers, I put the contents of my bag scattered around the counter back in and make my way to work. I just can't shake the feeling that everything is tumbling down around me. *I knew this was all too good to be true. That doesn't mean this doesn't hurt.*

I take in a deep breath and call for the elevator, wiping my sweaty palms against my trousers. *Fuck, I can't do this–not without him.*

I let out a sigh and head toward the stairwell. Looks like I'm walking eighty-six flights down again today. Great.

CHAPTER SEVENTEEN

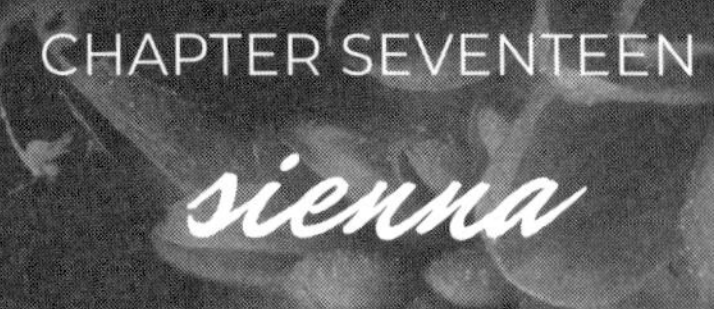

I climb up the stairs to my apartment. Today dragged like a bitch. I have been ignoring all of Keller's calls. The more I thought about it today, the more annoyed I am that he lied to me.

We might not be in an official relationship, but I thought we might be getting there. Now, him leaving in the middle of the night, finding blood-dripping clothes, leaves my mind reeling, debating if this whole thing is based on a lie. I shouldn't be shocked. No man has ever proven differently yet.

A brown parcel on my doorstep makes me stop in my tracks. It looks like someone had thrown it around in the back of the delivery truck. Picking it up, I spot it is addressed to me in shaky black handwriting. The smell of burning paper makes me hold my breath. It's that strong.

Putting the package under my arm, I unlock the door. The fresh scent of eucalyptus assaults my nose. The apartment is sparkling. Christ, Maddie must be bored without me to start a deep cleaning.

"Oh my god, you're home!" Maddie hurtles towards me at full speed, crashing into my still frame, wrapping her arms so tightly around me I can barely breathe.

"Did you miss me or something?" I laugh. This was just the welcome I needed after a shitty day.

"Of course, I did. Can't you see the whole place is sparkling? How was your dirty week with Mr. Sex God himself?" she asks, wiggling her eyebrows at me.

"Good," I respond matter-of-factly. I can't hide my emotions from Maddie. I never could. She always sees straight through me.

Her face pulls into a frown as she looks me up and down, as if assessing the situation. Grabbing my hand, she leads me into the lounge and plonks herself onto the sofa with a spring, patting the seat for me to join.

"Wait, we need wine," she mumbles as she sets off to pour two gigantic glasses of chilled rose. The woman can read my mind, I swear.

We spend the next hour delving into my doubts and frustrations. Whilst Maddie listens and nods, I can feel her brain ticking.

"Is it me? Am I the problem?" I let out a frustrated sigh.

"Maybe, just maybe, you need to let go of your past, Si. I am certain there is a reasonable explanation. A man can't be that obsessed with you and not be interested. You just run away at the first sign of trouble, too. You'll see; I have a good feeling about this one." She drains the last of her wine and sets the glass down on the table. "What on earth is that monstrosity of a package, anyway? I can smell it from here. Is the damn thing burning or something?" she says, pulling her nose up.

I snatch hold of the package and rip off the brown paper, which reveals a small, scratched black leather box.

Maybe it's an early Christmas present from my mom? Ha–that would be the first in a lifetime.

Lifting the lid up, the stench of burning flows out of the box. Gray ash and scattered half burned roses fill the box to the brim. A small, white envelope is placed on the top. Quickly ripping the envelope open, a white card is left which reads:

Sienna,

I'm hurt you threw out the roses I sent you. Let this be a message: I will burn anything that gets in my way. You will come back to me.

All my love,

J x

With trembling fingers, I throw the note back in the box and slam the lid shut. Since the night Keller threatened him, I hadn't heard a peep from Jamie. I thought this was over.

Maddie stays silent, her eyes wide as she stares at the box.

This isn't the Jamie I thought I loved, the man I was going to marry. My brain can't work out why he is still holding on to me, not letting me go.

"Sienna, I think you need to go to the police. This is getting weird now. First, he attacks you down an alleyway. I have spotted him outside our apartment window at least twice this week. And now, he's dumpster diving through our trash and sending you burnt roses. What if he wasn't who you thought? What if he really is dangerous, Sienna?"

I don't have a response to give her. I always thought I

could look out for myself. Now I'm just not sure. Unease fills my body as the tears begin to slip down my cheek.

A loud knock on the door makes us both physically jump. Before I can react, Maddie flies off the sofa and stomps over to the door, armed with a golfing umbrella she swipes from the stand next to the entrance.

"Jamie, I swear to fucking God, if you so much as step a foot in this apartment I will stab your eyes out, you fucking freak show!" she shouts through the door.

"It's Keller." His voice. It instantly makes my heart race.

Maddie turns to me, her eyebrow cocked.

"Let him in," I sigh.

As Maddie unlocks the catch, and the door flies open, nearly knocking her against the wall.

"Excuse me! Who do you think you are barging in here?" But she stops her verbal assault immediately as Keller looms over her.

Without so much as a greeting to Maddie, he beelines straight for me, concern etched across his features.

If looks could kill, Jamie would be 6 feet under by now.

Once he reaches me, he kneels down, taking my hands in his, searching my face.

"What's happened, Sienna? Did he hurt you?" Anger laced in his tone contrasts with the softness in his touch.

Shifting my eyes to the box, his gaze follows, and he sees the package. He leans across and opens the box, reading the note. His eyebrow cocks up as he does. He shoves the note back in the box and slams the lid shut, throwing it back down on the sofa with a huff. Grabbing my face in both of his large hands, he brings his forehead to mine.

"Sienna, I promise you. I will never let him hurt you or

even get close enough to touch you ever again. Baby, look at me," he whispers, his thumb stroking my face. I blink back the tears. I look at him, really look at him. He doesn't need to say anything, because love radiates from him, and his protection is just what I need at this moment. All I can do is give him a small nod as I bury my head in his chest. His musky scent gives me comfort as he wraps me up in a tight embrace.

His heart is thumping in his chest. I can feel it against my face. This man has the potential to kill with his bare hands. It has been more than obvious he's capable of that. He's built to be a machine. Everyone else might be fearful of him. I'm not. I love this side of him, my fierce protector. In this moment, I realize I don't want to be without him. Not for another day. I don't want to fight against my heart any longer.

"Take me home, Keller; make me feel safe. Make me yours." I whisper against his chest. His breath hitches at my words as he brings his mouth down to mine. The moment our lips touch, a spark ignites, my fear washes away, and I feel alive again.

"I have something I need to deal with. You and Maddie get ready here. Do *not* leave this apartment. Grayson will come and pick you up in an hour. I'll meet you at the club and then I will take you home, where you belong. I promise. You need to promise me something, too: no more running, okay? We need to stop denying what this is between us. You own my every thought; you are it for me. I have never gotten on my knees for anyone. I am the monster people kneel before. But I will always kneel before you, my goddess. I will worship you with every fiber of my being. A normal relationship is not something I can promise. I've never had one. But I want to try. Fuck, I want to try so hard to be worthy of you. The thought of you abandoning me today felt like someone had ripped my heart out and stomped on it. Be mine. Let me own your heart like you own mine?" I can hear the nervousness in his tone as he kneels before me, opening his heart to me.

His eyes search mine, looking for a response.

"I'm yours, champ, always, and only yours for as long as you'll keep me."

"I won't ever let you go. Now that I have you, you're mine forever," he growls as he leans in, giving me an earth-shattering kiss. A kiss that solidifies what we both know. This is it. We are it for each other, and I finally feel complete.

I peer over to spot Maddie with her back against the door, an infectious smile lighting the room. That girl loves love. She catches my eye and gives me a wink.

"Right, I better go get ready. If you kiss me anymore, I'm dragging you by the neck of that hoodie and having my way with you on top of all my fluffy cushions." I giggle.

"Well, I'm about to walk out of here with a rock-hard dick. So I'm all for this plan of you riding my cock," he replies as I swat his chest with my hand, trying to hold in a laugh.

"Go! I don't want a quicky. I want you, your mouth, and your cock all night long," I rasp as he lets out a low groan.

"Your filthy mouth kills me, woman."

Standing up, his raging hard cock tents those sexy sweatpants. He dips his hands in his pocket and pulls out two white tickets, handing them to me. Cocking an eyebrow, I take the tickets from his hand, giving him a questioning look.

“One of the guys–Luke, from the gym–is fighting at tomorrow night’s charity event in Madison Square. Me and Grayson have been training him up. I got you two tickets if you and Maddie want to come?”

A warm fuzzy feeling erupts in my chest as a smile lights up my face.

“Oh my god, yes! That sounds awesome! We would love to. Thank you.” I jump off the couch and place a quick peck on his lips before walking him to the door, even though I’m not wanting him to leave me.

I twiddle with my hair, like an infatuated teenager, while leaning against the doorframe. “So I’ll see you in a couple of hours then, champ.” I wink.

He pulls me into his embrace and I melt against him. “Wear something short and sexy for me. I can’t wait to have your ass grinding up against me,” he rasps, sex dripping from his tone.

Closing the door as his heavy footsteps echo down the hall, I fall back against it, trying to regain my composure. I am a complete hot mess. How I am going to get through tonight, I have absolutely no clue.

“I knew it. I knew he would be back in no time for you. Fuck, the way he looks at you like he wants to literally eat you up is so hot!” Maddie swoons as she reappears from her room.

“I’m scared, Mads. I am completely and utterly head over heels for this man. What if he’s no different from the rest of them? If he leaves, I honestly think he will take my whole heart with him. I’m strong, but not that strong.”

She wraps me up in her warm embrace, bringing instant comfort. “Oh, Si, what if he doesn’t? What if he is your twin flame, and you’re destined to spark each other for the rest of eternity? What you two have, not many people even get to have a taste of. So you grab it with both hands and you claim it. You own it. This is your time for happiness." Her voice is stern but laced with adoration.

Nodding into her embrace, I know she is right. I can feel it deep in my soul. Keller is, and always will be, the one for me. No matter what secrets he may be hiding, I will always choose him.

I get dressed in record time before Grayson shows up. I've picked out a tight satin black dress that hugs every curve, just stopping in the midsection of my thighs. I finish it off with red heels and red lip stain. There hasn't been time to wash and blow dry, so dead straight hair it is. Straightening highlights the caramel tones blended into the ends of my cascading hair. After a quick flick of mascara, I'm ready, with a whole ten minutes to spare.

Hearing a heavy knock on the door, I quickly make my way out of my room to let Grayson in. No doubt Maddie is running behind. Beauty takes time, and she certainly takes that mantra seriously. Shit, the last time Grayson saw me, my bare butt was squashed on his desk. But I can't even be embarrassed. It was fucking hot. Flinging open the door, I give Grayson a wide grin. He's leaning against the door frame, eyeing me up from head to toe. Not in a flirty way, more in a 'so this is what Keller is into' way.

"Well, how nice it is to see you fully dressed tonight, Sienna." He winks and strolls straight past. *Great start.* My mouth is still wide open as I watch him spread out on the couch and make himself comfortable.

"Sienna, can you zip me up?" Maddie shouts from her room. Before I can even step forward, she comes barreling out, tits on full display with her gold sequin dress wrapped around her stomach. My eyes go wide as she realizes we have company, the color draining from her face.

Grayson's eyes are glued to Maddie as an amused grin dances across his lips. "I'm more than happy to comply, sweetheart. Why don't you come take a seat," he says and taps his hands on his lap.

"Oh fuck off, Grayson. We all know I won't be putting this fine ass anywhere near you." She scoffs, but I can see the patches of red appearing on her chest. *Oh, this is interesting.*

Grayson is not anything like Maddie's usual type. She goes for tall, slim businessmen. Not big, burly boxers covered in tattoos, with a dirty mouth. No, that appears to be more my type.

Remembering my best friend is still currently half naked in the hall as Keller's best friend still gawks, I rush over and pinch together the dress and do the zip up, trying to hold in a chuckle as I do.

"I think he's into you, Mads," I quietly whisper.

Again, she scoffs and darts back into her room, slamming the door shut.

"Come on, girls, we need to leave in five. Grab your shit and let's get moving," Grayson demands, every word sounding regimental. It certainly gives me the wedge up my ass I need to get going. The quicker we get there, the quicker I get to Keller. Although I'm not too sure about leaving Maddie and Grayson together, they might kill each other by the end of the night.

Grayson leads us out of the apartment to his shiny white Audi, parked under our streetlamp. His attention snaps to a hooded figure lingering outside the apartment block next to ours. The figure is watching, but not making any move towards us. Funny, I have never seen anyone outside that block before, especially at this time of night. We live in a neighborhood full of older people and families, so a hooded man leaning against the wall is certainly a bit out of place. Grayson doesn't seem to flinch. He keeps his eyes on the man and opens his car doors for us, ushering us in.

I can hear him mumbling under his breath on the phone. I can't quite make out what he is saying other than, "Yes, I'm fucking sure." But as quick as I realize he is on the phone, he's sliding into the driver's seat and slamming the door. With that, he brings the car to life and speeds off, making my head slam back against the headrest.

"Do you have to drive like a fucking maniac, Grayson?" Maddie shouts from the back seat. Grayson, in return, just increases the volume of the music to full blast. These two are exhausting.

It's Friday night and The End Zone is already filled to the brim with eager New Yorkers dancing and drinking the stress of the week away.

By the sounds of it, tonight is a throwback R&B night, which safe to say, is an absolute winner in my books. Grayson nods us through security and hurries us past the dance floor, and past a second set of security, I'm assuming, to the VIP area.

"Keller's guests," Grayson tells the balding man in the black suit, who eyes us up and down and nods.

The VIP room, much like the rest of the club, is breathtaking. All black matte walls with gold furnishings. What I can imagine a billionaire's ideal strip club would look like.

The servers are all wearing tiny spandex shorts and crop tops, waltzing around with magnum bottles of champagne, giving the men an eyeful of their cleavage as they bend over to refill their glasses on the gold tables.

Grayson leads us over to a booth at the back of the area, the table already laid with three magnums and a tray of tequila shots. It's all great, but I just want Keller now.

I scoot up into the booth. Grayson squeezes in next to Maddie. "Touch me again. You'll find the heel of my stiletto wedged in your left eye."

"Fuck sakes, Maddie. I'm a big guy trying to fit into a fairly small booth. Trust me, I didn't want to touch you," he spits back, and her head flies around in shock.

Yep, Keller needs to hurry up and help me buffer this situation.

"Come on, you two. Play nice." I chuckle and pour out three glasses of champagne. The creamy bubbles dance on my tongue. Normally, I'm not a champagne kind of girl. I like my drinks sweet and sickly. But this is to die for.

The air in the room shifts, and all the attention darts to the VIP door. I know from the shiver running along my spine, it's him.

He nods past security and strides through like he owns the place. His entire persona drips power and wealth, and God damn, is he fine to look at. His black suit jacket and crisp white shirt–which has the first two buttons undone–emphasize the dark tattoos wrapping around his neck. Perhaps that's why I can't tear my gaze off him. Nor can any of the women here. But his dark eyes never stray from mine as he stalks his way over. Everyone watches as he does. I hadn't put much thought into the celebrity aspect of his life. Shit. What if he wants to hide me from the world?

Should I just keep it friendly in public? I am so out of my depth here.

As soon as Keller reaches me, he rests his hand on the table. Those sexy as sin veins protrude through his skin. I give him a small smile, still not having decided on how I should greet him in public. I feel the whole room watching us, waiting for his next move. Keller swiftly makes the decision for me as he bends forward and slams his lips against mine. I can feel him smile against my lips as he does. I've probably shattered the dreams of the women in here thinking they had a shot with him when he waltzed in. But he's all mine.

"Don't ever think I want to hide you, Sienna. I could feel your thoughts the second I walked into the room. I want the world to know you belong to me and that I am only owned by you," he rasps in his deep voice as he brings his nose down to mine.

I could literally melt on the spot. I have no doubts that I am soaked. How it's possible to be so turned on by someone every time they are in your space is beyond me.

He sits next to me in the booth. I catch Maddie watching our interaction. She looks so damn happy for me. I wonder if Keller has any decent friends I can set Maddie up with. He wraps his arm around my shoulder, pulling me flush against his side, and I melt into the embrace. A calm washes over me. He leans over and picks up a glass of champagne and downs it in one, tipping his head back, his Adam's apple bobbing as he does. God, even the way he drinks is delicious.

"Maddie," Keller nods, giving her a smile.

"Hi!" She blushes, giving him a small wave. No one is immune to Keller's charm.

"Oh, hi, Grayson. Hi, Keller. Thanks for picking my girlfriend and her bratty friend up and bringing them here," Grayson mocks.

Keller flicks up a brow, leaning over the table and grabbing his forearm.

"Shut it."

I shoot him a look as he sits back down. "They've been like this the whole time. I think secretly they are into each other," I whisper in his ear. He lets out a chuckle in response, continuing to sip his champagne.

"She's a woman. Of course, Grayson is into her," Keller replies, placing his hand on mine on the table. Electricity shoots through my fingers straight to my center. Sliding my hand from underneath his, I trail it slyly down the side of his body and down to his thick thigh, stroking up and down his rough denim jeans. His breath gets heavier the closer I get to his cock, and my fingers tingle as I continue to tease him. He doesn't stop me. He just stares straight faced onto the dance floor.

Could I really, here? I don't know what's gotten into me. This isn't how I behave. I seem to become a horny bitch whenever Keller is around me.

As if he senses my hesitation, he brings his lips to my neck, brushing against my sensitive skin.

"Don't you dare fucking stop, now. How far can you go?" A hunger stirs in his voice as he starts to nip at my neck. The room is so dimly lit it's hard to make out what anyone else is doing in the booths. Maddie and Grayson are too busy picking on each other and sipping champagne to even notice us anymore. *Fuck it.*

I inch my hand ever so slightly higher, slowly unzip the fly of his jeans and undo the button, trying not to move the top half of my body that's on display. His cock is straining against the material. Of course, Keller isn't wearing boxers.

Keller's massive frame fills the booth, so the table completely covers us. A low groan escapes his perfectly full lips, and there is a wild hunger in his eyes. That's enough to give me the confidence to grip the base of his cock and slowly start stroking up and down. "My greedy girl couldn't wait a couple of hours for my cock, could you? Hmm?"

I've never been brave enough to do this before. The thought of getting caught only fuels the fire within me.

"It's yours, baby, take it when you want it," he says, as I continue to pump my hand up and down. I'm so lost in the moment, my legs tightly squeezing together, and Keller's hungry eyes are eating me up. I fail to hear Maddie shouting over the music to get my attention. Keller's low cough brings me out of my haze as I snap my eyes to her.

"Oh, finally you're back in the room. We're just going to go for a dance and get some more shots. Are you guys coming or staying?"

"Oh, I'm definitely coming," Keller announces, giving me a wicked grin.

"Yep," I answer quickly, maybe too quickly. "We'll meet you there in a sec." With that, Maddie and Grayson slink off to the bar, leaving me and Keller alone in the booth, my hand still gripping his pulsing cock.

"Fuck, baby, you are insatiable," he murmurs, taking my lips with his.

"Only for you," I tease back, but I'm being deadly serious. Nuzzling my head into his chest, I let out a content sigh. He really is starting to become my happy place. The world is calm when he is with me.

The unmistakable smell of gasoline suddenly grabs my attention.

"Keller, why do you smell like gasoline?" I stop

pumping his cock as I wait for him to respond, and I see the annoyance flickering across his features.

"I torched your ex's car on my way here," he states it matter-of-factly with a shrug, no emotions showing on his face, yet his eyes are searching mine, waiting for a reaction.

Slapping my hand against his chest, I let out a laugh. "No you fucking didn't." He still doesn't react, just stays deadly still watching me, his cock still pulsing in my hand.

Once I manage to contain my laughter, I snap straight up to look at him. He's not joking. Not in the slightest.

"Why?" I ask, keeping my tone even.

Removing my hand from him, I create distance between us. *Would he really do this for me?* I'm not remotely pissed he did that. In fact, it's kind of hot that he would go to such measures to protect me. Plus, Jamie is a prick, so there is also that.

"Sienna, I warned you the first time we met. I'm not a good man. There is darkness in me. Now that darkness is there to protect you. I won't ever apologize for doing something to protect you. I can't lose you, and I sure as shit won't let anyone threaten you. I'll set the world on fire to protect you, and I won't ever let a single flame touch your beautiful skin."

Well shit. His words give me chills and my stomach does that strange, flippy thing.

I quickly put him back in his jeans and do them up, disappointment obvious as his jaw ticks, and bring both my hands up to cup his cheeks.

"Thank you." I smile as I bring my lips down to his, showing him how grateful I am, his eyes going wide at my response. If I need–no *want*–anyone fighting in my corner, I wouldn't want anyone other than Keller. I love this protective side of him.

"So, you don't mind me going around torching cars?" he questions, his eyebrow raised.

"You can try to scare me off all you want, Keller. I don't care. Trust me, I didn't grow up with a sheltered life. I don't just want the good parts of you, I want them all–the good, the bad, and the downright ugly. You just have to accept those parts of me, too."

A wicked smile passes his lips as he claims mine.

"You are fucking perfect, Sienna," he growls in my ear.

I'm about a minute away from jumping on his lap and letting him do whatever he wants to me. Begrudgingly, I break the kiss, our breathing heavy.

"Right, we best go find our friends, dance for a bit, and then I need you to take me home to show me how you own me." I snatch his hand and lead him out of the VIP area to the bar with him never more than two steps behind me.

Once we reach the bar, it's easy to spot Grayson towering above everyone else. He doesn't notice us. He is too busy giving a murderous glare to someone on the dance floor. I follow where he's scowling and spot Maddie grinding up against a random bloke, his hands roaming up and down the sides of her body as she throws her head back and laughs. She looks happy and free, just how she should be. Interesting to see Grayson's reaction. I'll have to store that one for later. Right now, all I want is Keller's cock inside me.

As if reading my mind, he grabs me by the waist, his breath hitting my neck. "I need to get you home. I can't fucking take much more of this, baby."

"Thank God. Yes! If I have to squeeze my legs together for one more minute, I'm going to get a bloody rash."

I feel him chuckle against my back.

"Grayson, you good to take Maddie home?" He points to her on the dance floor.

"Yeah, fine," he gruff's back, sinking his scotch. I'm surprised the crystal doesn't smash in his hands with the death grip he has on it.

Biting my bottom lip, I shoot Keller a questioning look. He just shrugs in response.

"Let me quickly go say bye to Maddie. Maybe see what's up with Grayson whilst you wait. He looks like he's going to strangle someone." Giving him a quick peck up on my tiptoes, I beeline into the jumping crowd of dancing strangers, making my way to Maddie.

As soon as she spots me, she lets out a high-pitched tipsy scream, shoving the poor bloke off her and giving me a big bear hug.

"We're heading off, Mads. Did you want a lift? Or Grayson's offered to take you home."

"Oh, Grayson can take me home. I like winding him up," she laughs, spying him out of the corner of her eye. Oh, he looks like he wants to kill her right now.

"One dance with me," she pleads, batting her long black lashes at me. *How could I say no?*

She quickly nabs my hand before I can answer and spins me under her raised arm as we sway to the music. During the song, the dance floor gets more and more crowded. I feel hands rubbing up and down my arms as I sway my hips to the music. The touch is light and then suddenly it's ripped off me, replaced by two powerful hands digging into my hips. As soon as his hands make contact, I know it's him. My body reacts instantly to him. Every damn time.

"I think you need a reminder of whose hands can touch you, princess," he growls as he lifts me like I weigh the same as a feather. Then he drapes me over his shoulder, like a complete caveman.

"Let me down, Keller, this is fucking embarrassing," I shout over the music whilst hitting his rock hard back. It actually hurts the palm of my hands. His back is that solid. My body vibrates as he chuckles beneath me. "Once I'm finished with you, you won't ever need reminding again," he says, forcefully slapping my ass, which burns right into my center, soaking my panties.

The crisp air surrounds my skin as we enter the back street. I hear the keys click and the car flashes open. Keller gently slides me into the passenger seat with a murderous look still sporting his face.

He doesn't say a word on the drive home, his hands gripping the steering wheel and his knuckles white. As if he is about to explode.

"Keller, if you think I'm going to apologize for dancing with a stranger, just be warned you'll be waiting a long goddamn time," I say, raising my voice. "Look at me," I demand. Protective and obsessed I love, but jealous caveman shit, I pass on. "I said I was yours and I meant it. Now get over yourself and get your head back in the room. It was harmless. I would never, I mean never, go out of my way to hurt you. The only man's hands I want on me are yours," I explain sincerely, hoping he gets the message.

"I'm sorry, Sienna. I just saw another man touching you and saw red. I can't help it when it comes to you. I can't fucking lose you. I've never had anyone to lose before. I don't think I could take it." He sighs.

Placing my hand on his thigh, I gently stroke up and down, trying to comfort him. "I promise I'm not going anywhere. I only want you, always."

"Good girl."

"Now drive quicker so I can get out of this tight dress and let you fuck me. It's all I've thought about all night," I tease.

"Oh, trust me. We will be going the full distance tonight. You'll be on your ass seeing stars by the time I'm finished with you, baby."

"That sounds like heaven."

CHAPTER EIGHTEEN

keller

She is the first person in my life to knock me on my ass, and I couldn't be happier about it.

We are inevitable. I don't believe in destiny and all that crap. But some other force of nature must have been at play when she was propelled into my lap.

I have my own perfect goddess, naked and kneeling in front of me. Her skin glistens as the New York skyline twinkles through the bedroom. She's ready and waiting for me to claim her, to own her.

There is nothing on this earth that could stop me from taking her, not just for now, but forever. I've had a taste and I can't let her go. Fuck the consequences. Nothing has ever stopped me from fighting for what I want, and I'm going to fight with everything I can to keep her.

I can be worthy of her. I might not deserve her, but I can try. She settles the monster within me. If I can win this fight and be rid of my ties to the mafia, not only can I keep her safe, I can drop the mask. I can be who she needs me to be. A simple smile lighting up her features is enough to calm my inner rage.

Fuck, the way she looked into my soul and thanked me for torching her prick of an ex's car was confirmation she is it for me. She doesn't only accept my darkness, she fucking loves it. The dirty little princess wants the monster to protect her, own her, and devour every inch of her. So that's what I'll do. For the rest of my time on this earth, I will dedicate it to worshiping her the way she deserves.

"Where do you want me to start?" Trailing my fingers over her face, I pry open her mouth. A quiet moan slips past her lips, shooting blood straight to my dick.

"Do you want to be fucked with my fingers, or does my greedy girl want my mouth devouring her pussy as I fuck you with my fingers?" I rasp as I use my index finger to tip her chin up to face me. A red blush slowly forms on her cheeks and sparks the pure hunger in her eyes.

"I want it all, Keller. Show me what you've got. No hiding from me anymore. Your deepest, darkest urges. Show me. Please, *Sir.*"

Fuck, this woman. I bring my lips to hers and place a gentle kiss. I need to remind her–fuck, remind myself–this is more than rough, dirty sex.

"Let's get one thing straight. I will *always* treat you like the princess you deserve when we're outside the bedroom. But when we are in here, I'm going to fuck you like a whore."

A devious grin spreads across her plump lips, her eyes shimmering with desire. She takes in my words and I feel her breath hitch. I know she wants this, too. I could feel it the second she landed on my lap. She is my perfect firecracker.

She gives me a slow nod.

"Show me." Her eyes light up.

I tighten my grip around her neck and tug her to stand

upright, taking some of the weight with my other hand on her waist. My mouth is just inches from hers as I close the distance between us. I can feel her erratic, warm breath hitting my face, the remnants of expensive champagne still with her.

"I'm going to tie your wrists together. I know how much you love touching, but not tonight. Tonight is all about you. I'm going to bring you right to the edge of pleasure and crashing back down, over and over, until you're writhing in pain. Only then will I fuck you. Is that what you want, baby? Do you want to be completely and utterly at my mercy? All of your pleasure solely in my hands?"

Moments pass, our heavy breaths the only sound in the room.

"Yes-yes, Keller. I want it all." Her voice is barely a whisper.

Unable to contain my hunger any longer, I crash my lips to hers, taking everything I can get. Slipping my tongue into her mouth, I lap up the taste of champagne as I probe. There's something sexy about her nakedness rubbing against my fully clothed form. She's completely exposed, completely trusting me. All the power lies entirely in my hands. The hands that are used to inflict pain are the same ones that will bring her ultimate pleasure.

Abruptly, I break the kiss, unable to take anymore. My dick can barely last when I'm around her.

"Lay on your back on the bed, legs spread." My voice is deep and commanding.

She responds immediately, swaying her hips as she makes the short walk to the bed, sensually crawling up onto the mattress, her pussy on full display as she does. My goddess knows exactly what she's doing.

Once in position, I yank open the top drawer of my

chest, rummaging through the contents to find the white cotton wrap. It's the first thing I can think of to tie her wrists with. I can't wait to use the same wrap on my hands for my next match, which might be my new good luck memento before a fight. I smirk as I slam the draw shut.

I stalk back to Sienna, spread perfectly on her back on my bed, her hair splayed above her head, creating a halo around her. I watch as her perky tits lift with each breath. I climb on top of her, my knees on each side of her hips as I unravel the crisp white wrap, letting it drape through my hands. Grabbing both of her wrists with one hand, I start wrapping around them, pulling them tight as I loop under and start wrapping between her hands, tying the end back through.

"Good girl."

"Keller, please do something. I'm about to fucking explode over here. Please touch me; do something, anything." Desperation laces her tone.

"Patience, baby."

I pepper light kisses from her wrists, moving all the way down her arms, inch by inch. When I get to her neck, the delicate flesh just below her ear tempts me, and I bite and suck, leaving love bites in my wake.

She lets out a whimper in response.

Fuck, seeing my marks on her body does something to me.

Continuing down her body, I switch between gentle kisses and bites, elevating the contrast between pleasure and pain.

"I bet if I bury my head between your legs, you'll be fucking dripping. Shall we see?"

I feel her nod her head against the bed. Not good enough.

"Words, Sienna," I demand.

"Fuck, Keller. Put your fucking head between my legs, now!" she almost shouts.

I chuckle. We've barely started, and she's already teetering on the edge. She needs reminding who's in charge here. I quickly lift myself off her. I don't want to, but she needs to know.

Now standing over her, her body sagging in defeat, she tries to close her knees slightly. Snatching my hand out, I slam her knees back down to the mattress.

"You don't get to make demands here, baby, and you sure as shit don't get to hide your pussy away from me. In here, it's all mine." Hesitating, I watch her for a moment. "Now stay still like a good girl, and keep that mouth shut. Okay?" I see her lips form into a tight 'o' before she snaps them shut and nods.

Dropping to my knees at the edge of the bed, my hands grip around her thighs and lightly skim my tongue from her entrance all the way up to her clit. Her back instantly arches off the bed, and I spread my hand across her smooth stomach and press her back down, keeping her still. She lets out a huff in frustration as I do. I continue skimming the tip of my tongue up and down until I can feel her legs start to inch closer, and I can feel the slightest vibration from her trembling on my tongue. Immediately, I retreat and sit back on my heels as her body goes limp in defeat.

"You don't get to come until I say so, okay, baby?" I remind her, pausing, to let her take in a few breaths. I spy her shiny white teeth chewing her bottom lip. Resting on my heels as I kneel before her, I take in her sheer beauty, her perfect pink pussy glistening before me, drenched in her juices. *If I were to die right now, I'd die a fucking happy man,* I think as I lick my lips, debating how to bring her to the edge next. I know I can't take much more. I need to sink into her soon. My cock is throbbing so hard I can't concentrate. Rising to my feet, I rip off my shirt, the buttons flying through the air. I don't have time to unbutton them. And I bend down to slip off the jeans restraining my cock, finally joining Sienna in being completely exposed.

Her eyes eat me up as she slowly takes me in, settling her gaze directly on my cock. *My greedy princess.* I smirk. Striding to the edge of the bed, I flip her onto her stomach. She lets out a shriek as she lands face first on the mattress, her hands still bound above her head. Leaning forward, I grip her hips and pull her closer, so her ass is in the air, resembling the cat stretch Grayson loves to get me to do after training. I bet I don't look anywhere near as sexy in the same position.

"Fuck, baby, you are fucking gorgeous. This pussy was made perfectly for me. Don't worry, it won't be long until I fill you up. I can't fucking take much more."

She responds by pushing back her hips and wiggling her ass, thinking she can tease me.

I draw my hand back and firmly slap her left cheek. Her screams fill the room as she darts forward, the red mark already forming on her pale skin.

"Oh my god, Keller!" she sobs, moisture dripping down the inside of her thighs, her breathing heavy as she brings her ass slowly back towards me. *I knew it! My greedy girl loves it.*

I grab her red ass cheek and slide my other finger along her wet slit.

"You are fucking dripping, baby. Did I really get you that wet by spanking you?" I rasp, as I continue to rub my fingers along her seam. A moan escapes her lips, like music to my ears. "You want me to do it again, princess? How about harder this time?"

"What? No."

Her voice is strained, which makes me laugh as her ass grinds up against me.

I spank her ass again as I slide two fingers into her entrance. Her back arches as she lets out a primal scream.

"Fuck, Keller, I can't hold it anymore," she pleads, still fucking my fingers.

"My greedy girl, it looks like I'm going to have to get more creative with you."

Her breath hitches as I bring my mouth down to her spanked ass and bite her flesh. She comes apart beneath me, trembling around my fingers as she screams out my name.

I don't need to be told twice. I rest my knees on the edge of the bed and smother her body under mine. Her silky skin rubs against my chest. Slinking my arm between her legs, my fingers find her clit and pinch. She presses herself forward, her face smashing into the duvet even further to stifle her screams.

Dragging my fingers back towards her entrance, I tease my index finger in, letting out a low groan as her walls tighten against me. Just the thought of her squeezing against my cock makes me pick up the pace. Adding two more fingers, I increase the pace, her breathing matching the movement. I can feel her pussy clenching against me. My fingers are drenched in her juices.

She responds to me so perfectly, every fucking time. Her hips meet my pace, thrust for thrust. We were made for each other in every way possible.

I slow my assault, removing my fingers, and trail them up each ridge of her spine along that sexy tattoo. When I reach the back of her neck, I tighten my grip as she pulls her head back and lets out a moan. It's the sexiest fucking sound, her breathy moan. It almost sends me over the edge without her even touching me. Just watching her come undone, completely at my mercy, has me ready to explode.

"Keller, please. I need you inside me. I need you to fuck me. I can't take it anymore," she almost sobs, her voice barely a whisper. I can just about hear her through the sound of the blood pumping in my ears.

Her words send a shooting pain straight to my chest. I can never deny my goddess, and right now, I feel the same desperation as her.

Not wasting another second, I flip her back over to face me. Never in my life have I wanted to so desperately look someone in the eye while I fuck them. I want everything with this woman. I want her to see me. I want to see her exposed. I want–no–I crave her intimacy. She needs to see and feel how I feel about her. She spreads her legs wide, her knees pressing into the mattress, inviting me in as the bed dips, and I position my cock at her glistening entrance.

I slowly push myself inside, going inch by inch so she can adjust to my size.

"Fuck, Keller," she moans, her voice deep and raspy. "More."

Leaning over her, careful not to squash her, I take my weight on my wrist above her head.

"You feel so good wrapped so tight around my cock. It's fucking perfect. You, Sienna, are fucking heaven on earth. I don't think I could ever give this up."

"Good job you aren't giving this up. Now hurry up and fuck me. Fuck me like you own me, like the dirty whore that I am."

Every ounce of preservation I had flies out the window

as I pound in and out of her, the sound of our bodies slapping together vibrates around the room, muddled with the screams escaping Sienna's lips.

Nothing in my life has ever felt this good, not even winning my first world title. This takes the belts.

My heart is hammering in my chest as I feel my release building. I'm so fucking close. Slamming my lips onto hers, I claim her mouth as I continue my assault, using my spare hand to find her clit as I smother it in her juices. I'm on the edge of the cliff, about to jump. Every vein feels like it's about to explode. I can't take it anymore.

"Now, Sienna. Come for me, baby."

That's all it takes, and she screams out my name, writhing beneath me as the walls clench so tight around my cock, milking my orgasm. I follow quickly behind her, releasing everything I have into her. Our sweaty bodies are entangled with one another, our breathing heavier than if we'd run a marathon, and pure euphoria seeps through my body.

"Fuck, Sienna, that was... Fuck, I don't even have words for it." I sigh, bringing my forehead to hers.

"I know," she just about manages through fluttering eyelashes, her big blue eyes piercing into my soul.

Staying where we are, catching our breath, I ride out what is the most intense orgasm of my entire life. I slowly lean forward and undo the ties on her wrists. Gently rubbing them and bringing them to my lips to sprinkle delicate kisses where they were bound. Her features soften as she watches me.

"I'm keeping these. My new good luck charm." I wink just before stealing a quick kiss. A few moments later, I nab a cloth from the bathroom rail and run it under a lukewarm tap. Catching myself in the mirror, I look wild, but surprisingly free. My usual angry features are not even remotely evident. That's the effect she has on me.

Returning to the bedside, I gently sweep the cloth up the inside of her legs and between. She's now resting on her forearms, watching my every move intently. I can feel the cogs of her brain ticking from here.

"Whatcha thinking, baby?"

"Is it like that for you with all the other women?"

"Never," I reply simply. A smile dances across her lips.

She bats me away with the palm of her dainty hand. Even with full force, she wouldn't move me an inch. But it's cute she tries. I steal a quick kiss as I wrap my arms around her waist and roll us onto our sides, gently lifting her head to land on the fluffed Egyptian cotton pillow. Pulling her body into me feels perfect; spooning her back flush against me simply fits.

"Sleep now, princess," I whisper against her hair, pulling the stray strands laying over her cheek behind her ear.

Those three little words lay on the tip of my tongue. Something holds me back. I've never said those words to a woman before, hell I've never said them to anyone. But there is no denying how I feel. She is it for me.

Her breathing steadies, a slight whistle every time she breathes out. Closing my eyes, I settle my head and absorb the delicious scent of peach invading my senses. My brain is completely quiet, another effect she has on me. Not only the beacon of light to my dark, the calm to my storm. Sleep comes easily with her wrapped in my arms.

CHAPTER NINETEEN

Christmas is in full swing, New York is twinkling, and now apparently, so is my apartment. Maddie has been busy turning the place into a bloody grotto, complete with a bright red 'Scrooge' sign tacked to my door.

I can't lie, though. The waft of cinnamon drifting through the room from the bubbling saucepan of mulled wine is delicious. The one thing I will never moan about over Christmas is the copious amounts of amazing food and drink.

Maddie takes Christmas incredibly seriously. The first couple of Christmases we spent together, she was mortified at how 'grinchy', as she calls it, I am. Whilst she is Buddy the elf in woman form, practically swinging from the tinsel hung on the ceiling. She's a bundle of excitement throughout the whole month of December.

I'd never experienced a Christmas like it. Growing up, my mom and dad tried to make it special despite having no money. That was, until my dad left. From then on, you wouldn't have even known it was Christmas. All the other kids excitedly ran into school to show off their new toys, bellies full. I would sit and watch from the back of the class, tears stinging the backs of my eyes as I had nothing to show, nothing to be excited about.

Then Maddie happened. The woman is relentless in her pursuit of happiness. It's infectious. Now I can confidently say, I don't *mind* Christmas. I do, however, draw the line at that stupid racket Slade song on repeat.

This year Maddie has gone even further to spread the Christmas cheer. I think she's worried I might ditch her for Keller over the holidays, and the thought of going back to her parents, still unmarried and without a boyfriend, makes her skin crawl.

"Maddie," I shout as I walk through the hallway.

"In here!" Her voice is just about inaudible over the excessively loud Christmas playlist she has going on.

As I reach her, she's busy slamming a rolling pin on top of a round pile of dough, white flour smothered over each counter and smeared across her face. She gives me a wild grin. "I'm making Christmas cookies!"

"I gathered," I chuckle, tossing my handbag down and darting into the kitchen to help before the place looks like a drug gang lives here.

"Are you okay, Mads? The place looks amazing. But this is extreme, even for Mrs. Claus here." I bounce my hip against hers, gently trying to press her for more.

Wiping the small beads of sweat from her forehead with the back of her arm, she lets out a deep sigh. "I just feel super lonely. I really thought I'd have someone to spend Christmas with this year." She stares blankly at the beige ball of dough she's excessively rolling, now near flat as a pancake. I wince at her words, feeling bad for not being around very much the last few weeks.

"Hey Maddie, you know I'll always spend Christmas with you. Hell, whenever you need me, I will always be there."

I wrap her in a tight embrace. She always spends so much time making sure everyone around her is happy that she overlooks herself.

"I don't mean you, silly. I know you won't go anywhere. You made a solid deal to have Christmas with me until we run out of Christmases. I mean, I just wish I'd find someone to love me. Like you've found with Keller."

I wrap her tighter so she drops the death grip on the rolling pin. "I promise you, your time will come. The universe is just waiting to send you the perfect man at the perfect time so all your stars can align."

Snapping her head up, she pushes from my embrace. "Ha! You just admitted you and Keller are in looooooove," she teases, so I give her a dramatic eye roll.

"I did not say that. You're putting words in my mouth."

"Keller and Sienna sittin' in a tree."

"Stop it, Maddie," I warn as I whack her arm, causing her to burst out into a fit of infectious laughter. So much so that I can't help but join her.

Once all twelve oddly cut gingerbread men cookies are safely baking away in the oven, Maddie gives me clear instructions to remove them from their furnace in precisely eighteen minutes. She's gone off to get ready for Keller's charity boxing match later this evening. "Oh Si, a package came for you earlier today," she says, poking her head out of her room. "I stuck it on your bed. I checked the label, and looks like it's from a legit company. Looks fancy as fuck, actually. Rather than some more burned crap from Jamie." Going back into her room, she calls over her shoulder. "Don't forget the cookies."

"I'll try," I shout back. She has absolutely no faith in my domestic skills.

I haven't ordered anything, so I am more than intrigued by what's been delivered to me. I quickly dart to my room to see.

A large, rectangular, shiny black box rests on my bed. It's finished off with a silky gold ribbon, tied in a perfect bow on the top. My shaky hands gently pull the lengths of the bow, then I lift the lid off and toss it on the bed, revealing layers of thick, black tissue paper. A gold envelope nestled on top catches my eye.

Grabbing the note, I rip the top open and pull out the card.

"An outfit fit for a goddess. You are my goddess, Sienna. Wear this tonight so I can tear it off you later. All my love, Keller x x "

Tears threaten to fall as I pull apart the tissue to reveal a stunning gold sequin material. Pulling the dress out of the box, I hold it up and admire its beauty. Thin, gold chain straps connect to a plunge line dress which trails down longer on one side. It would just about brush past my knee. I hang it on the back of my door, the sequins reflecting the light and sparkling around the room. A long, rectangular black velvet box rests in the packaging. Surely not. This dress is glitzy enough as it is. And I don't imagine Keller is the kind of guy to go jewelry shopping in his spare time away from the gym.

Inside the box rests a thin gold chain necklace with a dazzling princess-cut diamond. The way the light reflects and the clarity of the stone, there is absolutely no way this is zirconia. This right here is the real deal. Simply stunning and elegant, a perfect pairing with the dress. This must have cost more than my month's wages. Shit, probably even more than that, knowing Keller. That man doesn't hold back when it comes to buying fancy things.

Snapping the jewelry box shut, I place it on my dresser and grab my phone. No new notifications, not that I expected anything. Keller was training all day with Grayson and then heading home to get ready for tonight. He and Grayson are heading down early to help Adam get ready for his fight. Apparently, if he can win this, there are some top promoters there who could launch his career. I'm sure with Keller on his side, he won't have any problems with that, anyway.

So, Maddie and I are being picked up at 7 pm by Keller's driver. Which is fine. But I just miss him. It's only been a few hours and I'm like a lovesick puppy. Quickly navigating to my texts, I pull up mine and Keller's mostly dirty chat.

ME

I absolutely love the dress. Should I be worried about your taste in women's clothes? Something you do often? xx

Ok, that wasn't quite what I was trying to get across. Shit.

ME

That came out wrong, but thank you. P.S. I'm very much looking forward to seeing how it sparkles on your bedroom floor. P.P.S. That necklace is FAR too much as a gift, Keller. I don't need extravagant gifts. Only you.

Right, that sounds better, less passive-aggressive. I blame my Scorpio tendencies. That jealous streak just doesn't know how to chill, clearly.

As I'm drying my hair, my phone lights up in the corner of my view.

SEX GOD KELLER

If I don't see that necklace wrapped around that pretty little neck of yours, there will be hell to pay. Your ass will be red raw.

A blush crosses my cheeks as I remember him doing exactly that a couple of nights ago. Boy, was it H.O.T. He knows my desires, inside and out. He knows how to push each and every one of my buttons to absolute perfection. Pair that with our intense connection, sparks literally fly every single time. He's set a fire within me and I have no intentions of ever putting it out.

Another ping drags me from my thoughts.

SEX GOD KELLER

Not that a spanking is much of a punishment for my greedy goddess. Maybe I'll have to get more creative with you. You are going to be the most stunning woman in the room tonight. I'm not sure I am going to be able to keep my hands off you.

My pussy is throbbing as I read his words. My fingers start to move the towel away from my legs as another message pops up.

SEX GOD KELLER

And if you even THINK about putting those fingers anywhere near that perfect pussy right now, I suggest you stop. Be a good girl and remember who it belongs to.

How the hell did he know that's what I was going to do?

SEX GOD KELLER

Put the damn necklace on. I promise it won't be the only necklace you'll be wearing tonight. See you soon, princess. xxx

Carefully undoing the clasp of the necklace, I wrap it around my neck. It delicately falls just between my collarbones and illuminates against my pale skin. Dropping the towel that was wrapped around me and covering my breasts with my forearm across my body, they are looking super perky the way I am pressing them against my body. I quickly snap a picture and send it to Keller.

ME

Got it, boss, the necklace is on... see?

A response immediately comes through.

SEX GOD KELLER

Fuck Sienna, now I gotta go take a cold shower.

Chuckling to myself, I put the phone down and run to get the cookies before the place burns down. Once that's done, I continue getting ready. Going for a look that will compliment that dress, I swipe a light gold shimmery eyeshadow on my lids and a quick flick of black liquid eyeliner. He wants a goddess? Well, tonight he's getting one.

After styling my hair to cascade down one shoulder with bouncing curls, I finish the look with a nude matte lipstick. The dress is a statement enough. I just need to provide a body whilst the material steals the show.

I rifle through my messy drawers in search of the sexiest lingerie I can find and settle for a crotchless lace red thong that looks perfect against the light tan on my skin. But I decide against a bra as the dress looks like it will hold me in all the right places without one. It fits like a glove, emphasizing my figure in all the right places. The plunging neckline does wonders for my boobs and the way it ruches up on one side gives me the perfect hourglass figure. I'm glad I managed to smear some instant fake tan on. I look like I'm glowing. Every ounce the goddess I know Keller is going to devour, and I cannot wait.

7 pm rolls around a lot quicker than expected. Peering out of our living room window, I see a blacked-out Mercedes pull up outside. I shout at Maddie to hurry up. She still hasn't appeared out of her room yet. No doubt redoing her hair for the hundredth time. Eventually, she strolls out, her eyes go wide and her mouth drops open when she sees me.

"Fuck me, Sienna! You look stunning. That dress; I take it that was the package from Keller. Boy, that man has style!" Excitement radiates off her as she speaks.

Maddie is wearing a simple, tight black dress matched with killer silver stilettos and a leather jacket. Her bright blonde hair is in a simple yet elegant updo, framing her face with wavy curls. She could wear a sack and still look like a model.

"Awe thank you, Mads. You're looking hot tonight, too. Trying to impress a certain trainer?" I say, wiggling my brows at her.

A blush creeps up her chest as she looks away. "No, he's the last person I want to impress," she snaps back too quickly.

"Okay, okay," I say as I surrender my arms and back away, laughing as I do. Sometimes she is just too easy to wind up.

As soon as we show our tickets at the door, two massive bouncers escort us through the building, down a side passage away from the crowds. They don't say a word, and we just follow. Trying to keep up with their long strides in heels is a bit of a task.

Despite the corridor being nearly empty, the sound of the chattering of thousands of people behind the wall vibrates around me, sending waves of excitement through to my core.

I've never been to a boxing match before. I certainly didn't expect a near full capacity turnout for a charity event. Although I should never underestimate Keller. I often forget he's famous; when it's just me and him, that doesn't even come into the equation. To me, he's my Keller with a filthy mouth and a devilish grin that worships the ground I walk on. To the rest of the world, he's a famous heavyweight boxer living a glamorous, playboy lifestyle.

Little do they realize, he spends his evenings curled up watching Netflix with little old me. Although the media around him is kept to a minimum, I assume that's Keller's doing, and I don't think anyone would really fancy facing Keller's wrath.

He made it clear in the club the other night that he doesn't want to hide me from the world, which gave me warm fuzzy feelings inside. I don't want to complicate anything for him. He has a massive fight coming up. He could become the undisputed heavyweight champion of the world. With the focus and dedication he's been putting into training, and from the snippets of information he's shared with me, there is no doubt in my mind Keller will come out on top. I don't see any opponent coming up to even match him.

The security guards usher us into the arena through big

double doors. The music blares and the lights are dim, but it's still bright enough to see the thousands of people occupying the space, singing and chanting.

We keep walking and walking; the ring getting closer and closer as we reach an empty front row only mere feet away from the ring. He gestures for us to take a seat as he nods and speaks into his earpiece, not so much as a "Have a nice evening ladies" as he storms back off.

A row of stern-looking judges, I assume, sits in the next front row to my right. As soon as my butt touches the seat, a young girl in black and white shorts and a crop top passes Maddie and me glasses of bubbles with a fake smile and flits off.

I glance to my left as Maddie quickly locks her phone and stuffs it straight in her bag, her eyes wide as she spies to see if I'm looking.

"Everything okay, Mads?"

She shifts in her seat, avoiding me. What on earth has got her acting so strange?

"I, um, was just replying to a text. Nothing really."

"Well, it doesn't look like nothing. You look like you're about to pop a blood vessel."

The lights fade out to black as the music erupts through the arena, sending goosebumps along my body. Blue spotlights illuminate. The screen is filled with the image of Luke, his face covered by his blue robe, head down, as he makes his entrance. Another fighting machine, he means business. I can't take my eyes off the man walking right behind him. My Keller. His face unreadable, looking absolutely edible in a black tux, his dark eyes piercing through the screen. He follows Luke to the ring surrounded by a wave of black-suited security guards.

He strides down the walkway with power. He gives

Luke a hard pat on the back and pulls his head into his shoulder as he leans down and whispers something. Luke nods and continues up into the ring with Grayson. After Luke's opponent does his walkout, the lights brighten, and the crowd goes quiet as they introduce the fighters. The atmosphere is electric. I'm on the edge of my seat, anticipating the start of the fight.

By the seventh round, Luke has the upper hand. That much is clear, even to me. His opponent looks sloppy. Keller and Grayson's shouts bellow through the arena. His opponent is on wobbly legs, failing to land any of his weak punches. *Seriously, I could give this guy a run for his money.*

Now, I don't have a clue about boxing, but I've seen Keller box, so I know how it should look. His opponent backs against the ropes as he lands a weak body shot on Luke's torso, only opening him up to a right uppercut that sends him flying. It's almost in slow motion as his face crumples and blood spurts out of his eyebrow as he thumps to the floor. The crowd erupts, and Maddie and I are out of our seats, excitedly squealing. The ref counts to eight, and he doesn't get up. Luke thrusts his glove up in victory as Keller and Grayson jump the rope and run to hoist Luke up onto their shoulders. Their faces beaming with pride as if they've watched their kid go off on their first day of school.

Keller's eyes snap to mine and don't leave as his lip turns up to a smirk. He brings his free hand up to his lips and blows me a kiss with a wink, which sends a shiver down my spine. I squeeze my legs together in an attempt to stop the ache.

It may not be Keller's fight, but the entire room is in awe of him. He walks around the ring like he owns the place. His natural habitat. All eyes are on him. I don't blame them; he is looking fine tonight.

He ducks under the red ropes and jumps off the ring, determination in his demeanor as he sets his sights on me. The cameras follow his every move as his hooded eyes fill the screens around the room. He's stalking straight toward me. The room is filled with chatter, but at this moment, all I can focus on is him reaching me. The anticipation has me almost salivating as he makes his way over.

"You look fucking amazing, baby" he rasps as he crouches down to my level.

"You don't scrub up too badly yourself, champ," I say as I chew my bottom lip.

Before I know it, his hands are gripping both of my cheeks as he crashes his mouth down to mine with pure hunger and desire. I close my eyes and sink into the kiss, forgetting where we are and the fact our not so PG make-out session is being blasted across the screens.

"God, I've been waiting what feels like fucking hours to do that," he moans.

"Keller, what about the cameras? Everyone's staring at us," I say, shifting uncomfortably in my seat. This is his world, not mine.

Keller turns towards one of the cameras pointed at us on the side of the ring and winks before turning his attention back to me. Claiming my lips again, he sticks his middle finger up behind him towards the camera. I smile against his lips. I think he got the message across as when I glance back up to the big screen above the ring, it's back to showing Luke and his celebrations.

"I want the world to know you're mine, baby. But as soon as they make you feel uncomfortable, just tell me, and I'll soon get them to back the fuck off, okay? This is one of the shittier aspects of my life. I try to keep those cock-sucking vultures and their cameras out of my face as much as possible." He says this with sincerity laced in his tone. I never doubt Keller's threats. That's probably why there's so little about him online. They're probably shit scared to get on his bad side. Hell, I wouldn't envy the person on the other end of his wrath.

"Honestly, it's fine. I just don't want to bring any more unwanted attention to you."

I completely forget Maddie is sitting right next to me as Keller gives her a soft smile and nod. I watch as she gives him one of her signature 'fuck off' tight-lipped smiles and spins her attention back to the ring. What on earth has he done to piss her off?

Furrowing my eyebrows, I turn my attention back to Keller. "I have no idea," I whisper, and he simply nods.

"I have to run back with Luke and Grayson real quick. Don't go anywhere, we'll meet you back here and head back all together."

"Sounds good to me," I hum and plant a quick peck on his lips. He turns to walk away. "Don't keep me waiting too long," I shout loud enough to get his attention as I wiggle my eyebrows at him. Oh, he knows. Shaking his head with a chuckle, he jogs back to the ring.

"Maddie, want to explain what in the fuck that was about?" I ask sternly, starting to lose my patience with her now. She's been acting strange since that message earlier.

She sighs and pulls her phone out of her silver clutch and pulls up an article, eyeing me cautiously.

"Si, I didn't want to ruin your night. I thought maybe it was a misunderstanding or an old image. But he's wearing the same tux, same day old stubble, and slicked back hair. It was taken tonight. I'm so fucking sorry." A sadness creeps into her voice as she death grips her phone, pulling it into her chest.

"What was taken tonight? You're sorry about what? Jesus, Maddie, speak in English. You're near giving me a panic attack!"

I can feel my heart flutter in my chest, my palms sweating. For Maddie to be this wound up, there must be something seriously wrong. I can't take it anymore. I reach over and pry the phone from her vise grip.

My eyes scan the screen, my mind trying to keep up with what I'm seeing. ***'Is this the mysterious woman keeping Keller Russo off the market?'*** It's splashed across the top of the page. I feel sick. With trembling hands, I keep scrolling down the article. The first picture sees a smiling Keller helping a stunning brunette out of the car. Her long, manicured fingers are wrapped around his forearm as she looks up and smiles at him. Her long, toned legs are on full display.

Rage fills me. My ears are ringing as I look at the next photo, tears threatening to spill.

No, Sienna, a man will not make you cry. Never again.

The next one sees them walking into the arena together, arm in arm, smiling as they walk stride for stride, looking every part the celebrity couple the world would expect from him.

"Can we go, please?" I say with a shaky breath.

Maddie simply nods, her expression somber, as she clasps my hand with hers, and we join the swarm of people heading toward the exit. I don't even give Keller a second look as I walk out.

Back at the apartment, I tear the dress off, leaving it in a pile on the floor. My phone has been turned off and sits on my nightstand, and after pulling on the first set of pajamas I find, I head to Maddie's room. I don't want to be alone tonight, left with my thoughts. She gives me a warm smile and scoots over towards the wall, lifting the duvet for me to join. I let my head sink into her plush goose feather pillows.

"One day, I'll stop making you comfort me when my heart is broken." I try to make light of the situation, but she always sees right through me. She gently strokes my hair.

"Don't be silly. That's what best friends are for. Get some sleep. You never know, maybe things will look different in the morning"

She is always the optimist. Rolling away from her, I sigh and turn out the lights. My sleep is anything but settled and I toss and turn, images of Keller and that woman haunting me.

I really thought he was different.

CHAPTER TWENTY

A series of aggressive knocks on the door stirs me from my afternoon nap. The noise hammers through my ears. I've ignored every single one of Keller's calls since the catastrophe that was last night. Now I've had the day to think about it. I'm pissed off, but I know I should have heard him out. I panicked and ran in typical Sienna style, except this time, I have a man that won't back down.

"Jesus fucking Christ, I'm coming!" I shout, as I throw my legs over the side of the bed and drop myself off the edge with a thump. This best be important or I swear to God.

Not even bothering to get changed from my thin vest top and bright pink shorts that barely cover my ass cheeks, I pad out of Maddie's room and head towards the irritating noise.

The closer I get, the more the knocking assaults my ears. Shit, am I about to be arrested? No, they'd just smash the bloody door down, wouldn't they?

"Open up, princess."

Stifling a yawn with my hands, my head still fuzzy from this abrupt wake up call, I unlock the door and open it a notch to peek through.

Keller stands there, his hair styled the same as last night. There's a slight darkness pooled under his eyes, like he hasn't slept. His black hoodie hugs his bulging biceps. And those damn gray sweatpants. If I wasn't so angry, I'd be salivating at them.

"What do you want, Keller?" I snap.

"You gonna let me in or what, baby?" His husky tone sends electricity straight to my pussy. She clearly hasn't woken up to get on the same page as my brain yet.

I don't have the energy to fight with him right now. If the continuous door knocking is any indication, he isn't going to piss off until I let him in.

Without a word, I swing open the door and gesture for him to come past, holding the door open, and giving him the most sarcastic grin I can muster. He barges straight past me, his eyes rake up and down my body, and the cocky prick licks his lips and waltzes into the living room.

I stomp into the room and stand by the entrance, hands on hips, glaring at him.

"Late night?" Jealousy laces my tone. I can't help it. I can only blame my Scorpio tendencies.

"Fuck, baby, you are so hot when you're all possessive."

I see red. "Are you serious right now, Keller? Who is she?" I spit, not holding back anymore. Physically pressing my feet on the floor to stop myself from going over to him.

"If you're referring to those articles a little birdie has told me you've been reading, that woman would be my PR manager, Stacey. She needed a lift, so I gave her one. Simple as that."

I believe him, despite my deep-rooted trust issues; every fiber of my being believes him.

"You want to talk about why you stormed off before even speaking to me about it? Fuck, I'm no relationship expert here, but I don't think that's the way we handle shit like this. You have a stalker ex, Sienna. I was losing my mind worrying about you. Luckily, Grayson had Maddie's number and managed to ease my worries. You don't run from me–there's no point. I'll always find you."

He says this last part as he takes a step towards me, and my heart mends with every move he makes. I back up until I'm met with the wall. His hands slam against it, caging me in against his body, his warm breath beating down on my face.

"I shouldn't have left. I saw the pictures and my heart shattered. After what happened with Jamie, I feel like I'm just waiting for everything to go up in flames around us." A single tear rolls down my cheek as I explain.

Maddie clears her throat from behind us, which makes me jump. She offers a quick smile and wave as she maneuvers around, straight into the kitchen, putting the kettle on. She's trying to look busy, but I know full well she's spying out of the corner of her eye.

"I have something for you, princess," he says as he starts lowering his sweatpants. I gasp in horror, grabbing his hands to stop him, knowing Maddie is only meters away, watching. Ushering him to the bedroom, his delicious gray sweatpants still hang below his ass. I had to stop him from giving Maddie the full show of his downstairs. I can hear her chuckling echoing through the apartment.

A mischievous glint in his eyes flutters as he pulls down his boxers as soon as I slam my bedroom door shut.

I grab his hand to stop him. "For fuck's sake, Keller. Do

you really think I'm in the mood for that right now? I'm so pissed off I don't even want to look at you, let alone fuck you!" I'm trying to keep my eyes from traveling to his cock.

A deep chuckle escapes his lips as he shakes my hand off his forearm with ease, continuing to slip his boxers down, his eyes never breaking contact.

God, no matter how hard I try, this man just turns me on, even if I want to punch him in the jaw at the same time. He stands there in all his glory. A plastic wrap covers the area just above his pubic bone, and I only notice once I stop ogling his cock.

He slowly removes the clear tape surrounding the plastic. This man has an obsession with tattoos, I'm sure.

Taking a step back, my eyes focus on the script of black ink and almost bulge out of their sockets. I cannot believe what I'm seeing. Resting just above his cock, in a beautiful dark font reads "PROPERTY OF SIENNA". It's delicate and beautiful, which makes it stand out like a sore thumb against his array of black angry-looking tattoos.

"W-why would you do that? You do realize that's permanent, right? After last night, who knows if we are actually even together anymore!" I say, trying to keep the desire off my face. The man can read me like a book. But I want to mess with him a little.

"Branding myself with your name wasn't enough?" His brow cocks up as he speaks.

"It's there in ink. I belong to you. Forever. Be angry all you want, even better. How about you fuck me like you hate me, then I will fuck you like I love you? How does that sound?"

He loves me?

"You don't love me, Keller." The words burn my throat as I speak. *He feels this, too?*

"Marry me?" he whispers. My eyes snap up to his. All I am met with is pure adoration in them, making my heart flutter.

"You- w-what?" I stutter. Surely he can't be serious?

"I'm deadly serious, Sienna. One day, you will be mine forever. The look on your face tells me I have a bit more to do to get you on the same page." He's rubbing his jaw while drinking me in.

Am I ready? Could I marry him? I couldn't imagine living another day without him.

"Move in with me?" he asks. "I want you consuming my entire life–in my head, my heart, and my home. Does that prove how into this I am? You are it for me, Sienna. No one else, not now, never."

A smile spreads across my face. "Yes," I reply instantly. No hesitations when it comes to him, I'm ready to dive in head first. Fuck the consequences. I just want him.

A devious grin flashes across his face as he stalks towards me, eating me up with his eyes. "I can't wait to wake up and eat that delicious pussy for breakfast. Every. Fucking. Day."

I melt.

Keller swiftly closes the distance between us, scooping me up as I wrap my legs tightly around his torso. His rock-hard cock rubs against my bundle of nerves, and I involuntarily let out a moan as he throws us down on the bed. Capturing my lips with his, he mumbles, "Too many clothes, baby".

I couldn't agree more.

I WAKE UP WITH A START AS MY PHONE BUZZES NEXT TO MY HEAD. Holding in a yawn, I pick it up, not wanting to interrupt Keller from his peaceful slumber. Although he looks very uncomfortable in my poxy bed.

My body freezes as I see the name flashing across the screen.

Mom.

With trembling fingers, I slide across to accept the call, taking in a deep breath, bracing myself for the abuse that will no doubt be hurled at me.

"Hi Mom," I whisper.

"Nice to see my daughter whoring it out with a rich boxer in New York. Living the dream whilst I'm here in a pokey flat with no heating. You've not even bothered to send me any money for months." As she rambles in her drunken slurs, I pinch the bridge of my nose and shut my eyes.

"I bet you're pleased with yourself. You finally trapped a man with money to look after you like the stuck-up princess you are. You are the reason your dad left me; you ruined our lives."

Tears threaten to spill as I listen.

"Well, good luck keeping that one. He will soon get bored with your shit like the rest of them. You, Sienna, are my biggest regret, a waste of space. No one will ever love you, just like me."

"Shut up." I finally snap. "You're my mom, why do you do this to me? Why can't you just be happy for me? My whole life I've looked after us both."

All I wanted was for you to love me, to care for me.

Her evil laugh fills the speaker.

"I gave up everything for you, Sienna," she spits out in her venomous tone.

"No, you didn't. You've drunk your whole life away. I can't do this anymore, Mom," I sob. Why can't she love me? *Am I really that unlovable?*

"Oh, quit feeling sorry for yourself. You're pathetic. Look, I need money. Your new man is worth a few quid. Send me some over. It's the least you can do to repay me."

The bed sinks beneath me as Keller leans over and grabs the phone from my ear, giving me a small smile. Fury burns in his eyes.

"I suggest you stop calling Sienna. You don't deserve to even have her number. Your daughter is the most incredible woman I have ever met. No thanks to you. I will make it my mission to give her the most incredible life, filled with love and happiness, while you can continue to rot. You won't be receiving a single dollar from us. If you so much as think about contacting her again, I will take everything you have left away from you. I will break you to the point of no return. Don't underestimate the lengths I will go to for her. Now if that's everything, I suggest you fuck off."

I can't hide the shock on my face as he cuts the call and throws the phone to the end of my bed. He wraps his muscular arms around me and smothers me into his embrace, his strength creating a calmness within me. It's almost enough to forget my mom's disgusting words. Almost.

"Fuck, baby, I think I'd rather have no fucking parents than have a mom like that. I am so fucking sorry. You deserve so much better."

The realization hits me like a ton of bricks. All I need is him. He has made me feel more cherished, loved, and protected in these few short weeks than anyone ever has. He is the family I choose. I melt into his embrace and let the tears flow. A warmth radiates in my chest as he cuddles me, whispering sweet reassurances into my ear.

Maybe I don't need anyone else. Maybe Keller and Maddie are meant to be my family.

After a few minutes, my tears subside. I bring my face to Keller's and place a soft kiss on his lips.

"Thank you, I've spent so many years putting on a brave face, thinking I'm the problem when it's her. I don't want to ever be like her. I want to be happy, and you make me so happy, Keller."

A grin spreads across his face.

"Oh baby, you bring light into my life. Before you, there was literally only darkness. I've never had any family, so I don't know what you're going through. But don't ever forget that you have me, princess."

"Tell me what your childhood was like?" I ask, and he tenses against me.

"You don't have to if you don't want to. I'd just like to understand," I quickly add. He sighs and rests his chin on the top of my head, nestling me tighter into him.

"I can't lie to you. It was tough, especially the time before I met Luca. I was lost. I was angry. Angry with my birth parents, angry with the world and with myself that I couldn't find a way to make a family love me enough to keep me. That's where I got into street fighting. It was the only thing that made me feel alive, and I was fucking good at it. By the time I was fourteen, I was going out of my way to fight. I wanted the pain to make me feel something."

He takes in a deep breath, as if just remembering his past physically hurts him.

"That's when I met Luca, a kid so similar to me we had an instant bond. We looked out for each other and unleashed hell in the underground boxing scene. No one wanted us, so we spent most of our nights in abandoned units after running away from our foster homes, stealing what we could to survive. Then finally, Mrs. Russo came into our lives and knocked us into shape. I mean, she was too late to save me from my demons, but she kept me alive. If it weren't for her and Luca, I would never have gone pro."

"Oh, Keller," I sigh, stroking his face with my hand. I can see he's fighting to hold back the tears.

"I wish life could have been kinder to you. No kid deserves to go through that. You turned it around. I am so proud of you. I mean, look at everything you've achieved. It's incredible. You are incredible."

He gives me a sad smile, almost like he doesn't believe how amazing I truly think he is. I take his face in both of my hands and kiss his nose.

"I mean every word, Keller. There may be darkness, but there is always light. One day, I'll prove it to you. Maybe we were destined to find one another, to heal our pasts and create something great."

"I don't doubt that, baby. Me and you, we're inevitable."

CHAPTER TWENTY-ONE

keller

I've led a far from normal life. As I pack Sienna's final box of belongings into my SUV, I pause to watch her jog down the last flight of stairs, her messy bun wobbling on the top of her head. I have to admit this is the most normal I've ever felt in my life.

The thought of coming home to her every day and snuggling her to sleep makes my chest feel weird; like warm and fuzzy. It's a completely alien feeling, but I can't lie, I fucking love it. If that makes me a total pussy, then so be it.

Her smile is infectious. It makes me want to do everything I possibly can to keep it there. I love it. Shit. I love her.

Love. Hell, I don't know what love feels like. I'd bet all the money I have that this is it. Why else would the thought of her leaving me make me want to puke my guts up?

As I sit here staring out the windshield, I can't believe I asked her to marry me. She thought I was joking. I wasn't. If I can find a way to make her mine for eternity, it's fucking happening. The pure panic that ran through me when I couldn't find her after the fight just solidified everything for me.

As soon as I'd finished congratulating Luke, I made my way back to Sienna, only to find an empty seat. I frantically tried calling her over and over but her phone went straight to voicemail. My heart pounding, I raced over to Grayson, panic taking hold.

"Fuck, have you seen Sienna and Maddie? They're fucking gone?" I shout, catching the attention of the rest of the team, all now staring at me like I'm crazy.

What if Jamie's hurt her? I'm starting to think the worst.

Grayson grabs my shoulders, shaking me back to reality.

"Dammit, Keller, calm the fuck down. I'll text Maddie."

Pure fear now takes over, pure desperation to get her home, to get her back to me.

"Look. She's fine. They're on their way home," he says matter of factly as he shoves the phone in my face, showing me Maddie's message.

What the fuck...

So I'll settle for living together. For now.

She's giving us a month trial period, enough time to let Maddie sort out the finances and find a new roommate. She actually asked me how much half the bills would be. I don't think she quite realizes just how much money I have. Hell, I'm actually debating buying Maddie her own apartment just to ease Sienna's worries. Actually, fuck it. That's exactly what I'll do.

Just four weeks until my unification title fight, four weeks until I'm free. In this moment, everything feels like it's perfectly fitting into place. The last piece of the puzzle is about to slot right in. But for some reason, I can't shake the feeling that something is going to shatter everything.

"Everything okay?' she hums, searching my face from

the passenger seat, her fingers curling around my thigh. "Look, if you're having second thoughts now you've seen all the shit I'm bringing to clutter your life, just tell me." She shifts uncomfortably in her seat. Now that gets my full attention. I want to murder anyone who has made my firecracker feel less than she deserves, who's given her these fleeting moments of doubt that I wouldn't want her. She really has no idea.

Tipping her chin up to me with my index finger, I bring my lips down to meet hers. Never in my life have I been pussy whipped. I can't help it. She brings it out of me. Maybe it's those goddamn crystals she's packed.

"Mine," I mutter simply, as I feel her lips turn into a smile.

Revving the Escalade to life, I shift into gear and take us home. It's the first time I truly feel I have one.

"I can't believe I live here now," she exclaims, tossing her arms in the air. I can't help but laugh as I watch her, taking her in. She truly loves this penthouse. She lights up whenever she's here. It makes me feel in love with the place all over again.

Four exhausting hours later, gone is my black, white, and gray color scheme. Every room now has a touch of her, her fluffy pink pillows scattered over the bed. In fact, the only place that remains untouched is my kitchen. Our kitchen. Which figures, as she's already told me she can burn pasta.

We're now sprawled out on the leather couch, her head resting on a pillow placed on my lap as we watch our latest murder mystery series, my fingers idly stroking her silky hair.

"I really don't know what kind of monster can take someone's life without any remorse," she rambles, and my whole body stiffens beneath her. It's a good thing she can't see my face right now.

Monsters like me she means.

The simple statement plagues me with the reminder that this happiness I feel won't last. There's no way she could love a fucking monster like me.

"Hmm," I reply simply and snatch the remote, turning this shit over to the first Christmas film I come across. *Love Actually* it is. The loud crunching of popcorn stops as her body makes small heaving motions, almost as if she is trying her hardest to hold in a sob. I have no idea what's going on.

"Baby, are you okay? Are you crying?"

She shakes her head into my lap and brings her hands over to cover her face, hiding from me.

"Shh, it's ok. Whatever it is, just tell me," I whisper, moving her hands away from her face.

"No, it's silly. I'm fine, honestly."

I lift her small frame and she adjusts her legs to straddle me. I take her face between my hands, her red eyes are filled with tears as she sniffles. A snotty laugh escapes as she tries to hide her emotions from me.

"I don't care if you think it's silly. Tell me what's got you this upset and let me fix it," I say as I chase a tear from her cheek.

She lets out a defeated sigh, avoiding my eyes.

"I just struggle so much with Christmas. I can't remember ever celebrating with my parents, even when they were together. The only memories I do have are of my mom getting drunk and smashing up any presents that I did get. Now, every year, Christmas just reminds me of how lonely my childhood was, how I don't have a family."

My poor girl is almost as broken as me. We both have an

emptiness inside us. Until Mrs. Russo, I, like Sienna, had never celebrated a Christmas or a birthday. I know how it feels to be unwanted, unloved. I chose to fill my void with darkness. It was too late for even Mrs. Russo to save me.

"Oh, baby, trust me, I know how that feels. Every year I hoped it would be different, that finally, I would have a family to care for me. That was all I wanted for Christmas, really. It never happened. Even by the time Mrs. Russo found us, it was too late. I was already a monster."

"Oh, Keller, I'm so sorry. I wish it could have been different for you. Hell, I wish life could have been different for both of us."

I nuzzle my head into her neck to try and compose myself for a few breaths.

"Well, how about we start our own Christmas traditions? What if, every year, we sit and watch a marathon of films with popcorn? Hell, I'll even wear a Santa hat if that makes you happy. We might both have had shitty upbringings. Maybe together we can forget about that shit, even if it's just for a little while."

A smile forms across her lips as she brings her nose to mine.

"You'd do that for me?"

"I'd do anything for you, baby. I promise, this year I'll give you a Christmas that will make you smile, and then every Christmas after that. Deal?"

"Deal."

I have no clue what I'm doing. All I know is I want to do anything to make this goddess smile.

"Now, if you want to sit and watch this film, I think you better get your pussy far away from my dick. Otherwise, we won't be watching any of it."

Her cheeks flush in response as she giggles. Lifting

herself off my lap, she swipes the popcorn back up off the floor and moves to sit at the other end of the couch. There's a mischievous glint in her eyes as she shoves her hand in the box and starts hurling the popcorn at my head, her bubbly laughter filling the room.

I let out a chuckle and shake my head, picking up the stray popcorn on my lap and bringing the sugary ball to my lips. *Who eats this sickly shit?*

"Oh, is that how you want to play it?" I tease, launching myself across the sofa, caging her underneath me as she tries to wriggle out of my hold, tears streaming down her face as she belly laughs. I tickle her sides. The scene is so funny that I can't help but laugh. We're behaving like children, but I've never been happier.

"Keller, please! Oh my god, it hurts!" she manages between her fit of giggles.

I bring my lips down to kiss her sweet popcorn flavored mouth, biting down on her bottom lip and giving her a grin. My phone vibrating in my pocket brings me out of my love filled haze, and digging it out, I see Luca's name flashing. Reluctantly, I lift myself off Sienna and press a quick peck to her forehead. "I won't be long, baby. I gotta take this," I say as I hit accept and stroll towards my office.

"Luca."

"Keller, is now a good time to talk?"

The door clicks as I close it behind me and make my way over to my reclining leather sofa, spotting a new white envelope displayed front and center of my dark oak desk.

"Yes, I'm in my office now"

"We have a problem, brother."

Shit.

"The Falcones aren't backing down. Despite Mario refusing to sell the drugs to them, they've made an attempt on our port. A fucking terrible attempt, mind you, but an attempt none the less."

"Okay, you want me to deal with them?" I scratch my fingertips over the stubble on my jaw.

"No." His answer is quick. "There's more."

"Fucking elaborate then, Luca," I grit out, starting to lose my patience.

"I had Rico stand watch outside Falcone's mansion last night to see if any of our fuckers were working with them. You won't believe this. He saw Sienna's ex rock up, enter the security code for the gates and stroll straight past the guards. He was there for two fucking hours and left empty-handed."

I pause, my brain absorbing the information.

What in the fuck would Jamie be doing with the mafia? He has yet to strike me as anyone useful.

"Did you find anything on him?" I question.

"Nothing unusual yet. Clean record. Your typical corporate American lawyer. We're missing something."

Clearly.

"Get the guys back on the search. We need to know everything. I can't have him putting Sienna in danger with the Falcones."

"You have my word. She will be protected at all costs. I'll get my men on it now and get back to you with an update. In the meantime, keep an eye on Sienna. Just in case we are missing something big with the ex. My gut is telling me something off, I just need to pinpoint what it is."

"Agreed."

I'm reeling with this new information. I know I have to keep my head straight to protect Sienna.

"Mrs. Russo is coming over for dinner tonight."

"Hmmm?" he mumbles.

"To meet Sienna. I know you've now met her a couple of times already, but I'd like you to get to know her, maybe while my dicks in my pants this time." I chuckle.

"Of course, I'll be there. You best keep it in your pants the whole time I'm there, or I swear to God," he threatens, amusement clear in his tone.

"You'll do what?"

A deep laugh echoes down the line.

"You got me there, brother."

Intrigue getting the better of me, resting the phone on my shoulder, I stroll over to the desk and pick up the white envelope. Peeling out the contents, I come face to face with an 8x10 print out of me kissing Sienna at the fight. A big red X is etched across Sienna's face.

What the fuck?

"Keller, are you still there?"

"Fuck, Luca, hang on a sec!"

Scribbled in thick black marker

'YOU HAVE A WEAKNESS.
SIENNA ANDERSON.'

I drop the paper onto the desk, picking up the desk chair and launching it across the room, smashing into the picture frames hanging on the wall, which smash to pieces across the floor.

"Keller! What the fuck is going on?"

Getting my breath back, scrubbing my hands over my face, my day old stubble scratching at my palms, I bend and scoop up my phone I've somehow dropped. Heat builds in my chest and I feel my heart beating hard.

"They know who she is Luca, They fucking know who

she is and what she means to me!" Rage burns inside me now.

"What do you mean, they know?"

"They sent a goddamn picture of me kissing her at the fight, with a big ugly red X over her face. Luca. They know who I really am."

"Fuck," Luca mutters.

Fuck, indeed.

"Don't do anything fucking stupid, Keller. Keep the beast inside until we have a plan. Do not fucking leave Sienna's side."

"I fucking know that, Luca," I snap back.

"Calm down, Keller. I'll alert the men and meet at your penthouse. Give us thirty minutes. In the meantime, keep your head straight. Okay?"

My fist is gripping the phone so tight. I can feel it; fury is taking over.

"Fucking words, Keller. Don't lose it. Not now; Sienna's there."

His words snap me back to reality. Sienna.

"Okay."

That's all I can muster at the moment. As I cut the call, I make my way back to the light, to the only person capable of bringing calm, and taming the monster. My goddess.

As I enter the room, her head snaps up over the back of the sofa. Her big blue eyes instantly lower my blood pressure. I remind myself she's here, she's mine, she's safe.

Sinking into the leather couch, I pat my lap. Without hesitation she straddles me. I bury my head into the crook of her neck and with a heavy inhale, I breathe in her sweet scent. The effect is better than any drug on this planet. She leans back and brings both of her soft palms to my cheeks, pulling my face to look at hers. She studies me intently, her eyebrow cocking up. "Is everything okay, champ? I heard glass smashing and your eyes are wild. You look like you want to kill someone."

I let out an involuntary laugh. She's hit the nail right on the head, and she doesn't even realize the truth she speaks.

Bringing my nose to hers, our foreheads touching. I don't want her looking into my soul, seeing the monster that's on the edge of exploding out of me.

"Everything will be fine. I promise."

I let out an exasperated sigh. It's now or never. With Luca and his men, the fucking mafia, on their way up to the penthouse, I need to let her in on some of it.

"Talk to me, Keller. Please." Her eyes plead with me.

"A threat has been made against you. I need you to trust me when I say no one will fucking touch a hair on your head." She stiffens, her worried eyes now searching mine.

"What kind of threat, Keller? Was it Jamie?" she whispers, her voice shaking.

"Right now, I don't know. Luca and his men are on their way here now. I should know more soon."

"Luca and his men? What is he? Some sort of gang leader?" she mocks, searching for an answer.

I don't respond. I can't lie to her.

"He *is* the mafia, baby."

"Don't be ridiculous, Keller. Your brother is not the *mafia,"* she says, mocking the word.

"I could not be more deadly serious right now, Sienna. He's the leader of New York's largest mafia organization. I promise you, he would never hurt you. He's coming to help protect you."

Her brows furrow as she digests my words. She's sitting on the lap of the mafia leader's right-hand man, his hitman. But this is a detail I won't be revealing today, if ever.

"Right, so you're telling me the leader of a ruthless gang that murders people is coming here right now, and they won't hurt me. Riiiight."

"I would never let anyone, and I mean anyone, hurt you, Sienna. You know that. I told you I wasn't a saint; I never pretended to be one. Right now, the only thing I care about is keeping you safe. Okay, baby?"

Fuck. I need her to understand.

"Okay, I trust you. Are you sure you're okay?" she says, as she brings her lips to mine for a soft kiss. My body slightly relaxes into her touch.

More than that, she trusts me.

I smother her in an embrace, wrapping my arms tightly around her delicate frame, almost to remind myself she's mine. Most women would run a mile with this kind of information. Not my woman. She's more worried about me than anything else. Never in my life has someone been concerned about how I am. I've never felt *this* kind of love.

"What are you going to do about the threat?" she questions, her voice muffled in my chest.

Hunt down every single one of Falcones' men and slit their throats, I think to myself as the elevator pings.

"I'll get the men in the office and then introduce you to Luca. Remember, above all else, he's a good man and my brother. He'll do anything to keep you safe."

I really hope she understands.

She simply nods and climbs off my lap, offering me a hand up from the sofa. That makes me laugh. If I was to take her up on the offer, she'd just fall straight on her face back on the couch. She might be strong for her petite frame, but I doubt she can lift over 200 pounds. I grab her hand anyway and take all my weight into my glutes as I rise off the couch. Keeping her hand in mine, we walk over to the elevator as Luca strides out, his eyes meeting mine and giving me a quick nod.

The fact that she has my back, that she's worried about me, stirs feelings deep inside my chest.

Stepping to the side, out walks six of his men. All dressed in black suits, leather loafers, and all with their signature slicked back hair. Luca must have warned them not to interact with me in front of Sienna, because they stand there unfazed by me, their faces expressionless.

Bar one fucker, whose eyes are glued to Sienna. He obviously didn't get the memo. I don't recognize him. I might stay in the shadows, but I know all of Luca's men. His eyes are running up and down Sienna's body, stopping for that second too long on her tits.

My protective instinct kicks into gear. "Office, now!" I bark at them. Their eyes go wide as they shuffle off, out of my sight. The prick smirks at me and carries on walking, and suddenly, possessiveness gets the better of me. I turn to a stunned Sienna and guide her chin up with my finger. "Just trust me, okay?" I ask and she quickly nods in return. Then I turn on my heel and stalk over to the prick, stopping him in his tracks. My hand laces around his throat, his eyes go wide in shock as I squeeze tightly on his windpipe.

"If I so much as see you glance in her direction again, I'll slit your fucking throat and leave you to bleed out on my floor. Now fuck off out of my sight." Violence drips from my tone.

A smirk creeps up his face as he nods. I loosen my grip and push him away, and he slowly steps around my body to follow the rest of the men. I bring my sights back on Sienna, who is still planted in the same spot I left her, flicking her gaze between me and Luca with an eyebrow raised.

Luca breaks the silence with a chuckle. “Always the hot head, this one.” He points at me, winking at Sienna.

“Really?” I cock my brow at him.

Closing the gap between him and Sienna, Luca offers his hand to her. She accepts as he brings her hand to his lips for a quick kiss.

“I’m sorry about this. I’m Luca Russo. It’s nice to finally meet you, *formally,* and see the woman that’s finally tamed the beast.” He winks at me.

Oh, he has no idea.

She offers him a small smile as she removes her hand at the first opportunity, still eyeing me.

Good girl.

“It’s nice to meet you, too, Luca,” she says sweetly, not an ounce of fear in her tone.

Clapping Luca on the shoulder, I find my words. “Right. Let’s get to the office before those fuckers start a fight amongst themselves in there.” Luca nods and heads off to the office.

Quickly reaching Sienna, I drop my head to hers.

“Thank you, baby. Thank you for trusting me,” I whisper. Propping up on her tiptoes, she presses her soft lips to mine for a slow kiss. Fuck, no matter where we are, this woman always has an effect on me.

“Stay in the living room. I won’t be long. Then we can go back to other more exciting things,” I say with a wink.

“I’ll be ready and waiting,” she quips back with a tempting smile. Stealing one more quick kiss, I reluctantly leave her and head to the office.

The shards of glass crunch under my trainers as I walk

into the office. Luca sits in a recliner that's now back at the desk.

"I see you had a tear up in here, Keller," Luca grins.

"It was either that or the Falcones, so the chair took the brunt of it. For now."

Luca clears his throat, takes up the picture of me and Sienna and crumples it in his fist before tossing it in the trash.

"Keller, I have a plan. I can't risk you before the fight. I can't let you lose your head and do more damage than good–to yourself, to Sienna, and to us. We're keeping close tabs on Jamie and the Falcones. They are a weak unit. We will exploit them and take them down. In the meantime, Enzo will keep watch of Sienna when you aren't with her," he says, pointing to the prick from earlier who has eyes for my girl.

My fists clench. "I don't fucking think so, Luca."

I storm past the men and stare out the window, taking in the skyline, trying to calm the rage inside of me. Usually, this makes me feel powerful, like I can take on the world. Today, it does nothing. I simply stare as the world goes by. I know Luca is right. I can't risk it. They know who I am now; my mask has been stripped. Thoughts of Sienna flood my brain. In that moment, I know what I have to do. Everything I do from this day on is for her and our future.

Everyone in the room is silent. The only noise is the irritating tapping coming from Luca's Zippo against the desk.

"Fine," I huff.

"I want two men protecting Sienna, and it sure as shit isn't going to be that limp dick," I say, pointing to the fucker that was eye fucking Sienna earlier. My eyes dagger into his. He doesn't even flinch. Maybe he isn't a complete waste of space.

"Enzo stays. He runs the best security service in the country. I give you my word."

"Enzo," Luca shouts. He snaps his head to him, giving him a slow nod. "Don't fucking eye up Keller's woman again, otherwise, I won't be able to stop him killing you. Okay?" Luca tells him, trying to keep a straight face.

"Of course," the prick responds, offering me a nod. Letting out a huff, I nod in response. Fuck it. I know I won't be leaving her side until this is over, so I will agree. For now.

"Okay, agreed. Keller. I trust you have everything under control here. I'm going to have to skip dinner–things to do, wars to start, and all that. I'll leave Enzo stationed in the building and send over Nico. I'll speak to you later."

With that, he stands and clasps his hand on my shoulder, giving it a squeeze, and strolls out of the office. His men follow behind. Leaving me and my rage to fester in an office of broken glass. I turn to the window, and for a moment, watch the sun setting across the skyline. But I don't see the colors as the darkness creeps in.

A soft knock of the door grabs my attention, and I twist towards the door. She peers her head through the gap.

"Can I come in?" she asks quietly.

"Yes, baby." Then reality sweeps in."Shit, be careful of the glass." I pounce over to the door before she can enter. Swinging it open fully, I lift her under her arms as she wraps her legs tightly around me. She doesn't need to say anything. Just feeling her heartbeat against my chest is soothing enough.

"Sienna," I sigh.

"Shh," she murmurs, bringing her index finger to my lips.

Never in my twenty nine years on this planet has someone had the balls to fucking shush me. Yet here she is, a goddess in real life, wrapped around me like a snake, telling me to 'shh'.

I don't know how I got to this point. But I am so fucking glad I have. With a mischievous glint twinkling in her eyes, her lips form into a grin.

My horny goddess is coming out to play.

She knows me too well.

I'd much rather be buried deep in her sweet pussy than slitting Falcone's men's throats, anyway.

"I know you, Keller. Fuck now, talk later," she whispers softly in my ear.

I don't know whether it's the way she understands me or the fact I am completely and utterly head over heels for her, but every nerve in my body is standing to attention. It's hard to hold back the primal urge to slam her against the wall and fuck her into oblivion. I hesitate, though, because I want to give her more, more than just a fuck. I want to give her everything.

Taking her bottom lip between my teeth, I nip, my cock straining against my pants.

"I want you in control now, baby. I am at your mercy, my queen. Do what you want to me and indulge yourself."

She's a natural submissive, but her fiery side tells me there's more in her, more I can coax out. What better way to show her she owns me than to give my full self over to her?

CHAPTER TWENTY-TWO

sienna

Something sparks inside me at his words.

Full control.

The powerful man is willing to give up the one thing he craves, for me. Control.

"You'll do anything I say?"

"Anything," he confirms.

I hesitate for a moment. Can I really do this? Can I really take control?

"You hold the power here, baby. You always have. Now take hold of it and show me what you've got. Give in to your desires."

Fuck.

I am so turned on right now, I can barely think.

"Okay."

He strolls us over to the bedroom. Kicking the door open with his foot and placing me down on to my feet. A wide grin spreads across his face. This man never ceases to amaze me.

"On the bed." I try my hardest to sound stern, I'm trembling with a mixture of excitement and nerves.

He strolls over to the bed and turns to sit on the edge.

"Wait." I panic and shout.

He stops immediately.

"I need you to take my clothes off," I say, whilst biting my thumb. He doesn't wait. He stalks over to me and slowly peels off my leggings. I put my arms up as he peels off my jumper. A wicked grin meets me as my head pops out from the material.

"Your turn," I tease.

He rips his clothes off and throws them into a heap on the floor, turning his back to me, his ripped tattooed back and his firm perky butt teasing me as he walks towards the bed, jumping dramatically backward onto the mattress with his arms wide.

His cock is already standing to attention, the veins protruding. I can see the glistening of pre-cum. I lick my lips.

"You can't touch me, not anywhere, unless I tell you to," I say, sounding as powerful as I can. He grunts and nods his head, digging his fingers into the duvet. He's already struggling, power rushes through me.

"I need something to blindfold you with."

"A tie. There are loads in the closet," he grits out.

I quickly pick out the first black tie I can find, the silky material brushing against my fingertips. Keller is still on the bed, his chest just heaving up and down as he waits for me. I clamber onto the bed and straddle him, purposely brushing my dripping sex over his cock. Just that alone sends pleasure to my core.

"Lift your head."

His eyes, now almost black, meet mine, and he's biting his bottom lip so hard, I'm shocked he's not bleeding. I fix the blindfold and drop a quick kiss to his lips.

"Jesus, baby, you're killing me already," he groans.

I smile in response.

I plant wet kisses all the way down his perfect body, kissing each rock hard abs as I do. Until I reach his Property of Sienna tattoo. I can't help but hum in appreciation of his gesture. It's hot as fuck seeing my name there in dark ink.

Mine. I love it.

I slowly lick across the tattoo. He knows exactly what I'm doing and a deep groan fills the room. I slide down him slowly and take a position on my knees between his legs, his cock throbbing under my palm. I lick the moisture from the top and his whole body vibrates.

"Fuck," he mutters, and I smile.

Taking him between my lips, his salty taste swirls around my mouth as he hits the back of my throat. Curling my tongue around as I bob up and down, I close my eyes and feel pleasure bubbling through me; I can't stop muffled moans from escaping my lips as I relish being so filled with his cock.

When I start caressing his balls, his hips thrust up and down to meet my movements. I push down hard on him to signal him to stop. This moment is all mine. His balls seize in my hands, and I know he's close. His breathing is frantic. He's pulsing in my mouth.

With one final suck, I lift myself back up and climb off the bed, watching his knuckles turn white as he tries so hard to remain in control of himself. It's a perfect sight, but I need a release.

I have an idea.

I clamber back over him on all fours until my breasts sweep past his face and I keep going, settling in a seated position, my pussy hovering right above his mouth.

"Baby, please," he cries out, tipping his head back into

the bed to try to reach me somehow. I can't help but giggle watching him. I slowly lower myself onto his face, taking the weight in my forearms, careful not to suffocate the starving blindfolded man beneath me.

His tongue connects instantly with my clit. My whole body rushes with intense pleasure. I moan in response to him. Fuck, even blindfolded, this man can still find my clit. He's perfect.

He laps me up ferociously, like a man starved. I ride his face to meet the pace of his tongue, my toes curling as the blood rushes to my head.

"Fucking sit on me, baby. I need more. I don't care if I can't fucking breathe, just sit the fuck down."

That lights the spark that sets me over the edge. I need this. I press my ass down as far as I can, his nose digging into my pubic area as he starts to suck and bite my pussy. My eyes roll back in my head as he eats me up like his last meal.

"Use your fingers," I moan, my eyes rolling to the back of my head. I'm so fucking close, I just need him to tip me over the edge. Two fingers slide into me and that sets me off. I come like I never have before. I can barely see as I ride his face and his fingers, soaking up the pleasure that's setting me on fire. I lean forward, giving him some space to breathe as I catch my breath, panting above him.

"Fuck, that was perfect."

My limbs are still trembling as I make my way back down his body, inching up his blindfold. I want to see all of him. His eyes hit me straight in the heart. Pure love greets me. I can't help it, I crash my mouth to his, my sweet taste still covering his lips, and grind my pussy over his cock.

"Please let me fuck you, baby. I can't take it anymore." The pain in his voice almost makes me feel sorry for him.

I push myself up and he squeezes his eyes shut. I find the tip of his cock and slide myself onto him, his cock filling me up perfectly as I stretch around him. I feel so full; I let out a gasp at the feeling, still sensitive from my last orgasm.

"Fuck." He groans, his mouth searching for mine.

"I want you to choke me," I blurt out. His eyes fly to mine, his eyebrow raised. I keep slowly pumping up and down on his cock as he stares at me, openmouthed.

"Not just grabbing my throat, I want to feel like I'm dying. I want to only feel you fucking me into oblivion. Can you do that for me?"

Nerves pit in my stomach as I wait for him to answer. The last time I suggested this with Jamie, he was disgusted.

"Oh, fuck yes. Fuck." He runs his hand aggressively over his face.

My cheeks flush in response.

"If it's too much or you feel like you might pass out, tap my chest, okay?"

"Yes," I say confidently.

His hand moves to my neck, softly stroking along my collarbones as he then wraps his hand all the way around my throat and squeezes. My body reacts by trying to suck in a deep breath through my mouth. The air doesn't make it to my lungs and my eyes go wide. My body is screaming for air. He ups the thrusts now, violently pounding into me. Blood thumps in my ears as he squeezes his hand tighter.

"Relax, baby," he softly whispers in my ear.

The soothing sound of his voice makes my muscles relax a little, the panic that was building subsiding for a second. The grip on my throat loosens slightly for a second.

"Breathe in a little for me, princess," he whispers.

I do as he says, the little bit of oxygen reaching my lungs. As soon as his hand wraps back around my neck even tighter, the only thing I can feel is his cock hitting that sweet spot and the hand closing around my windpipe. I'm balanced on the edge between, fighting for one to take over.

His other hand finds my clit and pinches hard. Shockwaves zip through my veins, and I'm hitting sensory overload. My lungs are now screaming for air. I claw at his hand around my neck; I need air. It's all too much. I'm about to come and pass out at the same time. Fuck.

The tightness around my neck is gone, and I fall forward, desperately gasping for breath. Keller gently kisses next to my lips as his hands now squeeze my ass checks, pushing them down on his cock as he pounds into me.

"Come for me."

That's enough to shatter me. Everything goes black as stars fill my vision. Keller swears in my ear as he makes his final thrust. Warm liquid spills out of me and down my thighs. My breathing is still erratic. My lungs–hell, my whole body–is on fire.

"Baby, look at me."

Our sweaty bodies are still stuck together. I meet his worried eyes. They're searching mine, making sure I'm okay.

"That was perfect. Thank you," I say with a smile. He moves a stray hair from my face and cups my cheek.

"You are perfect. That was the hottest thing I've ever experienced. I'm speechless."

A chuckle escapes me, and I bring my lips over his and lie on top of him, never wanting to leave this moment.

CHAPTER TWENTY-THREE

sienna

ONE MONTH LATER…

The sun is beaming through the window, lighting up our bedroom. A whole wonderful month has passed, which means I've officially been living with Keller for a month. A smile creeps up my face as I think about how safe, loved, and extremely satisfied I am in *every* aspect of my life.

Handing in my notice at the law firm has been a particular highlight. Another thing I can thank Keller for. David is pissed to not have me distracting him on the daily, but he's happy I'm finally pursuing my dreams. Something that would never have been possible without Keller and his growing list of deeds to make me happy.

First, he bought Maddie's apartment, so I didn't have to worry about her finding a new roommate or, in his words, "Her shacking up with some weirdo." Next, he made a considerable donation to Paula's charity. It means more budget to plan events for the kids, thus Paula needing a spare set of hands full time, a *paid* full time.

When she called, she was ecstatic, offering me the position of Head of Events. My only hesitation being it is considerably less pay than my family law gig. But Keller, being Keller, assures me, despite my argument, that he has enough money to last us ten lifetimes. I don't need to pay my half of Maddie's rent anymore, nor is he expecting anything from me for living with him. I know if I need it, I have a room at Maddie's. Not that I ever anticipated leaving Keller. Not for one second.

Every day, our connection strengthens. I can even say I enjoyed Christmas this year. Keller kept his promise. We invited Maddie, Grayson, Luca, and Mrs. Russo over for Christmas dinner. Mrs. Russo is the most wonderful, kind-hearted lady I have ever met. Her eyes light up when she speaks to Keller and Luca, and they pander over her just as much. Watching them interact, you'd never guess they weren't all related by blood.

Luca has grown on me. There's more to him than meets the eye, similar to Keller. They wear a mask of hard exterior when deep down they have hearts of gold. There is light beneath their darkness. They just need someone to bring it out of them, like Mrs. Russo does when she's around.

Don't get me wrong. Am I particularly thrilled about Keller's brothers being a mafia boss? Absolutely not. But I'm the last person to judge. Between Keller and Luca, I have never felt safer, more like part of a family. Maybe I should be running for the hills, but my gut tells me this is where I belong.

Maddie and Grayson spent the whole time either picking at each other, leaving Maddie red-faced and Grayson smirking, or totally ignoring each other's existence. I bet their drive home was a blast. I almost wish they would just fuck to get it out of their systems. It's clear to everyone around them they have undeniable chemistry, but they won't admit it.

The day was filled with fantastic food, laughter, and family. It was perfect. Everything was slotting into place, minus the minor issues of the threat to my life and Jamie. Keller doesn't give much away, other than he will protect me with his life, and it's being dealt with. In all honesty, I trust him. He hasn't given me a reason not to yet, and I wouldn't fuck with Keller and Luca. I know there is more he's hiding from me. I'm leaving it in his hands to reveal the truth when he's ready.

Maybe my thought process is clouded by my sheer love and infatuation with this man.

I only have another two weeks left at my job before my last day. Then we're jetting off to Vegas for Keller's unification fight. Every day, he trains religiously; if not at Kings Gym, then in his home gym. On days I work from home, he usually chooses to train at home, so I get one hell of a view whilst I work. Just in this brief space of time, I swear his muscles are even more defined. He looks bigger and stronger, if that's even possible. We've stuck to a protein packed diet, although he eats four times more than me; it's quite horrifying the amount of food he packs in before a fight.

He's even started giving me self-defense lessons every now and again. Which usually just end up with me spread out on the mat whilst he fucks me into oblivion. Much like how most nights end. One orgasm Sienna is no longer. Now we're talking at least five. The things this man, *my man,* can do with his fingers, tongue and cock are extraordinary. Not to mention being fucked up against the floor-to-ceiling windows eighty six stories above the twinkling New York skyline. It's almost like a dream. But I can't shake the feeling that one day I'm going to wake up and it really will be just that: a dream, a fantasy.

Keller starts to stir next to me. Despite this being the largest bed I've ever slept in, he doesn't let me go all night. His fingers now draw delicate circles on my abdomen, making me squirm from the ticklish feeling. This causes my ass to brush his hard cock, shooting tingles across my skin.

"Morning, baby," he murmurs against my back in his deep, raspy voice.

"Morning," I reply with a smile and snuggle back into him.

"I fucking love waking up with my cock on your ass."

He groans as he peppers light kisses along my shoulder blades, his short stubble scratching against my skin. A quiet moan escapes my throat as I tip my head back to rest on his muscular shoulder.

"You mean you just love waking up next to me? I'm more than just an ass to you. Aren't I?" I try to keep my tone neutral. He can't see my face, but I'm trying my best to hold in a laugh.

"If you don't know the answer to that by now, then I've failed you." He lets out a sigh.

Sometimes, I forget beneath his rock hard exterior, beneath that mask he carries, is a lost soul, a man who has never truly experienced being loved. I had a half-arsed kind of family and a string of shitty boyfriends. Keller had nothing, not even half-arsed parents. None. My heart breaks thinking about his childhood. The things he must have done to survive and become the man he is today, the man who has everything he deserves and more.

Turning round to face him, "Everything," I say, taking his face in my hands. His lips creep up into a smile. "My Champ. My King. My Everything. Always," I whisper, bringing my lips to his, pouring my love into this kiss. He breaks away, his dark eyes staring into my soul.

"My Goddess. My Queen. My *World.* Forever."

"I love you, Keller." The words tumble out of my mouth.

I snap my lips shut tight. It's been on the tip of my tongue for weeks. I just couldn't face the rejection. I mean, he's already told me he can't give me the fairytale ending. How could he love me back?

A few seconds pass that seem like a lifetime, his face unreadable.

Tears sting at the corners of my eyes as I feel the rejection coming. Sending me right back to the girl I was a few months ago, the girl who was never *quite* enough.

"Sienna, baby," he sighs, brushing his fingers through my hair.

Oh God, here it comes. I lower my gaze, almost bracing for impact. Tipping my chin up with his finger, my eyes meet his. His black eyes are gleaming with admiration.

"I love you. I love you so much it almost physically hurts. I will love you every fucking day until the day I die."

The tears that were threatening start spilling down my cheeks, as soft sobs leave me.

"Oh, baby, don't cry," he says, worry lacing in his tone.

"I-I'm just so happy Keller," I hiccup.

"It's you and me against the world. Forever."

He gives me his best lopsided grin as he proceeds to slowly lick the tears from my cheeks, going up one side and down the other. He consumes my whole heart, and now all I crave is for him to consume my whole body.

"I need you." The breathy whisper leaves my mouth.

"Like air to breathe. How could I ever deny you anything?"

Before I know what's happening, Keller's on top of me,

my hands pinned above my head, as he's glaring into my soul with hungry eyes. Lowering his head, he takes my lips with his. His tongue explores as he deepens the kiss, lighting the fire inside me.

"More, Keller."

I feel him smile against my mouth.

"My queen is demanding this morning," he teases, peppering kisses along my jaw.

Tightening his grip on my wrists with one hand, the other slowly, so slowly, trails past my breasts, along my abdomen, creeping closer and closer to where I need his fingers to be. I inch my legs apart even further, giving him as much access as possible. His fingers lightly brush past my pussy and continue down my inner thigh. I let out a moan, my whole body screaming for him to touch me. Then his fingers trail back up the inside of my other thigh and finally run up my soaking seam.

"You are fucking dripping for me, baby," he rasps.

Arching my back, he bends his head and takes a nipple in his mouth. Sucking, biting, and licking between my breasts.

"So ready for me, so perfect."

One of his fingers teases my entrance and slowly enters as I let out a moan.

"More. I need more," I beg.

He chuckles against my neck as another finger joins, pumping in and out at a steady pace. I already feel like I am about to explode around his fingers, but he quickly removes them and my body sags, frustration building. As if sensing my inner turmoil, his finger lifts my chin to meet him. His eyes sparkle with desire, with love.

"This isn't just a fuck, Sienna. I want to worship your

body. I want to *show* you how crazy I am for you. How much I love you."

I am speechless.

I'm used to powerful, in control Keller.

The man hovering above me now is gentle, loving, and all mine.

"I love you." They're the only words my brain can conjure up right now.

Taking that as his cue, he crashes his lips to mine for the most earth shattering kiss I have ever experienced. His cock rubs up and down my slit, taking all my juices. He lines himself up at my entrance and inches his way in. Pure ecstasy flows through my veins as he finally fills me. I am so full. He gives me a second to get myself together before he quickly pulls out and slams straight back into me, sending my head flying back and my back arching off the mattress.

"Jesus Christ, Sienna, it's like you were made for me," he grits out.

"Fuck me like you love me. Show me."

That sets a fire within him as his eyes spring open. He's on the edge just as much as I am.

Without missing a beat, he ups the momentum. The slapping of our skin radiates through the room.

"I. Fucking. Love. You," he forces out through deep breaths between thrusts. Taking my lips with his and biting down on my lower lip as he slams into me, grabbing behind my knee and pulling it up to my chest, giving him more access. His cock now hitting that sweet, sweet spot that is going to send me over the edge.

"I'm so close, Keller." My voice is low and quivering.

He doesn't speak, only grunts in response. We're both coming undone. I'm squeezing my eyes shut, as the pressure is almost all too much.

"Eyes on me, baby," his gravelly voice commands. Snapping my gaze straight to his, I see the torment dancing behind his eyes.

I can't hold it back any further. My whole body is alight as the sweat beads on my forehead.

"Now. Come now," he says through gritted teeth.

That's enough. I finally erupt, my whole body on fire as the orgasm shoots through me, and I scream his name from the top of my lungs.

I can faintly hear him roar my name over the ringing in my ears as he empties into me.

We lay there trying to catch our breath, sweaty foreheads meeting. Keller releases his grip on my wrists. My arms feel like dead weights.

"That was..."

I don't even have the right word to describe what just happened. He's right; that wasn't just a fuck. That was cementing our love, binding us together for life. It was perfection.

"Everything," he replies.

I can feel his love in every single part of me. I wrap my now tingling arms around his neck and draw him even closer to me, his weight squashing me into the mattress. His musky scent mixed with pleasure, filling my senses. Closing my eyes, I take in this moment, wanting this feeling to last forever.

I finally feel at home.

I ROLL OVER IN BED, SEARCHING FOR KELLER. I MISS HIS TOUCH.

I heard him creep out of bed a little while ago. As soon as he left, an emptiness washed over me. *God, I have it bad.*

The last few nights have been the same. He tosses and turns until he grunts and gets out of bed. Not before pressing a soft kiss to the back of my head, though.

He has his unification fight coming up in only a couple of weeks. He needs to sleep.

I toss back the duvet and check my phone for the time.

3 am. *Damn, it's the middle of the night still.*

I throw on one of his t-shirts. It hangs on me like a dress, and I head out of the bedroom to find him and bring him back to bed.

As I reach the bedroom door, the penthouse fills with the sound of Keller's deep chuckles. *What the hell is so funny this time of the morning?*

Intrigue getting the better of me, I make my way to the lounge, being careful not to make any noise as I walk over.

As I peer around the corner, I discover Keller sprawled out on the couch, a book in his hand, chest shaking as he laughs at whatever he's reading. *Keller reads? Hang on, I recognise that...*

My eyes go wide as I smash my hands to my mouth to hide my gasp.

The *black* book in his hand is mine, and it is absolutely filthy.

Shit shit shit. *I am so embarrassed right now.*

"Baby, what the fuck is a *nub?*" he shouts, still laughing his head off.

I storm over, my cheeks on fire, and snatch the book right from his hands. Well, I try, but Keller doesn't let go; he just grabs it back and holds it into his chest, tears pooling in his eyes.

I can't help but join him.

I don't know how long passes where we just laugh, him clutching the book. I regain my breath and make another attempt to steal the book back. It's a mafia arranged marriage, a spicy one at that.

He catches my wrist in his hand, throwing the book behind him.

"No, you can't take this off me. I'm just getting to the good bit. He's just tied her up in the basement. Is that the kind of thing you're into, my naughty goddess?"

"No, but I don't mind being tied up in the bedroom," I reply, a fire burning in my center. Something about seeing Keller so carefree and happy slams me right in the heart.

"Come here." He pulls me onto his lap, picks up the book and opens it in front of us, while I cuddle into his chest.

"I bite down on her nub, lapping her juices up." He starts to recite from the book in his deep voice, sending shivers down my spine.

"It's the clit, Keller. You don't have any trouble finding mine, either."

His chest vibrates beneath me, his laughter filling the room.

"Glad we cleared that up, baby. Want me to find your *nub* for you now?" he rasps with a mischievous glint in his eye.

"Read to me at the same time," I whisper, squeezing my legs together.

His fingers lift the hem of his T-shirt. I spread my legs over each side of his, my back against his chest. His index finger immediately finds my clit and starts to gently circle.

"How did I do?" he whispers in my ear.

I let out a moan in response, burying my head into his neck, his masculine scent assaulting my senses.

"Perfect, as always."

He starts reading again, but I can't concentrate on anything other than his deep voice vibrating against my ears. Until he slips two fingers inside of me, causing my back to arch against him. I snatch the book and toss it across the room.

"Hey! I was reading that," he pretends to whine.

I maneuver in his arms and turn to face him, straddling his lap, his rock hard cock rubbing against my pussy through his sweatpants. He gives me a pout and I crash my lips to his.

"Enough reading; more fucking. *Please.* And then you're coming back to bed with me."

"Your wish is my command. Now put that *nub* on my face and let me feast, *please.*"

I can't help but laugh as he slides his body down under mine while I hold on to the couch. He wastes no time in devouring me, his tongue lapping me up and down, biting on my clit. I ride his face until I see stars, his hands gripping my ass. Pure ecstasy fills my body as my climax rips through me. I tremble around his tongue. He continues to suck on my clit, as if proving a point he knows where it is.

I fucking love this man.

CHAPTER TWENTY-FOUR

keller

Fuck, I can't remember the last time I laughed as much as I did last night. Reading Sienna's filthy mafia book was certainly eye opening. But tonight, I want to do something special; I want to spoil my girl.

I grab Sienna's hand and walk her over to the elevator. She looks breathtaking in a short, little black dress and leather jacket. My cock is twitching just admiring her beauty. I'm taking her out to her favorite Italian restaurant. She's had enough of my pre-fight diet. I've trained so much these past few weeks, I need time to spoil my woman.

Her hand trembles in mine as we approach the elevator. Despite using this for the past month, she still seems scared. I keep asking why and she just brushes it off, saying she's a bit claustrophobic and scared of being stuck.

There's more to it than that. I know it. The fear that burns in her eyes every single time makes me wonder what exactly happened. She might think she hides her trauma well, but I know her, I see her.

Something about it isn't sitting right at all. I want to help her, but I can't if I don't know what I'm dealing with.

The elevator doors slide open and we step in. I do my now usual routine of wrapping her under my arm and settling in the corner, but this time the corner opposite the buttons. I remove my hands from around her shoulders and place a soft kiss on her forehead. I leave her there and walk over to the buttons and press the underground floor.

I watch cautiously as she nervously fidgets with her fingers, her chest heaving up and down. She's watching me, but I can see she's more focused on breathing. She really doesn't know how to do this without me. I hate seeing her like this.

The elevator starts to creep down, floor eighty highlights on the screen at the top. I turn my back to the buttons to face her and slyly move my hand behind my back, clicking the bottom two buttons. The emergency stop and lights.

We come to an abrupt stop and pure fear is evident on her face, her eyes open wide. It's the last thing I see before it goes black. I stand still. Her breathing becomes more and more frantic, like she's fighting for air. Every part of me wants to run to her and help, but she needs this. She needs to realize how strong she is.

The heart wrenching sound of her gasping for breath fills the small space, hitting me right in the chest. I can't see her, but I can sense her terror.

"Mom? No, please. I'm sorry. I'm so sorry. I won't ever do it again. Just please let me out, please don't leave me in here. I hate it," she cries out in pure panic. Thuds echo in the darkness as she starts beating on the walls as if she's a caged animal desperate to escape.

What the fuck? Guilt immediately shreds through me as I jab the lights button with my finger. I keep jabbing and nothing fucking happens. Oh fuck.

I just need to get to her first. I march through the darkness to her with my arms out, hoping to grab hold of her.

"Please, no. Please don't do this. I'm sorry, I'll be better," she sobs out, nothing but pain in her voice.

My foot bumping into something stops me. It has to be her. I lean forward with my hands to try to feel for her, but my hand connects with the mirror. I crouch down, using my hands to guide me. They end up on either side of her head, gliding down her soft curls and all the way down her body until I'm on either side of her arms.

"Baby, it's me. It's okay, you're okay. Everything's going to be fine. I promise you," I whisper into her ear, hoping and praying I can get through to her.

She doesn't respond, only with sobs, her body heaving under my palms. I swallow down the bile that threatens to come up at what I've just done. I never in a million years expected this to happen. My poor goddess. I tighten my grip on her arms and lift her up.

"No, no! Don't throw me in there! I can't do it. I can't. I'm sorry."

With every word she utters, my heart breaks a little more for her and the rage inside me boils. I want to kill her fucking piece of shit mother. I lift her up to maneuver her, to cradle her into me. She's like a screaming rag doll, clawing at my chest. My skin burns as her nails scratch at my neck.

"Baby, it's me, Keller. I've got you." But she continues to fight in my arms.

I hurry us back over to the buttons, squeezing her tight into my chest, to bring her some comfort, to bring her back to me from whatever hell she's entered. I keep smashing my finger into the button. On the last attempt, the elevator illuminates with bright white lights. I blink a few times to adjust to the sudden change and immediately look down. Her face is pressed so hard against me, I'm shocked she can still breathe. Her knuckles have a death grip on my shirt.

"Sienna, baby, I need you to look at me. It's okay. We're going to be moving now," I continue to whisper. She slowly peels her face from my sweater, her bloodshot, puffy eyes staring up at me, black makeup smeared all over her cheeks. Blood drips from the scratch marks on the side of her neck.

"I'm so fucking sorry, Sienna. I'm sorry this happened. I'm so sorry she did that to you," I manage to choke out. Tears burn my eyes.

Her chest heaves up and down erratically against me. She's looking at me, but she's not there. Her eyes have glazed over. I press the button back to level eighty-six. I need to get her up to the penthouse and bring her back.

The door pings open in no time, and I stride into the apartment, still holding onto her. My heart pounds in my chest as I make my way to our bedroom, throw back the duvet, and lay her gently on the bed, tucking her in right up to her neck. She doesn't move an inch the whole time. I get in and cuddle into her, pulling her into a tight embrace, stroking her hair, and whispering to her how much I love her. Over and over again. We are shrouded in darkness as her warm tears run onto my forearm.

"Sleep, baby. I've got you. I will never let that woman hurt you again. You are strong. You are incredible."

It's not until I feel her breathing settle, her body starts to release, that I finally feel like I can breathe again.

Fuck the penthouse, I'm buying us a mansion. No more elevators.

CHAPTER TWENTY-FIVE

keller

If someone told me I'd be declaring my undying love to a British bombshell a year ago, I would have laughed in their face. Now I'm here searching for houses to buy us to get us out of this penthouse. Somewhere we can start a family and avoid her ever having to use an elevator again. That memory will torment me for the rest of my life.

Me, the masked mafia hitman sworn off love. I thought I was put on this earth to fight—nothing more, nothing less. I had never even entertained the idea of having my own family. Until her.

The enchanting goddess brought me out from the dark and into her light. Shattering the mask I safely hid behind.

The darkness still lingers beneath the surface. It's there, waiting to be unleashed. Simmering since they made the threat to Sienna's life. They say a man with nothing to lose is dangerous. They should just wait to meet the man who has everything to lose.

I've given Luca time to do this his way. Falcone has backed off. They have made no new attempts on Luca's territory. Everything is running smoothly, *too smoothly.* Do I honestly believe mere threats would stop a rival mob from their attempts at power? Not a fucking chance.

The Falcones are ruthless; they have no morals. Which, in one way, is their weakness; they are too rash. But it makes them dangerous. You have to know your opponents inside and out to defeat them. It's the same motto as boxing.

I've spent the last few weeks meticulously watching my upcoming opponent's fights. I know his favored combinations, his southpaw stance. His preference to start a fight all guns blazing, which leads to him slowly tiring himself out. I have a clear plan on how to defeat him. I've never paid so much attention to detail to winning a fight before. This is now more than just a unification fight, a fight for my freedom. I'm fighting with all I have to be worthy of Sienna. To keep her.

Grayson's given me the day off training today. I need to rest before we jet off to Vegas tomorrow.

I start measuring and chucking spinach and a concoction of fruit into the blender, to create one of my usual disgusting looking green slop meals. At least after this fight, I can sink my teeth into a greasy burger with fries and enjoy an ice cold beer. I somehow need to persuade Sienna to drink her smoothie. She has barely eaten in the last few days. I can already see the weight dropping off her. Her face looks drawn. The sudden whirl of the blender startles her from her nap, where she's sprawled across the couch nestled in a white, fluffy blanket, almost the color of her complexion.

She has spent the last three days alternating between chucking her guts up and sleeping. Yesterday, I had to carry her in my arms to bed, as she was too dizzy to walk.

At first, I thought it was an after effect after what happened to her in the elevator. She promised me it wasn't that, and after a good night's sleep and lots of comforting, she was okay. That didn't really settle the guilt I felt for putting her in that situation, though. So, I panicked and called the doctor out who assured us it's just a viral infection that will pass. Not that it puts my mind at ease, knowing I have to leave for Vegas tomorrow and she is still not improving. The last thing I want to do is leave her. Not like this.

No matter how much she assures me she will be fine, even Maddie coming over to look after her doesn't ease my worries. What if something happens and I can't get to her? What if she needs me? I know she's strong, but I can't shake this feeling of dread in the pit of my stomach.

"How are you feeling, baby?"

"I'm okay, Keller. Stop worrying," she croaks as she yawns, nestling her head back into the pillow.

Pouring the contents of the blender into a tall glass, I take it over to her, letting her use my arm as a support to sit up as I bring the glass to her lips. She gives me a sad smile as she places her mouth gently around the glass, her nose turning up as she does.

"I-I can't," she stutters as she dry heaves, pushing the glass from her face.

"Baby, you really need to try something. You can't not eat or drink for days on end." I try to keep my tone light, not to sound too harsh. I'm worried.

"Let me just have another quick nap, then I'll try again, I promise." She offers me a smile to try to sweeten me up.

Before I can reply, her head hits the pillow again and soft snores leave her lips.

Gently lifting her head, I slide in close and rest her

pillow and head on my lap, stroking her hair as she smiles. Her breathing steadies, and she falls back to sleep.

"I love you, baby," I whisper.

"Hmmm," she softly moans.

It's only four days. I can cope with four days without her. I coped for twenty nine years on my own. But the thought of being separated from her just for a pathetic four nights makes me feel sick to my stomach.

Luca assured me Enzo will be standing guard to protect her 24/7. The rest of his men are busy protecting the territory. A war is brewing. I can feel it in my bones. What the catalyst will be which finally sets it off, I don't know.

CHAPTER TWENTY-SIX

God, do I feel like shit.

Every muscle in my body aches and every smell makes me gag.

"Si, I've made you a smoothie Keller left the recipe for. I'm under strict instructions to make sure you at least try to drink this. I've added extra strawberries, so it doesn't taste rank," Maddie says as she hands me a God-awful thick, browny green gloopy concoction. It actually looks worse than the one Keller makes. *Great.*

I swallow down the bile that creeps up my throat just looking at it. Covering my mouth with my hand, I shake my head at her. If I open my mouth to reply, I'm positive I will throw the small amount that remains in my stomach up all over her.

She gives me a sad smile, places the devil juice on the floor, and crouches down to my level, softly stroking my hair.

"Si, I've never seen you so sick. How long have you had this bug for now?"

"I-I don't know, feels like a lifetime," I croak out.

She pinches her features together. I can almost hear her brain ticking as she thinks.

"When was the last time you had a period? Jenny at work was just like this when she was really early pregnant with little Bobby. She could barely even stomach water without throwing it back up."

The blood drains from my face as I start to think back to when I last had a period. I am on the pill, but I know I've missed a few on the odd occasion over the last few months. I always just took a couple the next day and thought that would cover me. I usually get excruciating period pains for days before I'm due, and for the life of me, I can't think of the last time I even had to use my hot water bottle.

Shit.

"I-I don't know. Shit Maddie, I don't know."

My heart rate starts to quicken, and suddenly I feel like the room is one hundred degrees.

I don't even know if Keller wants kids. Fuck, what if he thinks I'm trapping him? I told him not to use a condom. Fuck fuck fuck.

The room starts to spin. "Maddie, I don't feel too good."

Concern washes over her face as she jumps up to help me sit up.

"Take some deep breaths with me, Sienna. It's just a panic attack. You're okay, I promise. Everything's okay. Just breathe. Focus on the breath going in and out."

Squeezing my eyes tightly shut, I breathe in for four and out for four with Maddie. After a couple of minutes, my body relaxes slightly. Passing me a glass of cold water, I take it from her with shaky hands, letting the cool liquid trickle down my throat.

"I think I should go get you some tests. Whatever the outcome, we've got this, okay? But you need to know one way or another. If you're not, then I'm calling a doctor. If it's a bug, you've had it far too long now."

She's right, I'm an adult. I can pee on a stick, easy.

"Okay."

"Are you sure you'll be okay if I pop out for 10 minutes? I'll just run to the shop and come straight back. If you need me, just call me."

I nod in response and flop back down on the sofa. Enzo had to go and sort out some personal emergency, but Nico was on his way up to take over. *I'm sure it will be fine.*

Maddie tucks me into the fluffy comforter and hands me the TV remote after flicking it onto the news.

"Hey look, it's a special program on Keller's fight. You can drool over your man while I'm out."

I let out a laugh. It hurts to do it, but I can't help it.

"Why do I need to drool over him on the screen when I have him in bed every night?" I wink at her.

"At least this bug hasn't killed your dirty sense of humor, Si."

With that, she grabs her coat and bag and heads out. The elevator pings as I settle in and watch my man on the screen.

Keller, the big softie, has been pandering around me like a mom for the last few days. I can tell he's worried about me. I doubt he's ever really had to care for someone other than himself up to now.

I had to physically rip myself away from him this morning so he could make his flight to Vegas in time. I'm absolutely gutted that I have to miss his big fight. I promised I would make sure I was awake to watch it and cheer him on from here. He knows he has my heart no matter where we are.

Since he left two hours ago, I have already had ten texts

and a phone call. I love that he is so obsessed with me, I can't lie. It feels good to be wanted. To be loved wholly and completely for exactly who you are.

I quickly type out a reply to Keller's latest message, asking how I am.

ME

I'm just watching your fight promo, cuddled up on the sofa. You are looking FINE in these videos, champ.

SEX GOD KELLER

Fine is my middle name, baby.

Shit, what is his middle name?

Another text pops up straight away.

SEX GOD KELLER

I don't have a middle name, in case you were wondering.

ME

Phew, I was panicking, thinking I didn't know you at all.

SEX GOD KELLER

You are the only one who knows me, really knows me.

ME

Good, let's keep it that way.

SEX GOD KELLER

I see this bug hasn't taken your sass away. I miss you already.

ME

Aww, my big, bad boxer boyfriend misses me.

SEX GOD KELLER

I think big bad boxer husband sounds better, don't you think?

ME

If you are going to propose, you better think of something better than a text.

In all seriousness, I would say yes in a heartbeat without even a ring. But I do draw the line at a text proposal.

SEX GOD KELLER

Oh trust me, baby, you'll know when I really propose to you. We're making our way to the airstrip soon. I love you always and forever. I'll call you when I land. xxxx

ME

Don't make me wait too long... I love you, too, my everything, always. Have a safe flight. Xxxx

Nothing could stop the grin forming on my face and the butterflies floating in my stomach. The elevator pings. I roll my eyes. Maddie must have forgotten something as per usual.

"What have you forgotten this time? You'd lose your head if it wasn't attached," I shout.

Weird, she doesn't respond.

Sitting myself up, I slowly pad out of our bedroom and into the living room, making my way to view the elevator.

All the air sucks from my lungs as I come face to face with him.

It's Jamie.

There's a murderous look in his bloodshot eyes. His face is gaunt and ashen, and his eyes have sunken into their sockets. Gone is the well-groomed businessman. A crazed drug addict stands before me. His thin lips slide up over his teeth into a sadistic grin, and shivers race down my spine. Fear spreads through my veins. I can't move, can't speak. I just stare at the creature my ex-fiancé has become. He stands still, his arms slack at his sides, staring at me. His expression, though, is bloodthirsty.

"I told you I'd be back for you, Sienna." His voice is gravelly. I barely recognize it.

"What-what do you want? How did you even get in here?" I say, attempting to sound brave, as I inch my hands into the front pocket of my hoodie, pressing the unlock button on my phone.

Jamie's wild eyes catch my movement, and he stalks toward me surprisingly fast. I back away from him until my shoulders bounce off the wall. *Shit.* Almost right in front of me now, his stench of BO laced with sickly aftershave assaults my senses, making me feel nauseous. When he reaches me, he trails his nose along my cheek and inhales deeply. I hold in my breath so I don't move. I can feel my heart pounding in my chest.

"God, Si, I've fucking missed you. I can't wait to have you back. And this time you won't ever be leaving me."

He's finally lost the fucking plot.

I try remembering Keller's words in our self-defense sessions. God, I wish I spent more time actually practicing the moves rather than fucking him.

No, I take that back. I regret nothing.

Mustering all the strength I have left, I slam my knee up, connecting with his balls. As he doubles over, I take the second of opportunity to run. My lungs squeeze as I gulp for air. My bare feet slip and squeak on the tile floor as I round the corner and head toward the bathroom. I reach out for the round doorknob, but my fingers only brush the metal and catch air as my hair is yanked, causing my head to snap back with it.

"No more running from me, Sienna." He's there again, pressing up behind me, his stink making me gag. "We need you to get the message across to your boyfriend and his brother."

We? Who the fuck?

Holding the back of my head, I try my hardest to wriggle free, clawing at his arms with my nails. He slams my forehead into the doorframe. Pain sears through my skull and stars twinkle in my vision. Tingling starts as darkness creeps in around me.

"Sleep now, *my* Sienna. We'll catch up later." I can barely hear him as the world starts to spin, and the floor rushes up to meet me.

My vision is hazy, as if someone is blowing smoke in my eyes. A sharp throbbing pain pulsates across my forehead, spreading around my temples. The sudden hit of ice cold liquid smothering my face snaps me into consciousness and instinctively I gasp for air.

A dark figure comes into view and I blink quickly to gain some focus, but it's no use. It's then I register the sharp pains radiating up my arms from my wrists. The hair on the back of my neck stands on end.

Panicking, I jerk to pull my wrists apart from their binds, almost shaking myself off the chair. I'm freezing and exposed. *Oh fuck, I'm near naked, too!* Goosebumps spread over my skin and I squeeze my eyes shut, trying and failing to cope with the panic rising in me like bile.

Memories of Jamie smashing my head against the door frame in Keller's apartment flood my brain and my body starts trembling.

No, no, please no.

I refuse to let him see me cry, but fear grips me tighter. I cringe and try jerking away as I feel his rough, icy fingers tuck my hair behind my ear.

"Well, well, well. Look who's finally decided to join the party," Jamie says, his voice dripping with malice.

My vision begins to clear as his face crowds mine. The stench of stale cigarettes almost chokes me, with his mouth just inches from my nose. Looking past him, I recognize my surroundings immediately. It's the same white kitchen counter where I caught him cheating. I'm bound to the same wooden dining chair I'd sat on for most evenings with him. Scanning the room, I spot at least seven other men all dressed in black suits with similar slicked-back hair. They could all be related. They look so similar. All watching me and Jamie, their faces expressionless. Similar to the men Luca brought around to Keller's not long ago.

More mafia men.

Snapping my eyes to his, I search for something, anything, to plead with the old Jamie that might be in there somewhere. But the man crouching before me is just a shell of the one I was once with. His eyes are wild and his pupils are dilated. He seems oblivious to the constant muscle tick by his temple. He just squats and stares at me with a sadistic grin etched on his face.

"Jamie, please." I try to sound sincere. Deep down, I want to tell him to fuck off, but I don't want to rile him.

He's too unpredictable. We've underestimated him once before. Who knows how far he will take this.

He doesn't respond, he just continues glaring at me with his crazed eyes. It's like a scene from Insidious.

"Why are you doing this, Jamie?"

A shiny object catches my attention and my gaze flicks to his hand. The sickening realization hits me. A fucking knife. The lunatic in front of me has a knife. As if noticing my fear, he runs the cool metal along the inside of my calf. I can feel the burning sensation of bile rising in my chest again.

"I can hear your heart pounding, Sienna. Not so brave now your big bad boyfriend isn't here to protect you. You fucking whore." A laugh skitters out of him and scrubs the back hand across his nose. "You don't realize what you've cost him, do you?"

This can't be happening. Tears sting the back of my eyes and I shake my head in disbelief.

"Why are you doing this to him? What's he ever done to you?" I croak out.

"It's not just me. Your boyfriend and his God Almighty himself brother have managed to piss off the Falcones." He tucks in his chin with an evil laugh.

"The Falcones?" My lips quiver. I'm so cold, it's hard to speak.

"Oh. Don't act dumb, Sienna. It doesn't suit you. They're your boyfriend's rivals. You know. Your hitman boyfriend? You really picked a keeper this time." His voice drips with anger.

"I don't understand. How does any of this involve you? You're a corporate lawyer, for God's sake, not part of the mob."

He shifts uncomfortably at my questioning, and his head does a quick jerk to the left. I've clearly hit a nerve.

"Well," he says, tapping the cold knife against my inner thigh, which makes me inhale sharply.

"I may have gotten into a little debt with Marco Falcone. I stumbled across some illegal substances and may or may not have taken them home with me. Turns out, the mafia don't like when you steal from them. I overheard them talking about Keller at the meet and came up with a brilliant idea, knowing that you were fucking him."

"This is why you've been stalking me, sending me burned roses and sending me all those texts?"

His eyes drop to where he's dragging the knife point along my delicate skin.

"Well, to start with, it was just to scare you. Enough to get Keller to give me some money to pay Marco off myself. But then Marco came up with a better deal. I kidnap and *kill* you. That *breaks* Keller and then shatters the entire organization around Luca. In return, I get a lifetime supply and all my debts paid."

The room spins as I take in Jamie's words.

He's going to kill me.

"You don't have to do this, Jamie!" I sob, my chest heaving.

"What have I ever done to you to deserve this?" I know it sounds desperate, but I am. I know Keller's not even in the same state right now. I don't have my protector.

I'm never going to see Keller again. The realization hurts more than any of the physical pain I am in.

Jamie doesn't respond; he merely chuckles and glides the cool metal's razor-sharp edge across my abdomen. Burning pain radiates in the wake of the knife cutting my skin. I watch in horror as a warm trickle of blood follows. God, I can't watch, but I can't look away.

This isn't real. Wake the fuck up, Sienna!

"God, you look fucking edible in this lacy underwear. How come you never wore anything like this for me?" Jealousy is clear in his voice as his tongue sloppily trails behind the knife, lapping up the blood.

He's clearly sick in the head. I'm never going to see Keller again. He's going to kill me. The horror of it settles in me and I shake my head vigorously.

"Keller will kill you for this," I spit, disgusted by him. If he's going to kill me, I won't give him the satisfaction of knowing my pain. I'm not the weak little Sienna he used to manipulate. I'm stronger now.

"Pretty hard for him to do in Vegas, don't you think, Sienna? Do you really think we didn't plan this? I've been waiting outside his penthouse for two days. Waiting for the fucker to leave. Even so, do you really think he could take on all of them?" He gestures to the men surrounding the room, watching.

He's grinning at me now, his teeth stained red with blood. *My blood.* Slipping his phone from his pocket, he shoves the camera in my face.

"Smile, gorgeous. Loverboy needs to see my handy work."

He takes me by surprise, and I stare into the three small, black cameras on the back of his phone. The camera clicks and he laughs to himself whilst typing and shoving the phone back in the pocket of his baggy tracksuit bottoms.

Zoning his attention straight back to me, a murderous glint flashes in his eyes as he lowers his head to mine, taking in a loud breath.

“What’s the matter, Sienna? I’ve never seen you this quiet,” he says, his eyes boring into mine.

“Fuck you!” I spit out at him, saliva splattering across his face before he wipes it off in disgust.

“You fucking stupid whore!” he screams as he hikes his leg up and smashes his boot into my ribcage.

Pain shatters through me as I tumble back with the chair, bouncing off the tiled flooring and landing on my left side. I let out a scream on impact, my whole body throbbing in agony, my ears ringing so high-pitched I can barely think. All I can see is his black steel-toed boots staring back at me as I lie helpless on the floor. I try with everything I have to free my wrists and ankles of my ties, but it’s no use. They won’t budge.

It feels like everything is in slow motion as he draws his left foot back off the floor.

“NOOOO!” I scream. I scream so loud it burns my lungs. Maybe, just maybe, someone will hear me and call for help.

His foot connects with my ribcage again, and pain sears through me, burning throughout my entire body, taking my breath away. All I want to do is wrap my hands around my stomach, an overwhelming need to protect our baby, but I can’t. I can’t free my hands. That in itself is killing me.

His foot connects with my ribcage again, and I’m gasping for air. All I can think about is the baby. I would have been a better mother than my own. I would have loved my baby more than life itself. Now, I’ll never get that chance.

“Please, Jamie, stop!” I manage, coughing pathetically. Each word splintering in my chest. I have to try anything to get us out of here.

“Shut the fuck up!” he shouts, lifting his boot again, this

time right in front of my face. He slams his foot forward, the impact straight into my cheek.

The pain is now taking over, consuming my entire body until I can no longer take it. I can feel my life draining out of me onto the cold floor.

My only thoughts in this moment: Keller.

He provides the warmth and the love I need to slip away. I can feel a small smile on my lips as I drift off.

I just hope he knows how much I loved him.

I imagine being wrapped in his embrace until I finally feel nothing.

CHAPTER TWENTY-SEVEN

The somber look etched across Luca's face quickly morphs to pure rage, and he smashes his phone against the steel walls of the aircraft. Shattering glass bouncing off the walls.

"FUUUUUCK!" he shouts frantically, running his hands through his hair.

He can't look me in the eye. Dread pools in the pit of my stomach. Luca is level-headed and able to control his emotions. This outburst means something is completely fucked.

"Tell me, Luca."

Finally, his eyes meet mine, but the words don't form. He just stares at me, pain evident in his features.

"For fuck's sake, Luca, whatever it is, we deal with it together. Now open your mouth and use your fucking words before I lose all the patience I have left."

"They have her, Keller. I'm so fucking sorry."

For a second, I don't think I hear right. Then it feels like all the air has been sucked out of the room.

Those four words slice me like a knife to the throat.

They can't. They can't fucking have her. This can't be happening. My mind is spinning.

Acidic bile rises up my throat. Aware we are in front of the rest of the mob, I feel their eyes on me. Watching, waiting for me to explode. Every part of my being wants to raise hell, burn the whole city of New York to the ground.

In this moment, everything I have ever loved is slipping to everything I've ever lost. My life is completely worthless without her.

"What happened to your deal?" I spit out, trying to retain the quivering in my voice.

"I don't fucking know, okay? Fuck! We'll get her back, brother. If it's the last thing I ever do, I will bring the light back to you," he replies, running his hands through his hair.

Unbuckling the belt, I jump up from my seat. "Tell the pilot to open the fucking doors, now," I rage, adrenaline pumping through my body as I march over to the exit. Grayson hurls his body in front of the aircraft door, blocking my path, and grabbing my sweater with both fists.

He's brave.

"Keller, sit the fuck down. Luca has men. They will get her back. You have to stay on this fucking plane. Everything you've worked for boils down to this fight. Don't lose your head. If you throw this fight, that's it. You're trapped. You want to be a better man, a man worthy of Sienna. Well, this is that opportunity."

"Don't fucking touch me." Snatching his wrists, I push them off me. He doesn't budge out of my path.

"Move Grayson. Fuck the fight. My life is worthless without her. So I suggest you either fucking come with me and help me dismember every one of those fuckers holding her, or shut the fuck up and sit down. Choice is yours."

I get it. He's never been in love. He's never cared about someone enough to lay his life down for theirs. I feel a hand grab my shoulder as I spin around, coming face to face with Luca. He gives me a slow nod and strides past me, gripping the exit door lever and pulling. "Get some fucking steps here now, you dumb fucks," he shouts to the men below, pure anger radiating off him. I assume that gets the message across, as the next thing, the metal steps are being connected to the exit latch, and we're making our way back onto the tarmac where the pouring rain lashes against my face. Through the haze of the downpour, a black Mercedes pulls up, and the driver opens the doors for us to jump in.

A message chimes through my phone as we make our way to my penthouse. Luca's men are either searching for her across the city or on their way to meet me. Every single man under Luca is on the hunt. Luca glances at my phone as I tap on the new notification from the unknown number.

An image fills the screen.

Sienna.

Wearing only her black bra and panties, her arms snaked around the chair, probably bound, and her ankles tied together. Tears stain her bloodshot eyes, deep red blood drips from her forehead down past her left eyebrow. I can feel her pleading with me through her eyes. Marks slashed across her stomach make me want to empty the contents of my own. Her piercing blue eyes, which always give her emotions away, are now filled with pure fear. I recognize the look. It's the same one I used to thrive on.

The only thing that keeps me from throwing my breakfast up is the fact she is alive.

"Send that over to Nico now. See what he can pull from that photo."

I nod and quickly forward it over. Another notification pops up. I quickly open it.

UNKNOWN

I told you I'd take her. That's what happens when you underestimate your opponent. I'm going to enjoy every second with her.

Jamie.

Fucking Jamie.

"It's her ex. He has her."

"FUCK!" I scream, smashing my fists into the headrest in front of me.

"We *will* get her back, brother. If it's the last thing we do, we will bring her back to you. You have my word. The Falcones are too uncoordinated compared to us. They're using a crackhead to do their dirty work, for fuck's sake."

I know we will because I won't stop until she's back with me. I will unleash hell on this city until she's home.

No one on this planet could stop me.

Another text pulls me from my murderous thoughts.

NICO

She's at Jamie's apartment. I've blocked the security feed and alerted our men to get there. Clean-up crew on standby.

He immediately sends through an address on West Street. I bark out to the driver and he puts his foot to the floor.

"Are we armed?" I ask Luca.

"Of course we are. A full selection in the trunk. I fucking told you they wouldn't be able to pull this off properly."

"She isn't safe just yet, Luca."

But she will be. If it's the last thing I ever do, I will make sure she is safe.

A BLOOD-CURDLING SCREAM ECHOES DOWN THE HALLWAY. IT'S her; I know, without a doubt. Without a second thought, I sprint towards the apartment door. I can just imagine Luca and Grayson wanting to shout at me to stop, but I don't fucking care. Her screams are getting louder and louder. It's all I can focus on. At least she is still alive, I tell myself.

"Keller, fucking stop!" Grayson hisses, grabbing my arm and trying to hold me back. "You don't know what you're walking into; you're no use to her fucking dead!"

It's no use. My strength is too much for him. Added to the pure rage burning inside me, they have zero chance of holding me back from her. Nothing in this world will stop me from getting her.

I don't give a shit. I can't take another second of the sound of her screams piercing my heart. Aiming my gun towards the door, I kick it open only to be met with silence. I immediately spot Sienna's limp body curled up on the wooden floor, crimson pooling next to her. The guns pointing at my head don't even register as I launch through the room to get to her.

"What the fuck have you done?!" I roar.

Grayson and Luca scream at me to stop. Bullets fly past my head, and the gunfire blasts in my ears. My vision is blurry as I collapse onto my knees in front of her, pull the knife from my boot, and cut her ties. Slow, shallow breaths escape her lips. My shaking hands, now covered in blood, pull her body into mine. Her unconscious form is unmoving.

"Sienna. Baby, can you hear me?" I'm failing to keep the rising panic out of my voice. My whole life feels like it's slipping through my fingers and I can barely keep a grasp on it. This can't be fucking happening. I can't lose her.

"Baby, please. You promised you wouldn't leave me. You promised, Sienna." A sob escapes as I stroke her sticky, blood-soaked hair.

The world around me fades out for a minute. All I can focus on is my perfect firecracker–motionless, bloodied, and bruised beneath me. Bringing my head down to hers, I nuzzle into her hair, warm tears running down my face.

Gunshots ring through my ears again, followed by thudding. Using my body as a shield, I lay on top of her and squint my eyes. Anything. I would do anything to protect her. She can live without me, but I could never live without her.

"Get her fucking out of here, Keller!" registers in my ears, and I look up.

Blood is splattered over white walls, lifeless bodies lay in heaps. Fuck, there must have been at least ten Falcone men in here. Scanning the area, I set my sights on Jamie. That little fuck is mine. Then a barely audible cough from beneath me grabs my attention.

"Keller?"

Her voice is faint as she struggles to breathe. Kissing her forehead, relief washes over me. "It's me, baby. You are safe now. I need you to grab onto my neck. Do you think you can manage that for me?" I need to get her out of here. She isn't ever leaving my side again. That is one thing I am fucking sure of.

She gives me a slow nod, and I help her maneuver her

arms around my neck as I bundle the rest of her body up, holding her tight against my upper body.

"Just hold on for five more minutes, okay, baby?" Sobs rack through her body, vibrating against me.

"Shh, it's okay. You're going to be okay, I promise you. No one will ever hurt you again," I stroke her head, buried in my neck, with the outside of my hand so the gun in my grip doesn't touch her. I'm doing my best to offer her comfort when on the inside, all I want to do is kill every fucker still standing in this room. Nothing would give me greater joy than watching life fade away from each and every one of them. I have the one thing in my arms that stops my desire to do that, the one thing that gives my life purpose.

The gunshot makes her jump in my arms, reminding me she doesn't belong in this world, and I squeeze her even tighter into me.

"It's okay, baby. It's Luca's men," I whisper as I look over and see Grayson, void of expression, shoot one of Falcone's men between the eyes point-blank. He doesn't flinch as his body slams to the floor in front of his feet. The tell of a true psychopath: taking someone's life doesn't faze us. He steps over the body as if it's a piece of trash on the sidewalk, immediately setting his sights on the next. Over in the kitchen, Luca has another man bent over the counter as he swipes a long kitchen knife across his throat in one swift movement. The whole apartment is a bloody war zone. Swiftly making my way out of the apartment, I head for the stairwell exit. Luca's car is parked right outside with a driver waiting.

"Just a couple more minutes, baby, and we'll get you to a hospital. Just stay with me until then." As I reach the last set of stairs, a figure catches my attention. I instinctively turn my body sideways to keep Sienna out of the line of fire. As I get closer, Jamie's psychotic grin stops me in my tracks.

"Move the fuck out of my way before you end up with a bullet wedged in your brain."

"You'd really give up everything for her. You really are the pussy they think you are," he snarls with disgust, pointing at Sienna.

He has no idea who I am or just how far I'd go to protect the woman I love.

The blood visibly drains from his face as I raise my gun, the suppressor pointing right at him.

"See, that's where you're wrong, Jamie," I say, edging closer and closer to him. "I'm not giving anything up for her. She *is* my everything, and I will stop at nothing to protect her." My gun is now pressing into his forehead. "Do you think I'm afraid of you? I kill men far bigger and scarier than you most nights. Without batting an eye, I can take a man's life. I reap pleasure from watching men quiver in fear as I slowly torture them. So do you honestly think I won't unleash carnage on this entire city for what you've done? *Do you*?" I shout, pure evil dripping from my tone. Sienna stiffens at my words. Fuck.

Jamie backs into the wall, the barrel of my gun still pressed firmly between his eyes. Every ounce of my being is screaming at me to end this, to pull the trigger. I hesitate as Sienna fidgets in my grip, knowing if I pull the trigger for her to witness, she'd never stay. She doesn't want to love a monster. Who would?

My grip on the gun tightens so much the veins of my hand could pop through the skin at any moment. Jamie stares me dead in the eyes, not flinching an inch. I underestimated this prick completely. One of the fundamental rules of boxing is to know your opponent inside and out.

How the fuck did I get him so wrong? I let my guard slip and nearly lost Sienna in the process.

Maybe I am meant to be just the monster.

"Do it. Please make this all stop," Sienna whispers in my ear. I know she's serious. Jamie's eyes bulge, darting to her back enclosed in my arms.

"Don't fucking listen to that dumb bitch. You really want to go to prison for that piece of ass? Trust me, I've been there, seen it and had it. It ain't all that."

I see red. The deep-rooted anger that has been bubbling within me erupts. I couldn't stop it if I tried. A bullet through the temple is an easy way out. Too quick. I let my gun clatter to the floor and relief washes over Jamie's features; color creeps back up into his cheeks. Without a second of hesitation, I grab his neck and squeeze hard enough to stop his breath. He's flapping against the wall, limbs flailing as he attempts to gasp for air, which only fuels me to tighten my grip around his throat. I can feel his pulse hammering in his neck. He's hitting my arms in a feeble attempt to get me off him.

"I fucking told you before, if you so much as touched her, I would end you. I don't make empty threats. You stupid fucking junkie." His arms now limply hit at me as his eyes bulge almost out of their sockets. Not a single ounce of regret displays on him, which pisses me off even more. With a last squeeze of the windpipe, he finally goes limp in my grip, all the air completely cut off and his life now ended by the hands of a monster.

I release my hold, and he collapses to the ground like a sack of shit. Any other time, I'd carry on like nothing happened, yet the realization hits me. She's witnessed what I am first hand. She just watched me take another man's life. There is no escaping that, certainly no denying it. But she's now safe. That's all that matters. She can hate me for the rest of eternity. At least I know she's safe.

"Baby, I'm sorry. I'm so fucking sorry. I wanted to be better. Better for you. For us." Wrapping my free arm around her tiny, frail frame, I collapse my head into her neck, her sweet peachy scent wafting up my nostrils. I know this will probably be the last time I get to hold her like this. Monsters like me don't get to keep the girl. I can take a man's life without hesitation. But the thought of losing her literally brings me to my knees.

"It's-it's okay, Keller," she stammers, her eyelids fluttering. She lets out a chesty cough and tiny red specks splatter across my white shirt.

"Sienna, stay with me, okay? I'm getting you help. I promise."

Beating open the door, darkness surrounds me. The street is eerily quiet. You wouldn't know a massacre is happening a few flights up.

An engine starts and bright lights illuminate the road. I dart towards the car and yank open the back door as the middle-aged Italian man jumps out of the driver's seat and helps me place Sienna across the back seats. I give him a nod. "Hospital. Now."

He simply nods in response. Edging to the other side of the Mercedes, I slip in and gently lift her head onto my lap. She doesn't even flinch when I move her. As we drive off, I spot Luca and Grayson in my peripheral, exiting the building, holstering their weapons and stalking toward the Audi behind us. Both of their faces dripping with crimson. Grayson swipes the back of his hand across his face, only smearing it more. Two predators fresh from a hunt.

Fear consumes me as the driver hurtles toward the

hospital. I sit deadly still, stroking Sienna's blood-soaked hair.

"I love you, princess," I whisper over and over again, praying with all I have she can hear me, that she can feel me.

The realization forms a pit in my stomach. I know what I have to do, no matter how much it will rip my heart out.

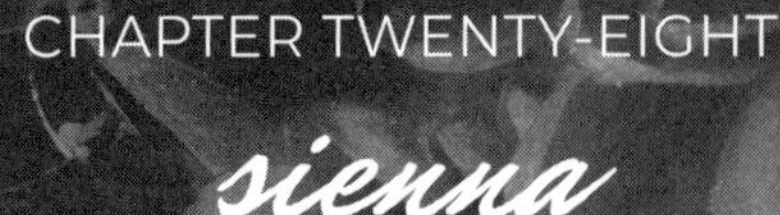

CHAPTER TWENTY-EIGHT

sienna

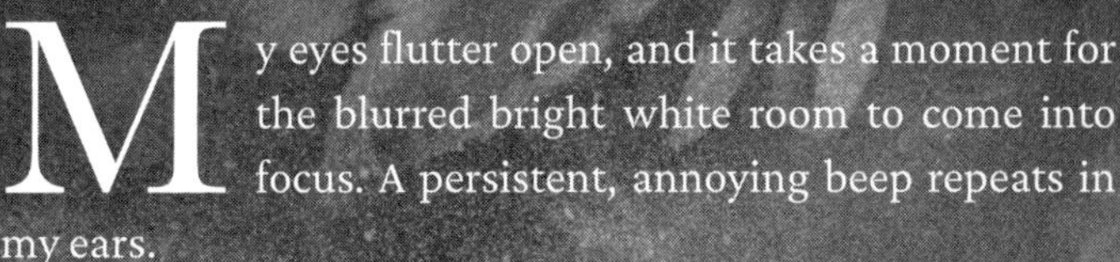

My eyes flutter open, and it takes a moment for the blurred bright white room to come into focus. A persistent, annoying beep repeats in my ears.

I feel as though I am floating on clouds, my body numb, bar the warm tingling covering my left hand. I can barely swallow. My throat is so dry. Letting out a small cough sends shooting pains through my ribcage.

Jesus Christ, was I hit by a bus?

Panic rises in my chest. I keep blinking in an attempt to clear my vision. I need to see so I can calm down. Images of Jamie standing over me, grinning sadistically, fill my mind. Ropes burning into my wrists. My arms pinned behind me. The cold blade. *No, no, no. Please don't let him be here.*

"Baby. Sienna!" The ragged voice I instantly recognize booms to my left. I don't have the strength to turn my head, but I know he's here. I know he's the warmth I feel around my hand.

"She's awake. Someone! Fucking get in here and help her, for fuck's sake!" he bellows.

Always my protector.

His bloodshot eyes stare back at me, pure panic and guilt etched across his features. His face provides some relief from the bright clinical lights burning my eyes.

"Keller?" I barely manage to croak out.

"Shh, baby, it's okay. You're okay." His voice shakes as he talks.

Knowing he's here brings me instant calm. The white walls, the beeping, and his panicked face–I'm in the hospital.

"Ah, Sienna, you're back with us, dear. How are you feeling? Does anything hurt?" a neutering female voice questions, as I scan the room to pinpoint where she is. By the glass door, I spot a small middle-aged lady with thick black-framed glasses and a jet black, razor-sharp bob. A stethoscope snakes around her neck, covering her white cloak. She gives me a smile as she walks over.

"I-I–" Letting out a cough, I try again.

"I feel numb," I croak. "What-what happened to me?"

"You were brought in two nights ago after the attack. You sustained a nasty head injury which caused slight swelling on the brain. We've kept you here in intensive care to monitor the swelling, which I'm pleased to report has significantly reduced. You do, however, have two broken ribs and some nasty bruising on your arms and legs, and stitches on the cuts on your abdomen."

I hear her words, but can barely focus on what she is actually saying.

"So, I'm going to be okay?"

"We want to keep you here for a few more days to monitor the swelling on the brain. As you have been dipping in and out of consciousness, we want to monitor to watch for any bleeds or further swelling. In the meantime, we will keep you propped up with painkillers to alleviate some of your discomfort. Run some further blood tests just to keep up on your vitals. Before we can think about discharging you." She speaks, barely moving her gaze from her clipboard.

"For now, we need you to rest and recover here. Your knight in shining armor could do with a break. He hasn't left your side since you were admitted." A smile forms on her lips as she speaks, nodding towards Keller perched next to me, gripping my hand so tight it's as if he thinks he'll lose me if he lets go.

"Thank you, Doctor."

"Great, get some rest, and I'll be back on my rounds in an hour to check on you." Moving the clipboard from her face, she offers me a soft smile before leaving.

I stare at the door, wracking my brains to piece together what happened. Jamie's voice taunts me.

"This is what you get for being a fucking whore, Sienna. I told you to come back to me, but you wouldn't listen. I can't wait for Keller to see you like this. Like the pathetic, useless bitch you are."

I remember him throwing me across the room like a rag doll; the men shouting at him to stop as he continued to kick me in the torso, over and over again. Each blow exploding pain throughout my body. I remember wanting to save my baby; the heartache that I couldn't almost killed me.

"Sienna? How are you feeling, baby?" Keller's soft voice brings me back to him.

I manage to turn my head enough to take him in. The look of a defeated man utterly breaks my heart. His jet-black hair is disheveled on top and there's a few days old stubble over his face. His dark blood-shot eyes are even darker as the circles shadow beneath. He looks broken. I've broken the strongest man on the planet.

His rough hands stroke my cheek as I sink into the feeling. Even now, his touch shoots electricity through me, almost bringing me to life.

Realization hits me like a ton of bricks.

He murdered Jamie with his bare hands.

He's a hitman for the mafia.

Luca is the fucking mafia.

I told him to kill Jamie.

This broken man before me, with tear-stained cheeks, killed a man to protect me.

Not one part of me feels any fear. I know deep in my soul, this man would do anything but hurt me. He is my protector.

"If you want me to leave, I'll go. I know you are probably petrified of me. I've hidden so much from you. You have every right to be pissed at me. But know this, Sienna, I would do it all again in a heartbeat for you. This is me; you've seen it all. There is no mask anymore." His voice catches as he speaks, and a single tear trails down his face.

This man carries the weight of the world on his shoulders and has never had anyone to share the burden, never had anyone to accept him for who he truly is. No matter who he is or what he's done, he is my Keller. My champ. I'll love him, not despite his flaws, but for them. Without him, there would be no life. He saved me, now I have to save him from himself.

"Keller, I need you to listen to me and listen to me properly. You are not a bad person. Yes, you may do horrendous things, but deep down that's not the true you. I told you I wanted it all, not just half of you. I will always love you, no matter what," I say as a sob catches in my throat.

His face remains still, emotionless, as he takes in my words. Each second he doesn't respond feels like a lifetime.

"Fuck, Sienna." He winces as he runs his hands through his hair, covering my hand with both of his and bringing his head down to them, hiding his face from me.

I feel like he's pushing me away. Why hasn't he told me he loves me back?

"Keller, please talk to me." Desperation is clear in my voice.

I can't lose him. I can't live without him. Why isn't he saying anything?

"You're scaring me, Keller. Please, just say something. I need you."

His tear-filled eyes lock on to mine, pure agony seeping through. Leaning forward, he places a soft kiss on my lips, the kind of kiss you give when you're saying goodbye to someone, not telling them you love them back.

"You are my queen, Sienna. I worship the ground you walk on every fucking day. I'm not worthy enough to be your king. You nearly died because of me, and I almost didn't make it to you in time. I can't live my life knowing I put yours in danger. As long as you are alive and safe, I'll be okay. I knew I couldn't keep you, but I tried anyway. I'm so fucking sorry, Sienna. You have brought me out of the darkness. I promise I will work day and night to maybe one day be the man worthy of your love. But just know I love you. I love you more than life itself. I love you enough to know I have to let you go. I will literally be ripping my own heart out and stomping on it. I'll take that, knowing you can live your life free and happy."

"No, no, no. Keller, don't do this. Don't do this to us. Please. I'm begging you!" Tears stream down my face like a river. A knife feels like it's being shoved into my chest.

A deep sob escapes him as he continues. "I am so fucking sorry. I hope one day you can forgive me. You will always be the only one to ever own my heart. Don't ever forget that. Never stop being my perfect little firecracker."

He stands, tears freely rolling down his cheek as he bends over and places a single, gentle kiss on my forehead.

I can barely breathe. All the air is gone. My heart feels ripped out with it. I feel empty. Alone.

"Am I not enough for you? Why can't you just love me and be the one man to stay in my life? Stop pretending like you aren't worthy of my love. You are. How am I supposed to go on with my life without you? You own my heart as much as I own yours. You're throwing in the towel on the one fight that could give you the world." Wiping the tears away with the back of my hand, I sniffle.

Bile rises in my throat as he can barely look at me. The man who can single-handedly strangle someone until they take their last breath doesn't have the balls to look me in the face and dump me.

"You can at least look me in my fucking eyes and tell me you don't want me. Be a man and tell me like you mean it. Tell me we are over." My voice gets louder and louder as I speak.

"Don't you dare ever say you aren't enough," he snaps. "I'm the one that isn't good enough for you. You deserve everything. That's why we have to be over, Sienna."

I let out a defeated sigh.

"Just leave, Keller. Join the rest of the men in my life that walk straight out the door. I'm done being the girl that wasn't quite good enough." I pull my gaze from him. The more I look at the hurt etched across his face, the more my chest aches.

I hear his heavy footsteps slowly make their way to the

door as it flings open and slams shut. As it does, I let out the breath I have been holding in and close my eyes, let the tears fall like a waterfall, letting out a blood-curdling scream as I realize I have been left with nothing, not even a working heart. I wrap my stomach tightly and crouch over as I rock back and forward, letting it all out.

My distress must have been heard out in the hallway as the doctor comes running through the door, all flustered. Rushing to my bedside and wrapping me up in a warm embrace, I feel nothing. I feel dead inside.

"Shh, Sienna. It's going to be okay," she hushes as she strokes my hair. She then places her small hand gently on my arm, wrapped tightly around my stomach. The tears keep on coming until my body eventually gives up, and I let my body sink into the darkness.

"The baby is okay. We have some more tests to do, but so far, everything looks fine."

I snap my eyes to hers, the blood draining from my face as my hand cradles my stomach.

Our baby.

That's the last thing I think of as the world fades into darkness.

CHAPTER TWENTY-NINE

keller

I left my soul in that hospital with her. A shell of a man walked out those doors. Hell bent on one thing.

Revenge.

Every mark, every bruise and broken bone will cost a life. That's at least twenty three, because I counted.

I slip back into the darkness and do what I do best, what I was born to do.

Hunt.

The love of my life, my title fight, my freedom. All gone. As the rain pours, dripping down my face, I slip my phone out of my pocket and dial Luca. He answers on the first ring.

"War has started. Enzo will stay and protect Sienna. You have my word no harm will come to her again."

Just hearing her name sends a sharp pain radiating through my chest.

"Grayson is on his way to the hospital to get you. I'll fill you in when you get here, not over the phone," he says, anger dripping from his voice.

"War is good with me. I'm ready to burn this city to ashes."

I disconnect the call before he speaks again. I'm not in the mood for chitchat. The only thing I'm in the mood for is killing every one of those Falcone fuckers. There's no way out for me now.

There's no Sienna to pull me from the darkness, no fight to focus on. All that's left is a monster with a taste for blood. One picture sticks in the forefront of my mind. Sienna slumped on the floor, lifeless, in a pool of blood.

If I'd have left her the hell alone, she would have been safe. The Falcones were after me and Luca and exploited Jamie's addiction to do it. That's why I had to leave her. Nothing will ever compare to the pain I felt breaking up with her, nor hearing her blood-curdling scream as I left. It took every ounce of strength left in me not to turn around and wrap her in my arms. That's all I wanted to do for the rest of my fucking life.

I should have known I didn't deserve to be loved in this life. I found it anyway, only to have it ripped from me.

CHAPTER THIRTY

keller

Twenty one days since I last held her in my arms.

Twenty one days since I last felt something, anything.

Enzo informs me daily of her recovery. He says that physically she is getting there, but she is still throwing up a lot. Emotionally, she is a mess. It fucking hurts knowing I'm the one causing her this pain.

When Maddie called me yesterday in hysterics, threatening to chop my balls off if I didn't sort my shit out, I almost dialed her number. *Almost.*

"She needs you, Keller. I'm so scared we're all going to lose her."

Her words have swarmed my mind ever since. I knew it was bad, but not this bad.

I squeeze my fingers around the sharp edges of the blade in my hand. As it slices through my flesh, warm liquid drips through my fingertips.

"You're a fucking psychopath."

I snap my head to the stupid pussy tied to the metal chair in the center of Luca's basement. Hit number fifteen–I don't know his name, nor do I fucking care at this point. All of Falcone's men are just numbers on my kill list at this point.

Why I haven't killed this mouthy little prick yet, I don't know. I thought getting revenge would make me feel something. Would tame the monster and distract me from the reoccurring screams I hear in my head, the heart-wrenching cries that barreled down the hospital corridors as I turned my back on the love of my life.

Instead, all it's done is make the screams louder. Every time I torture one of Falcone's men, all I can see is Sienna's face as I shattered her heart. They might have been the ones to physically hurt her, but I all but shot the final bullet. I killed the light in her. I'm worse than any of them.

My firecracker is made of strong stuff. I know with time, she will get over me. The thought of another man touching her, seeing her smile, and snuggling her to sleep, brings bile burning into my throat.

You chose this, you asshole. I shake my head and turn my attention back to my latest hit.

His face is swollen, blood spilling from the gash in his eyebrow. Yet he still sits there with a sarcastic smirk, as if he's enjoying the pain.

"Fuck, do you ever shut up?" I say as I slowly walk over to him, kicking the legs of the chair under him, sending him flying backward. His head bounces off the concrete floor. A few seconds pass and he doesn't move. Thank fuck, some peace.

Going back to my torture station, as I like to call it, I consider the shiny metal, clinical-looking tray resting on top of the fold-out table. An array of lethal blades is laid out perfectly in height order. Next to it, a pair of tooth extracting forceps smothered in dried blood with a neat collection of molars.

Maybe if I rip the rest of his teeth out, that will stop him from talking.

I hear him rustling on the floor a few footsteps away. A low groan escapes his lips. Snatching the cold instrument, my mind is made up. The teeth are going.

Luca's basement is arctic. The puffs of my breath linger in the air. New York is currently covered in a blanket of snow. I know Sienna would love nothing more than dragging me around Central Park and no doubt assaulting me with snowballs. She told me that back home in London they rarely get snow and when they do, it's the shit type that goes to slush. I'd love to witness her contagious smile again.

My phone vibrates against the metal tray, breaking me from my thoughts. Letting out a sigh, I pick it up. Every day I wait for her to finally make contact, to give me a reason not to lose myself to the darkness completely. So far, nothing.

Her name lights up my screen. I blink a few times to make sure I'm not hallucinating. It's been a long time since I slept properly. My finger hesitates over the green button. My heart wants nothing more than to pick up and tell her I was fucking wrong and beg her to take my sorry ass back. I quickly remember why I am doing this. I'd rather she be alive without me than dead with me.

The call cuts off and I sigh in relief. But that's immediately short-lived as the phone vibrates in my hand again. Just her name flashing on the screen gives me a warm feeling in my chest.

Fuck it.

"Sienna, are you okay?" I quickly ask, holding my breath as I wait for her reply.

"Huh? Yeah, of course, I'm okay. Why wouldn't I be? It's not as if I was kidnapped and then dumped in my hospital bed by the man I thought was the love of my life. Oh, wait." Sarcasm drips from her voice. She was never one to hide her emotions.

"No, I'm actually calling because I have a question for you."

"Ok, fine, but make it quick. I'm busy," I snap. I know I sound like an asshole, but I can't lead her on.

A moment passes. I can hear my heart racing in my ears as I wait for her to spit it out.

"Is Enzo single?"

Tightening my grip on the phone, my jaw clenches so hard I'm surprised my teeth don't shatter. I close my eyes and take a deep breath.

This fucking woman will be the death of me.

"Hellloo. Keller? Are you there?"

"Don't. You. Fucking. Dare. Princess," I manage to spit out, my mind reeling.

"You don't get to call me 'princess' anymore, you spineless piece of shit. Just answer the fucking question. Is he single, yes or no? I have an itch that needs scratching, and I kind of find that little scar across his cheek and his jet black hair sexy. I can't wait to wrap my fingers through it whilst he--"

"Enough!" I cut her off. "You belong to me. If you want Enzo to stay breathing, I suggest you stay away."

"Well, you've been a great help, Keller. I've gotta go have an itch scratched. Have a nice life, asshole.

"Oh, and by the way, I would have accepted you despite

your other certain, what shall we call it... pastime. You say being with you is dangerous, yet you leave me here all on my own, without your protection. You didn't even ask what I wanted. We both know Enzo has nothing on you. I have a hit on my head, regardless of being with you or not. I wanted it all with you, Keller. I loved you with every fiber of my being. Clearly, I wasn't good enough for you to make you stay. I have a pretty good idea what you've been up to, Keller. I hope it's worth it. I hope it makes you feel complete."

She cuts off the call. My mouth is gaping, my jaw almost touching the floor.

Loved.

She loved me, not loves.

She's right, I was supposed to be her protector. I let my doubts get in the way of what was important.

Now I've lost her.

I can't live like this anymore. This isn't me, not who I want to be, anyway. Tossing down the tooth extractor, it clangs against the metal tray, and feels like it's burned a hole in my palm. Maybe it's not too late, maybe I can fix this. All of it. Sienna saw all of me and still loved me, and I threw it back in her face out of fear. I was so close to having it all just three weeks ago. I want it all back, and that is exactly what I am going to do. Starting with re-arranging this fight and cutting my mafia ties.

I slide my phone into my pocket and head for the basement door, the prick on the floor asking where I'm going as I storm past him. There's a new spring in my step as I march into Luca's office. He's leaning back in his leather desk chair, frantically typing away on his phone, his brows furrowed. He drags his face from the screen and gives me a sad smile.

"I was wondering how long it would take." Amusement laces his tone.

I'm not stupid. I know he was watching everything unfold in real time through the security feed. I drop down with a thud onto his emerald green velvet sofa, wedged between two dark oak bookcases. Resting my foot on my knee and leaning back, I wait for his words of wisdom.

"Don't worry, I've spoken to Enzo. Sienna's not made any kind of pass at him this whole time. The only interaction they have is her scowling at him. She's winding you up, brother," he chuckles.

I'm glad he finds this fucking funny.

"I want out, Luca. I can't do this anymore. It's killing me."

A sadness passes over his features as he slowly nods, resting his elbows on his thighs.

"I need to be–no, I *want* to be–the man she deserves. I want to unify those belts and win back my girl and make her mine until the day I die. I can't do that working for you anymore."

His lips creep up into a smile, his perfect white teeth coming into view.

"I can't believe it took you this long to realize. It's been killing me watching you do this to yourself. I thought I'd lost you for good after you pushed away the one person who pulls you into the light. I've already spoken to the rest of the men, and we all agreed to let you go, we have a replacement in line. You and Sienna will always have our protection. A war is raging. You've been fighting in my corner for the last fifteen years now. It's my turn to repay the favor."

Relief flows through my entire body. It feels like the weight of the world has lifted from my shoulders. Finally, I can see a future out of the shadows, a future with my queen.

"But I'm going to need you to do two things for me. You're going to unify your belts. Channel that anger into the thing you were put on this earth to do: be the undisputed heavyweight champion of the world. Second, you are going to get your girl back. Grovel like no man ever before. You do *not* give up on her."

I stand and walk over to Luca, pulling him into an embrace as my emotions overwhelm me. *I'm finally free.*

"I can't tell you how much this means to me. I promise I won't let you down." I clap him hard on the shoulder. "I swear to God, if you need me, you call me. I will always have your back." We may not be brothers in blood, but I love him just as if we were.

"Come on, Keller. We both know I need to stand on my own two feet now. I need to take the lead and finish this. Trust me, I have a plan. I've learned from the best how to take care of myself. Now get the fuck out of here and get your girl."

"Well, I've got a fight to organize and one hell of an apology to plan."

"I don't think an apology is quite gonna cut this one. Persistence is key. Don't let her forget how perfect you are for each other."

I nod, turning on my heel, turning my back on the mafia and walking into my new life.

There isn't a force in the world that could stop me now.

"Let me know when to start my best man speech," Luca shouts down the hall as I leave.

Shaking my head, I let out a chuckle, the first laugh to leave my lips in weeks.

Sienna, baby, I'm coming for you.

CHAPTER THIRTY-ONE

I'm pretty sure I am close to dead.

The only reason I am still breathing at this point is for the tiny sliver of hope that remains in my shattered life.

My baby.

Every sip of water, every slice of toast Maddie forces me to eat is for the baby, not for me.

I don't want to be alive.

My mom was right. I am worthless, and no one will love me. I don't even deserve this child.

After my breakdown at the hospital, I haven't shed a single tear since. Not one.

I feel nothing.

I curl back into a ball and wrap my arms around my stomach, almost as if I am clinging on to the only part of my life I want. The bed dips as Maddie climbs in, wrapping her arms around me, her warm tears drip on my shoulder.

"Sienna, I know you don't want to, but I really need you to talk to me now. It's killing me watching you fade away. You haven't even shown a flicker of emotion since I picked you up from the hospital. Please, Sienna, just give me something. Let me know you are still in there somewhere."

Tears prick behind my eyes. It's the first time since he left that I have felt any emotion.

"I don't know what to do, Maddie. How am I supposed to live without him? How could he do this to me?"

Now I've started, I can't stop. It's like an explosion of pent-up emotion is erupting through me.

"How am I supposed to take care of a baby when I can't even get out of bed? How am I supposed to live the rest of my life without him? How am I ever going to be happy again? Tell me. Help me. What should I do?"

My body starts to tremble. Maddie tightens her grip, resting her hand on top of mine, over my belly.

"You will always have me, Sienna. I promise you. I am not going anywhere. I will help you every step of the way. But I need you to help yourself, too. I love you, but I can't sit here and watch you almost kill yourself."

A sob shakes my body as the tears finally escape. I can barely breathe as my chest heaves for air.

"I'm so sorry, Maddie. I'm so, so sorry."

"It's okay, Si. It will all be okay." She whispers more reassuring things as she strokes my hair, letting me cry my heart out in her embrace.

I cry and cry until there's nothing left. The world fades into darkness and I slip into a deep sleep.

After I finally wake, there's a nagging feeling telling me I need to shower. I need to do something. So, that's what I do. Despite my body aching all over, I make it into the shower and let the water scald me, let it distract me from the pain inside. I cry again until I can't physically force any more tears from my eyes.

I don't even bother looking in the mirror. I know it's not good.

After showering and throwing on some leggings and a jumper, I finally decide to brave it outside of my bedroom. With slow steps, I find my way to the kitchen and flip on the kettle.

"Maddie, do you want a coffee?" I shout and instantly regret it as pain shoots through my ribs, causing me to double over.

"Hey, it's okay. You sit down and I'll make them," she says as she snakes her arm around my waist, taking my weight and walking me to the couch.

The steam from the coffee fills my nose as I breathe it in, clearing my airways.

"How are you feeling, Si?" Maddie asks warily, waiting for me to break down.

"I mean, I made it out of my room, so I guess that's progress." I sigh, staring into my coffee.

"Have you thought about what you are going to do?" she questions.

"About?"

"The baby, are you keeping it? Are you telling Keller?"

Bile rises straight up my throat and into my mouth.

"Of course, I'm keeping it. And no, Keller doesn't need to know. I can't have him walking out on our child, too. I know how that fucks a kid up firsthand."

"Okay. Well, you have a check-up next week. Hopefully soon we will get to see the little bean on the screen!"

Her excitement makes me smile. I guess it's going to be

small steps to recovery. I just don't know how my heart will ever heal from this.

"David asked if he could pop over to see you later. Is that okay?"

No, not really. I don't want to see anyone.

"I guess so," I force out.

"Okay, I'll text him now. It might be nice for you to have your friends around you. We all want to help you, Si."

All I can do is nod in response.

A few hours later, David appears, dashing over to the sofa and smothering me in a hug.

"I'm so happy to see you. I've missed you, baby girl," he says, giving me his best grin.

"I've missed you, too," I lie. I can't miss anyone. I can't feel anything.

He plonks down on the couch between Maddie and me and snakes his arm around me, pulling me into his side.

Just like Keller used to do.

It's all too much; the room starts to spin, and all the air is being sucked out of my lungs.

I can't fucking do this anymore.

"Get out."

"What? What's the matter? Talk to me, baby."

Baby.

I jump out of his embrace, to my feet, staring at him, as hurt flashes across his features. That one word is enough to push me over the edge. Rage burns through me as I hear Keller's voice in my head.

"I said get out!" I scream as I fall to my knees, fighting for breath.

"Shh, Sienna. I've got you," Maddie whispers.

"I can't do this, Maddie. I can't live like this."

She walks me back to my room and helps me get into bed, tucking me in and turning out the lights.

"Just get some rest. I'll come in to check on you soon."

That's the last thing I hear before my mind switches off. I guess the only thing that will heal me is time.

CHAPTER THIRTY-TWO

ONE MONTH LATER.

Of course, the first day of my new job has to be at Kings Gym. The tragic story that is my life wouldn't have it any other way.

Pulling on my favorite pair of gym leggings. The ones that shape my ass perfectly, as Keller used to say, I pair them with a cropped black hoodie and bunch my hair into a high ponytail. Dragging a shimmery lip gloss across my lips, I'm ready to go. Today I feel better, thank God. I haven't even thrown up yet.

Butterflies dance around in my stomach in anticipation of how today will go. Will he be there? How will I feel when I see him? A million questions whirl around in my brain.

These hormones are sending me crazy, I swear.

Of course, he'll bloody be there. It's all over the news: *Keller 'The Killer' Russo has rearranged his unification fight.* Speculations fill the tabloids as to why he bailed on the last fight and how far from the truth they were.

I catch myself in the mirror. I've healed well, considering it's only been a few weeks.

On the outside, it looks like nothing has changed. I'm still the same Sienna, just skinnier and paler. On the inside, though, it's even worse. I'm a shit show. It's exhausting hiding my pain from everyone around me that cares, Maddie and David in particular. I can't bear their sympathy or their sad smiles, their walking on eggshells around me. So I plaster on my best fake smile and carry on with my day. I carry on. I power through, but inside I feel dead.

Keller ripped out my heart and took it with him without so much as a glance back. Now, I just feel numb. I'm back to my normal life. I'm starting my dream job. I'm living with my best friend again, my best friend who is nothing short of a lifesaver. She's dragged me back from the brink, yet again. Without her, I'm certain the darkness would have consumed me.

The thought of seeing Keller has me jittery. I've mourned our relationship and, in my head, I've cut him out of my memory. Yet, I know the minute I lay my eyes on him, everything will come flooding back.

He did and always will own every fiber of me. I just need to accept the fact our love story wasn't a fairytale. It was a fucking nightmare, but now I'm free. I'm miserable, but I'm safe and I'm free. I have more important things to concentrate on now.

As I grab my rucksack from the counter, Maddie whirls around. Giving me one of her big smiles, she races over to wrap me up in a hug.

"Good luck today, Si," she whispers in my ear.

Resting her hands on my shoulders, she leans back to look me in the eye.

"You stay strong. You've survived all of this without

him. I'm so proud of you." Her eyes glisten over as she speaks.

I give her a small nod. "Thank you, Maddie. I couldn't have done this without you."

I give her a quick peck on the cheek and head out.

Enzo is quick on my tail as I exit the building. I snap my head round and scowl, our usual interaction at this stage.

He doesn't want to babysit me as much as I don't want to be babysat. But neither of us fancy arguing with Luca and Keller at the moment, so we get on with it. He is always the gentleman. He opens the passenger door and nods as I slide in, then jumps into the driver's seat.

I turn my neck to look at him and open my mouth to speak, but the words don't come.

His eyebrow twitches up as he turns on the ignition to the jeep.

"I hear you have an itch that needs scratching by me, Sienna," he says, in his thick Italian accent.

Don't get me wrong, he's totally my type. Tall and muscular with jet black hair, tousled in a rough quiff on top. Like me, he has piercing blue eyes, but they contrast against his olive skin perfectly. His white teeth emerge as he breaks out into a grin. The first time I've seen the man smile. *He should do that more often,* I think.

"Oh, God, I'm so sorry. I don't know what I was thinking. I wanted to piss Keller off and it was the first thing I thought of." A red flush of embarrassment creeps up my neck.

"The first thing you thought of was fucking me? Good to know." He winks at me.

Playfully whacking his arm, I let out a laugh. It feels nice to actually laugh.

"Sorry if I got you in trouble. In fact, I'm sorry for being a raging bitch since you started babysitting my sorry ass. I'm not usually such a cow, I promise."

A sadness flashes across his eyes, and he quickly recovers himself, shuffling in his seat.

"I know how it feels to lose the one person you love in this life, Sienna. It fucking guts you and leaves you a shell of a person. But your person is still here. You never know, maybe there is hope for your heart after all."

He shuffles in his seat, gripping the steering wheel so his knuckles turn white.

"Keller made a mistake–a fucking big one. He did it for the right reasons. He sacrificed himself for your safety. I would do the same thing. It might hurt, but maybe think about why he did it. You know he loves you fiercely, maybe too much. You two need to heal apart to come back fighting stronger together. Don't give up too soon." There's a softness in his tone as he stares out of the windshield.

"Maybe. Thank you for understanding. Shall we call this a truce?" I ask, resting my hand lightly on top of his.

"A truce is fine by me."

We stay silent for the rest of the journey to Kings Gym, my mind reeling at how my day would play out.

The excited chattering of kids fills the gym as I walk in, tossing my coat on the stand. Grayson spots me immediately and rushes over, pulling me into a bear hug. Wrapping my arms around his strong shoulders, he lifts me up and spins me around. I'm not sure what's got him so happy today, but I can't complain about this greeting. Already he's put me at ease. After gently placing me down, the smile on his face greets me.

"Are you okay? You look pale." His eyes flicker across my face as if assessing my injuries.

"I'm fine," I lie and give him a small smile, as I twiddle with the rim of my hoodie.

"Is he here?" I almost whisper, my eyes darting around the room as if he's going to jump out at me any second. I'm not ready to see him.

Grayson nods as he chews his bottom lip.

"Maybe just hear him out. What harm can it do?"

It could finally break me.

Paula rushes over to me, her white hair pulled into a ponytail which swishes as she moves. Her signature red lipstick is perfectly painted on.

"Sienna, darling, you made it," she says, wrapping me in a big hug. People clearly have a thing for hugging today. It's like I almost died. Oh, wait.

"Let me look at you." Gripping my forearms, she leans back and scans me from head to toe, assessing for injuries. Unless she can see into my brain, she won't see anything.

"I'm so happy to be back at work," I lie. I'm happy to be working with the kids; it's just the choice of the venue that's my issue.

"Come on. We need to see Keller in the office to iron out the formalities for this session. I need my head of events there." She winks, grabbing my hand and pulling me through the gym.

Fuck.

My heart is almost pounding out of my chest. I've never had one, but I could be having a heart attack now.

"Come in!" his voice bellows after her knock. Paula swings open the door. He's there, sitting at his desk, his dark eyes piercing my soul.

It feels like all the oxygen sucks out of my lungs, and a high-pitched ringing fills my eardrums. I rub my sweaty palms along my thighs, hunching over to try and catch my breath. I'm losing it, that last grip I have on reality, slipping.

An electric current shoots from my shoulder. It's him. He's touching me.

"Don't touch me!" I shriek, now almost hyperventilating. The next thing I know, I feel like I'm floating and hear the door slam. The cool leather presses against my skin as I sink into the couch. Squeezing my eyes shut and clenching my fists, I focus on my breathing. Just like Maddie and I practice.

I slowly creep my eyes open, and Keller's worried face fills my vision.

"Baby, it's me. Are you okay?" There's concern in his raspy voice as he strokes my hair out of my face. I bolt myself upright to be rid of his touch. It's too much, he's too much.

"Paula, can we have a second?"

"Yes. Yes, of course. Sienna, I'll be just outside." Her eyes wide as she turns and leaves.

"What was that, Sienna? Are you still sick?"

"I'm no concern of yours anymore, Keller," I snap. Gone is the panic, replaced by pure rage.

"You'll always be my concern, baby."

"You don't get to call me that anymore. You don't get to care. You lost that right when you walked out on me. I'm broken beyond repair. What you did is worse than Jamie. I healed from that. The scars you left me with will run for eternity."

He goes stiff at my words, and his jaw ticks.

"One day, I promise you I'll heal every single scar. I won't give up until I prove myself to you, Sienna. I've never, ever stopped loving you. I'm going to show you, prove to you I'm worthy of you."

"Good luck. You'll be waiting an eternity. I'm not sure I have a heart left to love with. No thanks to you. Maybe in another lifetime, we can get it right, but not this one."

He cups my face with both his hands and lifts my chin so I'm forced to meet his eyes. I want to shake him off, yet my mind and body don't seem to be communicating. "Tell me you don't feel this. Tell me you don't love me anymore."

"I-I don't," I stutter. I can't bring myself to say the words.

"Say it. Say, 'I don't love you, Keller.'" His nose is now touching mine.

Goosebumps erupt across my skin. My damn body always reacts to him, no matter how pissed I am.

"I-I–" Nope, still no words. I let out a deep sigh, dropping my gaze to the floor.

"Baby, look at me."

I do. He consumes me. He says jump, I ask how high, like a puppet. And he's my master.

"I am so fucking sorry. I wish I could go back in time and change that day. I should never have left you. You were better off without me, that's what I thought. A part of me still does. But I can't live without you, Sienna. You own my mind, body, and soul. You saved me. I'm just so sorry I ruined us. Please forgive me. I'm begging you to give me another chance."

A single tear escapes his bloodshot eyes. This powerful hitman kneels before me, begging for forgiveness, pouring his heart out. Part of me wants to jump into his arms, tell him I love him and that everything will be okay.

But it's not enough.

His words aren't enough to mend my broken heart, to trust he won't break me again.

"It's not enough," I sigh. I can't bring myself to look at

him. Taking in a deep breath, I find the words I need to let out for closure.

"Words mean nothing, Keller. I appreciate your apology, I really do, but I need more. I need someone that knows I'm enough, enough to stay when it gets tough. I need someone that's all in. You don't know what it means to love. Maybe in another lifetime we'll find each other and have the fairytale ending we deserve."

Tears threaten to spill as I pick myself up and walk out the door, not giving him a second glance. The strongest man on the planet breaking to pieces in front of me didn't give me any satisfaction at all.

The session goes on without a hitch. The kids all have a blast with Grayson. Keller never appeared again. Saying my goodbyes to them all and giving Paula a quick hug, I meet Enzo outside, and he walks me to his blacked out Jeep parked across the street.

"Tough day?" he asks as we set off home.

"That's one way to put it," I mumble, and he merely nods in understanding, turning up the music to fill the silence.

The phone blaring in my eardrums wakes me with a start. It feels like I closed my eyes five minutes ago.

Paula's name flashes on the screen. *Shit.*

"Hello," I croak out, my mouth as dry as the Sahara after spending most of the night being sick. Who was it that named this morning sickness? Fuck, I wish it was just in the morning and not all day and night.

"Sienna, oh my god. You have to come and meet me. Something absolutely incredible has happened and I need you here. You can't miss this," she rambles. It's far too early for this kind of excitement.

I quickly remember she's my boss before I moan down the phone and respond like a petulant child.

"Ok, just text me the address. What sort of time are we thinking?" I ask, in hopes she'll say something at least four hours from now.

"Can you be there in an hour?"

Lord, give me strength. I check the time: 6:30 am.

"That… should be ok. I'll text you when I'm on my way."

"Oh, Sienna, I can't wait to see your face."

It best be good.

An hour later, Enzo is pulling up outside a unit towards the outskirts of Manhattan. Safe to say he was less than impressed with my early wake up call. He looks as tired as me, with his hair disheveled and eyes still a slight tinge of red.

The best I could muster was a pair of black leggings with a knitted dark gray dress, and I quickly threw on my Doc Martens and a black puffer. New York still hasn't let up on the freezing weather, so I'm glad I grabbed my chunky scarf and gloves before I left.

"Well, this is the address," Enzo dryly announces, as he pulls into a derelict industrial unit housing two large metal structures. The one on the left has a large lilac sign with 'The Hideaway' written in white lettering. Zipping my coat up, I make my way over to the brightly lit entrance. I'm guessing Paula's in here.

As I step over the entrance, I stop dead in my tracks. In front of me stands a completely renovated unit, sectioned into different areas. Scanning the room, there's a foam-floored play area brimming with brightly colored toys, a collection of chairs huddled in the corner around a floor to ceiling bookcase, filled with book collections. The back corner is a mini boxing gym, complete with black-padded flooring with a red canvas punching bag hanging from the ceiling. I can hear rustling from behind the double doors. "Paula, are you in here? It's me, Sienna," I call out.

Paula appears from the doorway, her shiny white hair curled and that red lipstick painted on her lips. How she looks this good at the crack of dawn I'll never know. Excitement radiates from her as she spots me.

"Oh, Sienna, darling. Isn't this just wonderful?!" she announces, flinging her hands in the air.

"I mean, yeah, this looks great, but am I missing something?"

God, have I forgotten some crucial information here? The place is great, but I have no idea what it has to do with me being here at 7:30 am on my day off.

"Well, Sienna, this is The Hideaway. A safe space for our kids should they need it. Complete with a new office for us to work from."

"Wow, that's-that's great Paula. Why didn't you tell me about this sooner? I could have helped. Do we have the funding for this?" I blurt out without even thinking.

I've seen our accounts. We are nowhere near ready to have this kind of setup yet.

"You'll have to thank Mr. Russo himself. He's funded and designed this whole place. He's spent weeks perfecting it, working closely with the kids to build their ideal hideaway."

A smile creeps up my face.

This place is perfect. My thoughts immediately go to Max; he would love this space.

"Wow, I don't know what to say. This is absolutely perfect. I can't wait to see the kids' faces. This is going to be game changing for us, Paula." Excitement is bubbling through me as I speak, the first genuine emotion I've felt in a long time, and I have Keller to thank for that.

"Mr. Russo has a kind heart beneath that hard exterior. He tells me he was a product of the state's foster system. He had a tough time; he knows how important this is for them. Speaking of..." Her eyes twinkle as she speaks of him.

I nod along as she speaks, a knot forming in my stomach as Enzo's words replay over and over in my head.

"Maybe it's not too late."

Muffled sobbing catches my attention from behind the stud wall in front of me. I shoot Paula a questioning look.

She drops her head slightly, letting out a small sigh.

"It's Max."

Dread fills my stomach.

"What's happened? Is he okay?"

That poor kid never catches a break. He's only seven, for Christ's sake.

"His mom's missing. I found him living at home on his own. He's been there for the last two days. I couldn't get hold of her to sign off on his boxing training next week, so I popped around. Found him crying his heart out on a stripped bed, shouting out for his mom."

"Shit."

Anger simmers. My heart breaks for him. He's been through far too much already. That goddamn woman needs a slap.

I tiptoe over to the doorway; Paula grabs my hand, bringing me to an abrupt stop.

"Keller is in there with him. Max was asking for him, so I called him and he came straight here. He's been with him since 5 am. Heart of gold, that one."

I slowly nod in response, nerves filling my stomach.

I'm doing this for Max, not for Keller. Max needs me. My heart flutters in my chest. I can't help my reaction to Keller, even if I try.

She releases my hand and I peer through the doorway. My breath catches in my throat as I take in the sight before me, tears welling in my eyes. It's a little bedroom, complete with bunk beds on either side of the wall. Little Max sits on Keller's lap, nestled tightly against him, muffling his sobs. His chest heaves up and down whilst Keller cuddles his small body with his muscular arms, his head resting on top of Max's.

My feet are planted on the floor. I can't move. My stomach erupts into butterflies. At this moment, the hatred I feel fizzles away. I forget what he did.

Keller's eyes, filled with sadness, shoot to mine as he gives me a small smile, one I can't help but return.

My legs move without thinking. I dart over to them and perch down on the bed next to them. Max's tear-stained face peels from Keller's chest to look at me.

"Max, baby, are you okay?" I ask, as I gently stroke his short blonde hair.

He quickly nods and throws his head back into Keller.

"Thank you," I mouth to Keller, not wanting to interrupt their moment. He seems to have it under control.

I stand to leave and Keller's hand shoots out to mine. Bolts of electricity pass through my fingers, lighting my whole body.

"Stay. Please."

His eyes are pleading with me, so I sit back down. His

powerful arm wraps around my shoulder and pulls me into his side. I settle into this familiar feeling and suddenly start to feel whole again as I place my arm around Max and close my eyes.

We sit quietly together with Max. As the little boy's heart-wrenching sobs continue to fill the room, all three of us cuddled together.

Almost like a family.

"Max, darling, how about we go get some hot chocolates? We can get them with extra cream and marshmallows if you like. What do you say?"

Paula's interruption yanks me back down to reality. Max's sobbing subsides for a second as he looks to Keller for reassurance. Keller simply smiles and nods to him. Max peels himself from Kellers's lap and pads over to Paula, not before turning to give us a bright smile, a naughty smile even, and then runs off towards the front door.

"I'll see you both later. Sienna, this is our new office now, so meet you here Monday morning?"

"Sounds good to me, Paula."

She gives us a quick wave and ushers Max out.

My attention now zeroes in on the warmth of Keller's touch, and I jolt away from him and jump to my feet. Hurt is clear on his face as he then bows his head.

"I have to go. Thank you for being there for Max. You're great with him, Keller."

"Can I show you something?"

His bloodshot eyes snap to mine. Despite looking as though he's barely slept, he is still so sexy.

"I don't think that's a good idea."

I don't trust myself around him. I want to hate him, but I just can't.

"Please."

Enzo's words dance around in my brain. The image of Keller cuddling a broken little Max. This might be a massive mistake, but something inside me screams at me to say yes.

"Okay."

CHAPTER THIRTY-THREE

keller

When Paula called early this morning, I didn't hesitate to jump in the car and come to Max. I knew how it felt to be abandoned. Hell, I was in his shoes once. All I wanted was for someone to tell me it was going to be okay.

Maybe if I did, I would have turned out a hell of a lot better.

As I walk Sienna to the car parked around the back of the unit, her eyes never meet mine, and she twiddles her thumbs while she walks. My heart is racing, being so close to her. All I want to do is scoop her up into my arms and tell her how much I miss her, how much I fucking love her.

I know I can't.

I'm so worried about her. She has no spark. She must have lost over ten pounds now. Her face is drawn, which just emphasizes the gray haze on her complexion.

It fucking kills me that I have done this to her.

I've pushed her too far; so far, I don't know if she will ever forgive me. The moment back in the room where she melted into my embrace, all the tension built up within her visibly left her body. It felt like I was home. For those few minutes, everything was right in the world again.

On the drive to our destination, she keeps her eye line straight out the windshield, her nervous tell evident as she picks at the skin surrounding her chipped maroon fingernails.

"So, what is it you wanted to show me?" she asks.

"Ah, now that would ruin the surprise, baby."

Her breath just slightly hitches at my words. Shit, I don't want to scare her away before we even get there. After seeing the panicked state she got into after seeing me at the gym the other day, I realized I had a long way to go to get back into her heart. I just hope her hatred isn't stronger than her love for me.

We drive in silence. I catch her glancing at me a few times. Just having her back in my company brings calmness to my life.

Pulling into the drive, I stop outside the large, black metal gates, lowering my window. The icy breeze blows into the car. Leaning over, I pad in the security code–*110620*. The night we met–a night that changed the course of my life forever.

The gates slowly open, and I make our way down the gravel drive, either side surrounded by acres of green, sparkling in the morning frost. Finally, the magnificent mansion comes into view. A fifteen bedroom estate, painted white, with ivory climbing to the roof. It might not look perfect now, but it will once I've finished with it.

I park next to the gray stone, round water fountain, and let out the breath I'm sure I've been holding since we entered the gate. Sienna's eyes fixate on the building before her, her plump lips slightly ajar.

"Wow."

“Wanna come see inside?”

“Oh my gosh, yes! This is the kind of place you read about in books. It’s beautiful.”

The excitement in her voice makes my heart flutter.

I lead her in through the archway to the wooden front door. Grabbing the key from my jeans pocket, I slip it into the lock and push, motioning for her to walk over the threshold. Her face lights up as she scans the home. Our home. One day, I hope.

A grand staircase greets us as we walk through. Don’t get me wrong, this place needs a facelift. It needs those finishing touches to bring out its character. That’s the plan, a place for us to create together and call our home forever. Everything at the moment is outdated, from the orange tinted kitchen units to the dark red frayed carpets. Despite that, Sienna is still in awe of its beauty.

It’s why I bought the damn place. As soon as I saw the listing, I envisioned Sienna sitting cross-legged by an open fire, surrounded by her filthy book collection all stacked in her ceiling-high bookcase. I imagined the gym we could build, the nursery, the acres of land for a dog to run around. Money doesn’t mean anything to me. I want a home, a family. I want it all, only, with her.

Turning her attention to me, she cocks a brow. “So, I’m assuming this place is yours?”

“You’d be correct.” I close the distance between us, desire crackling through the air.

“Apart from one minor detail,” I say, as I tuck a loose strand of hair behind her ear. She shivers under my touch.

“And what would that be?” she asks playfully, her pearly white teeth appearing from her grin.

“This place is *ours*, not mine,” I whisper. Her body stiffens in response.

"Why?" she says as she lets out a breath.

"I want us to build a home together. Something we create that we love every inch of. A place to grow a family. As soon as I saw the listing, my mind immediately thought of you. I saw us growing old here together. I couldn't bring myself to go back to the penthouse after what happened there. The guilt has been eating me up. I don't expect you to forgive me right now. I don't expect you to want to move in with me, either. I... just wanted to show you how serious I am about you, about our future. This house and I will be here waiting until you're ready."

I hope it doesn't take long, but I'm prepared to wait for as long as it takes for her to find her way back to me.

"Oh, Keller," she sobs, nestling her face into my chest. I stroke her silky hair as she lets it all out. Tears sting my eyes as I take in a shaky breath. I've broken her. Wetness soaks through my hoodie. These are tears I have caused.

"Shh, Baby. I'm so sorry, Sienna. I'm so sorry I've hurt you so badly." I choke out the words.

"Why did you have to leave me?" her barely audible voice whispers through sobs.

Using my thumbs to hook under her chin, I pull her head up to look at me. As she sniffles, I gently pad under her eyes, chasing her tears away. "I promise you I will never, ever leave your side again. I will never cause you pain like this again. I will cherish your heart over my own. I will love you until the day I die, and then I'll love you through eternity." My voice breaks as I let it all out to her.

"I'm starting to understand, Keller. It just fucking hurts so much that you could break my heart like that. That you could break me."

"I know. I would give up everything I have to go back in time and stand by your side. I thought I was protecting you by ripping out my own heart. I was completely and utterly wrong. For the rest of my life, I will regret that." I offer her a sad smile. "I love you, princess. Always and forever. Even if you never forgive me, you'll always own my heart."

We stare into each other's eyes for a few moments, nothing else matters.

"Kiss me," she whispers, so quietly I barely register her words.

Stunned, I look at her, her eyes red and blotchy, her skin pale, yet she's still the most beautiful woman I have ever laid eyes on.

"I said, 'kiss me'," she repeats, this time louder.

Lowering my lips to hers, I capture them with mine, slowly deepening the kiss. Pouring every ounce of love into it. My hands wrap around her hair as my tongue slips into her mouth, lapping her up, our teeth clattering together. She tastes like fresh mint. My cock twitches against my jeans in response, as I let out a low groan into her mouth.

"I've missed you so much, baby," I say as I take her mouth again, this time hungrily. Her arms wrap around my neck.

Regretfully, I pull myself from her, instantly missing her lips on mine. I have to do this the right way. Shock is written across her face as she stands there staring at me, her cheeks flushed and hair now wild, her swollen lips just daring to be taken again.

"I want to do this right, Sienna. I want you to come back to me with your whole heart. No doubts, no concerns, both feet in, ready to live the rest of your life with me."

I can't believe I'm doing this. I have to.

She isn't ready. I can still sense her nervousness around me. She doesn't trust me.

Her arms fold over her chest. "You're doing this to me

now? You're really turning me down?" she shouts, pain flickering through her eyes.

"Yes." The words fall out of my mouth. "All in, baby. I need you all in. I can feel it. You aren't there yet, so I have more work to do."

She lowers her head and lets out a sigh. That's when I wrap her up in a tight embrace and whisper in her ear, "This isn't a goodbye. I'm not giving up–not now, not ever. Everything here will be here waiting for you to come home."

"I can't keep doing this, Keller. Just take me home and leave me alone." She lets out a defeated sigh, and I do as she wishes, the ride home in complete silence. She gets out of the car and slams the door, not even glancing back my way as she storms into her apartment.

Fuck.

I HEAD STRAIGHT TO THE GYM TO DO WHAT I DO BEST. PUNCH shit.

"FUCCCK!" I scream, as I erupt a barrage of punches into the heavy bag. Releasing every ounce of devastation that consumes my body into the leather. It's the only way I know how to cope: to fight. Every muscle in my body is screaming at me to stop. Sweat drips off my forehead into my eyes, my lungs are on fire.

Smashing my head into the bag, I grip around it and take in some deep breaths. Spiraling. I'm spiraling into the darkness, and I've just pushed away my only hope into the light.

I can feel the stares of the rest of the gym beating into

my back as I stand there, almost hyperventilating into a punching bag.

If I'm going to win this fight in a couple of weeks, I have to get my head straight.

That's when it hits me.

The fight.

She wants me to fight for her, to prove to her I'll never abandon her again.

And that's exactly what I'm going to do.

CHAPTER THIRTY-FOUR

sienna

A loud knock at the door startles me from my daydreams as I stare at the amber liquid pouring into my coffee mug. The first week at The Hideaway has flown by. Every day we've had tons of new inquiries to deal with, meaning more and more kids turning up through the doors. It's great to be helping so many kids, but I am exhausted. I physically had to drag myself out of bed this morning and into the shower, every movement an effort.

That reminds me: I need to call the doctor's today. After they discharged me from the hospital, it's been a waiting game to schedule an ultrasound to see if my baby is okay. *Our baby.*

Swiping up the coffee mug filled to the brim, I pad over to the front door and fling it open, only to be greeted by no one.

A black box tied with a shiny gold ribbon lies by my feet. Crouching down, I pick it up and close the door, making my way back to the kitchen.

"Oooh, what's that? Looks fancy," Maddie muses, as she flits into the kitchen, sporting a similar tired look to me. Her hair is bundled on the top of her head and there is mascara smudged under her eyes.

"Not a clue," I respond deadpan, staring at the box, itching to rip it open.

"Well, open it, then. There might be something good in there."

Pulling the bow apart, I lift the lid to reveal another small, black velvet box and a white letter. Keller's all caps handwriting glares at me on the envelope.

"OPEN ME FIRST."

Ripping open the seal, I unravel the letter. Two rectangular tickets falling onto the countertop.

To my Queen,

I can't win this fight without you in my corner.

I want to give you the fairytale you deserve.

I want to make you smile every day.

I want to worship you every night.

I want to love you with everything I have.

I want to make this right.

Without you, there is no light.

That little black box holds the key to my heart for the rest of eternity.

If you're ready to own every inch of me, bring it with you to my fight. Do not open it a second before I tell you.

A driver will pick you and Maddie up at 11 am next Thursday to take you to a private airstrip so you can fly to Vegas. A hotel is booked for the two of you for four nights at the MGM Grand and for two tickets for my fight.

I'm ready to fight for it all.

Are you?

I love you.

My Goddess, My Queen, My World.

Always yours,

Your Champ x x x

My shaky hands place the letter to the side, and my vision blurs from new emotion. Damn hormones.

Maddie rushes over, wrapping me up in a warm hug.

"It's okay, Sienna. Everything is going to be okay. I promise."

For the first time in a long time, I believe her.

I'm going to fight for what I want.

I can't deny my heart any longer.

"How do you fancy a trip to Vegas next week?" Cocking my eyebrow, I turn to Maddie.

Her face lights up with excitement. "Shut the fuck up! Oh. My. God." She grabs the tickets from the side, shaking them in the air.

"Yes, yes, yes, yes. A million times, yes!"

The spark in me lights back up with a new determination. I'm going to get my man back.

Grabbing the smooth velvet box between my fingers, I

twiddle it in front of my face. I want to open it; surprises kill me. But I'm going to trust him. Keller always has a plan. I'll just have to wait a few days. I place it, with the tickets, back in the bigger box, then slide it across the counter, away from me, and resist the urge to peek.

"Well, looks like we're off to Vegas, baby."

Maddie bounces in excitement. "Is it too early to pop some champagne?"

"I wish," I chuckle, rolling my eyes at my excitable best friend.

"Oh shit, sorry! Does this mean you forgive him?"

"Yes," I reply with certainty.

"If he ever does anything to hurt you again, I'll kill him with my bare hands."

The thought alone of Maddie even attempting to hurt Keller has me erupting in a belly laugh.

"I'm being serious. I know people."

Oh, Maddie. She has no clue.

"Okay, okay. Noted Mrs. Smith."

"In all seriousness, Si, I'm happy for you. He brings out a spark in you no one else ever could. You deserve this. You both deserve a lifetime of love."

I pull my best friend back into an embrace. I know she longs for the same thing. "Thank you, Maddie. I love you."

"I love you, too, Si. Now, go get ready for work. The quicker you go, the quicker you get home for some non-alcoholic prosecco and karaoke session with yours truly."

Shaking my head with a laugh, I do just that.

Just one more week until my heart is mended.

"What do you mean you've had to move my appointment back? I have a flight to catch; I leave at 11." I nearly shout down the phone, anger boiling as Patricia, the *ever helpful* doctor's receptionist, continues to tap her acrylics on the keyboard, making me want to rip those nails from her fingers.

"We had an emergency. I can get you in at 10:20."

It's only round the corner. If I can get back from the appointment by 10:50, I won't miss the lift to the airport.

"Fine," I huff.

"See you then, Miss Anderson." Sarcasm drips from her snotty tone.

I cut the call and slam my phone down on the sofa.

Fucking bitch.

We stacked our luggage next to the front door. Clearly, we've taken enough for a month's trip to Vegas, but we need multiple outfit choices for Keller's fight. I'm already starting to show, and I want to surprise Keller with the news. Therefore, all my outfits are justified. Or so I'm telling myself, anyway.

"Jesus, who were you shouting at this early?" Maddie asks.

"The stupid bloody doctor's receptionist. They moved my appointment forward to 10:20 instead of 9:20. If I don't take this one, I have to wait another three weeks, *apparently*."

"Huh, why are you going to the doctor?" Concern shows on her face as she speaks.

"It's just a check-up. You know, after what happened, they want to make sure the little one is growing okay."

"Do you need me to go with you?"

"It's okay; you just get packed and ready to go. I promise to bring back a scan picture."

I give her a smile to hide my nerves. Today I find out if they are healthy. After everything, it would be a miracle to have even gotten this far. *Please be okay, my little one.*

THE CLINICAL SMELL ASSAULTS MY NOSE AS I WALK INTO THE doctor's office at 10:18 on the dot. I can't risk that bitch in reception telling me I've missed my appointment.

Patricia signs me in, shooting me a fake smile with her stupidly long glittery nails, still jabbing into that damn keyboard, making my ears want to bleed.

"Miss Anderson?" a doctor calls.

Following him into a private room, I spy a blue bed laid out in the center and a monitor standing next to it.

My palms begin to sweat. I wish I had Keller with me right now. He deserves to be here. I didn't want to add any more worry to him before his fight. I have to know they are okay before I tell him anything. Plus, he wants to surprise me with this black box, which is still killing me. So, then, I can do the same.

"So Miss Anderson, let's get you up on the bed. If you can lift your sweater and just tuck under your pants, we can have a little look through the ultra scan."

"Okay." I nod, as I take a deep breath and get up onto the bed. With shaky fingers, I lift up my top and expose my stomach.

"This will be a little cold, okay?"

I simply nod, holding my breath as I wait.

The monitor springs to life, black and white floating across the screen. Squinting, I try to make out anything, but it's no use; it's all just a black and white blur.

The doctor pushes further into my stomach with the cold probe, sliding it up and down. The whooshing on the monitor remains the same. As the moments pass, dread fills me.

"Ah-ha! There you are, little one."

My eyes snap up to the screen as a rapid heartbeat fills the room.

A little alien-looking thing wiggles on the screen.

Our little alien.

After taking a few measurements, he confirms I am roughly twelve weeks pregnant. I've left with a mountain of paperwork and appointment reminders. Due to the trauma I've been through recently with my symptoms, they want to keep a close eye on me. Our little alien looks to be thriving. Another fighter to enter the world.

As I exit the building, my emotions threaten to bubble over, until I quickly check the time on my phone.

11:15.

Shit! I race back to the apartment, my lungs burning as I run up the stairs and throw the door open.

Maddie stands staring into a cup of steaming coffee.

"Has the driver left?"

A frown crinkles her forehead as she nods.

"Did you explain to him what happened?" Irritation is clear in my tone.

"Obviously. He didn't give a shit. As soon as I told him you weren't here, he rolled the window up and drove off. A complete miserable asshole. I've even tried calling Grayson, but he just went straight to voicemail."

"Why can't anything just go right in my life for once?" I shout, snatching my phone out of my coat pocket and dialing Keller, who goes straight to answerphone.

Fuck it, I will get to Vegas.

The thought of Keller believing I wasn't turning up for him when he needs me makes me feel physically sick.

"Looks like we're slumming it in commercial then. You grab the laptop and I'll grab my credit card. We *will* get to Vegas."

CHAPTER THIRTY-FIVE

keller

"How much longer can we hold take-off?" I quiz the co-pilot, whose standing hand on hip glaring at me.

I've already demanded ten extra minutes and now his patience is wearing thin.

Well, so is mine, asshole.

Luca's hand firmly grips my shoulder from the seat next to me.

"Keller, we have to go. We can't wait for her to *maybe* turn up. You have a weigh-in this evening. If she were coming, she would have been here by now. I'm sorry." His tone is rough with regret.

Sadness overtakes my body as I sag back into the leather seats, admitting defeat.

The haunting realization slamming into me like a ton of bricks.

I've lost her.

For good this time.

CHAPTER THIRTY-SIX

keller

My satin robe skims along my forearms as I pace the room, throwing swift jabs into the air.

Where the fuck is Grayson? It's ten minutes before I walk out.

The nerves never go away. My twentieth professional fight and I'm still jittery with adrenaline.

My body stills at the sound of Sienna's sweet voice; it can't be.

"I'm his girlfriend. I have to see him. It's an emergency. Just let me through." Her voice creeps louder and louder.

Fuck this.

"Let her through. Now!" I bellow, and the guards part like the red sea, allowing Sienna to come into view. Her icy blue eyes pierce into me, and my breath hitches as she launches toward me. She's glowing. I can hardly believe my eyes. Her face lights up as she reaches me, her infectious smile brings my heart back to life. She leaps into my arms, and I dart out to catch her, my damn gloves getting in the way.

Sienna's legs hook around my waist. How, in that black dress, I don't know. She nuzzles into my neck, and her warm breath beats against my skin, sending shockwaves straight to my cock. I bury my head into the top of her hair, taking in my favorite scent. Her. That peach washes over me, and all the nerves and the dread dissipates in this moment. I see no one else but her.

"I love you, Keller. I love you so fucking much. Without you, I can't live. I'm miserable. I feel like half of my heart is missing."

I choke on a sob and bury my head further into her.

"I forgive you, Keller. Now, please forgive yourself. Let the darkness go. Drop that mask. I want it all, forever," she rambles almost breathlessly as she gets her words out.

The best words anyone's ever said to me.

"Oh, baby," I croak out. "I fucking love you, Sienna. I need you like I need air to breathe. Without you, my life's meaningless. You, my queen, are my light in the darkness. And I promise I will spend every damn day of the rest of my life worshiping you."

"Keller, wrap it up. It's time," Grayson announces from beside me. I am so wrapped up in Sienna, I almost forget where I am.

Her gaze sears with mine, her eyes swimming with emotion, with love. I see the flicker of desire burning in the background. She peers over my shoulder and then brings her lips to meet my earlobe, gently grazing along the lobe.

"Go out there and show them how a World Champion fights. Then come and find me and show me how one fucks," she says in a sultry tone.

A hunger glimmers in her hooded eyes, and I quickly steal a kiss, slamming my lips to hers as she moans into my mouth.

My dirty girl is certainly back.

Unwrapping her legs, she slides down my body and straightens her dress. Her red fuck-me heels accentuate her toned legs, making my mouth water.

Damn. Do I have plans involving them later.

"I'll see you on the other side, princess. Practice screaming my name at the top of your lungs." I give her a wink as she slaps my ass when I breeze past her.

I chuckle to myself as I make my way to the walkout. This fucking woman will be the death of me. My firecracker's found her spark, and now I'm minutes away from the biggest fight of my life, sporting a semi.

I wouldn't have it any other way.

Now to win this fight and get the girl... forever this time.

THE MGM GRAND IS FULL TO THE RAFTERS, OVER SIXTEEN thousand fans cheering as I make my way to the walkout. The crowd goes silent as the lights shine on the walkway. It's now or never.

DMX's 'X Gon' Give it to Ya' blasts through the arena, sending chills down my spine.

Security gives me the nod. I bow my hooded head and make the slow walk to the ring.

The crowd cheers my name; I'm the home fighter and I have their support. Yet none of that matters. All that matters is having my woman behind me, fighting in my corner.

I duck under the ropes and stride to my red corner. Grayson and my team are all sporting my signature black and red branding. We stand and wait for my opponent,

Dmitry Selimov. He stands three inches shorter and ten pounds lighter. He might have the upper hand on speed, but I match that tenfold with my power.

The last few weeks, I've trained. I've studied. On my feet, I am lighter. I'm ready.

He enters the ring, his bald head reflecting against the bright lights.

"Go give him hell, Keller. Be smart. Take your time; he's rash. Defend and strike," Grayson shouts over the roaring of the crowd, his spit hitting the side of my face. I nod in return. I know the plan. I have lived and breathed it for weeks. Opening my mouth wide, he shoves in the guard, and I rotate around as he removes the robe. All 240 pounds of pure muscle are on display for the world.

The white-haired ring announcer, suited in his black bowtie, proceeds to start the fight. Only a few moments before the bell goes. The crowd morphs into a sea of blurred faces, all bar one. The only face here tonight that matters.

"Tonight, ladies and gentlemen, you are going to witness a moment in history. A title fight to crown the undisputed heavyweight champion of the world. In the red corner, we have Keller 'the KILLER' Russo." The crowd wildly cheers my name. "From New York, USA, weighing in at 241 lbs, the current IBF, WBO and WBA heavyweight champion. With an impressive 19 wins, 18 by knockout. In the blue corner, we have Dmitry 'the Hitman' Selimov. Flying in from Moscow, Russia, weighing in at 230 lbs, holding the WBC belt. A record of 15 wins, 10 by knockout. I want a clean fight tonight."

We tap gloves and give each other a nod, jogging back to our corners.

"MGM Grand, Let's get ready to RUMBLE!!!"

Ding, ding, ding.

The moment I hear the bell ring, the nerves disappear. I see nothing other than my Russian opponent charging toward me.

Dmitry makes the first move, a sloppy left jab which I easily duck away from. I retaliate with a quick combination. His gloves are up as he defends. This is just my warm up. I won't unleash the beast for another four rounds, at least.

We dance around the ring, him throwing sloppy combinations. He wasn't expecting me to have perfected my footwork, and I'm quick to dart away from his predictable punches.

The bell signals the end of the round as I make my way back to the corner, but not before giving Dmitry a killer grin.

"Keep the pace, Keller. He's playing you. We know he fights better than this. He's trying to find your weakness. Don't fucking give him one," Grayson barks.

"Got it, boss," I say before my guard's put back in.

As the rounds progress, Dmitry gets stronger, neutralizing my attacks with uppercuts. He's been going through the gears up to now, but it seems like he's reached his top. I've only just started.

Each round, Grayson assures me I'm on the upper foot. We're dancing around, throwing punches, and defending. Waiting for the moment one of us slips.

Round 7: the bell rings. I need to end this now. I'm done pussy footing around. My lungs are burning, every muscle screaming at me to take him out. I land a series of hits; Dmitry stumbles but recovers quickly, leaving me open for an attack. He unloads a series of shots. I'm quick to cover my face with my gloves as he unloads body shots straight into my ribs. The pain sears through my body. That only ignites the beast inside me. My back against the ropes, he launches his right glove toward my head and misses, leaving his weakness open. I duck left from his glove and quickly switch to attack, throwing a barrage of punches as he leaves himself exposed.

Dimitry is clearly exhausted as his chest is heaving for air. He jabs his left hand straight at me, connecting with my jaw. I don't feel the pain. Quickly shaking my head, I decide this is it.

With his left arm still out, he's mine to take. I unleash an assault of uppercuts on the right side of his body, which sends him stumbling backward, his knees wobbling. The opportunity stares me right in the face.

His eyes go wide as my right uppercut connects with the underside of his jaw. Sweat sprays off him as his head darts back and his body follows. He stumbles once before he drops, thudding to the canvas.

The ref flies over, crouching beside him. He taps–1, 2, 3. On all fours, Dmitry slowly lifts his head. He doesn't have the strength to pull himself up. 5, 6, 7, 8. He slams his head back on the canvas.

I fucking did it!

The stadium erupts. Sweat merged with my blood drips over my eyebrows. I thrust my left glove into the air to signify my victory. Grayson and my team leap over the ropes and rush towards me.

"You fucking did it, Keller. I'm so fucking proud of you." Grayson grabs my shoulders and slams his body against mine.

That's when I spot her.

The world goes still.

In a room of over sixteen thousand people, she's the first one I see. The only one I see.

Her dazzling blue eyes pierce into my heart as she wipes

away her tears, overcome with emotion. She's standing and clapping hysterically. Awareness creeps over her features as she gives me an earth-shattering smile and blows me a kiss. I give her a wink and mouth, "I love you."

She has no idea what I've got up my sleeve.

CHAPTER THIRTY-SEVEN

I gasp as his glove connects with the side of Keller's jaw. His body barely moves an inch in response to the hit.

I may not be a boxing expert, but I know my champ is the better fighter here. Every punch he throws is more powerful than the last. The sweat coating his strapping physique glistens under the lights. With every punch, his strong muscles ripple. He belongs up there. He owns those titles.

I can't lie. Watching him compete in the ring is making me hot.

Even with his eyes burning with focus, he looks sexy. It could be the hormones or the lack of sex these last few weeks. I squeeze my legs together and shuffle awkwardly on the seat, just imagining massaging every single worn out muscle on his body.

Pull yourself together, Sienna.

Distracted by my thoughts, it all happens in slow motion. Keller's right glove connects perfectly with the underside of his opponent's jaw, sending him hurtling through the air and landing with a thud.

The room goes silent as the ref counts to eight.

The longest eight seconds of my life so far.

Holding my breath, I stand, chewing on my fingernails.

The referee throws up Keller's right arm in victory, and the entire room erupts with cheers.

"Holy shit, Sienna. He fucking did it!" Maddie exclaims from the seat next to me, jumping up and down, clapping, spraying her champagne all over the floor.

Emotion overcomes me. I'm so proud of him. Tears flow freely down my cheeks as I break out into a smile. These are happy tears.

Wiping them away, I join the chants of his name filling the arena. I can't take my eyes off him. Every part of me wants to leg it over there and pounce on him. I don't think being tackled by a security guard is a clever idea, though.

Goosebumps erupt all over my skin as Keller's dark gaze meets mine and he mouths, "I love you." A warm fuzzy feeling melts my insides.

God, I love this man.

The ring is now buzzing with different men, all dressed in similar dark outfits, buzzing around Keller. He's posing with all four of his belts covering his body, two wrapped around his waist and one draped over each arm. Once they are removed and the camera stops flashing, one of his team passes him a black microphone as the lights illuminate the ring in white, leaving the crowd in darkness.

"We fucking did it. Undisputed Heavy Weight Champion of the fucking world." His deep voice booms throughout the entire arena, the crowd whooping in response.

"First up, I want to thank my best friend and trainer for kicking my ass into shape and reorganizing this fight," he says as he nods to Grayson, who's beaming at Keller like a proud dad.

"There's also someone else here in the crowd tonight."

All the air leaves my body as two security guards zone in on me. My heart is pounding through my chest. "Come on up here, baby, and bring that black box."

Shit. The box. Maddie's eyes on stalks and her jaw is almost on the floor; I look at her, almost pleading for help.

She quickly snatches my clutch off the floor and rummages through, thrusting that small black box into my shaking fingers.

"Go, Sienna. Go get your man."

The tall security man offers me his hand. I graciously take it. I need someone to lean on. My legs are wobbling all over the place in these red heels. He ushers me up the stairs to the ring, pulling the ropes apart as I duck underneath. Keller's abs greet me as I straighten up the other side.

"What are you doing, Keller?" I whisper in embarrassment, keeping my head down.

I hear him let out a full bellied chuckle. It eases me for a second. He leans down, heat radiates off him as he whispers only loud enough for me to hear.

"This is our moment, baby. Pass me that box."

He holds out his palm. I instantly recognize those familiar white hand wraps and a blush creeps over my cheeks in the memory of that night.

He drops down to one knee with a thud, the floor vibrating beneath me.

I let out a gasp as I cover my quivering mouth with my trembling hands.

"Sienna. From the moment you hurled your perfect body on my lap and grabbed my dick like a gear stick, I knew you were it for me."

The crowd erupts into a mixture of laughs and cheers. A hiccupped laugh escapes my lips, jolting my body. Tears threatening to explode any second.

"When I lost you, I lost myself. I lost everything I'd ever wanted. My world crumbled. You keep my world spinning, you bring me literally to my knees. I want to spend every second of every day loving you how you deserve to be loved. Like the queen that you are. You've dragged me out of the shadows. Taught me how incredible it is to be loved and love in return."

Warm tears spill down my cheeks as he speaks. His eyes are filled with the warmth of his love, yet worry drips from his tone. Slowly opening the box displayed in front of me, the glimmering emerald-cut diamond appears, twinkling under the stage lighting.

Holy shit.

"You own my heart, Sienna. It will only ever be you. Please give me forever. Marry me?"

His words penetrate every wall I've put up around my heart, shattering my resolve. My hands instinctively place themselves across my lower abdomen. "Yes." The simple word falls from my lips. "Yes, yes, yes," I sob, darting towards him, dropping to my knees to meet him on the floor.

He grips the back of my head and smashes his lips down onto mine, pouring every ounce of passion and love into his kiss.

"I fucking love you," he mumbles through kisses.

The flashing and clicking of the cameras brings me back

into the room. I wrap my arms around his neck, his sticky, sweaty skin rubbing against my arms.

"How does tomorrow sound?" his deep tone sends shivers down my spine as he whispers just for me to hear.

"I'd prefer tonight." I don't want to wait to become his forever. I already am.

CHAPTER THIRTY-EIGHT

keller

I slip the ring onto her left finger, the sparkling diamond all I can see through my blurry vision.

"We love you, Keller."

The world stops as I spot her left hand shooting to cradle her lower stomach. I can barely see straight as my brain fumbles for words.

"We?"

"Yes, we." She lets out a nervous laugh.

Stunned. I fall to my knees before her again, gripping both hands around her small hips, lowering my head to nuzzle into her lower stomach. *Our baby.*

I squeeze my eyes tightly shut as sobs rack my body. Sienna's dainty fingers stroke my hair as I let it all out. All the pain of the last few months—hell, my whole life—pours out of me. It's not every day you win the world title, get engaged, and find out you're going to be a dad.

Placing a soft kiss on her stomach, I stand, then reach to cup her jaw. Worry dances across her features. I need to tell her, to show her how fucking much this means to me.

"We're going to have the family we always deserved,

Sienna. This kid is going to have all the love we never experienced. Thank you for giving me the greatest gift I could ever wish for."

A smile of pure relief washes over her as I take her hand in mine and squeeze, pulling her body flush against me.

"Let's get out of here and go start our happily ever after. I can't wait another fucking second to devour that perfect pussy. It's been far too long since I've had a decent meal."

WE FUMBLE INTO MY PRESIDENTIAL SUITE. THE REMAINS OF HER clothes fly through the air.

Breaking the hungry kisses, she bends over to unbuckle those sexy, red fuck-me heels.

"Leave them on," I growl from above her.

Her hands freeze in response, a devilish smirk creeping across her lips.

"Stand up," I command.

She does as I say, her perfect tits on display and only a silky red thong covering her pussy.

"Good girl."

She lets out a low moan in response, sending blood rushing straight to my dick, already strained against my black suit trousers.

My *wife.*

Pride fills my chest as I take her in. Ready and waiting, wetness dripping down the inside of her thighs.

Did we just get married in a chapel in Vegas with a fat Elvis reciting our vows?

Abso-fucking-lutely.

She didn't want the big wedding with the white dress.

The only people we needed were already here. Maddie and Mom cried throughout the entire ceremony while Grayson wrapped a strong arm around Maddie's shoulder. Luca still managed to sneak his best man's speech in, totally furious he didn't get to plan a bachelor party beforehand.

I didn't care what wedding we had. As long as we both said 'I do', that was good enough for me.

"Now, Mrs. Russo, what am I going to do with you?" I say, stalking toward her, wrapping her hair around my fist and tilting her head back to expose her delicate neck. Her pulse hammers against her pale skin.

I bite hard into her neck, and she lets out a gasp.

"Let me hear you, wife. I want this entire hotel to hear you scream for your husband tonight," I rasp, trailing my tongue up her neck towards her jawline, leaving a wet line behind.

"Fucking delicious."

Slipping my hand beneath her silky thong, I part that perfect pussy with my fingers, using my middle finger to run down her slit towards her entrance.

"Fucking soaking for me, baby."

"Mmmhmm," she hums in response, her eyes fluttering shut.

"Spread those legs for me," I command, and she shuffles her feet. I spy those red heels moving beneath me.

"Good girl."

With further access granted, I slide one finger into her tight pussy, her walls gripping my fingers, smearing them with her juices. I add a second and a third. Continuing my assault on her neck. Red, primal teeth marks appear, so I pepper gentle kisses on each of them. She rides my hand with ferocity, a deep moan escaping her lips.

I drop down to my knees for the third time tonight, as

I'm sure I will for the rest of our lives. Her eyes glisten with desire as she watches me, chewing on her swollen bottom lip.

"Please, Keller," she begs.

My wife only deserves to come on my face or my cock.

"Hands on my head and your leg up on my shoulder. I want to see all of you."

Her red heels drift past my head as she opens up for me, giving me the perfect view of her dripping pink pussy. I can't help but let out a groan at the view. Like a man starving, I dive right in and bite on her clit, her moans filling the room is music to my ears.

"More, Keller. I need more." She hums and tightens her grip on my hair, burning my scalp as she pulls. It's a welcome pain.

I vowed to worship her, to give her everything I had, and that's exactly what I'll do.

For the rest of my life.

Thrusting my fingers into her, I lap her up with my tongue. I feel her tightening around my fingers as she starts to quiver. Slowly removing my fingers, I grab both her ass cheeks and squeeze them tight in my grip. Using my strength to keep her upright and force her to smother my face, I unleash a frenzied attack on her clit. I might not be able to breathe, but I don't fucking care.

I wasn't joking when I said I'd die for her.

An orgasm rips through her as she frantically rides my face, pushing her ass into my tight grip.

"Oh, my god. Fuck, Keller!" she screams out, as I only tighten my grip on her, lapping up her orgasm as she stumbles back down to reality.

"Jesus fucking Christ, Keller. That was incredible. You

can do that every day, if you want," she says, her voice raspy as she tries to catch her breath.

I smile against her inner thigh and place a soft kiss there. The erection in my shorts is throbbing now.

"You are incredible, baby," I mutter as I slowly remove her leg from my shoulder and steady her by gripping her hips. Those damn shoes are going to need a shrine in the new home. Standing, I brush the long strands of hair away from her face. She smiles as I do.

"I love you, Wife."

Her smile widens as she places her warm hand on my cheek, running her thumb along my bruised cheekbone.

"I love you, Husband."

Taking her mouth with mine, the taste of her still covering my tongue. As I lap mine around hers, she's groaning into my mouth. I kiss her with everything I have and it's making me fucking hot.

"Turn around, baby. Both hands on the wall."

Her perfect round ass comes into view, and a deep moan escapes my lips.

I trail my finger down the tattoo that runs along her spine, slipping between her cheeks, and she snaps her head around in warning.

"One day," I promise.

She simply raises a brow. Undoing my pants, I swiftly rip them off along with my boxers, releasing my raging hard on, come already spilling out of the tip. I position myself at her entrance, guiding my cock up her wet slit. Her hair spans across her back. I gather it in one hand, wrap it tightly around my fist and slam my cock into her while she's bent at the waist, resting her hands on the wall. A gasp escapes her as she adjusts to my size. I drag myself all the way out and slam right back into her, causing her to jolt forward.

"Fuck, Keller. More," she grits out.

I don't need to be told twice.

I pound into her over and over again, my hips slapping into her ass.

"Jesus Baby, you feel so fucking perfect. I won't last long."

Pressing my body against her back, I reach around her torso and lower my hand to find her clit. Her legs begin to tremble around me as my release rages so close. Our heavy pants fill the air.

"Come for me, baby. Come now."

An orgasm rips through me, setting my whole body on fire.

"Fuck!" I roar as I spill into her.

She meets my orgasm with her own, her head flying backward as she screams my name again. I slowly slip out of her. Her body sags against mine as I do. I spin her around to meet me and wrap her in a tight embrace.

"That-that was perfect," she whispers.

Her eyes meet mine and are filled with love. The rest of her looks freshly fucked. Perfect.

"You are perfect, baby. Now, let me carry my wife to bed," I say as I bend down and scoop her up. She lets out a high-pitched shriek as I do. I playfully slap her bare ass as I stroll into our bedroom for the next few nights. And then we go home to start the rest of our lives.

CHAPTER THIRTY-NINE

The natural light streams in the room as I lay snuggled on my sleeping husband's side.

My husband.

A smile takes over my face as I watch his chest rise and fall steadily. Clearly exhausted after arguably the most life-altering day of his–no–our lives.

I'm married to the undisputed Heavyweight Champion of the World. I'm having a baby with him.

We finally get to right the wrongs of our pasts, to give a child the loving home we always dreamt of ourselves.

Placing a quick peck on his rock hard abs, I throw off the duvet and peel myself off him. As I kick one leg over the side of the bed, I'm abruptly pulled backward, a powerful arm wrapped around my ribs.

"Morning, my gorgeous wife," he mumbles in his deep, sleepy tone.

Laying me on my back, he pins my arms above my head and straddles his legs on each side of my body. He pushes himself backwards onto his heels and proceeds to place a flutter of kisses along my stomach.

"Morning, little one."

I can't help but smile, tears welling as I watch him kiss my belly.

The man who once killed for me, the professional hitman, the man who believed he was a monster, is smiling to my stomach, placing the most delicate kisses, whispering to his unborn child.

Everybody may have a darkness in them, but there is always light.

"Good morning, husband."

He scoots his legs further down the bed, now trailing kisses down my thigh.

"I need my breakfast, wife. Open those damn sexy legs and let me feast."

A sexy grin forming, his dark hungry eyes searching mine. The man is insatiable.

"Didn't you get your fill last night?" I tease.

He forces my knees apart as he brings his body back up between us, his face now crowding mine.

"I will never, ever have my fill of you, baby."

Isn't that the truth? I press my lips to his. He smiles against them.

There is nothing I want more than to be worshiped by my king for the rest of my life.

Everyone wears a mask. You can never truly love all of someone unless you see beneath it.

I see Keller.

Beneath the darkness, he is my light, as I am his.

I never believed in fairytales; that is, until him. Our tale might be dark and twisted, but it's ours and it's perfect.

epilogue

SIENNA

SEVEN MONTHS LATER...

The door crashes open as Maddie comes barreling in. With her arms flung open wide, excitement bubbles off her, like the bright blonde curls bouncing around her shoulders.

"Where's my niece? Auntie Maddie needs snuggles," she says, stopping as she reaches me. Tiny Darcy is nestled between my arms, wrapped in a pale pink blanket, making the cutest little piggy noises as she sleeps soundly.

"Oh my god, Sienna, she is gorgeous. A perfect mix of you and Keller," she gushes, tears welling in her eyes. "Can I?" She motions to hold Darcy.

"Of course you can. Hey, baby, want to meet your Auntie Maddie?" I coo to Darcy.

She takes a seat on the couch next to me. As I carefully place Darcy in her arms, Maddie cuddles her into her chest. She's a natural.

I can hear Keller and Grayson chatting away, beers in hand at the kitchen island. I don't think Maddie has even realized they're here yet. Grayson clears his throat and Maddie's eyes snap to his, a small smile forming on her lips. Her expression is almost sad as she immediately focuses back on Darcy.

As soon as we got back from Vegas, I moved straight into Keller's new home. Our home.

We designed and decorated every room from scratch. It's perfect. The home already had an old worldly vibe that I wanted to keep, but also modernize. We went for darker colors to match the dark oak flooring. Our kitchen is a beautiful midnight blue with gold features, which almost makes me want to cook every night. Keller even installed a wall to ceiling bookcase in the lounge for me, with all my favorite spicy reads taking center stage.

Every last detail is perfect.

Keller cocks an eyebrow at me. I know what he's thinking. We've been debating for weeks when these two would finally get together. So far, nothing. Keller's adamant Grayson is a no go on relationships, but I'm always quick to remind him of how his own life changed. He now has the family he never dreamed he deserved.

Seeing the way he dotes over Darcy makes my heart feel full. The giant and his tiny princess; she has him wrapped around her finger at only a few days old. I knew she would. Beneath his rock hard exterior, he's a softie. Christ, he spent my whole pregnancy waiting on me hand and foot. It was bliss–massages on demand and gorgeous home-cooked Italian meals every day. He'd even sit and speak to her through my belly, telling her every night how much we loved her.

I give him a soft smile and he gives me one of his sexy winks in return. God, only five more weeks before I have the all clear to jump him. I've missed him in that respect.

"So, Maddie, anything new going on in your life?" I quiz her.

"Well, I have a second date tonight with Gregory. He's taking me to that new Mexican restaurant in Times Square," she gushes as Grayson coughs his beer out in response.

Interesting.

"So Gregory has the potential to be 'the one'?" I say, wiggling my eyebrows at her. Her face blushes. She's completely avoiding Grayson and Keller, who are both now staring dead at her.

"He's exactly what I think I need, so yeah, I guess there is potential." I can hear the hesitation in her voice.

As I go to respond, Keller stands up and puts his beer down on the coffee table, bee lining straight to me. Every damn time he enters my personal space, I melt. He totally consumes me. I'm sure I'm obsessed and always will be.

Leaning down, he places a sweet kiss on my forehead.

"I have to meet Elijah now quickly, baby. He's spending big bucks hiring out The End Zone on a Saturday Night for his and Samantha's wedding party. It's only right that I meet him in person."

I know he doesn't want to leave. But since leaving his old life behind, he's thrown himself headfirst into his boxing and the nightclub. The End Zone was recently voted the hottest club in Manhattan. Not that he needs the money. He added me to all his accounts after days of arguing. I didn't need his money, just him. Well, I saw the balances, and let's just say he wasn't joking when he told me he was a billionaire. I still feel weird even spending his money. I'll always continue to work at Young Minds with Paula. She can keep the funding since I am doing it on a volunteer basis.

"Take Grayson with you, please. He looks like he wants to murder Maddie. I'd prefer it if Darcy didn't witness a murder before her first birthday if we can help it," I whisper, and Keller chuckles in response.

He slams his lips to mine for a hungry kiss. I grip his face with both of my hands to deepen it.

"For God's sake, you two. You have God knows how many bedrooms in this place. Use them. It's burning my eyes," Grayson moans from the sofa. Keller's lips soften to a smile against mine as he places one final PG kiss to my lips. "I love you, my queen."

I can't help but feel giddy.

"I love you, champ."

He turns his attention to our little bundle in pink, still sound asleep in Maddie's arms. Crouching down, "Daddy won't be long, I promise, princess. I love you." He places a delicate kiss on top of her fluffy black locks.

She definitely has her dad's coloring, that's for sure.

"Come on, Grayson. You're coming with me."

"Fine," he huffs in response as they leave.

"Don't forget Paula's bringing Max over to meet Darcy later," I call out after him. I know he wouldn't have forgotten. He loves that boy like a son. We both do.

"I wouldn't miss that for the world," he shouts back.

We're in the process of adopting him. His mom never returned and signed her rights away. Paula's currently fostering him whilst Keller pushes the paperwork through. We wanted to make sure everything was perfect with the house and his little sister had made a safe arrival before telling him the news. I can't wait to make this a home for us all.

Maddie's shoulders sag in relief as the door closes behind them.

“Want to tell me why you’re messing around going on dates with this Gregory, when it’s quite clear you are head over heels in love with Grayson?”

Her eyes widen, then she lets out a shaky breath.

“There was a kiss–the best kiss of my life, Si. Now he won’t even talk to me. I’m so confused. I still want to hate him, I really do, but I can’t. What is wrong with me?” she sniffles, as tears roll down her cheeks, and I wrap my arms around her.

THE END.

afterword

Thank you so much for reading. I hope you loved Keller and Sienna's story. This is just the start of the series!

You can continue with Maddie and Grayson's explosive story in Detonate, which is available on Amazon and Kindle Unlimited now: **https://books2read.com/u/4XeERL**

COMING SOON IN THE SERIES:

The Boss, Luca, will get his happily ever after in Devoted. Releasing September 30th: **https://books2read.com/u/3GGoad**

The series will conclude in Frankie's book, Detained, in January 2024.

https://books2read.com/u/3yQ6ge

about the author

Luna Mason is an Amazon Top 50 bestselling dark romance author based in the UK. If she isn't writing, you'll find her with her head in a spicy book. To be the first to find out her upcoming titles you can subscribe to her newsletter here:

https://dashboard.mailerlite.com/forms/232608/79198959451506438/share

You can join the author's reader group to get exclusive teasers, be the first to know about current projects and release dates. And also a chance to win giveaways.

Luna Mason's Mafia Queens